P9-DMB-322

THE
BOURNE
DOMINION

ROBERT LUDLUM'S™

THE
BOURNE
DOMINION

A NEW JASON BOURNE NOVEL BY
ERIC VAN LUSTBADER

GRAND CENTRAL
PUBLISHING

NEW YORK   BOSTON

This book is a work of fiction. Names, characters, places, and incidents are the product of the author's imagination or are used fictitiously. Any resemblance to actual events, locales, or persons, living or dead, is coincidental.

Copyright © 2011 by Myn Pyn, LLC

All rights reserved. Except as permitted under the U.S. Copyright Act of 1976, no part of this publication may be reproduced, distributed, or transmitted in any form or by any means, or stored in a database or retrieval system, without the prior written permission of the publisher.

Grand Central Publishing
Hachette Book Group
237 Park Avenue
New York, NY 10017
www.HachetteBookGroup.com

Printed in the United States of America

First Edition: July 2011

10 9 8 7 6 5 4 3 2 1

Grand Central Publishing is a division of Hachette Book Group, Inc. The Grand Central Publishing name and logo is a trademark of Hachette Book Group, Inc.

The publisher is not responsible for websites (or their content) that are not owned by the publisher.

Library of Congress Cataloging-in-Publication Data
Lustbader, Eric.
  Robert Ludlum's The Bourne dominion / Eric Van Lustbader.—1st ed.
      p. cm.
  ISBN 978-0-446-56444-1 (regular ed.)—ISBN 978-1-4555-0010-9 (large print ed.)
  1. Bourne, Jason (Fictitious character)—Fiction. 2. Intelligence officers—Fiction. I.
Title. II. Title: Bourne dominion.
  PS3562.U752R643 2011
  813'.54—dc22
                                      2011000856

In loving memory of Barbara Skydel

Thanks to

Sam Gold, Ken Dorph

Prologue

JASON BOURNE EELED his way through the mob. He was assaulted by the bone-juddering, heart-attack-inducing, soul-shattering blast of music coming from ten-foot-tall speakers set on either end of the enormous dance floor. Above the dancers' bobbing heads an aurora borealis of lights splintered, coalesced, and then shattered against the domed ceiling like an armada of comets and shooting stars.

Ahead of him, across the restless sea of bodies, the woman with the thick mane of blond hair made her way around gyrating couples of all possible combinations. Bourne pressed after her; it was like trying to push his way through a soft mattress. The heat was palpable. Already the snow on the fur collar of his thick coat had melted away. His hair was slick with it. The woman darted in and out of the light, like a minnow under the sun-beaten skin of a lake. She seemed to move in a shuddering jerk-step, visible first here, then there. Bourne pushed after her, overamplified bass and drums having highjacked the feel of his own pulse.

At length, he confirmed that she was making for the ladies' room, and, having already plotted out a shortcut, he broke off his direct pursuit and plowed the new route through the melee. He arrived at the door just as she disappeared inside. Through the briefly open door the smells of weed, sex, and sweat emerged to swirl around him.

He waited for a pair of young women to stumble out in a cloud of perfume and giggles, then he slid inside. Three women with long, tangled hair and chunky, jangling jewelry huddled at the line of sinks, so engrossed in snorting coke they didn't see him. Crouching down to peer under the doors, he went quickly past the line of stalls. Only one was occupied. Drawing his Glock, he screwed the noise suppressor onto the end of the barrel. He kicked open the door and, as it slammed back against the partition, the woman with ice-blue eyes and a mane of blond hair aimed a small silver-plated .22 Beretta at him. He put a bullet through her heart, a second in her right eye.

He was smoke by the time her forehead hit the tiles . . .

Bourne opened his eyes to the diamond glare of tropical sunshine. He looked out onto the deep azure of the Andaman Sea, at the sail- and motorboats bobbing at anchor just offshore. He shivered, as if he were still in his memory shard instead of on Patong Beach in Phuket. Where was that disco? Norway? Sweden? When had he killed that woman? And who was she? A target assigned to him by Alex Conklin before the trauma that had cast him into the Mediterranean with a severe concussion. That was all he could be certain of. Why had Treadstone targeted her? He racked his brain, trying to gather all the details of his dream, but like smoke they drifted through his fingers. He remembered the fur collar of his coat, his hair, wet with snow. But what else? The woman's face? That appeared and reappeared with the echo of the flickering star-bursts of light. For a moment the music throbbed through him, then it winked out like the last rays of the sun.

What had triggered the memory shard?

He rose from the blanket. Turning, he saw Moira and Berengária Moreno Skydel silhouetted against the burning blue sky, the blindingly white clouds, the vertical finger hills, umber and green. Moira had invited him down to Berengária's estancia in Sonora, but he had wanted to get farther away from civilization, so they had met up at this resort on the west coast of Thailand, and here they had spent the last three days and nights. During that time, Moira had explained what she was doing in Sonora with the sister of the late drug czar Gustavo Moreno, the two women had asked for his help, and he had agreed. Moira said time was of the essence and, after hearing the details, he had agreed to leave for Colombia tomorrow.

Turning back, he saw a woman in a tiny orange bikini high-stepping like a cantering horse through the surf. Her thick mane of hair shone pale blond in the sunlight. Bourne followed her, drawn by the echo of his memory shard. He stared at her brown back, where the muscles worked between her shoulder blades. She turned slightly, then, and he saw her pull smoke into her lungs from a hand-rolled joint. For a moment, the tang of the sea breeze was sweetened by the drug. Then he saw her flinch and drop the joint into the surf, and his eyes followed hers.

Three police were coming down the beach. They wore suits, but there was no doubt as to their identity. She moved, thinking they were coming for her, but she was wrong. They were coming for Bourne.

Without hesitation, he waded into the surf. He needed to get them away from Moira and Berengária because Moira would surely try to help him and he didn't want her involved. Just before he dived into an on-coming wave, he saw one of the detectives raise his hand, as if in a salute. When he emerged onto the surface, far beyond the surf line, he saw that it had been a signal. A pair of WaveRunner FZRs were converging on him from either side. There were two men on each, the driver and the man behind him clad in scuba. These people were covering all avenues of escape.

As he made for the *Parole*, a small sailboat close to him, his mind was working overtime. From the coordination and meticulous manner in which the approach had been made, he knew that the orders had not emanated from the Thai police, who were not known for either. Someone else was manipulating them, and he suspected he knew who.

There had always been the chance that Severus Domna would seek retribution for what he had done to the secret organization. But further speculation would have to come afterward; first he had to get out of this trap and away to keep his promise to Moira to ensure Berengária's safety.

Within a dozen powerful strokes he'd come to the *Parole*. Hoisting himself over the side, he was about to stand up when a fusillade of bullets caused the boat to rock back and forth. He began to crawl toward the middle of the boat, grabbing a coil of nylon rope. His hands gripped either gunwale. The WaveRunners were closer when the second fusillade came, their violent wakes causing the boat to dance and shudder so violently, it was easy for him to capsize it. He dived backward over the side, arms pinwheeling, as if he'd been shot.

The pair of WaveRunners crisscrossed the area around the overturned boat, their occupants looking for the bobbing of a head. When none appeared, the two scuba divers drew down their masks and, as the drivers slowed their vehicles, tumbled over the side, one hand keeping their masks in place.

Completely invisible to them, Bourne was treading water under the overturned boat, the trapped air sustaining him. But that respite was short-lived. He saw the columns of bubbles through the transparent water as the divers plunged in on either side of the boat.

Quickly he tied off one end of the nylon rope to the starboard cleat. When the first of the divers came at him from below, he ducked down, wrapped the cord around the diver's neck, and pulled it tight. The diver let go of his speargun to counter Bourne's attack and Bourne ripped off his mask, effectively blinding him. Then he grabbed the speargun as it floated free, turned, and shot the oncoming second diver through the chest.

Blood ballooned out in a thick cloud, dispersed by the current rising from the deep. Bourne knew it wasn't wise to stay in these waters when blood was spilled. Lungs burning, he rose, breaking the surface under the overturned boat. But almost immediately he dived back down to find the first diver. The water was dark, hazy with the gout of blood. The dead diver hung in the mist, arms out to the sides, fins pointing straight down into darkness. Bourne was in the midst of turning when the nylon rope looped around his neck and was pulled tight. The first diver drove his knees into the small of Bourne's back while he hauled on the rope from both sides. Bourne tried grabbing at the diver, but he swam backward out of the way. Though it was clamped shut, a thin line of bubbles trailed from the corner of Bourne's mouth. The rope was cutting hard into his windpipe, holding him below the surface.

He fought the urge to struggle, knowing that this would both pull the rope tighter and exhaust him. Instead he hung motionless for a moment like the diver not three feet away, twisting in the current, playing dead. The diver pulled him close as he drew his knife to deliver the coup de grâce across Bourne's neck.

Bourne reached back and pressed the PURGE button on the regulator. Air shot out with such force it caused the diver to loosen his mouth, and, with a thick plume of bubbles, Bourne tore the regulator free. The cord loosened around his neck. Taking advantage of the diver's surprise, Bourne freed himself. Turning, he tried to pinion the diver's arms, but his adversary drove the knife toward his chest. Bourne knocked it away, but as he did so the diver wrapped his arms around Bourne's body so he couldn't surface to get air.

Bourne pressed the diver's octopus—the secondary regulator—into his mouth and sucked air into his fiery lungs. The diver scrabbled for his regulator, but Bourne fought him off. The man's face was white and pinched. He tried again and again to position the knife so that it would cut Bourne or the octopus, to no avail. He blinked heavily several times and his eyes began to turn up as all the life drained out of him. Bourne lunged for the knife, but the diver let it go. It spiraled down into the deep.

Though Bourne was now breathing normally through the octopus, he knew that following a purge there would be very little air left in the tanks. The diver's legs were locked around him, ankles crossed. In addition, the nylon cord had become entangled with both of them, building a kind of cocoon. He was working on freeing himself when he felt the powerful ripple. A chill rolled through him, rising from the depths. A shark came into view. It was perhaps twelve feet long, silvery black, slanting unerringly upward toward Bourne and the two dead divers. It had smelled the blood, sensed the thrashing bodies in the water transmitting the telltale vibrations that told it there was a dying fish, possibly more than one, for it to feast on.

Struggling, Bourne swung around, the diver in tow. Unbuckling the harness of the second diver's air tanks, he pushed them off. Immediately the corpse sank down amid its black clouds of blood. The shark changed course, heading directly for the body. Its mouth hinged open and it took an enormous bite out of the diver. Bourne had given himself a respite, albeit a short one. Any minute now more sharks would be drawn to join in a feeding frenzy; he had to be out of the water by then.

He unsnapped the first diver's weight belt, then pulled off his tanks. Then he fitted the mask over his face. Taking one last aborted breath, he let the tanks go—they were out of air, anyway. The two of them, locked in a macabre embrace, began to rise toward the surface. As they did so, Bourne worked on the nylon cord, unwinding it from around them. But the diver's legs were still imprisoning his hips. Try as he might, he couldn't unlock them.

He broke the surface and immediately saw one of the WaveRunners bouncing over the water directly at him. He waved. In the mask, he was hoping the driver would assume he was one of his divers. The WaveRunner slowed as it neared him. By this time, he'd managed to untangle the rope. As the craft swung around, he grabbed onto its back. When he tapped the driver on the knee, the WaveRunner took off. Bourne was still half in the water, and the vehicle's speed loosened the diver's death grip. Bourne pounded on the diver's knees, heard a crack of bone, and then he was free.

He swung up onto the WaveRunner and broke the driver's neck. Before he tossed him into the water, he unhooked the speargun from his belt. The driver of the second WaveRunner had seen what was happening and was in the process of turning when Bourne drove directly at him. The driver made the wrong choice. Drawing a handgun, he squeezed off

two shots, but it was impossible to aim accurately on the bucking vehicle. By this time Bourne was close enough to make the leap. He swung
the speargun, launching the WaveRunner's driver off the vehicle even
while he took control of it.

Alone, now, on the sapphire water, Bourne sped away.

Book One

1

THEY'RE MAKING US look like fools."

The president of the United States glared around the Oval Office, fixing his eyes on the men standing almost at attention. Outside, the afternoon was bright and sunny, but in here the tension in the room was so oppressive it felt as if the president's own private thunderstorm had rolled in.

"How did this sorry state of affairs happen?"

"The Chinese have been ahead of us for years," said Christopher Hendricks, the newly minted secretary of defense. "They've begun building nuclear reactors in order to wean themselves off oil and coal, and now as it turns out they own ninety-six percent of the world's production of rare earths."

"Rare earths," the president thundered. "Just what the hell are rare earths?"

General Marshall, the Pentagon's chief of staff, shifted from one foot to the other, clearly uncomfortable. "They're minerals that—"

"With all due respect, General," Hendricks said. "Rare earths are elements."

Mike Holmes, the national security adviser, turned to Hendricks. "What's the difference and who the hell cares?"

"Each of the rare earth oxides exhibits its own unique properties," Hendricks said. "Rare earths are essential for a host of new technologies including electric cars, cell phones, windmills, lasers, superconductors, high-tech magnets, and—to many in this room, especially you, General, most important of all—military weaponry in all areas crucial to our continued security: electronic, optical, and magnetic. Take, for example, the Predator unmanned aircraft or any of our next-generation precision-guided munitions, laser targeting, and satellite communications networks. They all depend on rare earths we import from China."

"Well, why the hell didn't we know about all this before?" Holmes fumed.

The president plucked a number of sheets off his desk, holding them up like washing on a line. "Here we have Exhibit A. Six memos dated over the last twenty-three months from Chris to your staff, General, making the same points Chris has made here." The president turned one of the memos around and read from it. "'Is anyone at the Pentagon aware that it takes two tons of rare earth oxides to make a single new energy windmill, that those windmills we use are imported from China?'" He looked inquiringly at General Marshall.

"I never saw those," Marshall said stiffly. "I have no knowledge—"

"Well, at least someone on your staff does," the president cut in, "which means that, at the very least, General, your lines of communication are fucked." The president hardly ever used foul language, and there ensued a shocked silence. "At worst," the president continued, "there's a case to be made for gross negligence."

"Gross negligence?" Marshall blinked. "I don't understand."

The president sighed. "Clue him in, Chris."

"As of five days ago, the Chinese slashed their export quotas of rare earth oxides by seventy percent. They are stockpiling rare earths for their own use, just as I predicted they'd do in my second Pentagon memo thirteen months ago."

"Because no action was taken," the president said, "we're now good and screwed."

"Tomahawk cruise missiles, the XM982 Excalibur Precision Guided Extended Range Artillery Projectile, the GBU-28 Bunker Buster smart bomb"—Hendricks counted the weaponry off on his fingers—"fiber optics, night-vision technology, the Multipurpose Integrated Chemical Agent Detector known as MICAD and used to detect chemical poisons, Saint-Gobain Crystals for enhanced radiation detection, sonar and radar transducers..." He cocked his head. "Shall I go on?"

The general glared at him but wisely kept his venomous thoughts to himself.

"So." The president's fingers drummed a tattoo on his desk. "How do we get out of this mess?" He did not want an answer. Depressing a button on his intercom, he said, "Send him in."

A moment later a small, round, balding man bustled into the Oval Office. If he was intimidated by all the power in the room, he didn't show it. Instead he gave a little head bow, much as someone would when addressing a European monarch. "Mr. President, Christopher."

The president smiled. "This, gentlemen, is Roy FitzWilliams. He's in charge of Indigo Ridge. Besides Chris, any of you heard of Indigo Ridge? I thought not." He nodded. "Fitz, if you would."

"Absolutely, sir." FitzWilliams's head bounced up and down like a bobblehead. "In 1978 Unocal bought Indigo Ridge, an area in California with the largest deposit of rare earths outside of China. The oil giant wanted to exploit the element deposits, but with one thing and another they never got around to it. In 2005 a Chinese company made a bid for Unocal, which Congress stopped because of security concerns." He cleared his throat. "Congress was worried about oil refining getting into Chinese hands; it had never heard of Indigo Ridge or, for that matter, rare earths."

"So," the president said, "simply by the grace of God, we retained control of Indigo Ridge."

"Which brings us to the present," Fitz said. "Through the efforts of you, Mr. President, and Mr. Hendricks, we have formed a company, called NeoDyme. So much money is needed that NeoDyme is being taken public tomorrow in an enormous IPO. Some of what I've told you is, of course, in the public domain. Interest in rare earths has quickened with the Chinese announcement. We've also been taking the NeoDyme story on the road, talking the IPO up to key securities analysts, so we hope that they will be recommending the stock to their clients.

"NeoDyme will not only begin the mining of Indigo Ridge, which should have begun decades ago, but also ensure the future security of the country." He pulled out a note card. "To date, we have identified thirteen rare earth elements in the Indigo Ridge property, including the vital heavy rare earths. Shall I list them?"

He looked up. "Ah, no, maybe not." He cleared his throat again. "Just this week our geologists delivered even better news. The latest test bores have given indications of the presence of a number of socalled green rare earths, a tremendously significant find for the future, because even the Chinese mines don't contain these metals."

The president rolled his shoulders, which he did when coming to the crux of the matter at hand. "Bottom line, gentlemen, NeoDyme is going to become the most important company in America, and possibly—I assure you this is not an overstatement—in the entire world." His piercing gaze rested on everyone in the room in turn. "It goes without saying that security at Indigo Ridge is a top priority for us now and into the foreseeable future."

He turned to Hendricks. "Accordingly, I am this day creating a top-secret task force, code-named Samaritan, which will be headed by Christopher. He will liaise with all of you, draw resources as he sees fit from your domains. You will cooperate with him in every way."

The president stood. "I want to make this crystal clear, gentlemen. Because the security of America—its very future—is at stake, we cannot afford even one mistake, one miscommunication, one dropped ball." His eyes caught those of General Marshall. "I will have zero tolerance for turf wars, backbiting, or interagency jealousies. Anyone holding back intelligence or personnel from Samaritan will be severely disciplined. Consider yourselves warned. Now go forth and multiply."

Boris Illyich Karpov broke the arm of one man and jammed his elbow into the eye socket of the second. Blood spurted and heads hung. The stink of sweat and animal fear rose heavily from the two prisoners. They were bound to metal chairs bolted to the rough concrete floor. Between them was a drain, ominous in its circumference.

"Repeat your stories," Karpov said. "Now."

As newly appointed head of FSB-2, the Russian secret police arm built by Viktor Cherkesov from an anti-narcotics squad into a rival of Russia's FSB, inheritor of the KGB's mantle, Karpov was cleaning house. This was something he had longed to do for many years. Now, through a deal made in strictest confidence, Cherkesov had given him the chance.

Karpov, leaning forward, slapped them both. The normal procedure was to isolate suspects in order to ferret out discrepancies in their answers, but this was different. Karpov already knew the answers; Cherkesov had told him all he needed to know about not only the bad apples in FSB-2—those on the take from certain *grupperovka* families or what business oligarchs remained after the Kremlin crackdown of the last several years—but also the officers who would seek to undermine Karpov's authority.

No one was speaking, so Karpov stood up and exited the prison cell. He stood alone in the sub-basement of the yellow-brick building just down the road from Lubyanka Square, where the rival FSB was still headquartered, just as it had been since the time when it was overseen by the terrifying Lavrentiy Beria.

Karpov shook out a cigarette and lit it. Leaning against a dank wall, he smoked, a silent, solitary figure, locked within thoughts of how he would redirect FSB-2's energies, how he could build it into a force that would find permanent favor with President Imov.

When his fingers began to burn he dropped the butt, ground it beneath his heel, and strode into the neighboring cell, where a rotten officer of FSB-2 sat, broken. Karpov hauled him up and dragged him into the cell with the two officers. The scuffling commotion caused them to lift their heads and stare at the new prisoner.

Without a word, Karpov drew his Makarov and shot the man he was holding in the back of the head. The percussion was such that the bullet exited the brain through the forehead in a spray of blood and brains that spattered the two men bound to their chairs. The corpse pitched forward, sprawled between them.

Karpov called out and two guards appeared. One carried a large reinforced black plastic lawn bag, the other a chain saw, which, at Karpov's direction, he started up. A puff of oily blue smoke rose from the machine, and then the two men went to work on the corpse, beheading then dismembering it. On either side, the two officers looked down, unable to tear their eyes away from the grisly sight. When Karpov's men were finished, they gathered up the pieces and dropped them into the lawn bag. Then they left.

"He didn't answer questions." Karpov looked hard from one officer to the other. "His fate is your fate, most certainly, unless..." He allowed his voice to die off like smoke rising from a fire that was only just starting.

"Unless what?" Anton, one of the officers, said.

"Shut the fuck up!" Georgy, the other, snapped.

"Unless you accept the inevitable." Karpov stood in front of them, but he addressed Anton. "This agency is going to change—with you or without you. Think of it this way. You have been granted a singular opportunity to become part of my inner circle, to give me both your faith and your fealty. In return, you live and, quite possibly, you prosper. But only if your allegiance is to me and me alone. If it wavers so much as a little, your family will never know what happened to you. There won't even be a body left to bury, to comfort your loved ones, nothing, in fact, to mark your time on this earth."

"I swear undying loyalty to you, General Karpov, on this you can rely."

Georgy spat, "Traitor! I'll tear you limb from limb."

Karpov ignored the outburst. "Words, Anton Fedarovich," he said.

"What must I do, then?"

Karpov shrugged. "If I have to tell you, there's no point, is there?"

Anton appeared to consider a moment. "Untie me then."

"If I untie you, then what?"

"Then," Anton said, "we will get to the point."

"Immediately?"

"Without a doubt."

Karpov nodded and, moving around behind the two, untied Anton's wrists and ankles. Anton stood up. He was careful not to rub the rawness of his wrists. He held out his right hand. Karpov stared fixedly into his eyes, then, after a moment, he presented his Makarov butt-first.

"Shoot him!" Georgy cried. "Shoot *him*, not me, you fool!"

Anton took the pistol and shot Georgy twice in the face.

Karpov looked on without expression. "And now how shall we dispose of the body?" This was said in the manner of an oral exam, a final, the culmination, or perhaps the first step in indoctrination.

Anton was as careful with his answer as he was thoughtful. "The chain saw was for the other. This man...this man deserves nothing, less than nothing." He stared down at the drain, which looked like the maw of a monstrous beast. "I wonder," he said, "have you any strong acid?"

Forty minutes later, under bright sunshine and a perfectly blue sky, Karpov, on his way to brief President Imov on his progress, received the briefest of text messages. "Border."

"Ramenskoye," Karpov said to his driver, referring to Moscow's main military airport, where a plane, fueled and fully manned, was always at his disposal. The driver made a U-turn as soon as traffic allowed, and stepped on the accelerator.

The moment Karpov presented his credentials to the military immigration official at Ramenskoye, a man so slight Boris at first mistook him for a teenager stepped out of the shadows. He wore a plain dark suit, a bad tie, and scuffed, dusty shoes. There was not an ounce of fat on him; it was as if his muscles were welded into one lithe machine. It was as if he'd honed his body for use as a weapon.

"General Karpov." He did not offer his hand or any form of greeting. "My name is Zachek." He offered neither a first name nor a patronymic.

"What?" Karpov said. "Like Paladin?"

Zachek's long, ax-like face registered nothing. "Who's Paladin?" He snatched Karpov's passport from the soldier. "Please come with me, General."

Turning his back, he started off across the floor and, because he had Karpov's credentials, Boris, quietly seething, was obliged to follow him. Zachek led him down a sporadically lit corridor that smelled of boiled cabbage and carbolic, through an unmarked door, and into a small, windowless interrogation room. It contained a table bolted to the floor and two blue molded-plastic folding chairs. Incongruously, there was a beautiful brass samovar on the table, along with two glasses, spoons, and a small brass bowl of white and brown sugar cubes.

"Please sit," Zachek said. "Make yourself at home."

Karpov ignored him. "I'm the head of FSB-2."

"I'm aware of who you are, General."

"Who the hell are you?"

Zachek pulled a laminated folder out of the breast pocket of his suit jacket and opened it. Karpov was forced to take several steps closer in order to read it. SLUZHBA VNESHNEY RAZVEDKI. He reared back. This man was head of the counter-insurgency directorate at SVR, the Russian Federation equivalent of the American Central Intelligence. Strictly speaking, FSB and FSB-2 were confined to domestic matters, though Cherkesov had expanded his agency's mandate overseas without generating any blowback. Was that what this interview was about, FSB-2 encroaching on SVR's territory? Karpov now very much regretted not having brought up the subject with Cherkesov before he had taken over.

Karpov slapped the veneer of a smile on his face. "What can I do for you?"

"It's more what I—or, more accurately, SVR—can do for you."

"I very much doubt that."

Karpov was close enough to snatch Zachek's credentials as Zachek was about to put them away. Now he waved them like a flag of war on the battlefield. In his mind he heard the sounds of sabers rattling.

Zachek held out Karpov's passport, and the two men exchanged prisoners.

When Karpov had put his passport safely away, he said, "I have a plane to catch."

"The pilot has instructions to wait until this interview has ended." Zachek crossed to the samovar. "Tea?"

"I think not."

Zachek, in the process of filling one glass, turned back to him. "A mistake, surely, General. We have here the finest Russian Caravan black tea. What makes this particular blend of oolong, Keemun, and Lapsang souchong so special is that it was transported from its various plantations through Mongolia and Siberia, just as it was in the eighteenth century when the camel caravans brought it from China, India, and Ceylon." He took the filled glass by his fingertips and brought it up to his nose, breathing in deeply. "The cold, dry climate allows just the right touch of moisture to be absorbed by the tea when it is nightly set down on the snow-covered steppes."

He drank, paused, and drank again. Then he looked at Karpov. "Are you certain?"

"Quite certain."

"As you wish, General." Zachek sighed as he put down the glass. "It has come to our attention—"

"*Our?*"

"The SVR's attention. Do you prefer that?" Zachek's fingers waggled. "In any event, you have piqued the SVR's attention."

"In what way?"

Zachek put his hands behind his back. He looked like a cadet on the parade ground. "You know, General, I envy a man like you."

Karpov decided to let him talk uninterrupted. He wanted this mysterious interview over with as soon as possible.

"You're old school, you came up the hard way, fought for every promotion, bodies of those weaker than you littered behind you." He pointed at his own chest. "I, on the other hand, had it comparatively easy. You know, it occurs to me that I could learn a lot from a man such as yourself." He waited for Karpov to respond, but when only silence ensued, he continued.

"How would you like that, General, mentoring me?"

"You're like all the young technocrats who play video games and think that's a substitute for experience in the field."

"I have more important things to do than play video games."

"It pays to familiarize yourself with what the competition is up to." Boris waved a hand. "Now get to the point. I don't have all day."

Zachek nodded thoughtfully. "We simply want to ensure that the arrangement we had with your predecessor will continue with you."

"What arrangement?"

"Oh, dear, you mean Cherkesov flew the coop without informing you?"

"I have no knowledge of a deal," Karpov said. "If you've done your research, you know that I don't do deals." He was through here. He headed for the door.

"I thought," Zachek said softly, "that in this case you would make an exception."

Karpov counted to ten and then turned back. "You know, it's exhausting talking to you."

"Apologies," Zachek said, though his expression indicated anything but. "The deal, General. It involves money—a monthly figure can easily be arrived at—and intelligence. We want to know what you know."

"That isn't a deal," Karpov said, "it's extortion."

"We can bandy words all day, General, but as you yourself said, you have a plane to catch." His voice hardened. "We do this deal—as we did with your predecessor—and you and your colleagues are free to wander the globe, far beyond the scope of FSB-2's charter."

"Viktor Cherkesov created our charter." Karpov turned the doorknob.

"Believe me when I tell you that we can make your life a living hell, General."

Boris opened the door and strode out.

It was just over 665 miles from Ramenskoye to the Uralsk Airport in western Kazakhstan, a flat and ugly stretch of land, barren, brown, desiccated.

Viktor Delyagovich Cherkesov was waiting for him, leaning against a dusty military vehicle, smoking a black Turkish cigarette. He was a tall man with thick, wavy hair, graying at the temples. His eyes were dark as coffee and unreadable; he'd seen too many atrocities, had given too many orders, had himself participated in too many crimes.

Karpov walked over to him with a quickening pulse. Part of his deal with this devil was that in return for the keys to FSB-2 he would, from time to time, grant favors. Of what sort, he had not bothered to ask; Cherkesov would not have told him. But now the first summons had arrived and Karpov knew that his obligation to the former head of FSB-2 had come due. Denying him his request was not an option.

Cherkesov offered a cigarette and Karpov took it, leaned in to catch the flame from Cherkesov's lighter. He despised the harshness of Turkish tobacco, but he wasn't about to refuse his former boss anything.

"You look good," Cherkesov began. "Ruining other people's lives suits you."

Karpov cracked a wry smile. "And your new life suits you."

"Power suits me." Cherkesov threw down his cigarette, the end burning bright against the cheap tarmac. "It suits both of us."

"Where have you been since you left us?"

Cherkesov smiled. "Munich. Nowhere."

"Munich *is* nowhere," Karpov affirmed. "If I never see that city again it will be too soon."

Cherkesov shot out another cigarette and lit it. "I know you, Boris Illyich. You have something weighing on your mind."

"SVR," Karpov said. He'd been seething the entire flight. "I want to talk with you about the deal you made with them."

Cherkesov blinked. "What deal?"

And then everything fell into place. Zachek had been running a bluff, hoping to take advantage of the fact that Boris had been in his new job less than a month. He told his former boss about the repugnant interview at Ramenskoye, leaving out no detail, from Zachek's approach at Immigration to his last line as Boris had walked out the door of the windowless room.

During this discourse, Cherkesov sucked ruminatively on the inside of his cheek. "I'd like to say I'm surprised," he said at last, "but I'm not."

"You know this man Zachek? There's something smarmy about him."

"All flunkies are smarmy. Zachek does Beria's bidding. Beria is the man you need to watch out for." Konstantin L. Beria was the current head of SVR and, like his notorious forebear, had amassed a reputation for violence, paranoia, and malevolent trickery. Konstantin was every inch as feared and despised as Lavrentiy Pavlovich Beria had been.

"Beria was afraid to come near me," Cherkesov said. "He sent Zachek on a fishing expedition to see if you could be turned."

"Fuck Beria."

Cherkesov's eyes narrowed. "Careful, my friend. This is not a man to be taken lightly."

"Advisement taken."

Cherkesov gave a curt nod. "If relations deteriorate, contact me." He flicked his lighter open and closed, the clicking like that of an insect moving through a field of grass. "Now to the matter at hand. I have an assignment for you."

Karpov watched the other man for any sign of what he was about to say. He found none. Cherkesov was like that, his face closed as a bank vault. Military jets sat, tense and watchful, on the tarmac. Now and again a mechanic would appear; no one came near the two Russians.

Cherkesov plucked a bit of tobacco off his lip, ground it to powder. "I need you to kill someone."

Karpov let out a breath he had not been fully aware he'd been holding. Was that all? He felt a wave of relief flood through him, and he nodded. "Just give me the details and it will be done."

"Immediately."

Karpov nodded again. "Of course. Immediately." He took a drag on his cigarette, one eye slitted against the smoke. "I assume you have a photo of the victim."

Cherkesov, smirking, drew a snapshot out of his breast pocket and handed it over. He watched, curious and avid, as all the blood drained from Karpov's face.

He met Karpov's eyes with a knowing smile. "You have no choice. None whatsoever." His head tilted. "What? Is the price of your success too high?"

Karpov tried to speak, but he felt as if Cherkesov were throttling him.

Cherkesov's smile broadened. "No, I thought not."

2

JASON BOURNE, IN a hotel on the edge of the Colombian jungle, awoke into darkness, but he did not open his eyes. He lay on the thin, lumpy mattress for a moment, still wrapped in the strange web of his dream. He'd been in a house of many rooms, with corridors that seemed to lead to places in which he was blind. Like his past. The house was on fire and filled with smoke. He was not the only one in it. There was someone else who moved with the stealth of a fox, someone who was looking for him, someone who, with murderous intent, was very close, though the thick, choking smoke hid him completely from view.

At what precise moment dream became reality he couldn't say. He smelled smoke; it was what had awakened him. Rolling out of bed, he was engulfed in it, and once again his dream reared up in his mind. He made for the door and stopped.

Someone was waiting for him, just on the other side of the door. Someone armed. Someone with murderous intent.

Bourne backed up, grabbed a scarred wooden chair, fragile seeming as kindling. Opening the door, he hurled the chair through the doorway. Even as he heard the answering gunshots, he exploded across the threshold.

He struck the gunman's wrist with such force that a bone snapped. The weapon hung by nerveless fingers but the gunman wasn't done yet. His kick caught Bourne in the side, slamming him against the opposite wall. The gunman, having given himself breathing room, moved through the smoke like a wraith, swinging the butt of the gun—now gripped in his other hand—into the side of Bourne's head.

Bourne went down and stayed down. The smoke was thickening, and he could feel the heat as the flames licked closer. Down on the floor the air was clearer, it gave him an edge his opponent had not yet figured out. He kicked out at Bourne, who grabbed the shoe in mid-flight, twisted it so that the ankle cracked. The gunman shouted in pain. Bourne, on his knees, punched him hard in the kidneys then, as the body started to crumple, grabbed the back of the gunman's head and slammed the chin against his knee.

Smoke engulfed the hallway. The flames had reached the head of the stairs and threatened to turn the second floor into an inferno. Grabbing the gunman's weapon, Bourne launched himself back into his room. As he sprinted across the floor, he crossed his arms over his face and, leaping, crashed through the glass and wood of the window.

They were waiting for him on the other side. There were three of them, converging on him as he hurtled to the ground from the second-floor window in a hail of shattered glass. He caught one, in a bright wink of blood the barrel of his gun scoring a line down the man's cheek. He buried his fist into the belly of the second man, who doubled over. Then a gun muzzle pressed hard into the back of his neck.

Bourne raised his hands and the man with the gashed cheek ripped the gun from his grip, then punched him in the jaw.

"¡Basta!" the man behind Bourne commanded. "Él no quiere ser lastimado." He's not to be hurt.

Bourne calculated that he could take these three, but he remained unmoving. These people weren't out to kill him. They had started the fire. The one lurking outside his door could have kicked it down and tried to shoot him, but he didn't. The fire was to herd him, as were the shots fired in the hallway. He hadn't been expected to engage the gunman in the hallway.

Bourne had a strong suspicion who had sent these men, so he allowed them to tie his hands behind his back and jam a hemp sack over his head. He was bundled into a hot, cramped vehicle that stank of gasoline, sweat, and oil. They rumbled off into the jungle, the lack of shocks telling him that he was in some sort of run-down military vehicle. Bourne memorized the turns, counting to himself to get a rough approximation of how far they had come. All the while, he used the sharp metal edge behind his back to begin sawing through the flex that bound his wrists together.

After perhaps twenty minutes, the vehicle came to a halt. For some time, nothing happened, except a sharp and sometimes vitriolic exchange in idiomatic Spanish. He tried to make out what was being said, but the thick hemp and the peculiar acoustics of the vehicle's interior made it virtually impossible. He was summarily hauled out into the coolness of deep shade. Flies and mosquitoes buzzed, a falling leaf brushed against the back of his hand as he was pulled forward. The acrid stench of a latrine, then the odors of gun oil, cordite, and sour sweat. He was pushed down onto what felt like the rough canvas of a folding camp stool and there he sat for another half an hour, listening. He could hear movement, but no one spoke, a sign of ironclad discipline.

Then, abruptly, the hemp sack was removed and he blinked in the dusky light of the forest. Looking around, he found himself in a makeshift camp. He noted thirteen men—and that was just in his field of vision.

One man approached, flanked by two uniformed counterparts, heavily armed with semi-automatics, handguns, and ammo belts. Bourne recognized Roberto Corellos from Moira's detailed description. He was handsome in a rough, hard-muscled way. And with his dark, smoldering eyes and intensely masculine presence, he possessed a certain charisma that was certain to resonate with these men.

"So..." He drew a cigar from the breast pocket of his beautifully embroidered guayabera shirt, bit off the end, and lit up, using a heavy Zippo lighter. "Here we are, hunter and prey." He blew out a cloud of aromatic smoke. "But which is which, I wonder?"

Bourne studied him with great care. "Funny," he said, "you don't look like a convict."

A grin split Corellos's face and he made a broad gesture. "That, my friend, is because my friends at FARC were good enough to spring me from La Modelo."

FARC, Bourne knew, stood for "Revolutionary Armed Forces of Colombia," the left-wing guerrillas.

"Interesting," he said, "you're one of the most powerful drug lords in Latin America."

"In the world!" Corellos corrected, his cigar lifted high.

Bourne shook his head. "Left-wing guerrillas and right-wing capitalists, I don't get it."

Corellos shrugged. "What's to get? FARC hates the government, so do I. We have a deal. Every now and again we do each other favors and, as a result, the government fuckers suffer. Otherwise we leave each other alone." He puffed out another fragrant cloud. "It's business, not ideological. I make money. I don't give a fuck about ideology.

"Now to business." Corellos bent over, hands on knees, his face on a level with Bourne's. "Who sent you to kill me, señor? Which one of my enemies, eh?"

This man was a danger to Moira and to her friend Berengária. In Phuket, Moira had asked him to find Corellos and deal with him. Moira had never asked him for anything before, so he knew this must be extremely important, possibly a matter of life or death.

"How did you find out I was sent to kill you?" Bourne said.

"This is Colombia, my friend. Nothing happens here that I don't know about."

But there was another reason he hadn't hesitated. His epic encounter with Leonid Arkadin had taught him something about himself. He was not happy in the spaces between, the dark, solitary, actionless moments when the world came to a standstill and all he, an outsider, could do was observe it and feel nothing at the sight of marriages, graduations, memorial services. He lived for the periods when he sprang into action, when both his mind and his body were fully engaged, sprinting along the precipice between life and death.

"Well?" Corellos was almost nose-to-nose with Bourne. "What do you have to tell me?"

Bourne slammed his forehead into Corellos's nose. He heard the satisfying crack of cartilage being dislodged as he freed his hands from the flex bindings he'd surreptitiously sawed through. Grabbing Corellos, he swung him around in front of him and locked the crook of his arm around the drug lord's throat.

Gun muzzles swung up but no one made a move. Then another man strode into the arena.

"That's a bad idea," he said to Bourne.

Bourne tightened his grip. "It certainly is for Señor Corellos."

The man was large, well built, with walnut-colored skin and wind-swept eyes, dark as the inside of a well. He had a great shock of dark hair, almost ringlets, and a beard as long, thick, and curly as an ancient Persian's. He emitted a certain energy that affected even Bourne. Though he was much older, Bourne recognized him from the photo he'd been shown so many years ago.

"Jalal Essai," Bourne said now. "I'm wondering what you're doing here in the company of this drug lord. Is Severus Domna moving heroin and cocaine now?"

"We need to talk, you and I."

"I doubt that will happen."

"Mr. Bourne," Essai said slowly and carefully, "I murdered Frederick Willard."

"Why would you tell me that?"

"Were you an ally of Mr. Willard's? No, I think not. Not after he spent so much time and energy pitting you against Leonid Arkadin." He waved a hand. "But in any event, I killed Willard for a very specific reason: He'd made a deal with Benjamin El-Arian, the head of the Domna."

"That's difficult to believe."

"Nevertheless, it's true. You see, Willard wanted Solomon's gold as badly as your old boss at Treadstone, Alexander Conklin, did. He sold his soul to El-Arian to get a piece of it."

Bourne shook his head. "This from a member of the Domna?"

A slow smile spread across Essai's face. "I was when Conklin sent you to invade my house," he said. "But that was a long time ago."

"Now—"

"Now Benjamin El-Arian and the Domna are my sworn enemies." His smile turned complicit. "So you see, we have a great deal to talk about after all."

Friendship," Ivan Volkin said as he took down two water glasses and filled them with vodka. "Friendship is highly overrated." He handed one to Boris Karpov and took up the other, holding it high in a toast. "Unless it's between Russians. Friendship is not entered into lightly. Only we, of all the peoples of the world, understand what it means to be friends. *Nostrovya!*"

Volkin was old and gray, his face sunken in on itself. But his blue eyes still danced merrily in his head, proof if any was needed that, even in his retirement, he retained every fiber of the superbly clever mind that had made him the most influential negotiator among the heads of the *grupperovka*, the Russian mafia.

Boris poured himself more. "Ivan Ivanovich, how long have we known each other?"

Volkin smacked his livery lips and held out his empty glass. His hands were large, the veins on their backs ropy, popped out, a morbid blue-black. "If memory serves, we wet our diapers together." Then he laughed, a gurgling sound in the back of his throat.

Boris nodded. A wistful smile lifted the corners of his mouth. "Almost, almost."

The two men stood in the cramped, overstuffed living room of the apartment in central Moscow where Volkin had lived for the last fifty years. It was a curious thing, Boris thought. With the money Ivan had amassed over the years, he could have had his pick of any apartment, no matter how large, grand, or expensive, and yet he chose to stay in this insular museum of his with its hundreds of books, shelves stocked with souvenirs from around the world—expensive gifts bestowed on him by grateful clients.

Volkin stretched out an arm. "Sit, my friend. Sit and put your feet up. It's not often I am visited by the great General Karpov, head of FSB-2."

He sat in his usual spot, an upholstered wing chair that had been in desperate need of re-covering fifteen years ago. Now its oxblood hue had all but receded into a formless, colorless mass. Boris sat opposite him on the chintz sofa, mildewed and battered as if it had been salvaged from a shipwreck. He was shocked by how thin Ivan had grown, how stooped, bent like a tree battered by decades of storms, sleet, and drought. *How many years has it been since we last saw each other?* he asked himself. He was dismayed to discover that he couldn't recall.

"To the general! A pissant's death to his enemies!" Ivan cried.

"Ivan, please!"

"Toast, Boris, toast! Revel in your time! How many men in their lifetime have achieved what you have? You are at the pinnacle of success." He rolled his thin shoulders. "What, you're not proud of what you have accomplished?"

"Of course I am," Boris said. "It's just that..." He let his voice trail off.

"Just what?" Ivan sat up straight. "What's on your mind, old friend? Come, come, we share too much for you to be reticent with me."

Boris took a deep breath and another slug of the fiery vodka. "Ivan, I find myself, after all these years, in the jaws of a trap and I don't know whether I can extricate myself."

Volkin grunted. "There is always a way out of a trap, my friend. Please go on."

As Boris described the deal he had made with his former boss and what Cherkesov had asked for, Volkin's eyes turned yellowish, feral, his innate cunning rising like a deep-sea creature to the surface.

At length, he sat back and crossed one leg over the other. "The way I see it, Boris Illyich, this trap exists only in your mind. The *problem* is your relationship with this man Bourne. I have met him several times. In fact, I even helped him. But he is an American. Worse still, he's a spy. In the end, how can he be trusted?"

"He saved my life."

"Ah, now we get to the nub of the problem." Volkin nodded sagely. "Which is you are a sentimentalist at heart. You think of this man, Bourne, as your friend. Maybe he is, maybe he isn't, but are you prepared to throw away everything you've worked toward for the last thirty years to save his skin?" Volkin tapped the side of his nose. "Consider that this is not a trap at all, but a test of your will, your determination, your dedication. All great things require sacrifices. This, in essence, is what sets them apart from the ordinary, what *makes* them great, out of the reach of ordinary civilians, attainable by only the very few, individuals willing and capable of making such sacrifices." He leaned forward. "*You* are such an individual, Boris Illyich."

Silence engulfed them. An ormolu clock ticked the minutes off like the beating of a heart pulled from a victim's chest. Boris's gaze fell upon an old czarist sword he'd given Volkin many years before. It was in beautiful shape, well oiled, lovingly rubbed, its steel glowing in the lamplight.

"Tell me, Ivan Ivanovich," he said, "what if it were you Cherkesov ordered me to kill?"

Volkin's eyes were almost all yellow now, a cat's eyes, full of mysterious, unknowable thoughts. "A test is a test, my friend. A sacrifice is a sacrifice. I would trust you to know that."

La Défense rose like a post-modern stranger at the extreme western edge of Paris. And yet it was a far better solution exiling the hightech business district of the city to La Défense than allowing modern construction to spoil Paris's gorgeous architecture. The gleaming green-glass Île de France Bank building sat midway along the Place de l'Iris, which ran like an aorta through the heart of La Défense. On the top floor, fifteen men sat on either side of a polished marble table. They wore elegant made-to-measure business suits, white shirts, and conservative ties, even the Muslims. It was a requirement of the Domna, as was the gold ring on the forefinger of the right hand. The Domna was probably the only group in existence where the two major Muslim sects, Sunni and Shi'a, peacefully coexisted and even helped each other when the occasion called for it.

The sixteenth man commanded the head of the table. He had a cruel mouth, a hawk's beak for a nose, piercing blue eyes, and skin the color of wild honey. By his left elbow and slightly behind him sat the lone woman, notebooks open on her lap. She was younger than the men, or at least seemed so, with her long red hair, porcelain skin, and wide-apart eyes, transparent as seawater. Occasionally, when the man at the head of the table extended his left hand, she passed him a sheet of paper in the crisp, professional manner of a nurse handing a surgeon a scalpel. He called her Skara and she called him Sir.

When the man at the head of the table read from the printout, everyone in the room listened, except perhaps for Skara, who had memorized the entire contents of her constantly updated notebooks, which she considered far too sensitive to be digitized.

The seventeen people inhabited a room made of concrete and glass into which had been embedded a network of electronic gear that would foil even the most sophisticated attempts at eavesdropping.

The directorate heads of the Severus Domna had convened from the four corners of the globe—Shanghai, Tokyo, Berlin, Beijing, Sanaa, London, Washington, DC, New York, Riyadh, Bogotá, Moscow, New Delhi, Lagos, Paris, and Tehran.

Benjamin El-Arian, the man at the head of the table, finished addressing the men at the table. "Frankly, America has always been a thorn in our side. Until now." He curled his hand into a fist. "Our goal is within our grasp. We have found another way."

For the next ten minutes El-Arian explicated every detail of the new plan. "This will, by design, put a great deal of pressure on myself and the other American members, but I have every confidence that this new plan will gain us far more than what was in place before Jason Bourne derailed it." He continued with a few more words of summation, then called an adjournment.

The others filed out, and El-Arian used the intercom to call in Marlon Etana, the Domna's most powerful and, therefore, influential field agent.

"I trust you are about to assign someone to terminate Bourne," Etana said as he approached his leader. "He murdered our people in Tineghir, including Idir Syphax, who was beloved by all of us."

El-Arian smiled toothily. "Forget Bourne. Your assignment is Jalal Essai. Since betraying his sacred trust to us, he has caused us considerable inconvenience. I want you to find him and terminate him."

"But through Bourne's interference we lost our chance at Solomon's gold."

El-Arian frowned. "Why do you remind me of something I already know?"

Etana's hand curled into a ball. "I want to kill him."

"And leave Essai free to do more damage?" He placed a hand on the other's shoulder. "Trust in these decisions, Marlon. Carry out your assignment. Remember the dominion. The Domna is counting on you."

Etana nodded, turned, and, without a backward glance, left the room.

All was silence in the vast echoless place until Skara rose. "Five minutes," she said without looking at her watch.

El-Arian nodded and stepped to the north-facing window. He stared down at the wide road, the foreshortened people. He was a scholar, a professor of archaeology and ancient civilizations, a formal man with an almost regal bearing.

"This will work," he said almost to himself.

"It *will* work," Skara said as she came up beside him.

"What color?"

"Black. A Citroën." She breathed against his shoulder. Her scent was curious, cinnamon and something slightly bitter, burnt almond, perhaps. "Three minutes from now no one will remember it."

El-Arian nodded again, almost absently. The familiar frisson coming off her still made him slightly uncomfortable. He thought fleetingly of his wife and children safe, protected by many layers, but so far away.

"Who will I be tomorrow?"

He turned to see her slender hand extended. Reaching into the breast pocket of his jacket, he produced a thick packet.

Opening it, Skara found a passport, her new legend, a first-class air ticket with an open return, credit cards, and three thousand American dollars. "Margaret Penrod," she read off the open passport.

"Maggie," El-Arian said. "You call yourself Maggie." He tilted his head slightly as his gaze returned to the street below them. "It's all in the legend."

Skara nodded, as if satisfied. "I'll memorize it tonight on the plane."

"There's Laurent," El-Arian said, indicating a figure in a dark suit exiting their building. He could not keep a certain excitement out of his voice.

Skara drew out a disposable cell phone and punched in Laurent's number. At once, a pre-programmed code was transmitted. El-Arian had already commenced his mental countdown. Laurent gave a little shiver and, drawing out his cell, checked its screen.

"What's he doing?" El-Arian said.

"Nothing," Skara assured him. "He must have felt the pulse, that's all."

El-Arian frowned. "He shouldn't have felt anything."

Skara shrugged.

"Can he do anything about it?"

"Not a thing."

At zero minus fifteen, a blur appeared in his peripheral vision, and he shifted his gaze to the oncoming black Citroën.

El-Arian craned his neck. "Is he calling someone?"

Skara's shapely shoulders lifted and fell. "There's no need to worry."

The next instant El-Arian understood her certainty. The Citroën struck Laurent so hard he flew perhaps ten feet in the air. He hit the ground, lay there for several seconds, then, astonishingly, began to move, trying to crawl back to the curb. The car swerved to allow its right-hand tires to crush his head, then it sped off so fast that by the time bystanders started to rush out into the street it had vanished.

3

CORELLOS WAS GETTING antsy. Bourne could feel his body tensing in advance of the moment when he believed that he could take Bourne unawares.

"This is the moment," Bourne said. "There won't be another."

Jalal Essai nodded, but Bourne could see the burning hatred in his eyes. Years ago, Bourne had been sent into Essai's house to retrieve a laptop. To a man like Essai, there was no greater transgression than the invasion of his house, where his family ate and slept. This was the essential dilemma: Essai could not forgive Bourne, and yet he was being forced to put aside his bitter enmity in order to get what he now wanted. Bourne did not ever want to be in his damnable position.

All around Bourne, Corellos's men put down their weapons.

"*Hombre*, do you know what you're doing?" Corellos's voice was drawn tight as a bowstring.

"I'm doing what needs to be done," Essai said.

"You can't trust this bastard. He was sent here to kill me."

"The situation has changed. Now Mr. Bourne realizes that killing you will be counterproductive." He cocked his head inquiringly. "Am I correct, Mr. Bourne?"

Bourne dropped his hold on Roberto Corellos, who took one staggering step away then stood under Essai's stern gaze, trembling with barely suppressed emotion. Blood dripped from one nostril. Stalking to where one of his men stood, Corellos lifted an arm and wiped his nose on the sleeve of his shirt. The man made the mistake of staring at Corellos's nose. Corellos tore the AK-50 out of his grip and beat him to his knees with the butt.

Bourne was busy working out the relationship between the two men. Before this encounter he would not have believed that Corellos would take orders from anyone else. His command of his dominion was absolute; none dared challenge him, including the new, rising order: the Russian, Albanian, and Chinese mobs. His clear subservience to Jalal Essai was both puzzling and intriguing. *He's entered a new and larger arena,* Bourne thought. *Essai has enticed him into the Domna's sphere.* And then he thought: *What prize has Essai offered him?* And the most important question of all: *What is Essai up to?*

Allowing himself to be captured had paid off. He'd sensed that the men had been sent by Corellos, but Essai's shocking appearance had led him into another world, one in which his interest was heightened.

Essai spread his hands in an inclusive gesture of amity. "There are camp chairs over there under that tree. Let's all sit down, break bread together, drink some tea, and talk."

"Pick up your damn weapons, *maricóns,*" Corellos growled, glaring from one man to another. And then, tossing his head, "Bring tequila, lots of it," he shouted to another of his men, a direct slap at Essai who, as a Muslim, was not allowed to drink alcohol.

As they seated themselves, Essai smiled a secret smile, his eyes holding the smolder of a banked fire, as if he had already devised a suitable punishment for Corellos's disrespect. Not now, not tomorrow or the day after. Patience was one of the unofficial seven pillars of Islam, whereas Corellos was hot-tempered, given to sudden eruptions of violence. In fact, Bourne knew the comment to be an attempt to regain some of the face the drug lord had lost in front of his men. Not that that would mitigate the offense in Essai's eyes. These two might be partners, he observed, but they sure as hell didn't like each other, a state of affairs that might prove useful in the future.

Essai watched Bourne, completely ignoring Corellos as the drug lord, bent over, tipped a full bottle of tequila over his nose. Snorting out blood and booze, he drank in long, greedy swigs, his eyes fizzing with rage. Essai had arranged his camp chair so that he faced Bourne. It was thus clear that Corellos was to be an observer of this conversation, rather than a participant.

"The Domna has you in its sights," Essai began.

"It already tried to kill me in Thailand." Bourne sat back. "So now it's the other way around."

Essai, Bourne, and Corellos were handed posole in a terra-cotta bowl, along with a wooden spoon. Corellos spat in his and, with a backhanded slap, sent it spinning away. He returned to his tequila, the bottle glinting in a leopard spot of sunshine as he tilted it up.

Essai nodded. "Possibly. Nevertheless, you have wounded them gravely, and believe me when I tell you that they will not stop until you're dead."

"The feeling is mutual."

Essai peered at him from out of fathomless eyes. "I believe you mean that." He sighed, put down his bowl, and laced his fingers in his lap.

Bourne tried to discern whether Essai was resigned or satisfied. Possibly he was both.

"I know you don't trust me." He shrugged. "Frankly, I'd feel the same were I where you're sitting now." He leaned forward, elbows on knees. "But I'll tell you something: You royally screwed the Domna. The plan was to use the cache of Solomon's gold to create a new gold standard, undermining America's currency. Now, of course, you've swept that off the table. Countless time and money has been irretrievably lost." He applauded. "Well done!"

So far as Bourne could tell, there wasn't even a hint of sarcasm in his voice.

Abruptly, Essai's expression darkened. "If only that were the end of it. Unfortunately for both of us, it's only the beginning."

"I assume Plan B will have the same dire consequences."

"Possibly, or it could be worse." He shrugged.

There ensued a strangled silence, at the end of which Bourne said, "You're telling me you don't know what Plan B is." ·

"Other than that it will extend the length and breadth of the Domna's dominion into the United States, no." He smashed a mosquito against his forearm and wiped away the resulting drop of blood. "I can see the disappointment on your face."

"*Disappointment* hardly covers it. I can't imagine why you wanted to talk with me."

As he began to rise, Essai said, "The Domna has put out a sanction on you."

"It won't be the first, and it won't be the last," Bourne said, unimpressed. "I'll survive."

"No, you don't understand." Now Essai stood, too. "In the Domna's world, a sanction is never undertaken lightly. Never simply doled out to the highest bidder. It is sacred."

Bourne watched Essai levelly. "Meaning?"

"Meaning the death blow will come at a time and a place even you will find surprising." He lifted a forefinger. "And it will be dealt by someone…"

"Yes?"

Essai took a breath. "The fact is, I need you, Mr. Bourne."

Bourne just managed not to laugh in his face. He did shake his head, though.

"I know, it's difficult to fathom—for me as well, believe me." He took a step toward Bourne. "But it's true what they say: Reality makes strange bedfellows, and, frankly, I cannot imagine stranger bedfellows than the two of us." He shrugged his shoulders. "Nevertheless…"

Bourne waited. He wasn't going to do Essai any favors; he wasn't going to keep the strange conversation going. But the fact was he didn't dislike Essai, and he hadn't liked his original assignment of breaking into his house. This mortal transgression he couldn't put off on Alex Conklin, even though the order originated with his late boss. Conklin either had had no inkling what the consequences of Bourne's assignment would be, or didn't care. But Bourne had—he knew how a Muslim would react to his home being invaded—and still he had obeyed orders. The fact was, he owed Essai. It was this debt that was keeping him here now.

"How long have you been siding against the Domna?" This was a crucial question.

"Many years," Essai replied without hesitation. "But it was only last year that I decided to break with them openly."

"What were you going to do with the information on the laptop I stole from your house all those years ago?"

"I was planning to take it and make my escape," Essai said. "But you put an end to that."

A silence engulfed them so stifling it seemed to silence even the insects and the haunting birdcalls.

Essai spread his hands, palms up. "So here we are, in the godforsaken jungle, being eaten alive by mosquitoes and green-headed flies."

He stepped away from the now drunken Corellos, who was clutching the near-empty tequila bottle like it was a ten-dollar whore. Bourne followed him into the dense undergrowth. A couple of Corellos's men eyed them with ill-disguised contempt, then, growing bored, spat and went to get beers out of a cooler.

"These Colombians," Essai said in that conspiratorial tone he could turn on and off at the drop of a hat. That's all he said, as if those two words spoke volumes, and they did. Bourne was aware that Essai felt he was better than these people, and maybe he was right. He was certainly better educated, more aware of the outside world, but perhaps that was missing the point. These Colombians, even the least educated of the lot, possessed a concentration of energy that, like a cyclone, could leave devastation in its wake in a heartbeat. Death cared nothing for education or self-awareness; it was the great leveler.

There was something crucial Bourne needed to know. "I was under the impression that once you were in Severus Domna, you were in for life. What led you to break with it?"

"At one point the Domna stood for something genuine—a meeting of the minds between East and West. It was a noble undertaking, a bold design, but it was like trying to mix oil and water. Gradually, so subtly that virtually no one was aware of it, the Domna changed." He shrugged. "Perhaps it was the ascendance of Benjamin El-Arian—though much as I despise the man, that would be a simplification of the process. El-Arian was and is the lightning rod, no doubt, but the disease infecting the Domna is widespread. It's gone too far to stop it."

"What disease are we talking about?"

Essai turned to him. "I know a little about you, Mr. Bourne, so I know that you are familiar with the Black Legion."

He was talking about the group of disaffected ethnic Muslims the Nazis brought back from the Soviet Union during World War II. The Muslims, who deeply hated Stalin, were trained by the SS, formed into units, and sent to the Eastern Front, where they fought with uncommon ferocity against the troops of their former motherland. The Black Legion had a number of powerful friends within the Nazi hierarchy. During the last days of the war, its soldiers were pulled out of the Eastern Front and sent to safe havens, where the allies couldn't touch them. Thus, they were scattered, but they never forgot. Decades later, they re-formed around a mosque in Munich, which was now widely regarded as one of the epicenters of Islamic fundamentalist terrorism.

"I've dealt with the Black Legion," Bourne said. "But it's been silent for more than two years—no manifestos issued, no attacks attributed to it. It's as if they fell off the edge of the earth."

"Allah wills it," Essai said. "This my heart knows." He wiped his forehead with the back of a hand. He was used to extreme heat, but the humidity was making a mess of his clothes. "In any event, the Black Legion, after suffering a number of defeats—at least one of them, I understand, by your hand and will—has turned its attention, shall we say, inward."

He glanced around, as if gauging and analyzing the position of Corellos and every one of his men. "For decades, elements high up in the Munich Mosque have had their eye on the Domna. They saw its aims as a direct threat because, as you know, the Mosque wishes nothing less than the domination of Islam in the Western world. The Mosque has been behind the steady influx of Muslims into Western Europe as well as agitating them to demand more rights, more power and influence over the local governments.

"Once, the Mosque had two or three of its people inside the Domna. Now it holds a majority, including Benjamin El-Arian. Now the Domna, with more global reach than even the Mosque possesses, is the greatest threat to world peace that we have ever seen."

Bourne thought about this for some time. "You're a family man, Essai. You're playing a too-dangerous game."

"You of all people know how dangerous." A slow smile spread across Essai's face. "But the die has been cast, the decision made. I cannot live with myself if I stand by and do nothing to stop the Domna." His eyes blazed like black fire. "The Domna must be stamped out, Mr. Bourne. There is no other alternative for me, for you—for your country."

Bourne could see the hatred in Essai's eyes as well as hear it in his voice. This was a man of rigid principle, indomitable spirit, fierce in action, clever in thought. For the first time, Bourne found a measure of respect for the man. And again, he thought about how he had broken into his home, principally because he felt sure that Essai would never forgive him.

"My sense is we don't have much time to find out what the Domna's new plan is," Essai said.

There was another silence between them, just the whir of insects, the chitter of tree frogs, the leathery sound of bats swooping through the treetops.

Essai rose and walked a bit away from the encampment. After a time, Bourne joined him.

Essai stared off through the trees. "I have four children," he said after a long time. "Three now, actually. My daughter is dead."

"I'm sorry."

"It was years ago, like another lifetime." Essai bit his lip, as if pondering whether or not to go on. "She was a willful girl—not, as you can imagine, the best of traits in a Muslim household. As a child I could control her, but there came a time when she rebelled. She ran away three times. The first two, I was able to bring her back—she was only fourteen. But then, four years later, she ran away with an Irani boy. Can you imagine?"

"I imagine it could have been worse," Bourne said.

"No," Essai said, "it couldn't." He began to peel the bark off a tree, digging into the tree's flesh with his long, scimitar nails. "The boy was engaged to be married and, quite stupidly, he took her back to Iran with him. Don't ask me why, because to this day I have no idea."

"Perhaps he truly loved her."

Essai shook his head. "The things humans do..."

His voice trailed off for a moment, but his nails never stopped stripping the tree. Then he took a deep breath and when he let it out, the words came like water over-spilling a dam. "The inevitable happened, of course. My daughter was taken away from him and imprisoned. They were going to stone her to death, can you imagine! Iranis, what barbarians!"

He meant Sunni, of course, because though Iranis weren't Arabs like him, they were nevertheless Muslim. Sunni, rather than Shi'a, like him. The enmity that accompanied the schism between Islam's two main sects was as poisonous as it was irreparable.

"Fucking animals is what they are."

It was the first time he had used an expletive, and Bourne could see how much it took out of him, but his vehemence dictated he expel the curse from his system like an infection.

"So I went in—myself, myself. I got her out of prison, got her out of Tehran, got her out of Iran. I was on my way back home with her, on a ship crossing the Mediterranean, when the Domna appeared." Quite suddenly he turned his eyes on Bourne. "Six men. Six! That's how many they determined was needed. The Domna had warned me not to go to Iran, not to interfere, that peace needed to be kept within the High Council. To do that, they said, both Shi'a and Sunni were required to respect each other's traditions. 'But this is my daughter,' I said. 'My flesh and blood.' Otherwise, they said, a sectarian war would break out within the Domna and we would be no better than those we sought to control. I doubt they heard me, or if they did, they did not care. 'We remind you of the dominion,' they said. 'Nothing is more important.'"

His head swung away again. There was bark under his nails, and dirt. An ant crawled along one finger, wandering, lost.

"That was the last I saw of her, my daughter. Nothing more was said. I did nothing because . . . because then I was Domna and there was nothing to be done in the face of its collective will. It's true that I had lost a lot of blood and I was in pain." He raised his right hand so Bourne could see the ugly white knot, the scar in the center of his palm. "I had no strength left, I told myself, I was loyal, I told myself. But when I returned home and saw the look on my wife's face the lies I told myself evaporated like mist in sunlight." His eyes sought Bourne's. "Everything changed, do you understand?"

"You crossed the Rubicon."

Essai let that sink in, then he nodded. "I came home a different man, a man of war, a man with a blackened heart. My colleagues—those I had considered friends—had betrayed me. They had slipped away when I wasn't paying attention. They no longer belonged to the Domna—at least the Domna I had once admired. This was a new Domna, in thrall to the Mosque and its hideous Black Legion.

"Now all I can think of is revenge. The information on the laptop you stole was to be that revenge. I was going to steal the gold from under the Domna's nose, but that is no longer possible."

Bourne was about to reply when Essai waved away his words. "But Allah is great, Allah is good because in the fullness of time you have reappeared, you, the instrument of my revenge."

There was another silence. Night creatures chittered overhead and Corellos, eyes closed, chin on chest, began to snortle like a pig.

Essai gave a dry laugh, then cleared his throat. "I need your expertise, Mr. Bourne. You are the only one I trust to find out what the Domna's new plan is so that, together, we can stop it."

"I work alone."

"Odd, isn't it?" He hadn't heard Bourne, or if he had, he ignored him. "Using the word *trust*."

"We're both men of our word, yes?"

Bourne nodded.

The corners of Essai's eyes wrinkled. "Then this is what I propose—"

"I know what you want me to do," Bourne said.

"It's only what you were planning to do yourself. But now you have my assistance."

"I don't want your assistance."

"With all due respect, Mr. Bourne, in this instance you most assuredly do. The Domna is both large and powerful, its tentacles spread into every corner of the globe." He waggled his forefinger in Bourne's direction. "You think I am being melodramatic, but I assure you I am not."

"I'm going to do what I'm going to do."

Essai nodded, almost eagerly. "Understood. In return, I propose to tell you whom the Domna has sent to kill you."

Bourne shrugged. "I'll find out in due course. I know all the avenues, all the players."

"You won't know this one. As I said to you, the Domna has embarked on a sacred mission. Without my help, you may very well be destroyed."

"And I suppose you're planning to withhold this information until I deliver to you the information you want on the Domna."

"Nothing of the sort, Mr. Bourne. I want you to live! Besides, I told you that we're both men of our word. I'm going to tell you this instant." He took a step closer, his voice lowered. "Unless you stop him, your friend Boris Karpov will kill you."

4

YOU'VE BEEN MORE than fair with us, Mr. Secretary."

"Peter, I've asked you to call me Christopher," Secretary of Defense Hendricks replied.

Peter Marks, sitting beside his co-director, Soraya Moore, murmured his acquiescence.

"I have ideas for the resurrected Treadstone," Hendricks continued, "but before I voice them I want to hear from you two. How do you envision Treadstone going forward?"

The three were in the drawing room of Hendricks's town house in Georgetown, where they were beginning a strategy briefing. Hendricks's family, while from the upper crust of Washington society, was nevertheless lacking wealth, which meant that despite his blue blood he was possessed of a distinctly blue-collar work ethic. He was a striver, some might say an overachiever.

He was slim and tall with the upright bearing of a military man. In fact, he had served, briefly, in Korea, had been wounded in the line of duty, and had been duly decorated by the president himself before returning to the public sector. Until a year ago, he had been national security adviser.

Now that he was finally in the catbird seat, he was determined to implement a number of initiatives he had been formulating for years. The first—and frankly most important—was turning the resurrected Treadstone into his own organization, free of the impediments of CI, NSA, and Congress.

Hendricks had no great desire to circumvent the law. Nevertheless, he had observed that, from time to time, there was a need for a group of people—small, tightly knit, intensely loyal to one another and to America—to operate in areas impossible for those subject to oversight and scrutiny to go. Now, with the country under attack from various extremist terrorist factions both foreign and homegrown, was such a time.

To that end, Hendricks had hired Soraya Moore and Peter Marks. Moore had headed up CI's own black-ops group, Typhon, until being summarily fired by M. Errol Danziger, the monomaniacal new head of CI, and Peter Marks had been close to the former heads of CI. They knew each other well, had complementary temperaments, and were smart enough to think outside the box, which, in Hendricks's opinion, was what was needed in this new splinter war of a thousand cadres they found themselves in. Best of all, Soraya Moore was Muslim, half Egyptian, with a massively deep pool of knowledge, expertise, and hands-on experience in the Middle East and beyond. The two of them were, in short, the polar opposites of the sclerotic generals and career politicians that littered the American intelligence community like bird droppings.

Marks and Moore were opposite him on a leather sofa, the twin of the one on which he sat. His assistant, Jolene, stood behind, a Bluetooth earplug connecting her to her cell. Sunlight crept in between the thick curtains. Through the slice of visible window could be seen the shadows of the secretary's National Guard detail. On the low table between them were the remnants of breakfast. Cleo, Hendricks's gorgeous golden boxer, sat immobile against his leg, mouth slightly open, head slightly cocked, staring at her master's two guests as if curious about the long silence.

Soraya and Marks exchanged a quick glance, then she cleared her throat. Her large, deep-blue eyes and her prominent nose were the centerpieces of a bold Arabian face the color of cinnamon. She was possessed of a commanding presence that Hendricks found impressive. What he liked best, however, was that she wasn't girlie—nor was she brittlely masculine like so many females in a male-dominated structure. She was her own person, which he found refreshing as well as curiously comforting. He therefore weighed her words as carefully as he did those of Marks.

"Peter and I want to move on a tip that came through early this morning," Soraya finally said.

"What sort of tip?"

"Excuse me, Mr. Secretary," Jolene said, leaning in, "I have Brad Findlay on the line."

Hendricks's head whipped around. "Jolene, what did I tell you about interrupting this briefing?"

Jolene took an involuntary step back. "I'm sorry, sir, but seeing as how it's the head of Homeland Security, I assumed you—"

"Never, ever assume," he snapped. "Go into the kitchen. You know how to handle Findlay."

"Yessir." Cheeks flaming, Jolene beat a hasty retreat out of the room.

Marks and Soraya exchanged glances again.

Soraya cleared her throat. "It's difficult to say."

"It's not what you'd call a normal tip," Marks said.

Hendricks drew his brows together. "Meaning?" He had completely forgotten Jolene, the call, and his waspish reaction.

"It didn't originate from any of the usual suspects: disgruntled mullahs, opium warlords, the Russian, Albanian, or Chinese mafias." Soraya rose and went around the room, touching a bronze sculpture here, the corner of a photo frame there. Cleo watched her with her large, liquid eyes.

Soraya stopped abruptly and, turning, looked at Hendricks. "All these things here are known. This particular tip came from the unknown—"

The secretary's brow furrowed further. "I don't understand. Terrorism—"

"Not terrorism," Soraya said. "At least not as we have defined it so far. This is an individual who reached out to me."

"Why did he want to turn? What's his motivation?"

"That was still to be determined."

"Well, whoever your informant is, get him over here for a debriefing," Hendricks said. "I don't much care for mysteries."

"That would be the protocol, of course," Marks said. "Unfortunately, he's dead."

"Murdered?"

"Hit-and-run," Marks said.

"The point is we don't know." Soraya gripped the back of an upholstered chair. "We want to go to Paris and investigate."

"Forget him. You have more important matters to see to. Besides, who knows whether he was trustworthy."

"He had given me some preliminary information on a group known as Severus Domna."

"Never heard of it, and furthermore the name sounds bogus," Hendricks said. "I think this contact is playing you."

Soraya stood her ground. "I don't share that opinion."

Hendricks rose and crossed to one of the windows. When he'd first met Soraya Moore, he'd wondered if she was a lesbian. There was something about her—a balance, an openness, a willingness to accept the complexities of people that a lot of hetero women simply couldn't manage. Then he'd dived deeper into her jacket and discovered that her lover was Amun Chalthoum, head of al Mokhabarat, the Egyptian secret service. In fact, he'd called Chalthoum and had an interesting twenty-minute talk. Danziger had used her affair with Chalthoum as an excuse to fire her from Typhon. That was high on the long list of stupidities perpetrated by M. Errol Danziger since he'd come to CI. Typhon's invaluable contacts and deep-cover operatives were loyal only to her. The moment Hendricks had named her co-director of Treadstone, every one of them had come with her. So now he had a sense of how unique she was.

"All right," he said. "Look into it." Then he turned back to them. "But, Peter, I want you here. Treadstone is still in its infancy and the fact is I envisioned it as an agency with the ability to police and clean up the giant squid of our post–nine-eleven intelligence community. There are now two hundred sixty-three and counting intelligence organs created or reorganized since 2001. And that doesn't account for the hundreds of private intel firms we've seen fit to hire, some of them so beyond our control they're operating here in the States in the same manner they do in world war zones. Do you realize that at this moment there are eight hundred fifty thousand Americans with top-secret clearance? That's far too many by a staggeringly exponential number." He shook his head emphatically. "There's no way I will allow both my directors in the field at the same time."

Marks took a step toward him. "But—"

"Peter." Hendricks smiled. "Soraya has the field experience so she gets this assignment. It's simple logic." As they were leaving, he said, "Oh, by the way, I've been able to get the Treadstone servers access to all the clandestine services' databases."

After they'd gone, Hendricks thought about Samaritan. He had deliberately kept its existence from Peter, knowing that the moment he got wind of it, he'd want to become involved in the security of Indigo Ridge. Despite the president's clear warning, Hendricks wanted to keep Peter on Treadstone, which was his baby now, a long-held desire that he was not going to relinquish, even for Samaritan. He was taking a risk, he knew that full well. Should any of the others in the Oval Office meeting, especially General Marshall, suspect that he was holding back key personnel for his own use he'd be in an untenable position.

Ah well, he thought, *what's life without risk?*

He stepped back to the window. His roses looked bedraggled and forlorn. He glanced impatiently at his watch. Where was that damn rose specialist he'd hired?

It was quiet here, the house removed from the hubbub at the center of the city. Normally, he enjoyed that; it allowed him to think. But this morning was different. He had awoken with the nagging sense that he had missed something. He had already been married and divorced twice when he had met, married, and then buried his beloved Amanda. He had one son, from the second wife, now a marine in military intelligence, deployed in Afghanistan. He should have been worried about him, but the fact was he rarely thought about him. He'd had little to do with raising him; to be truthful, he might have been someone else's son. Without Amanda, he had no attachments, no sense of family, only place. Like a European, he valued property over cash. In a sense, this house was all he had, all he needed. Why was that? he asked himself. Was something wrong with him? In restaurants, at official functions or the theater, he encountered colleagues with their wives, sometimes with their grown children. He was always alone, even though, from time to time, he had one woman or another on his arm—widows desperate to remain part of the social scene inside the Beltway. They meant nothing to him, these women of a certain age, with tight, poreless faces, breasts pushed up to their carefully sculpted chins, in their long gowns manufactured to impress. Often they wore gloves to hide their age spots.

He was pulled away from his ruminations by the sharp sound of the bell. Opening the front door, he was confronted by a woman in her mid- to late thirties, her hair pulled back from her heart-shaped face in a tomboyish ponytail. She wore round steel-rimmed glasses, denim overalls atop a plaid man's shirt, frog-green clogs, and a floppy canvas sun hat.

She introduced herself as Maggie Penrod and presented her credentials just as she had with the bodyguards patrolling the property. Hendricks studied them. She was trained at the Sorbonne and at Trinity at Oxford. Her father (deceased) had been a social worker, her Swedish mother (also deceased) a language teacher in the Bethesda school district. There was nothing memorable about her except, as she leaned forward to take back her ID, her scent, which had a decided tang. What was it? Hendricks asked himself. He sniffed as inconspicuously as possible. Ah, yes. Cinnamon and something slightly bitter, burnt almond, maybe.

As he led the way outside to the sad-looking rose bed, he said, "What's an art history major doing—"

"In a place like this?"

She laughed, a soft, mellow sound that somehow stirred something inside him, long hidden.

"Art history was a totally unrealistic career choice. Besides, I don't do well in academia—too much skulduggery and intrigue."

She had a slight accent, doubtless a product of her Swedish mother, Hendricks thought.

She paused at the edge of the rose bed, hands on hips. "And I like being my own boss. No one but me to answer to."

Listening more closely, he became aware that her accent softened her words, lending them an unmistakable sensuality.

She knelt down, her soft, strong fingers pushing aside stillborn flowers, their edges tight, ruffled, and brown. Blood streaked her skin, but she seemed unmindful of the thorns.

"The roses are balled and the leaves are being eaten." She stood up and turned to him. "For one thing, you're overwatering them. For another, they need to be sprayed once a week. Not to worry, I use only organics." She smiled up at him, her cheeks aflame in sunlight. "It'll take a couple of weeks, but I think I can get them out of intensive care."

Hendricks gestured. "Whatever you need."

The sunlight slid over her forearms like oil, illuminating tiny white-gold hairs that seemed to stir beneath his gaze. Hendricks's breath felt hot in his throat.

And then, without his knowing quite how the words slipped out, he said, "Care to come inside for a drink?"

She smiled sweetly at him, the sun in her eyes. "Not today."

I don't believe it," Bourne said. "It simply isn't possible."

"Anything is possible," Essai said. "Everything is possible."

"No," Bourne said firmly, "it's not."

Essai smiled his enigmatic smile. "Mr. Bourne, you are now in the dominion of Severus Domna. Please believe me in this."

Bourne stared into the fire. Darkness had come and, with it, a fresh wild pig, which Corellos's men had trapped, scraped free of hair, and spitted. The rich odor of its melting fat suffused the campsite. He and Essai sat near the fire, talking.

Some distance away, Corellos was talking animatedly to his lieutenant. "Petty victories," Essai said, eyeing him.

Bourne looked at him inquiringly.

"You see how it is. He knows I can't eat pork and yet this is what he offers for dinner. If you ask him, he'll say it's a treat for his men."

"Let's return to Boris Karpov."

The enigmatic smile returned. "Benjamin El-Arian, our enemy, is a master chess player. He thinks many moves ahead. He planned for the eventuality that you might succeed in keeping the Domna from finding Solomon's hoard of gold." He turned his head, the firelight glinting off his eyes. "You've heard of Viktor Cherkesov, yes?"

"Until several months ago, he was the head of FSB-2. He left under mysterious circumstances and Boris took his place. Boris told me all this. Cleaning up FSB-2 has been a long-held dream of his."

"A good man, your friend Boris. Did he happen to tell you why Cherkesov abdicated his powerful throne?"

"Mysterious circumstances," Bourne repeated.

"Not so mysterious to me. Benjamin El-Arian contacted Cherkesov through the appropriate intermediary and made him an offer he couldn't refuse."

Bourne's muscles tensed. "Cherkesov is part of the Domna now?"

Essai nodded. "And now I can see by your expression that you have intuited the rest of it. Cherkesov offered your friend Boris a deal: He'd give him FSB-2 in return for future favors."

"And the first one is killing me."

Essai saw that Corellos, having finished giving orders, was coming toward them. He sat forward and, lowering his voice, said with some urgency, "You see what a clever fellow Benjamin El-Arian is. The Domna is no ordinary cabal. Now you know the extent of what we are up against."

As Corellos pulled over a camp chair, Bourne said, "There's still the matter of why I came here in the first place."

Corellos stared at him with stainless-steel eyes. Above him a tree grew with bark peeling off like strips of flayed skin. The air shimmered and danced with mosquitoes.

"Assurances," Bourne said. It was clear he was addressing both Essai and the drug lord.

Corellos made a soundless laugh, bared his teeth and snapped his jaws together like a villain in a Tarantino film. "My dead partner's sister is paranoid. I mean her no harm, all assurances given."

"The business was Gustavo's and yours," Bourne said. "Now it belongs to you."

"That's the line she fed you."

"She has no use for blood money derived from drugs."

Corellos spread his hands wide. "Then why did he want her to take it over?"

"Family. But she's not like him."

"You don't know her."

Bourne made no reply. There was something about the drug lord that brought out an instinctive animosity, like seeing a scorpion or a black widow spider. The creature might not be threatening you at the moment, but what about in the future? Bourne studied him. He was the polar opposite of Gustavo Moreno, whom Bourne had met years ago. Whatever else he might have been, Moreno was a gentleman—that is, when he gave his word it meant something. Bourne did not have that sense with Corellos. Berengária was right to be afraid of him.

During this buzzing lull, Corellos sat back, lounging in his chair so that it creaked like an old man's bones. "So. What *does* the *puta* want?"

"Berengária wants only to be left alone."

Corellos threw his head back and laughed. Bourne could see the thick red welt from where he'd begun to strangle him.

"*Bueno.* Okay, we go to the next step. How much does she want?"

"I told you," Bourne said evenly, "nothing."

"Now I know you're fucking with me. Come on, give it."

A thin breeze stirred the swarms of mosquitoes. The forest was dense with the sounds of insects, tree frogs, and small nocturnal mammals. Bourne wanted nothing more than to bury his fist in Corellos's face. Now that he had met him, he suspected that Moreno had left his half of the business to his sister to piss his partner off. They could not have gotten on personally.

"You might believe the bitch," Corellos said. "Doesn't mean I do."

"Just leave her alone and this will be at an end."

Corellos shook his head. "She has all my contacts."

"This came directly off her hard drive." Bourne handed him the computer printout Berengária had given him before he'd left Phuket.

Corellos opened it and ran his thick, callused forefinger down the list. "All here." He looked up and shrugged. "This is a copy." He waved it in the air. "It means nothing."

Bourne handed him the hard drive from Berengária's laptop.

Corellos stared at it for a moment. "Fuck me." Laughing, he nodded. "Done."

"If you come after her..." Bourne allowed the implied threat to hang in the humid air.

Corellos froze for half a second. Then he opened his arms wide. "If I go after the bitch, then come the fuck on."

5

G ODDAMMIT!" PETER Marks pounded his fist against the steering wheel as he was stopped short at a red light.

"Down, boy," Soraya said. "What's eating you?"

"He's lying." Peter hit the horn with the heel of his hand. "There's something going on and Hendricks isn't telling us what."

Soraya regarded him archly. "And you know this how?"

"That crap he fed me about why I need to stay here. He's resurrected Treadstone with your overseas network in place so—what? We can be nannies for the other clandestine services? It's fucking make-work, there's nothing real about it." He shook his head. "Uh-uh, there's something going on he doesn't want us to know about."

Soraya stifled a tart rejoinder and, instead, thought about Peter's supposition for a moment. She and Peter had worked together for a number of years in CI. They had come to trust each other with their lives. That was no little thing. And instincts had a lot to do with their mutual trust. What had Peter seen or sensed that she hadn't? To be honest, she had been so elated at being given the go-ahead to run down the death in Paris that she hadn't paid much attention to what went on after that. More fool, her.

"Hey, slow down, cowboy!" she yelled as he veered around the rear of a truck. "I'd like to live until at least tonight."

"Sorry," Peter muttered.

Seeing that he was really and truly upset, she said, "What can I do to help?"

"Go to Paris, get the investigation of your murdered source under way, find out who the hell killed him."

She looked at him skeptically. "I don't like leaving you in this state."

"You don't have to like it."

She touched his arm. "Peter, I'm concerned that you're going to do something stupid."

He shot her a glare.

"Or at the very least something dangerous."

He took a breath. "Do you think your being here would change any of that?"

She frowned. "No, but—"

"Then be on the first plane to Paris."

"You're planning something."

"No, I'm not."

"Dammit, I know that look."

He bit his cheek. "And before you leave, why don't you give Amun a call."

Soraya immediately bridled, thinking he was needling her. But then, when she thought further, she saw the wisdom of his suggestion. "You might be right. Amun could provide a different perspective on this mysterious group."

She pulled out her cell and texted: "Arr Paris tomorrow AM re: murder. Can U?"

She found her heart beating fast. She hadn't seen Amun in over a year, but it was only now, reaching out to him, that she realized how much she had missed him—his bright smile, his certain touch, the brilliance of his mind.

She frowned. What time was it in Cairo? Almost 10:30 PM.

As she was calculating, her cell buzzed: a text had come in. "Arr Paris 8:34 AM local, day after tomorrow."

Soraya felt a warmth suffuse her body. She flexed her hands.

"What's up?" Peter asked.

"My fingertips are tingling."

Peter threw his head back and laughed.

Essai drove Bourne away from Corellos's encampment. The headlights were on, illuminating the dirt track through the dense forest of Bosque de Niebla de Chicaque, but already a pinkish blue light stole through the branches, snatching shadows from along the ground. Birdsong, which had been missing during the depths of the night, ricocheted back and forth above their heads.

"We're heading west instead of east," Bourne said, "back to Bogotá."

"We're going to the regional airport at Perales," Essai said, "where I'll take a flight to Bogotá and you'll take the car. You need to go farther west, to Ibagué. It's in the mountains, about sixty miles southwest of El Colegio."

"And why do I want to go there?"

"In Ibagué you will seek out a man named Estevan Vegas. He's a member of the Domna—a weak link, as you might say in idiomatic English, yes? I was going to speak with him about defecting, but now that you're here I expect you'll have a better chance than I would."

"Explain yourself, Essai."

"With pleasure."

Now that they were away from Corellos's camp, Essai seemed more relaxed, almost jovial, if such a word could be applied to this taciturn, revenge-obsessed man.

"It's simple, really. I'm a known quantity within the Domna: a pariah, a traitor. Even with a man like Vegas with shaky loyalty to the group, my presence would be problematic. In fact, it might backfire, providing him with a reason to become defensive, intractable."

"While I am an unknown quantity," Bourne said. "Vegas will be more inclined to listen to me."

"That will depend entirely on your powers of persuasion. From what I know of you, another excellent reason for you to take my place."

Bourne thought for a moment. "And if he does spill?"

"Your intel on the Domna will be current. I, unfortunately, have been cut off for some time. I am now deaf and blind to the details of their plots and plans."

"Vegas lives in the middle of nowhere," Bourne pointed out.

"First of all, the term *middle of nowhere* doesn't apply to the Domna," Essai said. "Its eyes and ears are everywhere." They bumped onto a paved section of the road, though their speed slowed considerably because it was in desperate need of repair and potholes deep enough to throw an axle seemed to be everywhere. "Second, though Vegas may not know everything we need to know, he's bound to know someone who does. It will then be your job to find them and charm them out of the information. Then you'll take a flight out of Perales. Tickets will be waiting for you there."

"And while I'm trying to poke into the Domna's dark corners, what will you be doing?"

"Providing a distraction to cover you."

"What, exactly?"

"You're better off not knowing, believe me." Essai manhandled the vehicle around a dual pothole of staggering depth. "There's a spare sat phone in the glove box, charged and ready to go. Also a detailed map of the area. Ibagué is clearly marked, as is the oil field Vegas runs."

Leaning forward, Bourne opened the glove box and checked the contents.

"You'll find my sat number pre-programmed into it," Essai continued. "That way, we'll never be out of touch, no matter where we are."

They rumbled past a gorge with sheer rock walls and, a mile or two farther, an enormous waterfall crashing down a blood-red cliff with enormous, unending energy. The tree canopy became abruptly less thick, more light flickering, a Morse code through the tangle of branches.

They burst through the western edge of the trees. A riot of bougainvillea inhabiting a colonial stone wall shivered, shaking off the early-morning dew in the first slender shoots of sunlight.

Bourne looked out at the countryside. Due west was a chain of formidable mountains, shaggy with dense forest. In a couple of hours that was where he'd be headed.

"What can you tell me about this man Vegas?"

"He's crusty, belligerent, often intractable."

"Beautiful."

Essai ignored Bourne's sarcasm. "But he has another side. He's a longtime oilman. He has overseen the oil outfit out there for close to twenty years. By now, I think his veins must run with oil. In any event, he's strictly hands-on; he believes in a hard day's work, even at his age, which must be sixty—knowing him, possibly more. He's hard drinking, buried two wives, lost a daughter to a Brazilian, who seduced her, then spirited her away. He's never seen or spoken to her in thirty-odd years."

"Sons?"

Essai shook his head. "He lives with a young Indian woman now, but to my knowledge she's never been pregnant. Other than that, I don't know anything about her."

"What doesn't he like?"

Essai shot him a look. "You mean what does he like?"

"It's more important to know what to avoid saying or doing," Bourne said.

"I understand." Essai nodded reflectively. "He hates communists and fascists in equal measure."

"How about drug lords?"

Essai glanced at him again, as if trying to figure out where this line of questioning was going. He was smart enough not to ask. "You're on your own there."

Bourne thought for a moment. "What I find interesting is that he lost his child and now, when he's in the perfect position to have more, he doesn't."

Essai shrugged. "Too much heartache. I can relate to that."

"But would you—?"

"My wife is too old."

"My point. His woman isn't."

Peter Marks watched the gardener get into her SUV and drive away from Hendricks's house. He'd observed her feeding the roses, then spraying them from a pump canister. She had worked slowly, methodically, gently, murmuring to the roses as if she were making love to them. She drove off without a glance at the security personnel.

The four men assigned to the secretary were of great concern to him. If he was going to shadow Hendricks in an attempt to discover what he was hiding, he'd have to stay off their radar. He considered it a challenge, rather than a problem.

Peter had always faced challenges head-on—he'd run at them with a fervor that burned brightest when he was a teenager and young adult. He hadn't come out so much as been brought out by Father Benedict, his local parish priest. But unlike the other boys whom the father had taken behind the sacristy for holy wine and sex, Peter had told his father. He was ten when this happened, but he was a precocious boy and wanted to publicly denounce the priest the following Sunday during Mass.

His father had forbade this. "It will be far worse for you than for him," he'd told his son. "Everyone will know and you'll be branded for life." There was no mistaking the warning in his father's voice. Peter had experienced the magnitude of his father's anger and he wasn't eager to trigger it again.

That Sunday, when they went to church, another priest whom Peter had never seen before performed the Mass. He wondered where Father Benedict was. Afterward, on the church steps in the sunshine of late morning, he heard people talking. Father Benedict had been assaulted the night before on his way home from church. Beaten to a pulp was the phrase most used. He now lay in critical condition at Sisters of Mercy Hospital eight blocks away. Peter never went to see him, and Father Benedict never returned to his parish church, even though he was discharged from Sisters of Mercy six weeks later. In the intervening years, Peter had never spoken to his father about Benedict, though his suspicion was that the priest had been on the receiving end of his father's wrath. And now, of course, it was too late to ask—his father had died eleven years ago.

Peter's eyes cleared. Hendricks had emerged from his house. A black Lincoln Town Car had pulled up and the driver got out, opened the door for the secretary, who climbed in. One of the security detail followed. Two others got into their nondescript Ford, and the two cars pulled out in unison. Peter, avoiding the gaze of the fourth man left behind, began the tail, his memories trailing behind.

In high school and college, he had experimented with like-minded boys his age, always being careful because that was his nature. But then he'd become interested in the clandestine services and begun to take the appropriate courses. When he did so, his college adviser changed. He had never seen or heard of him before. In fact, he couldn't find him on the college's admin list. One day, the adviser called him in for a talk, the gist of which was that if Peter truly desired a career in the clandestine services he'd have to "button it up," as the adviser put it.

The subject was never raised again, but Peter, having been given a word to the wise, did, in fact, button it up, reading as he did about case after case where spies or men in sensitive positions were compromised because of their sexual proclivities. He fervently did not want to become one of those disgraced people. And he vividly recalled what had happened to Father Benedict. So he became a better celibate than Benedict had ever been.

He loved Soraya like the sister he never had, but he certainly was never in love with her. He wondered that he'd once been jealous of her affection for Bourne. He scoffed at that now. How could he have ever been jealous of Jason Bourne? He couldn't bear to have that man's shadowy life.

The cars rolled out of the tree-lined streets of Georgetown, heading due east toward the heart of Washington. Dusk was forming, filled with haze and uncertainty. He checked his car's clock. Any moment now, Soraya would be in the air, on her way across the Atlantic to Paris and her rendezvous with Amun Chalthoum. He'd called his friend Jacques Robbinet to give him the particulars of her visit. Robbinet, whom he'd met through Jason Bourne, was the French minister of culture. Robbinet was also one of the new leading lights of the Quai d'Orsay, the French equivalent of Central Intelligence, and so wielded enormous power both inside and outside France. Robbinet had assured Peter that he'd extend Soraya every courtesy in cutting through the Gordian knot of French red tape.

The two cars were slowing as they approached East Capitol Street. They passed 2nd Street, SE, and stopped in front of the Folger Shakespeare Library, one of the capital's more remarkable institutions. Henry Clay Folger had been chairman of Standard Oil, now ExxonMobil. He was cut from the same cloth as the great industrialist/robber barons John D. Rockefeller, J. P. Morgan, and Henry E. Huntington. However, Folger spent much of his later years amassing a staggering collection of First Folios of Shakespeare's plays. In addition, the library housed, in the original edition or facsimile, every important volume on Shakespeare from the invention of the printing press to the end of the seventeenth century, including a copy of every book on history, mythology, and travel that had been available to the playwright. In fact, the library possessed 55 percent of all known books printed in the English language before 1640. But the crown jewels of the collection were the First Folios, the sole textual source of over half of Shakespeare's plays.

As Peter watched Hendricks emerge from his bulletproof car, he wondered what the secretary was doing at the Folger. It wasn't as if he'd come to write a dissertation on Shakespeare or the England of the Tudors and the Stuarts.

Even more intriguing, none of his bodyguards accompanied Hendricks up the steps and into the building. Checking his watch, Peter saw that it was after four, which meant that the building was closed to the public for the day.

Peter was familiar with the premises. There was a side entrance used by the staff and, on occasion, the flock of scholars and fellows who were, at any given time, in residence. He drove around the block, parked, and approached the side door, which was discreetly tucked away behind a line of sheared boxwood.

Thick and solid, the door was made of stout oak, studded with Old

World bronze roundhead nails. It reminded Peter of the door to a medieval castle keep. He drew a pick out of his inside pocket. He'd carried a couple of these, which he'd filed himself, ever since he got locked out of his apartment five years ago.

Within thirty seconds he was inside, moving down a dimly lit corridor that smelled of filtered air and old books. The odor was both pleasant and familiar, bringing back days in his youth when he'd haunted used-book stores for hours at a time, scanning titles, reading chapters or even, sometimes, entire sections. Sometimes, it was enough just feeling the heft of a volume in his hands, imagining his older self, amid a library he himself had amassed.

He kept an eye out for the residents or security, but saw no one. He moved through rooms filled with books in glass-fronted cases crisscrossed by security wires, down more corridors, wood-paneled and hushed.

Gradually, he became aware of the murmur of voices and turned in that direction. As he moved closer, he recognized one of the voices: Hendricks. The other speaker was also male, his voice pitched slightly higher. As he approached closer still, it struck him as being naggingly familiar. The pitch, the cadence, the long-winded sentences without pauses for punctuation. And then, when he had crossed the room, the voices were so clear he was certain they came from the open doorway to the next room. A particular turn of phrase caused him to freeze.

The man Hendricks was talking with was M. Errol Danziger, the vampiric current head of CI. He had sacked Soraya, one of the reasons Peter had quit—he'd seen her demise at CI coming. And now Danziger was in the process of dismantling the proud organization the Old Man had built from the scraps left to him by those who had remodeled the wartime OSS.

Peter stole closer to the open doorway. *If Hendricks is cooking up a deal with Danziger,* he thought, *it's no wonder he doesn't want us to know about it.*

He could hear them clearly now.

"—are you?" Hendricks's voice.

"I couldn't say," Danziger replied.

"You mean you won't."

A deep sigh, probably from the director of CI.

"I don't understand the need for this high-school-level cloak and dag-ger. Why meet here? My office—"

"We weren't ever going to meet in your office," Hendricks said, "for precisely the same reason you weren't invited to the meeting in the Oval Office."

This was followed by what Peter could only characterize as a deathly silence.

"What is it you want from me, Mr. Secretary?" Danziger's voice was so drained of emotion it might be called robotic.

"Cooperation," Hendricks said. "It's what we all want, and by *we* I mean the president. In the matter of Samaritan, I am his voice. Is that understood?"

"Completely," Danziger said. But even at his close remove, Peter could hear the venom in that one word.

"Good," Hendricks said. Whether he had noted the bitterness in the director's voice or he'd chosen to ignore it was impossible for Peter to say. "Because I won't be saying any of this twice." There was a soft rustling. "Samaritan is on the strictest need-to-know basis. That means even the people you choose won't know about it until they arrive at Indigo Ridge. Samaritan is the president's number one priority, which means that from this moment forward it's our number one priority. Here are your orders. Have your people rendezvous with the others at Indigo Ridge forty-eight hours from now."

"Forty-eight hours?" Danziger echoed. "How do you expect— I mean, for God's sake, look at this list. What you're asking is impossible to mobi-lize in that time frame."

"Directors are trained to accomplish the impossible." Hendricks's implied threat was clear enough. "That will be all, Mr. Danziger."

Peter heard first one set of footsteps echoing on the polished floor-boards, then, some moments later, another. Both faded away into the distance.

Peter leaned back against the wall. Samaritan, Indigo Ridge—two clues he would have to follow. *Samaritan is the president's number one priority*, he thought. *Why did Hendricks agree to let Soraya go to Paris? Why didn't he involve us in Samaritan?* These were questions Peter knew he had to answer, and the sooner the better. He had an urge to text Soraya, briefing her on what he had just learned and asking her to come back to Washington, but his trust in her stayed his hand. If she thought this death was important enough to investigate personally, that was good enough for him. He'd learned that her instincts were impeccable.

Then his mind turned to happier thoughts. It looked like Danziger was standing at the precipice. Peter felt elated, especially because he had been given inside knowledge. Anything he could do to sabotage Danziger's part in Samaritan—whatever that was—would be a giant step in destroying his career and getting him out of CI.

Off with his head! Peter's silent shout pinballed around his mind, gaining energy with each successive carom.

Having dropped Essai off at the airport, Bourne stopped at a cantina on the western outskirts of Perales. He was hungry but he also needed time to think. The place was flyblown, with walls somewhere between mustard and adobe. The fluorescent lighting had a tic, and the heartbeat of the ancient iced drink cooler against one wall sounded erratic. There were two waiters, both young men, thin and harried. While scanning the paper menu, he noted faces, expressions, and the angles of repose of the other patrons, old men with skin like tanned hides reading the local paper, drinking coffee, talking politics, or playing chess, an exhausted-looking prostitute past her prime, and a farmer practically inhaling an enormous plate of food. A person on surveillance never held his body in the same way as a civilian. There was always a certain telltale tension in the back, neck, or shoulders. He also studied everyone who came in or out.

Finding nothing out of the ordinary, he ordered a drink and *bandeja paisa* with a side of *arepas*. When the *aguapanela*—sugarcane-sweetened water with a muddle of fresh lime—came he drank half of it at once, then settled back.

"There's a spare sat phone in the glove box, charged and ready to go," Essai had said. *"Also a detailed map of the area. Ibagué is clearly marked, as is the oil field Vegas runs."* That much he could buy, but Essai had made a mistake when he'd added: *"You'll find my sat number pre-programmed into it."* It was entirely possible—even prudent—for Essai to have a spare sat phone, and the map was a no-brainer. But the fact that he had pre-programmed his sat phone number into it indicated to Bourne that it wasn't a spare at all. Bourne asked himself whether it was possible that Essai had known he had been sent to find and kill Corellos. Maybe Corellos himself had told him, but, if so, it would have been long after Essai could've bought a second sat phone. All of this meant that it was likely Essai was lying when he said he no longer had a way to ferret out intel from the Domna. If so, then he had a man inside the group, someone who was loyal to him.

Bourne had never been completely sold on Essai's earnestness, but he didn't for an instant doubt his desire to destroy Severus Domna. In this one matter, he and Essai were aligned—they needed each other. They also needed to trust each other, but the trust was compromised because it pertained solely to the matter of the Domna's demise. After that, all bets were off.

The food arrived, fragrant and steaming. Bourne, suddenly ravenous, dug in, using the *arepas* to soak up the sauce as a combination fork and spoon. As he ate, his thoughts continued. Then there was the matter of the Domna enlisting Boris to kill him. The story was so outrageous he had been inclined to dismiss it out of hand. Until, that is, Essai had described the trap Benjamin El-Arian had laid for his friend. He knew Boris wanted to be the head of FSB-2 more than anything. In a sense, he'd dedicated his entire adult life to that end. If he had been given the choice between his heart's desire and protecting Bourne, what would he do? Bourne was shaken by the knowledge that he didn't know. Boris was a friend, true, and he had saved Boris's life in the temporary war zone of northeastern Iran, but Boris was a Russian through and through. His ethos was different, which made predicting his choices difficult, if not impossible.

The thought that, even at this moment, Boris might be hunting him sent a chill through him that could not be dispelled by Perales's blazing heat. He pulled out the sat phone from Essai's car and, placing it on the table, stared at it for a time. He resisted the urge to call Boris and ask him outright what had happened and where he stood. That would be an unforgivable mistake. If Boris was innocent he'd be mortally offended—in fact, now that Bourne considered it, he'd act mortally offended even if he was guilty. Plus, if Essai was telling the truth, Boris would have been given a warning, and Bourne would lose a vital advantage.

He swept the sat phone off the table as if it were a chess piece. No, he thought, the best thing he could do was to go forward one step at a time into the dark. He was used to that. He had burst from the darkness of an unknown life into this shadow world where everything in front of him was black as night. There was a pain inside him—the agony of unknowing—that he had lived with so long he often forgot it was there. And yet every now and again it rushed back at him with the power of an express train. Nothing in his past was real, nothing he had once done or accomplished, nothing he had felt, no one he had known or cared about. All had been obliterated by his fall into the void. He kept looking for the things that were now impossible to find. The occasional shards that came back to him from time to time only increased his sense of isolation and helplessness. Often, they were disturbing in their own right.

At once, he saw again the woman in the stall of the Nordic disco, the sheen of sweat on her face, the sardonic smile, the muzzle of the handgun she aimed at him. What make and model was it? He strained to remember, but all he could see was her face, devoid of fear or even resignation. He felt the fur collar against his cheeks. Her mouth had opened, those red lips parting. She had said something to him in the moment before he had killed her. What was it? What had she said? He had the impression that it was somehow important, though he was at a loss to say why. And then the memory slithered away from him, back into the blackness of a past that felt as if it belonged to someone else.

To lose everything—your very life—was an unspeakable agony. He was wandering in an unknown land. The stars overhead were arrayed in unfamiliar constellations, and the sun never rose. He was alone, the impenetrable darkness ahead his sole companion.

The darkness, and, of course, the pain.

6

SORAYA ARRIVED IN Paris early on a gray, rain-washed morning. She didn't mind. Paris was one of the only cities she loved in the rain. The slick surfaces, the melancholy mood mysteriously heightened the beauty and romance of the city, the modern-day crust sluiced away, revealing the facades of history, turning like the pages of a book. Besides, hours from now she would be seeing Amun. In the first-class lounge, she showered and changed into fresh clothes, then spent fifteen minutes applying makeup while she drank a cup of awful coffee and ate a croissant that tasted pre-packaged.

She rarely wore makeup other than a neutral lipstick, but she wanted to make an impression on Jacques Robbinet, whom she was also meeting today. However, it wasn't the minister of culture who met her outside of security but a man who introduced himself as Aaron Lipkin-Renais. His credentials identified him as an inspector with the Quai d'Orsay.

He was tall, reed-thin, with one of those unmistakable Gallic noses that rode before him like the prow of a pirate ship. He wore his hand-tailored suit as only the French can. A gentleman, she thought, because he offered his hand to her and bent low over it.

"The secretary sends his apologies," he said in a softly slurred English, "but a meeting at the Élysée Palace kept him from meeting you himself." The Élysée Palace was the residence and office of the French president. It was where the Council of Ministers met. He offered a self-deprecating smile. "I'm afraid you'll have to settle for me."

"Je ne crains pas le moins du monde," she replied with a perfect Parisian accent. I don't mind in the least.

Aaron's long, horsey face broke into a huge grin. *"Eh bien, maintenant, tout devient clair."* Ah, well, now everything becomes clear.

He took her carry-on from her, and as they walked together through the arrivals hall Soraya had a chance to study him in more detail. She judged him to be in his midthirties, fit for a Frenchman. Though she wouldn't call him handsome, there was nevertheless something appealing about him, a certain boyishness in his gray eyes and informal manner that countered strongly the inevitable crusty cynicism built up by intelligence work. She thought they would get along.

Outside, the rain had become a gentle mist. The sky seemed to want to pull apart its gauzy layers. It was exceptionally mild. A light breeze ruffled her hair. Aaron led her to a dark Peugeot waiting at the curb. When the driver saw them, he got out of the car, took Soraya's carry-on from his boss, and stowed it in the trunk. Aaron opened the rear door for her and she climbed in. As soon as he was settled in beside her, they pulled away from the curb and threaded their way out of the airport.

"M. Robbinet has booked you into the Astor Saint-Honoré. It's centrally located and is close to the Élysée Palace. Would you like to go there first and freshen up?"

"Thank you, no," Soraya said. "I'd like to view Laurent's body and then see the forensics report."

He took a file out of the pocket in the driver's-seat back and handed it to her. "You're half Egyptian, aren't you?"

"Is that a problem?" She looked into his gray eyes, searching for a sign of prejudice.

"Not for me. Is it for you?"

"Not at all."

She smoothed her hackles back down. Now she understood. Aaron was Jewish. With the recent huge influx of Muslims, Jews were having a harder time in France, especially Paris. Jewish children were being particularly targeted in schools. Almost every day, there was a report of a Jewish child being beaten by a gang of Muslim children. She'd recently read an alarming report that many Jewish families were leaving France altogether because increasingly they found the charged atmosphere unsafe for their children.

He smiled at her, and she could very clearly see herself in him—the Semitic heritage that Arabs and Jews shared but, tragically, could not bear to contemplate.

She smiled back and hoped that he saw the same. Then she opened the file and looked through the pages. There were several photos of Laurent taken by the forensics team in situ. It was not a pretty sight.

She sucked in her breath. "It looks to me as if the car struck him, then ran him over."

Aaron nodded. "Yes, it would seem so. There's no other way to explain the two sets of injuries—the first to his sternum and rib cage, the second to his head."

"They couldn't have been made in one strike."

"No," he confirmed. "Our coroner says definitely not." He tapped one of the photos. "Someone hated this man very much."

"Or didn't want him to talk."

Aaron gave her a sharp look. "Ah, the light dawns. So that is your interest in this murder. It has international implications."

"I'm not saying a word."

"You don't have to." That boyish grin again.

Soraya was appalled. Was she flirting with him?

They drove onto the Périphérique, the boulevard that girdled the city, and entered Paris via the Porte de Bercy. The moment the Peugeot hit the streets, Soraya felt the welcoming warmth of the city. The familiar streets seemed to beckon to her, smiling.

Soraya tore her gaze away from the old mansard-roofed buildings and returned to her reading. The body exhibited no marks other than those consistent with being run over. His blood work was still being parsed, but the preliminary results noted no elevated alcohol levels or noticeable foreign substances. She returned to the photos, looking more closely at the ones that showed an overall view of the crime scene.

She pointed to a small, vaguely oblong-shaped blob in the lower right-hand corner of photo number three. "What's this?"

"Cell phone," Aaron said. "We think it belonged to the victim, but the damage to it made it impossible to manually access the phone book."

"What about the SIM card?"

"Bent and creased," Aaron said, "but I took it myself to our best IT technician. He's working on getting the information out of it."

Soraya thought a moment. "Change of plan. Take me to the tech, then I want to see where the murder took place."

Aaron took out his cell, punched in a number, then spoke softly for several seconds. "The tech needs more time," he said when he folded away his phone.

"He's found something?"

"He won't say for certain, but I know this man—best to give him the time he needs."

"All right." Soraya nodded reluctantly. "Then let's go to the murder scene."

"As you wish, mademoiselle."

She grimaced. "Call me Soraya. Please."

"Only if you call me Aaron."

"It's a deal."

*D*ocumentos de identidad, por favor."

Bourne handed over his passport to the armed soldier. The man stared hard at Bourne while he flipped the passport open. This was the second roadblock Bourne had encountered. The Revolutionary Armed

Forces of Colombia had been extremely active in the past six months, much to the vexation of the country's president. And then had come the invasion of La Modelo prison that had led to Roberto Corellos's escape. In a fit of pique, El Presidente had begun flexing his military muscle. Bourne was sure the *federales* were looking to summarily execute any FARC rebels they came across.

The soldier handed back Bourne's passport and, without a word, waved him through. Bourne put the car in gear and set off after the caravan of semis in front of him. He'd been on the road several hours and was now high in the mountains.

Ibagué lay along the National Route 40 that connected Bogotá with Cali, then continued to the Pacific coast. It was on a plateau forty-two hundred feet above sea level on the eastern slopes of the Cordillera Central, the central range of the Andes Mountains.

The highway snaked back and forth in perilous switchbacks. Narrow shoulders plunged down hundreds of feet into needle-pointed pine forests or the remains of gigantic rockslides. Now and again he spotted great charred slashes in the pines, evidence of lightning strikes. The sky was enormous, a kaleidoscope of swiftly moving cloud formations and dazzling sunlight. The elevation and the Southern Hemisphere sun combined to lend everything an astonishing clarity, knife-edged and vivid. Above him, the black crosses of condors wheeled and banked in the high thermals.

According to Jalal Essai, he would soon come to La Línea—the longest tunnel in Latin America. It cut through the mountain known as Alta de La Línea and was meant to ease the traffic on the truck-clogged highway to the Pacific port of Buenaventura. The tunnel was so new it wasn't on his map, which lay open on the seat beside him. As Essai had warned, there was no cell service here, and his sat phone had no GPS function.

The traffic was heavy, the caravans of semis moving at identical speed, rolling around a long curve, following the contour of the mountain. And then, viewed at the apex of the bend, the mouth of La Línea gaped, a black hole into which the snaking traffic disappeared and, on the eastbound side, reappeared.

Bourne headed into the tunnel, a long, sleek tube that bored straight through the mountain. It was lit on either side with strings of argon lights whose cool, bluish light spun off the hoods of oncoming vehicles.

The traffic slowed, as was normal in tunnels, but the progress was steady. He passed the three-quarters mark and was beginning to see a glimmering of daylight in the distance when the line of trucks abruptly slowed. A sea of glowing ruby brake lights appeared and traffic came to a standstill.

Had there been an accident? Was there another roadblock? Bourne strained in his seat, craning his neck. There were no flashing lights, no sign of the telltale sawhorses the military used to block the highway.

He slipped out of the car. A moment later he saw a group of men threading their way between the lanes of vehicles, coming toward him. They were heavily armed with submachine guns, but they weren't wearing the uniforms of the Colombian army. A cadre of FARC insurgents had stopped the traffic. Why?

He saw the leader now, a broad-shouldered man with a full beard and coffee-colored eyes even the lurid glow thrown by the argon lights couldn't wash out. One man stopped at each vehicle, holding up a faxed photo to show the driver while the others checked out the car's backseat and trunk. The trucks took longer, as the soldiers compelled the drivers, often at gunpoint, to open the backs so they could inspect the contents.

Bourne cautiously walked closer, passing other drivers who had climbed down from their cabs and were talking nervously among themselves. All at once he saw the fax sheet clearly. He was staring at himself. The rebels were looking for him. No time to wonder why. Turning on his heel, he walked back to his car and rummaged through the glove box, which offered up a screwdriver and a wrench, both useful weapons.

Retreating on foot, he ducked down, slid underneath a semi, crawling backward. Three vehicles behind him, he came out at the rear of an open-bed truck. Grabbing onto the nylon cords that tied down a canvas cover, he swung up onto the rear. From that vantage point he saw more FARC soldiers approaching from the rear. Ahead or behind, there was no exit.

Untying a section of canvas, he dropped down into the truck bed. The hemp sacks were stamped with the name of a well-known plantation. He used the screwdriver to rip open a corner. The truck was transporting green coffee beans. Leaving the items he'd taken from his car, he reemerged onto the canvas and took a cautious look ahead. The FARC rebels were making headway. They were almost at his car. Once they saw that it was empty, they'd know their prey was somewhere close at hand. He needed to be on his way before then.

Stealing down to the tarmac of the highway, he crept along the side of the open-bed truck. The driver was standing against the side of the semi in front, talking nervously with another man, probably the driver of the semi or his relief. The door to the cab was open and Bourne slithered in. As Bourne watched, the driver took out a pack of cigarettes, shook one out, and put it between his lips. He dug in his pocket for a light, but couldn't find one. He turned around and began to walk back toward the cab of his truck.

Bourne froze.

Aaron stood in the street on Place de l'Iris. "This is where M. Laurent was hit," he said.

"Anything on the car that hit him?"

"Not much. The eyewitnesses disagree on the manufacturer. BMW, Fiat, Citroën."

"None of those cars look alike."

"Eyewitnesses," he lamented. "But we did get black paint off the victim."

Soraya was studying the roadbed. "Not much help there, either."

Aaron crouched down beside her. "The same eyewitnesses claimed he had just stepped off the sidewalk."

"He stepped out into traffic without looking?" Soraya looked doubtful.

Aaron shrugged. "He might have been distracted. Maybe someone called to him, maybe he remembered he had to pick up the dry cleaning." He shrugged in that totally Gallic manner. "Who knows?"

"Someone knows," she said. "The person who killed him." Something occurred to her and she stood suddenly. "Where was his cell phone found?"

Aaron showed her and she went back onto the sidewalk several paces. "Now, when I step down into the street, run into me."

"What?"

"You heard me," she said a bit impatiently. "Just do it."

She took out her phone and put it to her ear, then walked at a brisk pace to the edge of the curb and down onto the street, whereupon Aaron, running, hit her. Her right arm flew diagonally out, and if she had not held on to it her phone would have hit the street more or less where they found Laurent's.

A slow smile spread across her face. "He was talking on his cell when he was hit."

"So what? Businesspeople are on their cell phones constantly." Aaron appeared unimpressed. "It was a coincidence."

"Maybe it was," Soraya said, "maybe it wasn't." She turned toward his car. "Let's talk to your tech and see if he managed to pull anything from the phone or its SIM card."

As they were walking back to Aaron's car, she stopped and turned around. She looked at the building directly across the sidewalk from where the hit-and-run took place. Her gaze rose up the gleaming green-glass and stainless-steel facade.

"What building is this?" she asked.

Aaron squinted up through the noonday gloom. "It's the Île de France Bank building. Why?"

"It's possible that's where Laurent was coming from."

"I don't see why," Aaron said, checking his notes. "The victim worked for the Monition Club."

Another fact Soraya hadn't known about her would-be informant.

"It's an archaeological society with offices here, Washington, DC, Cairo, and Riyadh."

"When you say here, you mean La Défense?"

"No. The Eighth Arrondissement, at Five, Rue Vernet."

"So what the hell was he doing here? Getting a loan?"

"The Monition Club is quite wealthy," Aaron said, again consulting his notes. "In any event, I checked with Île de France. He had no appointment with anyone at the bank, he wasn't a client, and they never heard of him."

"So why was he here on a busy workday morning?"

Aaron spread his hands. "My men are still trying to find out."

"Maybe he had a friend there. Have you talked to his associates at the Monition Club?"

"No one knows much about him, he kept to himself, apparently. He reported directly to his superior, so no one could tell me what he was doing at La Défense. Laurent's superior is out of town until tonight. I have an appointment to interview him tomorrow morning."

Soraya turned to him. "You've been very thorough."

"Thank you." The inspector couldn't hide his smile.

Soraya walked to his car, but before she got in, she took one last look at the Île de France building. There was something about it that both drew and repelled her.

The semi's driver called to his pal, and the man turned and went back to where the other driver waved a book of wooden matches. The openbed driver leaned forward while the other one struck the match and held the flame to the end of his cigarette. He reared back, pulling the smoke deep into his lungs. The semi's driver checked nervously over his shoulder, measuring the FARC's progress.

Bourne quickly checked the seat and the glove box. Nothing. Then in the well of the passenger's side he saw a cheap plastic lighter. It must have fallen out of the driver's pocket as he was getting out. He grabbed it. He slithered out of the truck's cab and went farther down the line until he encountered a knot of drivers.

"*¿Hombre, sabe usted lo que está pasando?*" one of them asked. Do you know what's going on?

"FARC guerrillas," Bourne said, which got them even more agitated.

"*¡Ai de mi!*" another cried.

"*Escuchamé,*" Bourne said. "Does anyone have a jerry-can of gasoline; my truck is dry. If the rebels order me to move and I can't, they'll shoot me dead."

The men nodded their agreement with this grim assessment, and one of them ran off. A moment later he returned and handed Bourne the jerry-can.

Bourne thanked him profusely and departed. When he was sure no one was watching him, he climbed up onto the canvas of the coffee truck and disappeared back underneath.

Inside, he used the screwdriver to puncture the jerry-can near the bottom, so the gasoline slowly leaked out over a couple of the sacks. Then he lit it. The result was a whoosh of flames, followed by a cloud of thick smoke so acrid it was choking. Bourne, holding his breath, got out of there before more gas leaked out and the conflagration spread. His eyes were already watering. The smoke billowed up through the hole in the canvas. Bourne climbed down just as the canvas itself caught fire. Flames licked upward, and now the smoke billowed in earnest as the rest of the hemp sacks started to burn. The smoke quickly reached the tunnel's arched ceiling and, boiling, spread horizontally.

It took only moments for visibility in that part of the tunnel to erode severely. People started coughing and wheezing, their eyes tearing so badly they couldn't see. Shouts went up from the soldiers in the forefront. Then the basso voice of the commander bellowed through, calling for his men to retreat. But the smoke was too thick, and the soldiers were bent over, gasping.

Bourne sprinted through this chaos, shoving aside soldiers and drivers alike. The wrench was gripped in his right hand. A FARC rebel loomed out of the smoke, abruptly blocking his path with both his body and his submachine gun. Bourne slammed him across the cheek with the wrench, kicked him in the groin, and, as the rebel doubled over, slid past him. Another was on him almost immediately. Bourne could see the commander; he had no time to waste. Absorbing two punishing body blows, he drove home the screwdriver between two ribs, and the rebel went down.

Bourne came up on the commander from a different lane. Sliding across the hood of a vehicle, he grabbed the man, disarmed him, and, jerking him hard, pulled him, stumbling, toward the light at the far end of the tunnel.

The commander was gasping and trying to spit out the smoke. His red-rimmed eyes continued to brim with tears, which rolled down his pockmarked cheeks. He struck out blindly. He was very strong. It took a knife-edged blow of Bourne's hand to his throat to subdue him.

Bourne pulled him along as fast as he could, ignoring the commander's choked curses. He was beyond the perimeter of the advancing rebels. Up ahead, he could make out the jerry-rigged blockade of FARC vehicles: four jeeps and a flatbed truck FARC was using for provisions, weapons, and ammo transport. Two drivers, who had been smoking, had grabbed their pistols and were now aiming the weapons at Bourne. Then they saw their commander, his own Makarov pressed into the side of his head.

"¡Ponga sus armas hacia abajo!" Bourne shouted as he drove the commander forward.

When they hesitated, he slammed the barrel into the soft spot behind the commander's right ear. Blood spurted and the commander cried out. The rebels put their pistols down on the hood of the flatbed truck.

"¡Ahora se alejan de los jeeps!"

"¡Haz lo que dice!" the commander shouted through a fit of coughing.

The men backed away from the jeeps; Bourne shoved the commander forward into one and climbed in beside him. A rebel lunged for his pistol and Bourne shot him in the shoulder. As he spun away and fell to the ground, Bourne said, *"¿Tu turno?"* Your turn? The other rebel raised his hands and did not budge.

"¡Si vienen después de nosotros," Bourne called back to the men as he started the vehicle and put it into gear, *"lo mato!"* If you come after us, I'll kill him.

He stepped on the accelerator and they sped away from the smoking tunnel.

7

THE MOMENT PETER got back to Treadstone HQ, he fired up his computer, logged in his code name, using the algorithm of the day, and scoured all the clandestine services' databases for the word *Samaritan*. He wasn't surprised to receive a null finding. He sat staring at the blank screen for a moment, then typed in "Indigo Ridge."

This time he got an immediate hit. He read the government assessment with mounting fascination. Indigo Ridge, an area in California, was ground zero for the mining of rare earths. Rare earths, he read, were essential for rechargeable nickel hydride batteries—something he used every day, but never gave a thought to. The real name was lanthanum nickel hydride—a rare earth. Rare earths were used in every laser as well as in electronic warfare, jamming devices, the electromagnetic rail-gun, the Long Range Acoustic Device, and the Area Denial System used on the Stryker vehicle. The list of cutting-edge weapons needing rare earths was staggering.

The next paragraphs dealt with NeoDyme, the company created to mine the rare earths at Indigo Ridge. NeoDyme had just gone public, but it had the backing of the US government. Peter immediately understood the strategic importance of NeoDyme and Indigo Ridge. In that event, Samaritan was linked in some way with the rare earth mine. But what was its purpose?

Peter got up and stretched. He waved away Ann, his secretary, as he emerged from his office, went over to get himself some coffee and a stale doughnut. He stirred sugar and half-and-half into his mug, took it and the doughnut back into his office to have a think.

Ever since he could remember, sugar had been a great stimulator of creative thinking for him. As he chomped down on the doughnut, he thought about the meeting between Hendricks and Danziger. And then the thought came: What if Samaritan was an interagency initiative? That would make it huge, indeed. And again, Peter felt the sharp pang of being left out. If Hendricks didn't trust him, then why did he want Peter heading up Treadstone? It made no sense to him. Peter didn't like mysteries, especially when they cropped up in his territory. And then he thought of something else that made him sit up straight. In trying to find out about Samaritan he'd been able to access all the clandestine services' databases. Hendricks had told him that, almost as an aside. Odd, considering, so far as Peter was aware, it was an unprecedented coup. The various services were notoriously zealous in guarding their own data, even after the well-publicized revamping following 9/11. Being on the inside, Peter knew that plan was for PR purposes because the American public had to be calmed and soothed. The fact remained that when it came to interagency intel sharing nothing much had changed. The clandestine services community was still a feudal nightmare of separate fiefdoms, lorded over by political-minded mandarins jockeying for congressional funding while desperately staving off budget cuts and staff downsizing forced by the current economic climate.

Dusting off his fingertips, he took a swig of coffee and dived back into the top-secret soup he had at his fingertips, courtesy of his boss. At some point, he wondered whether Hendricks had had an ulterior motive in getting this access for Treadstone.

He couldn't help but wonder why Hendricks had told him about it in such an offhand manner. He was trained in suspicion, to see ulterior motives, to peer into the dim interiors of what people said and did. Had Hendricks been giving him a subtle clue to hunt around the database soup? But for what?

What if it had to do with Hendricks himself? He navigated to Hendricks's own computer and sat there for a moment, staring at the blinking box that asked for a security code. He thought about words that his boss might use. Sitting back, he closed his eyes, pondering the briefing at Hendricks's house this morning. He went over everything that had been said, every move the secretary had made.

Then he recalled Hendricks's curious parting line: "*Oh, by the way, I've been able to get Treadstone access to all the clandestine services' databases.*" He frowned. No, that wasn't quite it. His frown deepened as he struggled to recall the secretary's exact phrasing.

"Excuse me, Director."

He looked up to see Ann standing in the doorway. "What is it?" he snapped.

She flinched. She was not yet used to her boss's moods. "I'm sorry to bother you, but there's a problem at school with my son and I need a couple of hours off."

"Of course," he said, waving at her vaguely. "Go on." His mind had already returned to its original train of thought.

Ann was about to leave when she turned back. "Oh, I almost forgot. Before she left, Director Moore asked for an additional server to be added to her—"

"She asked for what?"

Peter had swiveled toward her and was half out of his seat. She turned pale, clearly scared half to death. Through his mounting excitement, he recognized this and willed his voice to modulate more normally. "Ann, did you say that Soraya asked for another server?"

"Yes. It's going to be installed tonight, so on the off chance you're going to be working late—"

"Thank you, Ann." He forced himself to smile at her. "As for your son, take as much time as you need."

"Thank you, Director." Slightly bewildered, she turned, grabbed her coat and handbag, and left.

Peter, turning back to his computer screen, thought long and hard about Hendricks's precise words. Then he had it: *"Oh, by the way, I've been able to get the Treadstone servers access to all the clandestine services' databases."*

Servers. Peter's eyes flew open. Why on earth had he said that when the servers had nothing to do with access? The Treadstone servers were where its own data was stored. He stared at the blinking box in the middle of the screen, asking its mysterious question. *Jesus Christ*, he thought, *could it be that simple?*

His fingers trembling slightly, he typed in the word: "servers."

At once, the box was replaced by a file tree. Peter stared in disbelief. He was inside Hendricks's computer. The secretary wanted him there, he was absolutely certain of that. He'd delivered a coded message to Peter. Why hadn't he been able to tell Peter outright?

Peter's first thought was that Hendricks was afraid his house was bugged, but he immediately dismissed the thought. The secretary's house and offices were electronically swept twice a week. So Hendricks was afraid of something else. Was it someone on the *inside*, one of his own people?

Peter stared at the screen. He had a sense that he would find the answer somewhere within the secretary's file tree. Leaning forward, he got to work with a feverish intensity.

This is utter madness," the FARC commander said as Bourne hurtled the stolen jeep down National 40.

"How did you know I was in the tunnel?" Bourne said.

"You will be followed to the ends of the earth." His name was Suarez. He hadn't been reticent about telling Bourne his name or the ways in which he was certain Bourne would die.

Bourne smiled. "There isn't one of your men who could get out of Colombia."

Suarez laughed, even though it caused him some pain in the area behind his right ear. "Do you think FARC is my only affiliation?"

Bourne glanced at him and that was when he saw the gold ring, gleaming on the thick forefinger of his right hand.

"You're a member of Severus Domna."

"And you are a dead man," the commander said flatly.

All at once he grabbed at the wheel. Bourne smashed the barrel of his Makarov down on the back of his hand, and Suarez bellowed like a maddened bull. He snatched his hand away, cradling it with the other.

"Fuck, fuck, fuck!" he cried. "You've broken it!"

"Relax." Bourne hummed to himself as they rocketed along. He deftly moved the jeep around lumbering semis and laden flatbeds.

Suarez, rocking back and forth in pain, said, "What the hell are you so happy about, *maricón*?"

For some time, Bourne occupied himself by flying past vehicles. Then he said, "I know how you knew where I was."

"No," Suarez said, "you don't."

"Someone at the last roadblock before the tunnel made me and radioed you, someone also with the Domna."

"This is true, but I am not following orders. Your death is a gift to a friend of mine, an enemy of yours."

He was whey-faced, the pain causing beads of sweat to break out at his hairline. He stared fixedly ahead, until his gaze strayed to the side mirror. A smile flickered across his lips and, in the space of a heartbeat, was gone. Bourne, who had been checking the rearview mirror every minute or so, saw the two motorcycles flicking in and out of the traffic behind him.

"Roberto Corellos has expended a lot of capital with us to have you killed."

So Corellos was taking revenge for Bourne having lost him face in front of his men. Now they were mortal enemies.

"You'd better buckle up," Bourne said.

He waited for the motorcycles to break free of the other vehicles behind him, then he accelerated. Putting on speed, they closed the distance between them. At the moment of their maximum acceleration,

Bourne trod on the brakes so hard that the jeep laid a layer of rubber onto the macadam of the highway. The vehicle swerved violently from side to side as he threw it into neutral, its transmission traveling down through the gears as its tires fought to grip the road.

The motorcycles shot past him and then, swerving mightily, braked, turning in a wide circle. Bourne forced the transmission back up the ladder and stomped on the accelerator. The jeep shot forward, slamming grille-first into the right-hand motorcycle, catching it broadside, throwing it completely off the highway. Suarez's forehead nearly went through the windshield. The motorcycle skidded wildly, the cyclist trying desperately to regain control as he skated across the width of the macadam. An instant later it crossed the narrow shoulder and disappeared over the mountainside.

A gunshot spiderwebbed the jeep's windshield and Bourne threw the vehicle into reverse, spun it around until it was headed directly at the second motorcycle. The biker was taking aim again with his handgun. The cycle was between the jeep and the mountainside with its vertiginous drop of hundreds of feet. Owing to the FARC roadblock, the oncoming traffic had been at a standstill. Now motorists were scrambling to get away from the chaos.

Bourne drove directly at the cyclist, whose pistol was aimed right at him.

"*Dios mio*, what the hell are you doing?" Suarez shouted. "You're going to get us both killed."

"If that's what it takes," Bourne said.

"The reports about you are true." The commander stared at him. "You're insane."

The motorcyclist must have thought so as well, because, after firing wildly, he took off in a spray of gravel. Braking, Bourne extended his left arm and squeezed off a shot. The motorcyclist's arms flew outward as he was launched off the cycle's seat. It slammed into a stalled car, which slewed into the truck in front of it.

Bourne took off down the highway, which, owing to both the FARC blockade and the fire in the tunnel, was now entirely deserted.

8

THIRTY THOUSAND FEET in the air, Boris Karpov sat in the jet-liner and watched the dove-gray clouds scroll past the Perspex window. As always, he had mixed feelings about leaving Russia. A Russian, he mused, was never truly comfortable outside the motherland. This was to be expected. The Russian people were special—extraordinary, really, once you took into account the terrible history they'd had to endure first under the czars, the Cossacks, then Stalin and Beria, a darkness constantly stalking his beautiful country. Altruism was not a well-known quality in the Russian mind-set—deprivation had made self-preservation the pri-mary motivating factor for so long, it was now hardwired into the Russian psyche—but in this respect Boris was different from his fellows. His love of Russia motivated him to want a better life not just for himself but for those people who were continually looking up at a light they could never attain.

The first-class cabin attendant asked if he had everything he needed.

"We're baking chocolate chip cookies," she said, bending over him with a smile. She was blond and blue-eyed—Nordic, he surmised—and had a slight accent. "You can have them with milk, chocolate milk, cof-fee, tea, or any of a dozen liquors."

Cookies and milk, Karpov thought with a wry smile, *how all-American.* "The classic," he said, making the attendant laugh softly.

"Mr. Stonyfield, you Americans," she said affectionately, using Karpov's legend name. And with a hushed whoosh of fabric against pantyhose, she returned up the aisle.

Karpov sank back into his ruminations. Of course Americans were born into the light, so they were used to looking down on everyone else. But what else could you expect from such a privileged people? Karpov did not know what to make of being mistaken for one of them. He waited for the reaction to come, and when it did, he realized that he was somehow humiliated, as if he were a country hick who had by some miracle been momentarily mistaken for a Yale graduate. The attendant's error had diminished him in some way he couldn't quite grasp, holding up to him the mirror of everything he had lacked from the moment he'd been born.

His parents had had little time for him, being locked in grim and silent combat to determine who could have the most affairs during the course of their marriage. There was never any thought of divorce; that would negate the rules of the game. Consequently, they scarcely noticed when Karpov's sister, Alix, died of an uncontrollable brain fever. Karpov had taken care of her, nursing her through her terrible and debilitating illness, first after school, then cutting school entirely to be with her. When she was transferred to the hospital he went with her. He formed the impression that his parents were relieved to have both the children out of the house.

"So gloomy," his mother would mutter as she made breakfast. "So damn gloomy."

But most mornings she failed to appear. Karpov sensed that she had never come home during the night.

"I can't stand it" was all his father could manage the mornings he did appear. He couldn't look at Alix, much less go into her room. "What's the point?" he responded to Karpov's question one morning. "She doesn't know I'm there."

On the contrary, Karpov knew that Alix knew when someone was with her. She often squeezed his hand as he sat beside the bed. He read stories to her from books he'd bought. Other times he read aloud the lessons from schoolbooks he deemed important enough to learn. Because of these sessions with his sister he discovered a love of history. What he loved best was to read to her about various periods in Russia's storied past, though admittedly some were depressing, awfully difficult to digest.

Karpov was at her bedside at the hospital when she died. After the doctor's pronouncement, a suffocating silence engulfed the room. It was as if everything in the world had stopped, even his heart. His chest felt as if at any instant it would cave in. The smell of antiseptic made him want to gag. He bent over Alix's waxen face and kissed her cool forehead. There was absolutely no outward evidence of the massive and brutal war that had gone on inside her brain.

"Is there anything I can do?" the attending nurse had said when he exited the room.

He shook his head; his chest was too congested with emotion to allow for speech. Echoes followed him down the linoleum-lined corridors, the pain-filled, inarticulate noises of the sick and the dying. Outside, the glowing Moscow twilight was filled with snow. People walked this way and that, chatting, smoking, even laughing. A young man and woman, their heads together as they whispered to each other, crossed the street. A mother pulled her little boy along, singing softly to him. Karpov observed these everyday occurrences as a prisoner will the sky and passing clouds outside his tiny, barred window. These things no longer belonged to him. He was cut off from them like a diseased limb cleaved from a tree.

There was a hole in Karpov's heart where Alix had resided for so long. The tears came and, as he walked aimlessly, watching the snow pile up, listening to the bells of St. Basil's, muffled and indistinct, he cried for her, but also for himself, because now he was truly alone.

"Sir?"

The attendant had reappeared with his milk and cookies, and Karpov shook himself like a dog coming out of the rain.

"I'm sorry," she said. "Shall I come back?"

He shook his head and she slid his tray out and set down the plate of cookies and the glass of milk.

"Still warm," she said. "Is there anything else?"

Karpov smiled at her, but there was more than a hint of sadness in it. "You can sit down beside me."

Her soft silver bell of laughter wafted over him like a cool breeze. "What a flirt you are, Mr. Stonyfield," she said. Shaking her head, she left him alone.

Karpov stared down at the cookies, not seeing them at all. He was thinking of Jason Bourne, he was thinking about what he was setting out to do, he was thinking of what his decision would mean not only for the present but for the rest of his life.

Nothing would ever be the same. The knowledge didn't frighten him—he was too used to the unknown for that. But he did have a queasy feeling in the pit of his stomach, as if a group of moths were fluttering there, directionless, waiting for the inevitable to happen.

It wouldn't be long now. That was the only thing he knew for certain.

Marcel Probst, the Quai d'Orsay IT tech to whom Inspector Lipkin-Renais had delivered Laurent's cell phone and its SIM card, was one of those Frenchmen for whom wine, cheese, and an arrogant sneer were the essentials of life.

Moments after she had arrived with Aaron, Probst made it clear via a sour, almost offended look that he did not like Soraya. Whether it was because she was Muslim or a woman, or both, Soraya could not say. Then again, he didn't seem entirely enamored of Aaron, either, so who could say. In any event, his face, sour as a prune, announced his prejudices like a warning sign on a highway.

Probst was dapper, well dressed, and in his late forties. In other words, the direct opposite of the American IT techs of Soraya's acquaintance. *Liberté, égalité, fraternité*, she thought as she stepped up to his workbench. It contained, among other paraphernalia, a laptop computer and an oscilloscope flanked by a pair of high-end bookshelf speakers.

"What do you have for us?" Aaron said.

M. Probst pulled on his lower lip, making it into a kind of teapot spout. "The phone itself is beyond even my skills," he said, "and the SIM card is a mess."

Apparently, he never met a consonant he didn't try to swallow. *Maybe*, Soraya thought, *they tasted like Brie.*

M. Probst cocked an eyebrow upward. "Was the instrument, by any chance, compromised while being transported here?"

"Certainly not," Aaron said. And then, somewhat irritably, "Have you found something or not? Get on with it, if you please."

M. Probst grunted. "The curious thing is that from what I can tell, the SIM card was wiped clean of information."

Soraya's heart sank. "From the damage?"

"Well, mademoiselle, that depends. You see, this SIM card was subjected to two forms of damage. The one as I have already mentioned is physical." He tapped the oscilloscope's spikily juddering line. "The other was electronic."

"What do you mean?" Aaron said.

"I can't be one hundred percent sure," M. Probst said, "but there is a strong indication that the card was subjected to an electronic pulse that wiped it clean." He cleared his throat. "Well, almost. There was only one thing salvageable," he said. "There is no doubt that it was entered after the electronic pulse, but before the phone was rendered useless."

"You mean in the instant before Laurent was struck by the car," Soraya said, and immediately regretted the interruption.

M. Probst glared at her as if she were a rat that had crawled into his sanctum sanctorum.

"I believe that is what I said," he said stiffly.

"Moving on," Aaron said, gamely, "let's get to what you salvaged."

M. Probst sniffed like a character out of Victor Hugo's *Les Misérables*.

"It's a good thing you came to me, Inspector. I very much doubt anyone else could have brought up so much as a kilobyte of information."

For the first time, a smile curved M. Probst's bloodless lips, thin as a miser's coat. It was clear he felt he had put the interlopers in their place. "Here is what was transferred to the SIM card in the last moment of the victim's life."

On the laptop screen, a single cryptic word appeared: "dinoig."

Aaron shook his head and turned to Soraya. "Do you know what that means?"

Soraya looked at him and said, "I'm starving. Take me to your favorite restaurant."

Miles away from La Línea, Bourne pulled off the highway into a dense copse of trees and overgrown brush. Exiting the jeep, he came around to the other side and hauled Suarez bodily out of his seat.

"What are you doing?" Suarez said. "Where are we going?"

He was a mess. The right side of his head was bloody, a huge bruise, standing up like a fist, scarred his forehead, and he cradled his bruised and swollen right hand.

Bourne dragged him along, hauling him to his feet when he occasionally stumbled. When they were completely hidden from the road, Bourne shoved Suarez against the trunk of a tree.

"Tell me about your role in Severus Domna."

"It won't help you."

When Bourne came at him, he held up his good hand. "All right, all right! But I'm telling you it won't do you any good. The Domna is completely compartmentalized. I move goods for the group when and if I'm asked to, but I don't know anything else."

"What kinds of goods?"

"The crates are sealed," Suarez said. "I don't know and I don't want to know."

"What are the crates made of?" Bourne asked.

Suarez shrugged. "Wood. Sometimes stainless steel."

Bourne considered for a moment. "Who gives you your orders?"

"A man. A voice on the phone. I never met him. I don't even know his name."

Bourne snapped his fingers. "Phone."

Suarez dug awkwardly in his pocket with his left hand and drew out the phone.

"Call your contact."

Suarez's head moved spastically back and forth on his shoulders. "I can't. He'll kill me."

Bourne took Suarez's swollen right hand in his and broke the pinkie. Suarez screamed and tried unsuccessfully to pull his hand away. Bourne shook his head and took hold of the next finger on the hand.

"Five seconds."

Sweat was rolling freely down Suarez's face, staining his collar. "*Dios*, no."

"Two seconds."

Suarez opened his mouth but nothing came out. Bourne broke the second finger and the commander nearly passed out. His knees gave out and he slid down the tree trunk. Bourne slapped his cheek. Suarez's eyes watered and he turned and vomited onto the ground.

Bourne imprisoned his middle finger. "Five seconds."

"*¡Basta!*" Suarez cried. "*¡Basta!*"

All the color had drained from his face and he was shaking in reaction to the trauma. He stared at his cell phone, clutched in his sweaty left hand. Then, as if snapping out of a trance, he looked up at Bourne.

"What . . . what do you want me to say, *hombre*?"

"I want his name," Bourne said.

"He'll never give it to me."

Bourne tightened his grip on the middle finger of Suarez's ruined right hand. "Find a way, *hombre*, or we continue where we left off."

Suarez licked his lips and nodded. He punched a button and a number popped up on the screen.

"Wait!" Bourne said and, reaching over, killed the connection.

"What?" Suarez said in that slightly dazed tone of voice that had come out of him ever since his fingers had been broken. "What is it? I did what you asked. Don't you want me to call him?"

Bourne sat back on his haunches, thinking. He knew who Suarez's contact was. He recognized the digits. Suarez was calling Jalal Essai's satellite phone.

9

CHEZ GEORGES, THE restaurant to which Aaron took Soraya, was a block from the Bourse—Paris's stock exchange. As such, lunch was attended mostly by suits, talking stocks, bonds, options, derivative swaps, grain and pork belly futures. Nevertheless, the atmosphere was Old World Paris before the advent of the EU, the euro, and the slow disintegration of French culture.

"First it was the Germans, then the Dutch," Aaron said. "And now we are encircled by what amounts to refugees from North Africa with no hope of integration, jobs, or prospects. It's no wonder they want to burn Paris to the ground."

They were sitting at the long banquette, facing each other, eating hanger steaks and the establishment's astonishing *frites*.

"The homogeneity of the French is under siege."

Aaron looked at her for a moment. "This is how we do," he said, using the English slang of American cops. This is the way we do things.

She laughed so hard she had to put a hand to her mouth in order not to spray food all over her plate.

His eyes crinkled nicely when he smiled. Despite that, the smile made him look younger, like a little boy whose joy is unadulterated by life's responsibilities and concerns.

"So." He put down his utensils and steepled his fingers. "Dinoig?" He spread his hands. "You have an explanation."

"I do." Soraya licked salt off the tips of her fingers. "The word is an anagram."

Aaron stared hard at her for a moment. "A code?"

Soraya nodded. "Admittedly a crude one. But it was meant as a fail-safe. In case my contact got into trouble."

"Terminal trouble." Aaron took a sip of the Badoit mineral water; he'd very kindly refrained from ordering wine.

Soraya dug in her handbag, pulled out a pen and a pad, and wrote "dinoig" on it. She looked at it for several moments before she said, "Since the anagram begins with a consonant, let's start with the assumption that the word begins with a vowel. Two i's and an o. There are only six letters, so the chances of both i's being in the center are virtually nil." Beneath "dinoig," she wrote "I." "Now it becomes easier because of our choices for a next letter; n makes the most sense."

Now the second line read "In."

"There." She looked up at Aaron and turned the pad around so that it faced him. Then she handed him the pen. "You finish it."

Aaron frowned for a moment, then he wrote down the next four letters and turned the pad back for her to read.

"'Indigo,'" Soraya read aloud.

Peter's back was killing him. He'd been working nonstop on Hendricks's files, opening the folders one by one since they were only marked with numerical designations: 001, 002, 003, and so forth. They were filled with memos, to-do lists, even reminders of birthdays and anniversaries. The files were remarkably devoid of anything interesting. He rose from his computer crouch, put his hands at the small of his back, and stretched backward. Then he went off to relieve his aching bladder. Peter liked to think while he peed. In fact, some of his best ideas had come to him while his bladder was emptying. There was something about the physical feeling of relief that set his brain to wandering down fruitful paths.

He stared at the wall. His eyes roved among the multitude of small cracks in the plaster, finding fanciful shapes as if they were clouds passing across the sky. Except these shapes were permanent. That being so, some of them had already become friends. There was the Roaring Lion, the Boy Holding Balloons, the Boxing Kangaroo, the Old Man with Drooping Earlobes. And then there was Houdini, the man with what to Peter looked like a lock around his waist.

"Good Lord!" Peter cried all at once.

Shaking and zipping up, he hurriedly washed his hands and virtually ran back to his computer terminal. Now, instead of going folder by folder, he scrolled down, looking for a file locked with an electronic encryption.

Sure enough, there was one, at the bottom of the folder tree. When prompted for a password, he typed in: "servers." Nothing happened, not that he was surprised. It would have been extraordinarily stupid for Hendricks to use the same password twice.

Peter twirled a pencil between his teeth, sat back, and considered his next move. What word would Hendricks use to safeguard this file? He tried Hendricks's birthdate, the date he was appointed secretary of defense, his address. Nada.

He sat there so long without moving his cursor that Hendricks's screensaver came on. He was looking at a beautiful green-eyed woman with high cheekbones and an open, smiling face. Fifteen seconds later the image faded out and another of the same woman appeared. This time, she was seen with Hendricks. They were holding hands on a bridge in Venice. The woman was Amanda, Hendricks's third wife. She had died five years ago. The scene changed again to a shot of Amanda in a formal gown, on the terrace of a huge stone mansion.

"*Idiot!*" Peter thought, smacking his forehead with the heel of his hand. He typed in: "Amanda."

Open Sesame. He was in!

The file contained two long paragraphs and one short addendum.

The long paragraphs seemed to be notes Hendricks had taken after a recent meeting he'd had in the Oval Office with the president; General Marshall, the Pentagon's chief of staff; Mike Holmes, the national security adviser; and someone by the name of Roy FitzWilliams. Peter was immediately reminded of the conversation between Hendricks and Danziger at the Folger he'd overheard piecemeal. *"We weren't ever going to meet in your office,"* his boss had said, *"for precisely the same reason you weren't invited to the meeting in the Oval Office."*

From what Peter read, the briefing concerned the extreme strategic importance of rare earth metals. The president had decided on an interagency task force, code-named Samaritan, to safeguard the Indigo Ridge mining operation in California. Apparently, the president had put Hendricks in charge of Samaritan and had given it the highest priority.

Peter had reached the end of the second paragraph and was wondering anew why his boss hadn't briefed him and Soraya regarding Samaritan when his gaze fell on the last, short addendum. With a shock that went through his body, he discovered that the paragraph was addressed to him:

Peter, I know you're reading this; you're more curious than George the chimp. There's something about this FitzWilliams character that disturbs me. Can't put my finger on it, which is why I want you to investigate him. Strictly down low and off the clock. The POTUS has read us the riot act about noncompliance with Samaritan. The work I'm asking you to do certainly falls into that category, so I urge you to be exceptionally careful. I know you will be. If you're wondering, you're the only one I trust with this. DO NOT use any of the normal channels to contact me re: your progress. Your findings here, ONLY. I can't stress enough how important your conclusions could prove. Good luck.

Estevan Vegas."

Bourne, having consulted his map, calculated that they were less than five miles from Vegas's home. He'd had to make a decision as to whether to try finding him at home or at the oil field. The long, dusty afternoon was fading, the sepia light like that in an old photograph. The day was dying, and, in any event, he wanted to approach Vegas in the presence of his Indian mistress.

"Who?" Commander Suarez said in a voice bleary with pain, fear, and the sour aftermath of adrenaline. "Am I supposed to know this man?"

"He's a member of Severus Domna."

"So what?" Suarez couldn't even shrug his porcine shoulders without wincing. "I told you, everything inside the Domna is tightly compartmentalized." He smacked his lips. "I need a beer. I'll bet you could do with one, too."

Bourne, driving very fast, ignored him. They were still climbing through the Cordillera mountains. He had rolled down his window. The air cooled the jeep's stinking interior; Suarez sweated like a wild boar.

"If you tell me one more time that you don't know who Estevan Vegas is," Bourne said, "I'll stop the car right now and throw you down the mountain."

"Okay, okay." Suarez resumed his sweating. "So I know Vegas. Everyone in the area knows him. He's a character. So fucking what?"

"Tell me about the woman he's living with."

"I don't know a thing about her."

Bourne pulled off the highway, put the jeep in neutral, and, turning, slammed his fist into Suarez's left ear. Suarez's head snapped back and he let out a low groan. The rich scents of plants and loamy earth pushed into the jeep.

"You've already pulled the guts out of me," Suarez said. "What the fuck more d'you want, *hombre?*"

"You're making this hard on yourself." Bourne struck him again, and the commander gagged. He bent over with his head between his knees. Bourne hauled him back up by the collar of his sweat-stained shirt. "Shall we continue?"

"Her name is Rosalita—Vegas calls her Rosie." He wiped blood and bile off his lips with the back of his good hand. "She's lived with him for, I think, five years now."

"Why?"

Suarez's eyes flared. "How the fuck..." His voice uncharacteristically petered out. "What I hear is that Vegas saved her from a margay—a female who'd just given birth. Rosie had had the bad luck to stumble across its den. She couldn't outrun it. It had mauled her pretty good, I heard, before Vegas, hearing her screams, shot the thing. He carried her back to his place and took care of her. She's been taking care of him ever since, so I hear."

"Ever meet her?"

"Who, Rosie? No, never. Why?"

"I'm wondering why he never got her pregnant."

Suarez was silent for several moments. Ahead of them, thick thunderheads, purple and yellow, the colors of the bruises on his face, were piling up. The air had turned heavy. There was a blue-white flash of lightning, and almost immediately, the silence was cracked open by a double rumble of thunder, following faithfully...as a dog follows its master.

"This storm will be a sonovabitch," Suarez said. He put his head back and closed his eyes.

A moment later the first fat spatters of rain rolled down the windshield. In no time at all the drumming began on the jeep's roof.

"My question has an answer," Bourne said. "Provide it."

Suarez's eyes popped open and he turned his head toward Bourne. "I hear there's a grave out behind their house. A very small one."

Bourne put his hands on the wheel, gripped it hard. "How long did the baby live?"

"Nine days, so I'm told."

"Boy or girl?"

"I heard boy."

Bourne thought about how fleeting life was, especially for some. Nine days was no life at all. But to Estevan Vegas and Rosie, it must have been everything. It had to be; that was all they had.

He put the jeep in gear and got back on the rain-pocked highway. They were very close to Vegas's house. He put on as much speed as he dared with such poor visibility.

Back when Amanda was alive, Hendricks looked forward to coming home after a long, hard day's work. These days he went jogging in Rock Creek Park. He went every day and jogged the same three-mile course. He liked jogging in the late afternoon, when the light was spent from the day's exertions and lay along the winding path he had chosen, like a river of molten gold; he felt all the stronger for it. He also liked the repetition. He had discovered a curious comfort in passing the same trees, the same curves and esses. Of course, they were never quite the same; the seasons saw to that. He particularly liked jogging in the snow, his breath white in front of him, the frost in his nostrils and on his eyelashes.

Cleo always accompanied him, her lithe golden body bounding, her black muzzle moist with saliva from her wagging pink tongue. She watched him with her liquid brown eyes, wanting to please him and at the same time, he imagined, feeling keenly the pleasure of her working muscles. Sometimes, he wondered what it would be like to be her, to run ecstatically on all fours, to feel pure joy, to have no knowledge of your impending death.

Of course, Hendricks and Cleo had company—his National Guard detail making certain the route in front and back of him was clear. He disliked their presence in this context, in a place of serene beauty when all he wanted was to be alone with his thoughts.

In a way, his detail saw to that, though it was entirely inadvertent. Anyone on the length of his run during the time he was there was pulled aside and grilled to within an inch of their lives. Then they were held under surveillance, almost as prisoners, until he had completed the three-mile course.

Today there were precious few people caught in the security net as he jogged by, Cleo loping beside him. But the sight of one person made him stop and turn back.

When he approached the cluster, one member of the detail stepped in front of him and asked him for the sake of security to kindly keep his distance.

"No, wait a minute, I know her," Hendricks said, looking beyond him.

Stepping around the guard, Hendricks approached the young woman in jogging outfit and Nike sneakers.

"Maggie," he said. "What are you doing here?"

"Good afternoon," the woman he knew as Margaret Penrod said. "Same as you, I imagine, having a run."

Hendricks smiled. "My mind says run but my knees insist I jog."

"Do I have to be kept here under guard?"

"Of course not." He lifted a hand. "You can jog with me. That is, if you can stand my relatively slow pace."

Maggie looked around at the grim faces of the detail. "Only if your hounds will let me."

"My hounds follow orders." He looked at his detail.

"Already body-scanned, sir," one of them said.

Hendricks could see the disapproval in his face. His jogging with someone not pre-approved weeks in advance was against protocol. *To hell with their protocol*, Hendricks thought. *This is my time.*

By now Cleo had come over, sniffing at Maggie's sneakers.

"Find anything interesting?" Maggie asked.

Cleo looked at her, and Maggie crouched down, rubbed the boxer behind one ear. Cleo leaned against her in ecstasy, her sides panting.

"She likes me."

Hendricks laughed. "Cleo falls in love with anyone who scratches her ears."

Maggie looked up at him. Her face had found the lowering sunlight and her eyes seemed to glow. "What about you?"

Hendricks felt his throat redden. "I—"

Maggie rose. "That was a joke. Just a joke."

"Come on." Hendricks rose up on the tips of his toes. "Let's go."

They moved off, Maggie careful to keep to his pace. Cleo bounded at his side or between them, maintaining contact, bumping his legs in sheer joy. The guards followed close behind. He could feel their tension and he imagined their eyes boring into Maggie's back, on alert for any sign of hostile action. He supposed they were concerned about

Maggie suddenly turning on him and snapping his neck like a dry twig.

Every once in a while Cleo glanced at her, as if wondering what was going on. Hendricks was wondering the same thing. As they moved along the familiar path, tree branches dipping in the wind as if waving or saluting, he realized that everything looked different—the shapes sharper, the colors more vivid. He saw details he hadn't noticed before.

He was jogging with Maggie beside him. It was happening because he wanted it to happen and, frankly, that astonished him because he hadn't wanted something like this in a long time, probably five years, not since Amanda died. He hadn't wanted to be with another female since then. How shabbily he had treated Jolene and the other females who flitted in and out of his life. When they said or did something that reminded him of Amanda, it threw him into despair. Worse, when they said or did something that was different from the way she'd said it or done it, he became enraged.

The embers of that despair-rage cycle were visible to him at last. And being visible, they cooled, their heat growing dim. He felt as if life had sprung up whole from the ground, had materialized before his eyes, and he thought, *What have I been doing with myself?* He felt ashamed of his behavior; that wasn't the way Amanda would want him to act.

And now, jogging along, feeling Maggie's heat, smelling her particular scent of cinnamon and bitter, burnt almond, he did something he hadn't been able to do before. He looked back over those five years. He had been wandering in a desert. Maybe it was a desert of his own making, he thought, but it was no less real for that. Now, at last, he thought he was ready to leave that barren place and rejoin the world in which he and Amanda had laughed and loved and talked and just, well, enjoyed each other in the pure way that Cleo enjoyed her runs.

Hendricks, feeling lighter, became aware that he was enjoying jogging. He was enjoying not being alone. Maggie said something to him and he said something back. A moment later, he couldn't remember what either of them had said, and, what's more, it didn't matter. He hadn't shied away from her, he didn't feel embarrassed or a need to run away. In fact, he wished the course was five miles, instead of three. So that when they came to the end, he turned to her and said, "Would you like to have some dinner with me tonight?" as if it was the most natural thing in the world.

She must have felt the same way, because this time she said, "I would like that very much."

Estevan watched the storm coming in over the horns of the Cordilleras while Rosie was preparing dinner. She worked slowly and methodically, as she always did. Her hands were strong and sure as they trimmed the meat, seasoned it, and set it to braise in a pan slicked with hot oil.

When the rain came, it slashed at the windows and rattled the loose roof tiles he had promised to fix but never had. She lifted her head and smiled, the familiar sound assuring her that everything was as it should be. The end of the day grew dark as night and, for a moment, he saw her reflection in the mirror, the livid scars the margay had made down both sides of her neck. Outside, the white cross Estevan had fashioned from hardwood rose stark as bleached bone from the spot beneath the tamarillo tree that had been her favorite ever since he had brought her to his house screaming and severely wounded.

She turned away from the window and, touching her upper chest, where matching scars rose like white welts, lowered her head, and wept silently. At once, he was at her side.

"It's all right, Rosie," he whispered. "It's okay."

"He's out there," she said, "in the rain."

"No," Estevan said. "Our child is in heaven, safe and secure in God's light."

There would never be another child, so the doctors told them. Estevan knew that she had expected him to throw her out, convinced that the infant's death was her fault. Instead he had treated her with even more kindness. Hearing her weeping in the night, he had held her tight, rocked her, told her to forget about what the doctors had said, that they would keep trying to have another baby, that surely, by the grace of God and Jesus Christ, His son, a miracle would befall them. That had been three years ago, but since then nothing had grown inside her.

She was transferring the meat to the pot of cut-up potatoes, onions, and chilies when they heard the alarm. He could feel her body tense.

"Don't worry," he said, leaving her in the kitchen. He rustled around the living room, making his preparations.

"*¿Son ellos?*" she asked. "*¿Han venido por fin?*" Is it them? Have they come at last?

When Vegas returned to the kitchen, he had a shotgun in one hand. "Look at the filthy weather." He dragged his fingers through his thick beard. "Who else could it be? If I was them I'd make my move now."

Vegas was beside her, one strong arm around her, pulling her close. He kissed her cheek, her temple, her eyelids, and she felt the familiar tickle from his mustache.

"*No te preocupes, hija mía,*" he said in her ear. "Everything is ready. They can't touch either of us. We're safe, do you hear me? Safe."

He left her then to see to the last of the preparations, which were elaborate. Placing the lid on the pot, she wiped her hands on her apron and moved to the den where Estevan was crouched over the equipment he had spent months installing and tweaking until everything worked to his complete satisfaction.

"*¿Los ves, mi amor?*" Do you see them, my love?

"It's a jeep." Estevan Vegas pointed to the green-and-black infrared image on the small screen just to his left. To his right was a laptop computer connected to the array. Vegas had installed a software package that identified the infrared images. It currently showed a closed-top jeep. "It's them," he said. "No doubt."

"How long?"

Vegas looked at the meter on top of the infrared projector. "Three hundred yards," he said. "They're close now."

Rosie placed her hands on his substantial shoulders.

"*Se acerca el final.*" It is the end.

"*Para ellos, sí, el final.*" For them, yes, the end.

Vegas's fingers danced over the laptop's keyboard and the image on the screen was wiped clean, to be replaced by images of the video cameras he had installed around the perimeter of the property.

For a moment all they could see were gray sheets of rain, and then all at once a shape—the jeep cutting through the rain, jouncing along the road to Vegas's house. Rosie, feeling Estevan's muscles bunch in tension, leaned farther over him. She inhaled the raw oil smell of him, so ingrained that nothing could erase it.

"*Cerrar ahora,*" he said softly, almost to himself. "*Muy cerca.*" Close. Very close.

"Will it work?" she breathed.

"Yes," he said. "It will work."

And then, a moment later, the fruits of his labor arrived. They saw the explosion just before they heard it. The explosives he had planted beneath the road detonated by the vibration of the jeep's engine.

The vehicle jetted into the air, for a moment out of range of the video cameras. When it appeared again, crashing to earth, it was in pieces, ragged, fiery, smoking, twisted, almost unrecognizable.

Almost.

Estevan Vegas breathed a sigh of relief. "*Ya está hecho.*" It is done.

The wreckage of the jeep, smoldering, guttered in the downpour.

"*Hay es el fin de ellos.*" There is the end of them. "But just to make sure." Vegas was not a man to leave anything to chance. This was how he had always lived his life; the philosophy had been good to him. It had made him a rich man.

He rose, took up his shotgun, and stepped to the front door. "Lock it behind me," he said without turning around, and Rosie moved to do as he asked.

He went outside and strode through the driving rain, looking for the dead men.

Book Two

10

BORIS KARPOV FOUND plenty to dislike about Munich. Like almost all Russians, he despised the Germans. The bitter taste of World War II was impossible to dispel; the Russian senses of outrage and revenge were ingrained in him as deeply as his love of vodka. Besides, despite the city's new motto, *"München mag Dich"*—Munich Likes You—Munich was easy for Boris to dislike. For one thing, it was founded by a religious order—the Benedictines—hence its name, derived from the German word for "monk." Boris had an atheist's staunch distrust for organized religion of any stripe. For another, it was in the heart of Bavaria, home of right-wing conservatism that had its roots in Adolf Hitler's hateful National Socialism. In fact, it was in Munich that Hitler and his supporters staged the infamous Beer Hall Putsch in 1923, an attempt to overthrow the Weimar Republic and usurp power. That they failed only delayed the inevitable. Ten years later, Munich finally became the stronghold of the National Socialists, who, among other heinous crimes, established Dachau, the first of the Nazi concentration camps, ten miles northwest of the city.

So yes, plenty to dislike here, Boris thought, as he instructed his taxi driver to drop him along the Briennerstrasse, at the beginning of the Kunstareal, Munich's art district. From there, he walked briskly to the Neue Pinakothek, the museum concentrating on European art of the eighteenth and nineteenth centuries. Inside, he stopped at the information booth for a map, and then made his way to the gallery that housed Francisco de Goya's *Plucked Turkey. Not a major work*, Boris thought as he approached it.

A group stood contemplating the painting as a guide went through her spiel. Boris, standing to one side, waited in vain for her to mention whether or not *Plucked Turkey* had been one of the paintings stolen by the Nazis. His mind clicked over his responsibilities. Before leaving Moscow he had issued orders to Anton Fedarovich and left the day-to-day running of FSB-2 to him. But by definition that had to be temporary, since Boris was still in the process of shaping the organization to his desires and hadn't yet weeded out all the dead potatoes. From the outset he'd given himself five days at most to deal with Cherkesov's assignment. He could not count on FSB-2 being run properly without him longer than that.

Eventually, the group moved on, leaving in its wake a man who remained contemplating the Goya. He seemed unremarkable in every way: medium height, middle-aged, salt-and-pepper hair with a bald spot on his crown. His hands were plunged deep into the pockets of his overcoat. His shoulders were slightly hunched, as if they were supporting an invisible weight.

"Good morning," Boris said in passable German as he came up beside the man. "Our cousin regrets he could not come in person." This contact was one of thousands cultivated over the decades by Ivan Volkin. As such, he was unimpeachable.

"How is the old gentleman?" the man said in passable Russian.

"Feisty as ever."

The coded exchange having been made, the two men strolled together through the gallery, stopping at each painting in turn.

"How can I help?" the man said softly.

His name was Wagner, most likely a field moniker. That was fine by Boris; he felt no need to know Wagner's real name. Ivan had vouched for him—that was enough.

"I'm looking for connections," Boris said.

A faint smile crossed Wagner's lips. "Everyone who comes to me is looking for connections."

They had moved on and were now in front of Friedrich Wilhelm von Schadow's *The Holy Family Beneath the Portico*, in Boris's view a thoroughly reprehensible subject, like all religious themes, though he could appreciate the clarity of the artist's style.

"Involving Viktor Cherkesov?"

For a time, Wagner did nothing but stare intently at the painting. "Von Schadow was a soldier first," he said at last. "Then he found God, went to Rome, and became one of the leaders of the so-called Nazarene Movement, dedicated to bringing true spirituality to Christian art."

"I couldn't care less," Boris said.

"I'm sure."

Wagner said this in a way that made Karpov feel like a philistine.

"As to Cherkesov," Boris pressed.

Wagner moved them on. He let out a sigh. "What, specifically, do you want to know?"

"He was just in Munich. Why was he here?"

"He went to the Mosque," Wagner said. "That's all I know."

Boris hid his consternation. "I need more than that," he said evenly.

"The secrets of the Mosque are closely guarded."

"I understand that." What Boris couldn't understand was what possible business Cherkesov's new master might have with the Mosque. Viktor seemed about the last person to be sending into that particular snake pit. Cherkesov hated Muslims even more than Germans. He spent most of his time in FSB-2 hunting down ethnic Chechen Muslim terrorists.

"It's exceedingly dangerous to poke into the Mosque's business."

"I know that, too." Boris was well aware that the Mosque in Munich was ground zero for many of the Muslim extremist terrorist groups the world over. The Mosque indoctrinated disaffected young men and women, fired their hopelessness, channeled their frustration into anger. Then it trained them into cadres, armed them, and funded their subsequent flares of violence.

Wagner thought a moment. "There is someone who might be able to help you." He bit his lip. "His name is Hermann Bolger. He's a watchmaker. He also watches the goings-on at the Mosque." His lips curled into a smile. "Amusing, no?"

"No," Boris said flatly. "Where can I find Herr Bolger?"

Wagner told him the address and Boris committed it to memory. They visited two more paintings for show. Immediately thereafter, Wagner left. Boris consulted his map, wandering through the remainder of the galleries for the next twenty minutes.

Then he went in search of Hermann Bolger.

The rain fell like shouted words, like commands to the troops, with the fatal crash of ancient armies locked in hand-to-hand combat. Bourne stood beside a vaulting pine, its black branches swept by the wind, battered by the rain.

From this vantage point, he witnessed the explosion rip the jeep apart, the pieces crashing down, in flames for only seconds before the torrent doused them. Twisted junk fountained in all directions, two parts landing within three feet of where he hid: the blackened steering wheel and Suarez's head, stinking, still smoking as if fresh from a barbecue pit. Suarez's lips, nose, and ears had been burned away. The remains of his eyes were smoking as if he were a creature from hell.

Bourne, seeing Vegas clomp down the front steps of his house, stepped back within the dense shadow of the looming pine. From this distance, he looked like he was wearing old-fashioned hobnailed boots. Bourne noted the shotgun he carried, but that was hardly his most dangerous aspect. Vegas's eyes were like living coals. His bloody-minded demeanor reminded Bourne of a grizzly he had observed in Montana protecting her cubs from a marauding mountain lion. He wondered whom Vegas was protecting himself and Rosie from. This electronic setup must have been weeks in the making; it certainly wasn't meant for Bourne.

Who then?

You're out of your mind," Suarez had said when Bourne had stopped the jeep a thousand yards from Vegas's house. "I'm not doing that."

"It's the only way you're going to get some medical help," Bourne had replied.

"Once you get out, what's to stop me turning the jeep around and getting the hell out of here?"

"The only way out is back down the mountain," Bourne said. The rain was so torrential it felt like being inside a waterfall. "You'll be driving with one hand. You're welcome to kill yourself any way you want."

Suarez had delivered a murderous glare, but a moment later he just looked glum. "What evil moon was I born under to have crossed paths with you?"

Bourne opened the door and a roar like the end of the world rushed into the jeep. "Just stick to the plan and everything will be fine. You make the direct approach. Vegas knows you. I'll come around from the rear. Are we clear?"

Suarez nodded resignedly. "My hand is killing me. I can't feel the fingers you broke."

"You're lucky," Bourne said. "Imagine how much worse the pain would be if you did."

Slipping out of the jeep, he was completely drenched in seconds. He watched Suarez slide awkwardly over behind the wheel and move off down the road toward the house.

Bourne had seen the first of the infrared camera posts and had immediately stopped the jeep, though he hadn't told Suarez why. It was disguised as a mile marker. He recognized the equipment because he'd come across the same scenario in a villa in the mountains of Romania several years ago. The system was highly sophisticated, state-of-the-art, but in the end Bourne had defeated it and gained access to the villa.

Even if Suarez had noticed the mile marker, Bourne doubted he'd know what he was looking at.

The infrared setup was a surprise. Bourne didn't want another, so he had decided to have Suarez drive the jeep the rest of the way while he explored Vegas's property on foot.

The proof of Bourne's prudence was at this moment staring up at him with empty eye sockets. He felt no remorse at having sent Suarez to his death. The commander was a stone-cold killer, and given half a chance he would have shot Bourne through the heart.

He watched Vegas move cautiously around the wreckage, poking here and there with the shotgun barrel. When Vegas found one of Suarez's arms, he crouched down, examining it closely. From that point on, he concentrated on body parts. Slowly, methodically, his search took him in concentric circles, farther and farther from ground zero, closer and closer to Bourne's position under the pine.

The rain was still torrential, the hidden sky coming apart with scars of lightning and booming thunder. Bourne's vision wavered, blended with a newly risen memory shard, which took over. Bourne had slogged through a near blizzard to get to the disco where Alex Conklin had sent him to terminate the target. The fast-melting remnants lay on the fur collar of his coat as he made his way through the packed club. In the ladies' room, he had fitted the silencer to his handgun, kicked open the door.

The icy blonde's face was set, almost resigned. Even though she was armed, she had no illusions about what was about to happen. Was that why she had opened her mouth, why she had spoken to him just before he had ended her life?

What was it she had said? He combed through the memory shard, trying to hear her voice. In Colombia, in the intense downpour, he heard a woman's voice shouting across the thunder, and now he heard the icy blonde's voice, so similar in pitch and in desperation.

"There is no—"

There is no what? Bourne asked himself. What had she been trying to tell him? He searched through what was left of the memory but it was already breaking up like an ice floe in summer, the images fading, becoming gauzy and indistinct.

A sound close by startled him back into the present. Vegas had found one of Suarez's legs, and, rising from his scrutiny of it, was looking around. He spotted Suarez's head and began to make his way toward it, a deep frown furrowing his brow. Bourne wondered whether he would recognize the burn-mutilated face.

He didn't have long to wait. Vegas came upon Suarez's head. Using the end of the shotgun barrel, he turned the thing around so it faced him. Immediately he reared back and, raising the shotgun to the ready, backed away, peering through the downpour with an ominous look in his eyes.

That was all Bourne needed. Vegas had recognized Suarez and had been unsurprised by his presence in the jeep. If Essai had been telling the truth, it was possible that Vegas had been preparing himself for an assault by the Domna. If Bourne was reading the situation correctly, Vegas was quits with the Domna and had been preparing himself for their violent response. This would explain why he and Rosie hadn't cut and run. There was nowhere he could go that the Domna couldn't find him. At least here he was on familiar territory; he knew it better than anyone they would send. And he was prepared.

Vegas was someone whom Bourne could respect. He was his own man; he'd made a difficult and obviously dangerous decision, but he'd made it nonetheless.

"Estevan," he said, stepping out of the towering pine's shadow.

Vegas swung the shotgun in his direction and Bourne raised his hands, palms outward.

"Easy," Bourne said, standing absolutely still. "I'm a friend. I've come to help you."

"Help me? What you mean is help me into my grave."

The noise of the rain was so great the two men were obliged to shout at each other, as if they were in a stadium filled with screaming fans.

"We have something in common, you and I," Bourne said. "Severus Domna."

In reply, Vegas hawked and spit at a spot almost exactly between them.

"Yes," Bourne said.

Vegas stared at him for a moment, and that was when Rosie appeared through the pines. She held a Glock in one hand. Her arm was extended, straight as an arrow, pointed at Bourne.

Vegas's eyes opened wide. "Rosie—!"

But his warning came too late. She had let herself get too close to Bourne. He grabbed her outstretched arm, swung her around, and, as he disarmed her, held her tight against him.

"Estevan," Bourne said. "Lower the shotgun."

Bourne could see Vegas's love for Rosie in the older man's eyes, and he felt a fleeting twinge of envy. The normalcy of the world of sunlight would never be his. There was no point dreaming about it.

The moment Vegas lowered the shotgun, Bourne released Rosie, who ran to her man. Vegas wrapped one arm around her.

"I told you to stay inside." Vegas's voice was gruff with worry. "Why did you disobey me?"

"I was worried for you. Who knows how many men they sent?"

Apparently, Vegas had no answer for that. He turned his bleak gaze on Bourne and the Glock still in his possession. "Now what?"

Bourne walked toward them. Seeing Vegas tense, he reversed the Glock in his grip. "Now I give you your gun back." He held it out. "I have no need of it."

"It was just you and Suarez?"

Bourne nodded.

"Why were you with him?"

"I ran into a FARC roadblock and took him hostage," Bourne said.

Vegas seemed impressed.

"We weren't followed," Bourne added. "I made sure of that."

Vegas looked at the Glock, then up into Bourne's face. Surprise was replaced by a spark of curiosity. He took the Glock and said, "I've had enough of this rain. I think we all have."

Hendricks almost didn't recognize Maggie when they met at the restaurant he had chosen. She had on an indigo dress and black high heels. But she wore no jewelry, just an inexpensive but functional watch. Her hair was loose, longer than had seemed possible when she was wearing a hat. In her baggy gardener's overalls she had seemed to have a tomboy's figure, but the dress shattered that illusion. Her long legs tapered to tiny ankles. Whoever invented high heels, Hendricks thought, must have been a man in love with the female form. Amanda had worn them only infrequently, complaining of how uncomfortable they were. When he had pointed out that her friend Micki always wore high heels, Amanda told him that Micki had been wearing them for so long she could no longer wear flats—the high heels had foreshortened the tendons in her arches. *"Barefoot, she walks on tiptoes,"* Amanda had told him.

Hendricks found himself wondering what Maggie would look like barefoot.

He was about to give his car over to the valet when Maggie waved the boy away. When she slid into the passenger's seat, she said, "I'd rather eat at Vermilion, so I made reservations there. Do you know it?"

"In Alexandria?"

She nodded. "Eleven-twenty King Street."

He put the car in gear.

"Have you been there before?"

"Once." He was thinking of his first-anniversary celebration with Amanda. What an amazing night that had been, starting with Vermilion and ending at dawn curled and drowsing in each other's arms.

"I hope you don't think I'm willful," she said.

He smiled. "I don't know you well enough."

She settled back in the seat as he pulled out into traffic, heading for the Key Bridge and Alexandria. Her hands were very still in her lap. "The fact is, I'm a dessertaholic—is that a word?"

"It is now."

Her laugh was low and liquid. He drank in her scent as if it were the bouquet given off by a single-malt scotch. His nostrils flared and he felt a stirring in his core.

"Anyway, there's a dessert at Vermilion—salted profiteroles—that's my favorite. I haven't had them in a long time."

"You'll have them tonight." Hendricks maneuvered around traffic, the car containing his detail for the night right behind him. "Two portions if that's your desire."

She looked at him. The oncoming headlights turned her eyes glittery.

"I like that," she said softly. "A man who's not afraid of turning me into a glutton."

They were on the bridge now, the city's monuments lit up, turning the evening sky gold and gray.

"I can't imagine you being a glutton."

Maggie sighed. "Sometimes," she said, "there's a certain excitement in overindulging."

He frowned. "I'm not sure I—"

"It's the forbidden nature of the act, do you know what I mean?"

Hendricks didn't, but he was beginning to wish that he did.

Y‌ou've never done anything forbidden, have you?"

Maggie, a martini in her hand, watched him from across the table at Vermilion, an atmospheric town house. Their table was beside a window, and from their second-floor perch they could watch the nighttime parade of young people—tourists and residents alike—as they passed by on the sidewalk below.

"You've always been the good fellow."

Hendricks was both nettled and fascinated that she had nailed him so quickly. "What makes you say that?"

She took a sip of her drink. It looked like it had twinkly lights in the center of it. "You smell like one of the good ones."

He smiled uncertainly. "I'm afraid you've lost me."

She put her drink down and, leaning forward, took his free hand in hers. Turning it over, she smoothed open his fingers so she could study his palm. The instant she took hold of him, Hendricks felt an electric pulse travel up his arm, into his chest, before settling in his groin. He felt as if he had stepped into a tub of warm water.

Her eyes flicked up to engage his, and he had the distinct sense that she knew precisely what he was feeling. A slow smile spread across her face, but it was without irony or guile.

"You're an older brother or else an only child. Either way, you were the firstborn."

"That's true," he said, after a moment's hesitation.

"That's why you have such a strong sense of duty and responsibility. Firstborns always do; it's like it's hardwired into them before birth."

Slowly and sensually, her forefinger traced the creases on his palm. "You were the good son, the good man."

"I wasn't such a good husband—at least the first time. And I certainly wasn't a good father."

"Your duty is to job and country." Her eyes seemed to gather him in. "Those things come first—they always did, yes?"

"Yes," Hendricks said. He found that he was inexplicably hoarse.

He cleared his throat, took his hand from hers, and drank half of his single-malt. This intemperate act caused his eyes to water, and he almost choked.

"Careful," Maggie said. "You'll bring your babysitters running."

Hendricks, his cheeks pink, nodded. He wiped his eyes with his napkin and cleared his throat again.

"Better," Maggie said.

He wasn't sure whether that was a question, in which case it would require a response. He let it go and sipped the remains of his scotch.

"So how many languages do you speak?"

She shrugged. "Seven. Does it matter?"

"Merely curious."

But it was more than that. Part of him, already infatuated, sat back with eyes closed, but the other part, the always vigilant good fellow, as Maggie herself put it, wanted to vet her. It wasn't that he didn't trust the government's vetting process—though he could name numerous cases where it had missed something vital—but rather he trusted his own instincts more.

He handed her a menu and opened his own. "What do you feel like? Or would you prefer to have the profiteroles first?"

She looked past the menu and smiled. "You're so sad. Is it me? Would you rather we do this another time, or not at all? Because that would be—"

"No, no." Hendricks found himself raising his voice to ensure that he stopped her. "Please, Maggie. Just…" He looked away, his eyes losing their focus for a moment.

As if sensing his shift in mood, she tapped the menu. "You know what I love here? The soft-shell crab BLT."

His gaze swung back to her, and he smiled. "No profiteroles?"

She returned his smile. "Now I think of it, tonight I just might want another kind of dessert."

11

WHEN JALAL ESSAI left Bourne, he boarded a flight to Bogotá and then ninety minutes later transferred to an overseas flight, just as he told Bourne he would do. After that, however, it was a different story.

He flew to Madrid and then to Seville, where he hired a car and began his journey to Cadiz on the southwest coast of Spain. Cadiz had a storied history. Depending on whom you believed, it was founded either by the Phoenicians or, following Greek legend, by Hercules. The Phoenicians called it Gadir, the Walled City. The Greeks knew it as Gadira. According to legend, Hercules built the city after he had killed the three-headed monster, Geryon, completing his tenth labor. In any event, Cadiz was Western Europe's oldest continuously settled city. It had passed through the hands of a number of legendary conquerors—the Carthaginians, Hannibal, the Romans, the Visigoths, and the Moors, who ruled Qādis between 711 and 1262. It was from the Arabic that the modern name, *Cadiz*, was derived.

Essai had cause to think on this history as his car jounced the seventy-some-odd miles from the Seville airport to the sandy spit on which Cadiz was built. The Moors had spent the most time in control of the city, and it looked it. Because of the sandy soil, there were no high-rises in Cadiz, so the skyline looked more or less the same as it had in medieval times. Though in Spain, the city had a distinctly North African aspect and feel to it.

Following the map engraved in his mind, he entered the walls of Casco Antiguo, the old city. The cream-colored house off the Avenida de Duque de Nájera overlooked Playita de las Mujeres, one of the city's most beautiful beaches. From the second-story rear windows all of Casco Antiguo presented itself like the history of southern Spain.

Essai had called from the airport in Seville. Consequently, Don Fernando Hererra was expecting him. He opened the thick medieval wooden door as soon as Essai turned off the car's engine.

Don Fernando, who lived in Seville but maintained this second home as an occasional getaway, wore an immaculate summer-weight linen suit the exact shade of cream as the outside of his house. Though he was in his early seventies, his body was nevertheless lean and flat, as if he had been constructed in two dimensions instead of three, the vivid blue eyes made all the more prominent by his leathery skin, dark, wind-burned, and sun-wrinkled. Apart from his eyes, he might have been mistaken for a Moor.

Essai got out of the car, stretched, and the two men embraced in the European style.

Then Hererra frowned. "Where is Estevan?"

"Estevan is fine. He's being protected," Essai said. "It's a long story."

Hererra nodded, ushering Essai into the cool interior, but his worried expression did not abate.

The house was built in the Moorish style, with a central open space cooled by fountains and the fronds of slender date palms, which clashed softly in the sea breeze.

Hererra had set out food and drink on a beaten-brass tray atop a folding wooden table. After Essai had washed, the two men sat amid the shifting shadows and the musical plinking of the fountains, eating the foodstuffs of the desert bedouins with only their right hands, as the Arabs do.

Hererra plucked a Valencia orange from a bowl. *"Ahora,"* he said. *"Digame, por favor."* Taking out a folding knife with a long, thin blade, he began to peel the orange. "Estevan is not simply an employee of mine, he's an old friend. I sent you to Colombia to fetch him and the woman and bring them back here before the Domna killed them."

"So it was a test."

Hererra separated an orange segment from the sphere. "If you want to think of it that way."

"How else should I think of it?" Essai was clearly upset. "You don't trust me."

"Estevan isn't here." Hererra popped the orange segment into his mouth, then in a blur of motion pressed the knife blade against Essai's throat. He pointed westward with his other hand. "Out there are the Pillars of Hercules. Legend says there is a phrase engraved on them: *Non plus ultra.*"

"'Nothing further beyond,'" Essai said.

"Unless you explain yourself, Essai, there is nothing further for you beyond this point."

"You have no cause for either anger or concern." Essai's head was tilted back in a vain attempt to get away from the blade. He could feel the cool metal pressing against the pulse in his neck, and he fought the urge to swallow, a sure sign of his fear. "You sent me to bring Estevan Vegas back. But in Colombia I got a better idea. In Colombia I met Jason Bourne."

Hererra's eyes opened wide. "You sent Bourne to fetch Estevan?"

"You know Bourne personally, Don Fernando. Is there anyone better for the task? He's certainly a better choice than I am, especially once I discovered that the Domna had readied its attack on Vegas."

Hererra's eyes darkened. He put the knife away, but he was far from relaxed. "What did you tell Bourne?"

"Not the truth, if that's what you're worried about. I told him that Vegas is a weak link in the Domna chain."

"That much is true."

"Lies require a certain amount of truth in order to be believable."

Hererra stared at the incomplete sphere of the orange and shook his head. "It's never wise to lie to Bourne."

"He'll never find out."

Hererra's eyes flicked up. "How do you know? Estevan—"

"Vegas isn't going to say a word to Bourne. He has no reason to and every reason not to."

Hererra appeared to consider this for a moment. "I still don't like it. You'll have to contact Bourne, tell him to bring Estevan and the woman here. It's too dangerous."

"There are tickets waiting for him in his name at a regional airport. When he gets to Seville, there will be a packet with the rest of the details." Essai shrugged. "It's the best I could do, under the circumstances."

"You should have manipulated the circumstances better," Hererra said sourly. "You had Corellos in your pocket. What more did you need?"

"Corellos is about as stable as a boat taking on water. The man's a walking time bomb."

"All this may be true," Hererra said, "but it doesn't change the fact that Corellos is still useful to me."

"Owning Aguardiente Bancorp isn't enough for you? It's one of the largest financial institutions outside the United States."

Hererra looked up into the clattering fronds beyond which the sky shone as blue as his eyes. "Aguardiente is my day job." He broke off another orange segment. "I need to be engaged at night." His gaze, lowering like the sun, settled on Essai's face. "You should understand that better than most."

Popping the segment into his mouth, he chewed reflectively for a moment, savoring the sweet-tart juice, then swallowed the pulp. "But this isn't about me, Essai. It's about Bourne."

He broke off a third segment, but instead of eating it he handed it to Essai. Then he waited, patient as a *rōshi* in a Zen retreat.

Essai sat with the segment balanced on the fingertips of his right hand, staring as if it were a sculpture he had just bought, not something to eat. "You know what he did to me."

"Invading your house is not something one forgives easily."

Essai was still staring at the orange segment. "Or at all."

Hererra grunted and put aside what was left of the orange. "Now I'll tell you a secret, Essai. Bourne invaded my house, too."

Essai's eyes snapped up to meet his, and Hererra nodded.

"It's true. He came to the house in Seville with a woman named Tracy Atherton, posing as—" He waved a hand dismissively. "What matters is that it was as much an invasion as his stealing into your home."

"And what did you do?"

"I?" Hererra appeared surprised by the question. "I did nothing. Bourne was doing what he had to do. He had no reason to trust me and every reason not to." He allowed his echo of Essai's own phrase to sink in before he continued. "There was nothing to do. It's all part of the territory you and I and he inhabit."

Essai frowned. "You think I've taken this too personally."

"I think you need to gain perspective."

"You ignore the differences between the Muslim and the Western worlds."

"It's the Western world you've chosen to live in, Essai. You can't have it both ways."

"He deserves—"

"You're using him to bring Estevan here; that's enough. I know this man better than you do. It would be a mistake to push your luck." Hererra pointed to the orange segment. "Don't disappoint me."

After a moment, Essai pushed the fruit between his lips and bit down.

Come, sit by the fire." Estevan Vegas patted the raised stone hearth. "You'll be dry in minutes."

Bourne stepped across the kitchen and sat beside the older man. Rosie was at the stove, seeing to dinner. Night had come on with a jaguar's rush. Lashings of warm yellow light from the gas lamps Vegas had lit kept the dark from drifting in through the windows. The storm had abated, but the sky was still thick with filthy clouds. Outside, the blackness was absolute, it was as if they had been transported to the bottom of a well.

"You were expecting Jalal Essai?"

Vegas raised his eyebrows. "Is Essai in Colombia? I have no knowledge of that."

"Then these elaborate preparations—"

Vegas's eyes slid away. "For...others."

Bourne took the older man's right hand in his, stretched out the forefinger. A pale circle of flesh bore witness to the ring that had been recently discarded. Vegas jerked his hand away as if Bourne had drawn it into the fire.

"I know about the Domna," Bourne said.

"I have no idea—"

"They are my enemies as well as yours."

Vegas rose abruptly. "This was a mistake." He backed away from Bourne. "As soon as your clothes are dry you will leave."

Rosie turned from the oven. "Estevan, where are your manners? You can't send this man out into the cold and dark."

"Rosie, stay out of this." Vegas's gaze remained on Bourne. "You don't know—"

"I know what it means to be a decent human being, *mi amor*."

She could have said more, but she didn't. Instead, her eyes willed Vegas's to meet her own. It was there the argument was decided.

"Fine," he grunted. "But first thing tomorrow morning."

Rosie's smile burst across her face like sunlight. "Yes, *mi amor*. As you wish." She pulled the roast out of the oven. "Now, *por favor*, offer our guest a drink before the poor man dies of thirst."

Bourne carried his *cachaça*—a fiery liquor made from fermented sugarcane—and stood by a window. Behind him, Rosie was making the final preparations for dinner and Vegas was adding another place setting at the table.

He saw only his face in ghostly reflection, which was fitting, he thought. *I'm only a shadow, moving through a world of shadows.* His thoughts turned to Jalal Essai. Was he still working for the Domna? He had certainly been moving contraband through Suarez and his FARC cadre. Suarez was a member of the Domna, but he was also a political creature. FARC had been Suarez's life, fighting against the Colombian government. So was Essai using him for his own purposes? But what could those purposes be? Was the story about his daughter a fabrication, as well? If so, then his plan for a murderous revenge against the Domna was also a lie. Bourne took a sip of the liquor. It was possible that Essai's grudge was against Benjamin El-Arian personally and not the Domna collectively. That scenario put an entirely new spin on the situation. If it had any basis in fact. The truth was, Jalal Essai was a complete mystery. Neither his actions nor his motives were clear.

Once again, Bourne thought, he was in a place where he could trust no one.

He was called to dinner by Rosie. When he turned, she was smiling sweetly at him, her arm outstretched to the waiting chair. In her own unconventional way, she was quite beautiful, Bourne thought, with her long black hair, coffee-colored eyes, and dusky-rose skin. She was trim, with little fat on her, testament to living in the middle of nowhere. She wore no makeup nor any jewelry, save for a gold stud in each earlobe. Her teeth were white and even, her mouth generous, her smile as warm as her manner. Bourne liked her, liked as well the manner in which she handled Vegas. It wasn't easy for females in such a *macho* society.

Vegas was already at the head of the table, which was laden with stew, potatoes, two green leafy vegetables, and fresh bread that, as Rosie explained, she had made that morning. Vegas said a brief prayer, then they ate in silence for some time. A carved wooden crucifix observed them coolly from its place on one wall. The food was delicious, and Rosie beamed when Bourne said as much.

"So," Vegas said, wiping his lips with a soiled cloth, "where is he?"

Bourne looked at him. "Where is who?"

"Essai."

"Then you do know he was in Colombia."

"I hoped as much, anyway. I was told he would come and take us away before—" With a quick glance at Rosie he stopped short.

"You can say the name, *mi amor*." She was eating slowly, with very small bites, as if afraid if she ate her fill there wouldn't be enough to satisfy her man and their guest. "I won't curl up and die."

Vegas crossed himself. "God forbid!" He scowled. "Never say such a thing, Rosie. Never!"

"As you wish." Rosie lowered her gaze to her plate as she commenced eating again.

Vegas redirected his attention to Bourne. "As you have witnessed, we are prepared for the inevitable, but I no longer want to stay where we will eventually become vulnerable."

"But the Domna is everywhere."

"Essai has promised us asylum."

"And you trust him?"

"I do." Vegas shrugged. "But honestly, what choice do we have?"

Bourne thought about that and decided that they had no choice. "Why is the Domna attacking you inevitable?" He put down his fork. "What have you done?"

Vegas was silent for a very long time. Just when Bourne was thinking he might not respond, he did.

"It's what I haven't done that has the *maricóns* worried." Vegas shoveled food into his mouth and chewed contemplatively.

Bourne waited in vain for him to finish. As Vegas took a swig of peasant wine, he said, "What did the Domna want you to do?"

Vegas smacked his lips. "Spy. They wanted me to spy on my employer and one of my oldest friends. He's the man who gave me a job when I was broke, a drunkard being thrown out of bars in Bogotá. And spending nights in one alleyway or another. I was young, then, foolish and angry." He shook his head. "*Dios*, so angry." He took another swig of wine, perhaps to fortify himself. "I made my living—if you could call it that—putting my old trusty knife to the throats of nighttime passersby and stealing their money."

He looked up at the crucifix and scratched the back of his hand. "I was lost, a wastrel, no good for anything, or so I thought. One night, my fortune changed. This man—my intended victim—disarmed me in the blink of an eye. To tell you the truth, my heart wasn't in that business— it wasn't in anything. But I had nothing else."

He shrugged, staring at the dregs of the wine in his glass. He moved to refill it, but Rosie slid the bottle out of his reach. He didn't go after it. Perhaps, Bourne thought, this was a daily ritual between them.

"What spark of life this man saw in me I can't say, but see it he did." Vegas cleared his throat as if he was struggling to keep emotion at bay. "He cleaned me up, took me to his oil field, trained me from the ground up. I found something within me—call it a home, I don't know. Anyway, it was a place where I felt safe, protected. I worked hard, I loved the hard work. It afforded me a pleasure so acute it was just shy of pain. And now here I am, many years later, having learned my lessons well, running his oil fields for him. I have an instinct for it. I believe he knew even when I did not." His eyes shone as his gaze centered on Bourne. "And in all those years—it's decades now—he never told me why he took me off the street."

"You never asked."

Vegas turned his head away, as if looking into Rosie's face would calm him. "That would have been a breach of whatever it was that brought us together." He sighed now, and pushed his plate away. "This is the man I was ordered to spy on." His head swung around and now there was the flint of genuine anger in his eyes. "It was a test, you see. A test of my loyalty. And I passed. My loyalty, now and forever, is to Don Fernando."

For a moment, Bourne thought he had misheard. "What is Don Fernando's family name?"

"Hererra. Don Fernando Hererra." Vegas continued eating.

Bourne smiled, still trying to figure out the vectors and implications of this crucial nugget of information. Suarez was moving contraband for Essai. Essai was somehow tied to Hererra, who owned the oil fields Vegas was managing. Hererra had also, somehow, come under the scrutiny of the Domna. Still to be determined: why. Not to mention how Jalal Essai and Hererra had hooked up.

Rosie cocked her head. "Why are you smiling, señor?"

"Don Fernando is a friend," Bourne said.

Vegas looked up. "How fateful! Essai did well in sending you here. You'll be our shepherd. Tomorrow we will begin our long journey to Don Fernando."

After dinner, Hendricks offered to drive Maggie home.

"Let's go to your place," she said. "I want to check up on the roses."

"Do I have to pay you overtime?"

She smiled. "This is for me."

She got out of the car as they pulled up to his town house. The following car slid to a halt a discreet distance down the block, but still well within range of getting to Hendricks before anything untoward could happen to him. He could imagine his guards worrying that Maggie would hit him over the head with one of her spiked heels.

In fact, Maggie, on the grass, had just taken off her shoes. They dangled from the crook of her forefinger as she stepped lightly across the jewel-box lawn to the rose bed. Kneeling, she whispered to the bushes, touching each one as if they were her children.

When she rose and turned to him, she was smiling. "They'll be fine. Better than fine. You'll see."

"I have no doubt." Hendricks led her up the brick stairs and opened the front door. All the lights were off for security reasons, and, as he shut the door behind them, they were bathed in a darkness striped intermittently by the streetlights. Occasionally, a powerful beam from one of the guards' flashlights passed across one of the windows.

"Just like prison," Maggie said.

"What?" He turned to her, startled by her comment.

"The guard towers. The searchlights. You know."

He stared at her, the hairs at the base of his neck stirring. She was right, of course, he—and all politicians at his level and above—lived in a kind of prison. He had never thought of it that way before. Or maybe he had. Hadn't Amanda mentioned something of the sort during their dinner at Vermilion? He passed a hand across his forehead. This evening and the one with Amanda were becoming confused in his mind, blurring. But that was utter nonsense.

Suddenly he became acutely aware that the two of them were standing in the semi-darkness. "Would you like a drink?"

"I don't know. How long am I staying?"

"That depends on you."

She laughed lightly. "What will your bodyguards say?"

"They're trained to be discreet."

"You mean our sex tape won't end up on Perez Hilton or Defamer?"

Hendricks felt a fluttering at the base of his belly. "I don't...I don't know who those people are."

She came over to him and he breathed deeply of her special scent. His throat constricted so badly he could barely get the words out. "Do you want to sleep with me?" He sounded like such a schoolboy!

But she didn't laugh. "Yes, but not tonight. Tonight I'd like to talk. Is that all right?"

"Yes. Of course." He cleared his throat. "But I haven't talked to a woman since..." He could not evoke Amanda's name, not here, not now. "In a long time."

"It's all right, Christopher. Neither have I."

He led her to one of the sofas—his favorite. He often fell asleep on it, late at night, with a report open on his chest. His bed still felt cold without Amanda lying beside him. He liked that Maggie called him Christopher, no one did these days, not even the president. He despised the term *Mr. Secretary*. It seemed to him something to hide behind.

As they had settled on the cushions, he reached for a lamp on the end table closest to him, but she stopped him.

"Please. I prefer it just the way it is."

The glare from the guards' flashlights had become more intermittent as they returned to their constant patrol. Pale bars of streetlight striped the rug at their feet, illuminated the bottoms of their legs. He saw that she had not put her shoes back on. She had beautiful feet. What was the rest of her like, he wondered.

"Tell me about yourself," he said. "What were your parents like?" He paused. "Was that too personal?"

"No, no." When she shook her head, her hair floated around her face like a liquid frame. "But there's not much to tell, really. My mother was Swedish, my father American, but they divorced when I was little and my mother took me to Iceland for five years or so, before returning to Sweden." This was true, enabling her to better sell the lie of her Maggie Penrod legend. "I came to the States when I was twenty-one, mainly to see my father, whom I hadn't seen since the divorce." She paused for a moment, staring into space. More truth was emerging than she had intended. What did that say about her? "I don't know who or what I expected to find here, but my father wasn't happy to see me. Maybe it was the illness—he was dying of emphysema—but really, it seemed to me that his imminent death would make him all the more grateful for my presence."

Hendricks waited a moment before speaking. "He wasn't, though."

"Something of an understatement."

Her smile was grim. It did something to her face he didn't like. He wanted to put his arm around her. But he made no move.

"He had forgotten I existed. In fact, he denied who I was, said I was an impostor out to get his money after he died. He said he'd never had a daughter. In the end, his nurse showed me the door. She was big and burly—I guess she had to be in order to carry him around. But she was so intimidating that I left without saying another word."

"Did you try to go back?"

"I was so hurt I couldn't make up my mind. By the time I decided to try again, he was already dead." She hated her father, hated everything about him, including his American crudeness at fucking another woman while he was still with Skara's mother, his arrogance at leaving her alone in Sweden with a small child he cared nothing about, his narcissism that insisted he had never given life to her. Leaving a wife was one thing, and might under any number of circumstances be excused, but to deny your child's existence was unforgivable.

Much to her dismay, she discovered tears rolling down her cheeks. Leaning over, elbows on thighs, she put her face into her hands. Her head was about to explode. She felt crushed underfoot, as if her heart was breaking all over again. But, so strangely that it made her dizzy, a part of her had separated itself, as if she were watching her own grief the way she might watch the rushes of a film, raw and overfilled with emotion.

Now Hendricks did touch her. He put a hand lightly on her shoulder.

"I'm so sorry," he said.

"Don't be," she said, not unkindly. "I can't—I *won't* be sorry for myself." Picking her head up, she turned to him. Her tear-streaked face seemed suddenly very young and vulnerable. "I don't often remember the past—and I *never* tell anyone about it."

Naturally, Hendricks was flattered. Recognizing that, she felt the divide within herself widen. In deep-cover work, there existed the possibility of wanting to be your legend, of feeling as if you never wanted to leave the circumstances in which you found yourself. This, Skara sensed, was what might be happening to her now. She was being drawn toward her Maggie identity and away from Skara. She was comfortable in this house, comfortable with Christopher Hendricks. He was not at all how she pictured him—the cynical, double-dealing, greedy American politician. The human face on the target was, she knew, the most dangerous aspect of cover work.

Hendricks, sitting next to her, was of course unaware of her thoughts. And yet, the connection between them he had sensed when they first met had strengthened and deepened during the course of the evening to such an extent that he felt the conflict within her, though he was unable to divine its nature.

"Maggie," he said now, "is there anything I can do?"

"Take me home, Christopher."

And she meant it from the bottom of her cynical, double-dealing, greedy heart.

Karpov took the U-bahn to the Milbertshofen stop and walked several blocks to Knorrstrasse. The watchmaker Hermann Bolger's shop was on the second floor of a narrow old-fashioned building incongruously sandwiched between an ultramodern branch of Commerzbank and the garish facade of a fast-food chain sandwich shop.

Outside, an ancient sign depicting clockwork innards creaked in the fitful filthy wind. The stairs were steep and very narrow, the gray marble hollowed by decades of foot treads. The stairway smelled faintly of oil and hot metal. A radio was playing somewhere above him, a sad Germanic song that made him clench his teeth. Boris passed a small window, through whose grimy panes he could just make out a cramped back alley lined with galvanized garbage cans.

Bolger's shop door was open and Karpov stepped in. It was a small space. The sad German song sung by a sad and smoky female voice swirled around the shop, emanating from the innards of the place. Three walls were filled with clocks on shelves. Boris peered at them; they all seemed to be genuine antiques. In front of him was a low counter with a glass top and sides. Inside were watches in stainless steel and gold—all, he saw, as he bent to take a closer look, custom-made, presumably by Herr Bolger himself.

Speaking of which, the proprietor was nowhere in sight. Boris rapped his knuckles sharply on the glass counter, then called out, his gaze fixed on the open doorway to the back room where, presumably, the watchmaker had his workshop. The song ended and another began, tearful nostalgia for the Weimar Republic.

Growing impatient, Boris went around the end of the counter and into the back room. Here the smells of oil and hot metal were more concentrated, as if Herr Bolger were cooking up an odd, industrial stew. Light came from a rear window overlooking, Boris assumed, the same back alley he'd glimpsed on the staircase. The music was unbearably loud. He stepped over to the radio and turned it off.

Silence flooded the workshop, and with it a smell that mingled with the others. It was a familiar and galvanizing scent to Karpov.

"Herr Bolger!" he called. "Herr Bolger, where are you?"

Making his way through the overstuffed space, he yanked open the ridiculously narrow door to the WC and said, "Dammit to hell!"

Herr Bolger, on his knees, presented his backside to Karpov. His arms hung down loosely, the backs of his hands against the tiny gray tiles. His head was in the toilet, submerged in water.

Boris did not bother to check the body. He knew a dead man when he saw one. Backing out, he went quickly through the shop. He was pounding down the stairs when he heard the high-low wail of police sirens. He continued down as fast as he could, stopping only at the front door to peer through the pane of beveled glass. At least three police cruisers were pulling up in front of the building, cops piling out, drawing their service pistols and heading his way.

Shit, Boris thought, *it's a trap!*

He turned and sprinted up the stairs. The window along the staircase was too narrow for him to squeeze through. He kept going.

Behind him, the front door opened, the cops rushing in. He'd had several encounters with the German police and was not anxious to have another.

Shouldering his way back into the watchmaker's, he darted into the back workshop and tried to fling open the window. It wouldn't budge. He tried the crusted swing lock, but it was stuck and the sash had been painted over so many times it was almost impossible to make out the seam between window and sill.

He could hear the police stomping up the stairs, calling out to one another as they progressed up toward the second floor. Boris heard the word "*Uhrmacher*," and all doubt evaporated as to their destination. Here they came.

He turned and, scrabbling among the late Herr Bolger's instruments, found what he was looking for, then scored the edges of the glass pane. Knocking it out, he caught it before it fell and smashed into the alley. The police streamed through Bolger's doorway. Without a second thought, Boris climbed through and, squirming uncomfortably, set the pane back in place.

He found himself on a brick ledge slanted down to keep the rain from seeping into the window. He edged to his right and almost slipped off. He grabbed onto a metal downspout bolted to the wall at intervals with galvanized brackets. The police were in the workshop. They had found the body. A loud commotion ensued. Someone was barking into a walkie-talkie, no doubt calling in the murder. Boris froze, aware that he couldn't remain here long. Sooner rather than later, someone was going to try to open the window, and then the glass pane he had wedged in would fall out.

Looking to his left, he saw that there was only more ledge all the way to the corner of the building. He took a chance and, grabbing the downspout with both hands, leaned out to see what was beyond it. His heart leapt: He saw an architectural detail—a niche into which he was sure he could wedge himself out of sight.

It was not that far to the ground, but jumping even from this modest height was out of the question. The two galvanized garbage cans below had spiked tops, presumably to keep out the prying paws of rats and the homeless. Besides, at any moment, he expected police to arrive at either end of the alley. In fact, he was surprised they hadn't already.

Tightening his grip on the downspout, he turned his face in to the building's facade. Then, leaning his upper body against the downspout, he swung his left leg around the metal tube and onto the ledge on the other side. Now for the tricky part. He had to transfer his weight from his right leg to his left. Doing this left him vulnerable until he was fully across. He was contemplating this when the glass pane he had wedged into its frame exploded outward and fell to shatter on the spiked lids of the garbage cans. He had to move now!

He transferred his weight. He still didn't have a completely secure foothold with his left leg, so he was obliged to put the bulk of his weight against the downspout. He swung and immediately heard a pop, then another. He looked down. Two of the brackets had popped off from the downspout, which was never meant to hold such weight. The downspout bowed out, and, for a terrifying moment, Boris was certain he was going to plummet straight down onto those wicked-looking spikes. Then he had transferred his weight completely, both feet were on the ledge, and, turning gingerly, he wedged himself safely into the niche. Just in time, too. The police were swarming all over the alley.

12

BOURNE AWOKE BEFORE dawn. Night's shadows still filled the corners of the living room. Rosie had made up their one upholstered chair with bed linens and a pillow that smelled deeply of pine. For a moment Bourne sat immobile. He had been dreaming of the Nordic disco, of the bright lights, the pounding music, and the woman in the bathroom stall. But instead of pointing a gun at him, it was her finger. Instead of being blond and blue-eyed, she was dark-haired and brown-eyed. She was Rosie. Rosie had opened her mouth to say something to him, something important, he was sure with that certainty that exists only in dreams. Then he had rocketed awake.

Why?

Was it movement? He looked around, but the room was still and serene. What then?

He rose and stretched his tight muscles. It was when he was moving through the first cycle of exercises he practiced daily that he understood.

The sound of an engine, still far away, had penetrated his sleep, drawing him back to Colombia. Grabbing a sturdy carving knife out of the handmade rack on the kitchen counter, he went outside, shivering in the chill. The rain was gone, but a silvery mist obscured the ground and swirled somnolently through the treetops. In the east, pearl gray was grudgingly giving way to the pallid pink of the moment before sunrise. He saw two battered jeeps behind the house. They looked like World War II issue.

The sound rose into the coming morning.

Bourne cocked his head, listening more closely. And there it was, still faint but unmistakable: *thwop-thwop-thwop.*

He turned and was about to run inside when Vegas emerged toting a SAM—a Russian Strela-2 shoulder missile launcher with what appeared to be a laser-guided SCS-132 photo optic scope.

Bourne laughed. "You weren't kidding about being prepared."

"It's not just me I have to protect now," Vegas said. "It's Rosie."

They both turned to the north and, breathless moments later, the helicopter appeared through the rising mist. As Vegas rested the missile launcher on his shoulder and peered through the scope, machine-gun fire whistled over their heads.

"Perfect!" Vegas said and squeezed the trigger.

The missile shot off with a boom that echoed through the mountains. The helicopter was still rising over the top of the mist-shrouded ridge when the missile struck it head-on. It burst into a fireball, spewing molten bits of metal and plastic like an erupting volcano.

By that time Bourne and Vegas had taken shelter behind one of the old jeeps.

"You'd better get Rosie," Bourne said. "We need to get out of here as soon as possible. Are these jeeps gassed up?"

Vegas nodded. "All part of being prepared."

He'd started to head off to the house when they both again heard the telltale *thwop-thwop-thwop!*

"I hope you have another missile," Bourne said.

Vegas sprinted into the house. The second Domna helicopter was rising over the same ridge as the first one, but it abruptly veered off, taking a more indirect route toward the house. The crew inside had obviously seen the fireball; they would be more cautious in their approach.

Vegas returned. "All loaded up!"

Slamming the launcher back onto his shoulder, he peered into the sight. The copter had taken refuge behind a stand of tall pines. Not that it mattered. The laser-guided sight would home in on it even if it dropped from view.

"Here we go!" Vegas cried, and Bourne took a step away from him. He squeezed the trigger.

Nothing happened.

The moment Soraya met Amun Chalthoum at de Gaulle she knew bringing Aaron was a mistake. She and Aaron had driven out prior to their morning meeting with Laurent's boss at the Monition Club, and the moment Amun had clapped eyes on Aaron it was hate at first sight.

Realizing this, she asked Aaron to hang back while she went to fetch Amun.

"Who the hell is he?" Amun said as he hefted his carry-on.

"Hey, we haven't seen each other for what, over a year? And this is how you greet me?"

"Yes, over a year and you show up with another man, and not a bad-looking one at that, considering he's French."

"It's business, Amun. That's Inspector Aaron Lipkin-Renais of the Quai d'Orsay." The moment she said Aaron's full name she knew she had made another mistake.

"What's a Jew doing in the Quai d'Orsay?" Amun's black eyes looked hard as marbles. He was a tall man, trim, but well built, with wide shoulders and powerful arms. He was both charismatic and forceful in his opinions and orders. His men obeyed him instantly and unquestioningly.

"He's a Frenchman who also happens to be Jewish." Soraya leaned in and kissed him on the mouth. Then she linked her arm in his. "Come along and meet him. He's smart and quick. You'll like him."

"I doubt that," Amun grumbled, but he allowed her to lead him across the concourse to where Aaron was patiently waiting.

To Soraya's dismay, the energy between the two men seemed both electric and toxic, and she knew that she had brought oil and water together trusting that, contrary to the laws of physics, they would mix. No such luck and, as the three of them walked in silence to Aaron's car, she felt her heart sink. A triangle had already formed, with her at the crucial axis point.

During the equally silent ride back into Paris, Soraya had time to observe this thoroughly distasteful side of Amun. True, he had been trained as a clandestine field agent, ordered to break up spy rings, including, she had to assume, those controlled by the Mossad from Tel Aviv. But having been born and raised in Cairo, he had been inculcated from a very early age in a hatred of Israelis and, by extension, all Jews. The Jewish question was a topic she had never bothered to bring up with him. Or, she wondered as she squirmed in her seat, had she deliberately shied away from the topic because she did not want to face what must inevitably be his bias? The possibility shamed and diminished them both. She felt sick at heart.

It was then that she felt the loneliness assail her. She had chosen this life, no one had forced her into it, but there were times, like now, when she felt as alone as an old woman at the end of her life.

Aaron's voice cut through the uncomfortable silence. "I think we ought to drop Mr. Chalthoum at his hotel. We have an appointment to keep."

"I don't have a hotel," Amun said in a voice that could freeze a charging rhino in its tracks. "I'm sleeping with Soraya."

"Then we'll drop you at her hotel."

"I'd rather come with you to this interview."

Aaron shook his head. "I'm afraid that's out of the question. This is Quai d'Orsay official business."

Allah preserve me from male pissing matches, Soraya thought. "Aaron, I invited Amun here because I thought his perspective might be valuable."

Aaron frowned. "I don't understand."

"The organization Laurent wanted to talk to me about is international. Its tentacles are everywhere, especially in the Middle East and Africa."

"We are talking about another extremist Islamic cadre—"

"We're not, and that's the point." Soraya was looking at Aaron, but she was keeping track of Amun's expression and body language out of the corner of her eye. "Laurent was able to tell me that this organization has brought elements of East and West together."

"That's been tried several times before without success, but in this current climate, I'd say it was impossible."

Soraya nodded, happy that the tone of the conversation had dropped below a simmer. "I would have said the same thing, but something about what Laurent said convinced me that he wasn't lying."

"And what would that something be?" Clearly, Aaron was skeptical.

"Septimius Severus, the Roman general, was born in Libya. It was Severus who increased the size of the Roman army by adding soldiers from North Africa and beyond."

Aaron shrugged, but Soraya could feel Amun leaning forward in the backseat. She had grabbed his attention.

"General Severus was married to Julia Domna, a Syrian, whose family came from the ancient city of Emesa."

"Go on," Amun said, his eyes alight.

"Laurent told me that the name of this organization is Severus Domna. If we heed history, its name tells us that Severus Domna has somehow managed to meld elements of the East with the West."

Aaron bit his lip as he contemplated the implications. "Could any secret cabal be more dangerous?"

Everyone in the car knew the ominous answer.

The second helicopter rose and shot toward them. The side-mounted machine guns started chattering, the air heating up, dirt, mud, and metal parts flying like shrapnel all around them.

"What the hell happened?" Bourne shouted over the noise.

"I don't know. I think the launcher is jammed!"

Vegas had the launcher off his shoulder and was peering hard at it. Bourne grabbed him and pulled him down to the ground behind the jeep as bullets pinged all around them. Then he took the launcher away from him.

"Go get Rosie and get the hell out of here," he said.

"We'll never make it!"

Bourne was keeping track of the swooping helicopter. "I'll distract them."

"You'll have to do more than that in order to escape."

"Let me worry about that." Bourne gave Vegas's shoulder a squeeze. "Now go, *hombre*. There's no time to lose."

Vegas tried to stop him, but Bourne hefted the launcher onto his shoulder and sprinted out from behind the jeep, heading for a stand of tall pines to the west of the house. The moment the pilot spotted him, the helicopter veered off in his direction.

Vegas used this opportunity to scuttle, crouched over like a spider, from the jeep toward the house. But before he got there, Rosie flew out the door and met him partway. She was carrying a small leather case that looked like an old-fashioned doctor's bag. Vegas put his arm around her shoulders, guiding her lower, and together they ran back to the jeep. Climbing in, Vegas started the engine and, reversing hard, turned the wheel, changed gears, and shot forward along the side of the house. But instead of heading down the driveway, he lurched off to their left, following a hunting path he used. Soon enough they were engulfed in the trees, out of sight of even the copter pilot.

"Where is Bourne?" Rosie said.

"Protecting us, I hope."

"But we can't just leave him there."

Vegas was concentrating on keeping the jouncing jeep on the narrow dirt path. Pine branches whipped at them, slamming against the doors of the vehicle, and every once in a while his vision was occluded by foliage whipping against the windshield. Had he not known the path so well, traveling it many times at night without a flashlight, he surely would have crashed by now.

"Estevan," Rosie prompted.

"What would you have me do? Turn around and go back?"

She said nothing, just stared straight ahead.

"We must trust him," he said. "Just as we trust Don Fernando."

"I think maybe you put too much trust in people, *mi amor*."

"Not people, friends."

"You put a great store in friendship, *mi amor*," she said.

"Without friendship what are we?" Vegas said. "We are set adrift without either obligation or responsibility. And when the storm comes—as it inevitably does—where are we to go?"

She leaned over and kissed him on the cheek. "This is why I love you."

He grunted. But it would be clear to a blind man that he was pleased.

A double line of tracer bullets tore up dirt, grass, and the thick mat of pine needles on either side of Bourne. He made it into the relative safety of the trees with seconds to spare. The young pine right behind him crashed down, sawn in half by the rip of machine-gun fire from the copter. Once beneath the branches, Bourne knelt down and checked the launcher. Vegas was right, it was jammed, and he hadn't the time to try to fix it. Instead he ejected the missile. It was an SA-7 Grail, with a powerful fragmentation warhead, an older version, Bourne saw. The warhead used a 370-gram TNT charge. Carefully, he took apart the missile, separating the TNT and the container of rocket fuel.

Then he searched through the underbrush, looking for a branch. The first was too long, the second too wet, but then he found a broken branch of the right thickness and length. It was knobbed like a medieval mace. Bourne hefted it, then swung it over his head several times. He thought it would do. Stripping off his jacket and shirt, he tied the sleeves of his shirt to two knobs on either side of the broken branch, then placed the TNT and the rocket fuel gingerly in the fabric. The sling he had made from his shirt held them both securely.

Separating the items, he launched himself up into the thickest pine, moving nimbly, but mindful of the payload he carried, extremely cautiously from branch to branch, rising higher and higher. As he climbed, he could hear the helicopter's engine more clearly. It was hovering, waiting him out. Every once in a while the pilot sent a volley of machine-gun fire into the copse, perhaps hoping for a blind hit or to flush Bourne from his sanctuary.

Bourne needed a place where he would become a visible target and also give himself sufficient room. It took him some time to find the right spot, but at last he did, a delicate crotch just beneath the tip of the pine. There he balanced himself, then raised his head, waiting to be spotted. The pilot, possibly emboldened by the fact that Bourne no longer carried the Strela-2 launcher, moved the copter in for the kill.

With the TNT and the rocket fuel loaded into his shirt-sling, Bourne cocked his arm and waited. The few seconds as the copter maneuvered to get the kill shot were nerve racking. Bourne judged the distance; he needed the copter in closer. Just a few feet now. Three, two, one.

The machine-gun fire started up just as Bourne swung his payload up and out of the jerry-rigged slingshot. The combined payload struck the helicopter's shiny metal skin, where the TNT ignited, setting off the rocket fuel.

Bourne ducked as the explosion ripped through the body of the aircraft, tearing it into pieces. He began to climb down, but the stricken copter came out of the sky with appalling speed. Its still-spinning rotors snapped off the tops of the pines and continued to saw into the trees, following the body as it crashed into the copse.

Bourne, shaken out of his perch, felt the intense heat, the violent spray of wood chips, and heard the rotors' rhythmic drumbeat of death as they came crashing and flailing directly for him.

13

INDIGO RIDGE. Peter had worked until the wee hours of the morning reading up on the California mine; how it had been started, then abruptly abandoned in the 1970s when China flooded the international market with rare earths, driving down prices and rendering Indigo Ridge too expensive a proposition. Mining rare earths was a long and complex process and was further complicated by the refining processes, which were different for each element. Flash-forward to the present, when China abruptly reversed course, cutting rare earth exports by 85 percent, stunning everyone including the supposedly bright lights at the Pentagon, the DoD, and DARPA. Now the Pentagon was screaming bloody murder. The unthinkable had occurred: The manufacture of its next-gen weaponry was being either delayed or canceled altogether because of the scarcity of rare earths essential for the components. While everyone else in the world was slumbering in ignorance, China had been buying up virtually all the rare earth mines outside the United States and Canada.

Dismayed, Peter continued downloading everything he could find on NeoDyme, the new public company charged to mine Indigo Ridge, and its head Roy FitzWilliams. He began to read. Then he pulled the chart on the IPO. NeoDyme had gone public yesterday at 18. In its first day of trading, it had plummeted all the way to 12 before flattening out for what looked to be less than an hour. Late in the trading day, a number of huge trades brought the stock all the way back to 16⅜, where it closed. A high-volatility stock, that was for sure, Peter thought. Reading the accompanying commentary he pulled off the CNBC and Bloomberg sites, he could readily see why. The investing gurus didn't know what to make of NeoDyme. Some felt that since it would take years to get the rare earths out of the ground and refine them, the stock would be dead money until then. Others, who seemed to have more knowledge of the strategic importance of rare earths, gave the opposite opinion: It was time to get in now.

Completely hooked, he continued to read, switching to a bio of Fitz-Williams. A BA in earth and mineral sciences from Penn State, an advanced degree from the University of New South Wales, Australia, then jobs in the uranium mines of Australia and Canada, a stint in the Middle East, including Saudi Arabia. Then he disappeared off the map for just over two years.

Peter spent the next hour running down leads for 1967–1969 on the Internet, always finding a dead end. Just as he was about to give up, he discovered a clue. An obscure organization called the Mineralization and Rare Metals Conference Board had held a regional meeting in Qatar in the spring of 1968 at which Fitz was the guest speaker. Another frustrating forty-five minutes yielded one more interesting nugget: Fitz was listed as a consultant for El-Gabal Mining.

Peter immediately looked up El-Gabal, a Syrian company, only to discover it was now defunct. There was precious little known about it or, indeed, any business in Syria. The country was not a member of the World Trade Organization and every large business like El-Gabal was controlled by the government, so accurate assessments of Syria's export profits, let alone a single company's, were impossible to find or even guess at.

A dead end, Peter thought, returning to FitzWilliams's CV. He returned from the Middle East to run Indigo Ridge, keeping his job even when the mine went more or less dormant in the 1970s. He'd been there ever since and now, riding the stratospheric resurgence of rare earth metals, had returned to an almost princely prominence as a major player in the rapidly emerging strategic field.

Peter sat back and pressed his thumbs into his bloodshot eyes. He was exhausted and would have dearly loved a cup of coffee, but at this hour the machine was out and, anyway, he didn't want to get up for fear of breaking his train of thought.

He considered for a moment more, then called one of Soraya's assets in Syria, gave him the rundown on Fitz and El-Gabal, and asked for as much intel as he could unearth. Then he accessed Hendricks's hard drive and posted what he had discovered to the pertinent file there.

Peter wanted to go on, but the figures, facts, and opinions had begun to whirl inside his head like a school of reef fish. He needed sleep. Picking up his coat, he dragged himself out of the office. The corridors were silent; only the soft whir of the elevator rising disturbed the peacefulness.

The elevator doors opened and Peter stepped in. He pressed the button for the garage level and leaned his head against the wall, already half asleep. The bell sounded as the elevator came to a halt, and as the doors opened he saw a hulking figure in the shadows of the fifth-floor corridor. The figure approached him with definite intent, and Peter's head came away from the wall. Light spilled onto the figure as it entered the elevator. The door closed, sealing them in together. Peter saw the service revolver at one hip.

"Evening, Director Marks."

"Hey, Sal."

Sal's blunt finger stabbed out and pressed the button for the lobby, and the elevator resumed its quiet descent. "Burning the midnight oil, huh?"

"As always."

Sal grunted. "I hear ya, but you look like you could use some sleep."

"That's an understatement."

"Well, you can rest easy. Everything's clear upstairs."

The doors opened at the lobby and Sal stepped out.

"Have a better one, Director Marks."

"You, too."

Moments later Peter stepped out into the garage. The low-ceilinged space smelled of concrete, gasoline, and new leather. His footsteps echoed off the walls and ceiling. There were very few cars in evidence. As he headed toward his, he dug out his key and, because of the chill, pressed the button for the pre-starter.

The engine roared to life. A heartbeat later the explosion knocked him flat on his back.

Bourne fell through the pine. Just above him came the crumpled helicopter's circling blades. But as they hit thicker and thicker wood they slowed, and then the tree's gummy sap began to work on the blades' central mechanism, acting as a fast-drying glue, slowing them.

Bourne, scrambling down, half falling, half leaping, was cut, scraped, and bruised in too many places to count, his eyes, mouth, and nose filled with wood chips, sawdust, and tiny bits of metal. But in the end the beautiful pine became his ally, its sturdy lower branches holding the wreckage above him long enough for him to swing the last several feet down to the ground.

Coughing and gagging, he ran to the house. Inside, he stuck his head under the faucet in the large soapstone kitchen sink, letting a continuous stream of cold water cleanse and revive him. He found the keys to the second jeep right where Vegas had told him he'd left them. Because of Vegas's often dangerous work in the oil fields, the bathroom was almost as well stocked as a hospital dispensary. He grabbed bottles of disinfectant and rubbing alcohol, and a roll of sterile gauze on his way out. In the main room, he poured the alcohol on the pile of wood by the fireplace, then stood back, lit a wooden match from a box in the kitchen, and chucked it onto the woodpile. The resultant whoosh of flames was gratifying. For good measure, he set the kitchen curtains aflame. The fire spread greedily. Satisfied, he left the burning house.

Outside, the pine that had protected him was in ruins. It, too, was burning. A piece of one of the helicopter's rotors, sheared off by the tree, had struck the second jeep, crumpling the driver's-side front fender but leaving the engine unharmed. Putting the vehicle in gear, Bourne backed out, turned, and took Vegas and Rosie's path, veering off to the left of the driveway, into the thick copse of trees.

He followed what he sensed was a hunting path through the woods. He drove cautiously, acutely aware of the path's tortuous twists and turns as it wound steeply down the mountainside. Every now and again, through a gap in the trees, he could see the steep drop-off, and he noted how close the path came to the near-vertical plunge down into the lower country at the foot of the Cordilleras.

He could hear birdsong, which heartened him. Birds were the first to fall silent at any threat, whether real or perceived. If he had to bet, he'd wager that the two copters were the extent of this attack on Vegas. Why would the Domna think any more firepower was needed?

After thirty minutes or so, the dirt path emerged from the woods into a clearing, a small meadow filled with tiny wildflowers. Beyond rose another stand of even taller trees—pines and firs, but also, as the woods continued down the mountainside, an increasing number of deciduous trees, even some tropical varieties in the hazy distance. The smoke from the mounting house fire played over this part of the mountainside like a noxious industrial smog, obscuring the rising sun, graying out the high sky.

Cutting diagonally across the meadow, Bourne could make out the tracks of Vegas's jeep. He followed these precisely. On the other side of the meadow, the tracks plunged through the woods for a short distance before veering to the right. Bourne could see why. Off to the left, the cliff face dropped off, possibly the result of a gigantic rockfall sometime in the past. Continuing straight on would mean certain death.

This new trail was narrower and rougher, the jeep jouncing precariously as it twitched and whipped branches that sometimes obscured Bourne's vision. Fifteen minutes of this ended just as abruptly as it had begun, and Bourne found himself on a snaking two-lane paved road. He recognized it as the one he and Suarez had taken up to Vegas's house. Another jeep, with Vegas and Rosie in it, was waiting for him on the gravel of the inner shoulder.

"*¡Fantástico! En verdad, me sorprende.*" Vegas was grinning. Fantastic! Truly, I'm surprised.

Rosie smiled at him. "*Pero yo no lo soy.*" But I'm not. "You'll have to tell us about your escape."

"But not now." Vegas slapped the palm of his hand against the jeep's door. "Anyone left alive?"

"Not from their side."

"*Cada vez mejor.*" Better and better. He squinted up the mountainside to the plume of smoke. "Big fire."

"Your house," Bourne said. "This way no one will know whether you or Rosie are dead or alive for days, maybe weeks."

"*Excelente.*" Vegas nodded. "Where to now, *hombre*?"

"The airport at Perales," Bourne said. "But both the *federales* and FARC have set up roadblocks on the main highway. Do you know a shortcut?"

Vegas's grin spread across the entire width of his face. "Follow me, *amigo.*"

Marlon Etana, having arrived by private charter plane in Cadiz at more or less the same time Jalal Essai drove in, stood dreaming as he looked at the beautiful ancient facade of Don Fernando Hererra's seaside house. Here in Cadiz, Etana felt the terrible weight of history in the palm of his hand. Marlon Etana—in fact, all the Etanas—were serious students of history. Marvelous businessmen in the purest sense of the word, they had the knack of spinning the knowledge they gleaned from the past into money and power. It was the Etanas who had founded the Monition Club as a way for Severus Domna to come together in various cities across the globe without attracting attention or using the group's real name. To the outside world, the Monition Club was a philanthropic organization involved in the advancement of anthropology and ancient philosophies.

It was a hermetically sealed world in which the sub-rosa members of the group could move, meet, compare work, and plan initiatives.

The Etanas had envisioned a cross-cultural cabal of businessmen, spanning both the Eastern and Western worlds, whose combined power and influence would eventually dwarf those of even the largest of the multinational corporations. *Duco ex umbra*, influence from the shadows—that had been the motto of the Etana family from time immemorial.

Marlon's great-great-great-grandfather—a giant among men—had laid out long-term plans for Severus Domna, a way to help the world grow together rather than splinter apart. It was a noble dream and, certainly, if he had lived long enough it might have come to fruition. But human beings are fallible—worse, they are corruptible, and influence is the great corruptor. Exceedingly rare is the man who can ignore its glittering temptation, and even some of the Etanas succumbed. Not the least of these was Marlon's father, who was weak-willed. In order to fend off a threat from a group inside the Domna, he had forged an alliance with Benjamin El-Arian. Rather than becoming his savior, the clever El-Arian happily arranged for the man's downfall. El-Arian had already lined up a rival group within the Domna and, with its help, proceeded to toss the elder Etana aside. Soon after, Marlon's father took his own life—a terrible sin. For an Islamic, the lowest level of hell is reserved for suicides, because Allah has forbidden it in many verses of the Qur'an. The one Marlon had memorized, upon looking at his father's blank face, was: *"And do not kill yourselves. Surely, Allah is Most Merciful to you."*

Marlon did not know whether his father believed that Allah had been merciful to him, or whether he felt he had been abandoned. All he knew was that he'd used what little strength was left inside him to cause an uproar inside Severus Domna, to cause outrage and, hopefully, out of that outrage the beginnings of a difficult debate concerning the soul of the organization.

Benjamin El-Arian, clever devil, had seen through the veil of the suicide and had forbidden any debate whatsoever. And so, Marlon, all that was left of the once mighty Etana dynasty, without whose vision the Domna would not exist, had been reduced to taking orders from

Benjamin El-Arian. He had become a whipped dog, begging for whatever scraps El-Arian saw fit to throw to him.

Just after noon, Marlon saw movement at the front door to Hererra's house. Jalal Essai and Don Fernando emerged. They spoke for a few minutes before shaking hands in the Western style. Hererra climbed into a car parked at the curb and drove off alone. When the car was out of sight, Essai turned and began to walk toward the water. Marlon followed at a discreet distance.

Essai's pace was no more than a casual stroll, he gave the impression that he had nothing to do and nowhere to go. He followed Essai along the crescent waterfront, where Essai picked up several newspapers from a kiosk vendor. About a mile farther on he approached a café with a blue-and-white awning. A red anchor logo was stitched onto the awning's center.

Marlon Etana observed Essai seat himself at a table facing the water and proceed to order lunch. Marlon took several deep breaths, then retreated a distance so he could keep Essai in sight but also have a wider field of vision. Stepping into the shadows of a doorway, he checked that his pistol was loaded and functional. Then he drew a noise suppressor out of his pocket and screwed it onto the end of the barrel. He gave himself over to one of his Zen-inspired deep-breathing exercises.

The moment he saw a figure pass by a second time, Etana walked briskly along the waterline, a man with an urgent purpose. The man followed. Benjamin El-Arian had set him on Etana to make sure he terminated Jalal Essai. And if by some chance Etana failed, the shadow would take over the mission.

Etana led his shadow to the far end of the beachhead, beyond the piers and harbors, out along a strip of beach whose unpleasant constitution ensured it was deserted until the middle of the night, when, he had observed, kids used it to party, drink, and have clandestine sex. Etana had found it a nauseating sight, another vivid example of the corruption of the West.

A fishing boat, turned keel-up, sat up on a block of wood. The boat was rotting, the keel line encrusted with barnacles, entwined with dried seaweed. A faint odor of decomposition floated off the impromptu structure, which, to Marlon, seemed appropriate. He chose a perch along the keel and shook out a cigarette. As he put the cigarette between his lips, he drew his pistol with its elongated barrel and, turning, shot the shadow between the eyes. There was some noise, but none at all when the body hit the sand.

Pocketing the pistol, Etana walked over to the shadow and, grabbing him by the back of his collar, dragged him the fifty or so yards to the upturned boat. With some difficulty, he jammed the corpse into the open space beneath the craft. It already smelled bad enough that a decomposing body would not arouse any attention for days, maybe a week. By then the seagulls would surely have done their work, and no one would be able to identify the corpse.

Dusting off his hands, Marlon Etana drew smoke deep into his lungs and started back the way he had come. There was no one around, no one to see him. Best of all, there was no one to report back to Benjamin El-Arian.

Now it was time, he thought, to engage with Jalal Essai.

Boris Karpov wanted to murder someone. If one of the German cops was still stalking the back alley—as they had been for the past three hours while the forensics team in the watchmaker's shop methodically went about its business—the German would have been a dead man.

In the darkness that had descended over Munich, Boris had found his legs spasming, cramping, then, worst of all, growing weak. His head pounded with his need to urinate. He felt that if he didn't pee soon his bladder would surely burst. And yet his mouth was as dry as a desert, his lips all but pasted together.

At last, the lights had gone out in Hermann Bolger's shop, the flashlights of the alley cops were extinguished, and, save for a dog barking hoarsely, all fell silent. Boris made himself wait another agonizing thirty minutes. Toward the end, he'd had to bite his lip to keep from moaning.

Finally, when he judged it safe, he swung onto the downspout and shinnied down. It was tough going because his legs were all but useless. Twice he felt his hands, slippery with sweat, lose their grip and he was obliged to try to clamp the metal with his knees. This worked, but just barely.

On the ground at last, he squeezed between two garbage cans, and, crouching down, peed like a female. He let out a soft groan of relief. The pent-up water went on and on, creating a veritable lake. Getting his legs to work was a different matter. His muscles were so tight that the pain almost overwhelmed him when he stood up.

Acutely aware that he needed to put as much distance as he could between him and Bolger's shop, he nevertheless spent the next several minutes stretching gingerly and then more vigorously. He had no choice, really; his legs wouldn't have taken him to the end of the alley without giving out. He cursed his time as an administrator when he'd failed to keep up with his often brutal exercise routine. While he worked out, silently and without respite, he concentrated on breathing slowly and deeply.

When his legs had returned to a semblance of normalcy, he set out for the far end of the alley. He heard the soft swishing sounds of traffic and, now and again, a drunken laugh or two.

At the mouth of the alley he stopped, more cautious than ever. A slow, dull drizzle wet the streets, just like in those American spy movies. The city was filled with the throaty rumble of approaching thunder. All of a sudden the rain came down harder, bouncing off the concrete sidewalk and the asphalt street. He put up the collar of his coat and hunched his shoulders.

He looked and listened for anything anomalous. He'd been blind-sided; a trap had been sprung where there should have been no trap. His security had been breached. How had it happened? There was only one person he had come into contact with since he had arrived in Munich: Wagner, the contact he had met at the Neue Pinakothek museum. And unless Karpov had been shadowed from the airport to the watchmaker's, it was Wagner who had informed someone at the Mosque of Boris's inquiries. Sensing a tail was more art than science, and Boris was a master at smelling a shadow—he was certain he had not been tailed.

That left Wagner, or whatever his real name was, and Karpov would be in danger until he terminated the security breach. The sensible thing to do was to call Ivan and inform his friend that Wagner was playing both sides. If anyone knew Wagner's real name and whereabouts it would be Ivan. He pulled out his cell phone and was about to punch in the number when a sudden flash of lightning illuminated a man standing in a doorway almost directly opposite the mouth of the alley. A moment later thunder cracked and boomed.

Boris put the phone to his ear as if he were actually making a call and spoke as if in a conversation with someone. Meanwhile he forced his eyes to look left and right, down the street, ignoring the now heavily shadowed doorway dead ahead.

He pocketed the phone, then, hands deep in the pockets of his coat, emerged from the alley and headed left, hurrying through the rain. Three blocks along, he entered a *biergarten*. It was warm and bustling and smelled of wurst and sauerkraut and beer. An enormous skylight ran the length of the establishment, giving the illusion of being outdoors without the weather problems. Shaking off the excess wetness, he wound his way around patrons and servers and took a seat at a long table near the rear.

Abruptly famished, he ordered everything he had smelled when he came in. The beer arrived almost immediately in an enormous ceramic-and-metal stein. He took two quick gulps and set the stein down. On either side of him jolly Germans were drinking and eating, but mostly shouting, singing, and laughing, obnoxious as hyenas. It was all Karpov could do not to get up and walk out. But he was here for a reason and he wasn't going anywhere until he ascertained whether or not the man in the doorway had followed him.

Since he had sat down almost a dozen people had entered the *biergarten*, none of whom had set off any alarms. Mostly they consisted of families or young couples, arm in arm. Watching them, Boris strained to remember the last time he had walked arm in arm with a woman. He doubted he was missing anything.

His food came and, just as he was tucking into his gleaming, fragrant bratwurst, a figure stepped through the front door. The hair on the backs of his hands stirred. He put the bite of wurst into his mouth and chewed meditatively.

He had expected the man from the doorway across from the alley, but this was a woman—a young one, at that. Boris watched her covertly as she shook out her umbrella, then collapsed it before taking a look around the restaurant. He was careful not to meet her gaze, concentrating on spearing a potato slippery with grease. He popped the morsel into his mouth, washed it down with some beer, and looked up. The young woman had taken a seat at the end of a table, on the side facing him. She was between him and the front door.

Karpov had had enough of this nonsense; these people were either bad at their job or amateurs. He laid his knife and fork on his plate, took the plate in one hand, his beer stein in the other, and got up.

As the hour had grown later, the *biergarten* had become downright raucous, more and more of the patrons transformed into red-faced drunks. Threading his way through the crowd, he decided amateurs were the worst kind of adversary. They didn't know the rules, which made them unpredictable.

There was a small gap between the young woman and her neighbor— a thick-necked German, stuffing his face and guzzling beer. When Boris nudged him to move over, the fat German looked up, his eyes glaring.

He was about to say something, but Karpov beat him to it. "*Sie haben Fett über ihr ganzes Gesicht.*" You have grease all over your face.

Fatty grunted like a pig and, wiping his mouth with the back of his hand, heaved his bulk over.

"*Danke, mein Herr,*" Karpov said, climbing into the space rather clumsily so that he deliberately jostled the young woman slightly.

"*Je suis désolé, mademoiselle.*"

Her head jerked around. He was gratified to see that his French had startled her. Then a door slammed shut in her eyes and she turned away, staring down at a magazine she was holding. It was in English, Boris saw, not German. *Vanity Fair.* She was reading a story on Lady Gaga, one of those perfectly idiotic pop stars who could exist only in America.

He returned his attention to his meal. Some time later, she lifted the magazine so a plate of Wiener schnitzel could be placed in front of her. She took a look at it, wrinkled her nose in distaste, and, pushing the plate away, resumed her reading.

Boris swallowed a chunk of bratwurst and hailed a passing server.

"Noch ein Bier, bitte." Another beer, please. The server nodded. Just as she was turning away, Boris added, *"Und eine für die junge Dame."*

The young woman turned to him and said more tartly than sweetly, "Thank you, no."

"Bring it anyway," Karpov shouted to the back of the disappearing server.

She had dark hair and a cream complexion, with that quintessentially pretty look only American women have: healthy, vibrant, with perfectly symmetrical faces. In other words, bland as Wonder Bread. Once, several years ago in New Jersey, he had actually eaten a couple of slices of Wonder Bread spread with Peter Pan peanut butter. The cloying sweetness of the sandwich had dissolved into an unpalatable paste in his mouth, and he had gagged.

He turned to the young woman and said in English, "Aren't you going to eat your schnitzel?"

"Please." She dragged out the word: *puh-leez.*

Boris eyed the breaded veal cutlet. "Yeah, that'll put a couple of pounds on you, for sure."

This use of American slang caused her to finally look at him. "What's your story?"

"Gosh, Midge," he said with a plastic malt-shop accent, "I was just about to ask you the same question."

She laughed. "'Midge'! I haven't heard that name since I stopped reading *Archie* comics." She apparently made a decision, because she held out her hand. "Lana Lang."

He took her hand in his. It was cool, the edges more callused than he had expected. Maybe not an amateur, he thought. "You're joking, right?"

"Uh-uh." Her smile could be wicked. "My dad was some huge Superman fan."

"Hello, Lana Lang. Bryan Stonyfield."

"I know who you are," she said very softly.

Boris, who had not let go of her hand, tightened his grip. "How would that be? We've never met before."

"I'm Wagner's daughter." She slipped her hand from his and put more than enough euros on the table to cover both their meals. "Now you must come with me, no questions asked."

"Wait a minute," Karpov said, bristling. "I'm not going anywhere with you."

"But you must," Lana said. "You're in mortal danger. Without me, you'll be dead before dawn."

14

THEY MADE THE trip down the mountain without difficulty. Bourne had been correct in trusting to Vegas's local knowledge. His shortcut bypassed all the federal military roadblocks, as well as any of Suarez's FARC patrols looking for their commander.

Bourne reconnoitered the airport and its environs, looking for hostiles and finding none.

"You can't go into the terminal looking like that," Rosie said as she got out of Vegas's jeep.

Bourne looked at himself in the rearview mirror. There were smears of blood all over him, and his clothes were ripped.

Rosie dug into her bag and came out with a handful of money. "Stay here," she said.

Bourne was about to protest but the look in her eye stayed him. He watched her head into the terminal and counted off the minutes. At fifteen, he resolved to go in after her.

Vegas leaned against his jeep, smoking. "Don't worry, *hombre*. She can take care of herself."

As it turned out, Vegas's trust in her was well placed. Rosie emerged from the terminal swinging a white paper shopping bag. She had bought Bourne a shirt and a pair of jeans, along with underwear and socks. As he stripped off his bloody and shredded shirt, she climbed in beside him.

"Ah, good," she said when she eyed the bottle of disinfectant and the roll of gauze he had taken from the bathroom in Vegas's house.

She worked expertly on his naked torso, dabbing at all the cuts, scrapes, and abrasions he had collected in his fall from the pine tree. All the while, Vegas smoked his cigarette and grinned hard at Bourne.

"*¿Ella es una maravilla, verdad?*" She's a wonder, isn't she? "*¡Tú debe verla en la cama!*" You should see her in bed!

"*¡Estevan, basta!*" But she was laughing, somehow pleased, just the same.

She got out of the jeep then and turned her back so Bourne could strip off the rest of his clothes and pull on the ones she had bought for him.

Two hours after their rendezvous on the road, Bourne limped over to the Perales airport check-in counter. The limp was false, as was his London accent. To his surprise, there were not one or two, but three open tickets waiting for him under the code name *Mr. Zed*. He was pleased to discover that Essai had paid for everything in cash; there were no credit card numbers on the ticket or voucher receipts. He asked for a wheelchair when the time came to pre-board his flight. He booked his ticket under the name of Lloyd Childress, a British national, according to one of the two remaining passports he carried. He had ditched the third before he had left Thailand because the Domna had found him under that identity.

Afterward, in a secluded part of the modest departures terminal, Bourne told the pair what he had discovered.

"Essai left tickets for all three of us to Bogotá with a connecting flight to Seville, via a stop in Madrid," Bourne said quietly. "There's also a rental car voucher for when we arrive in Seville. Essai says final instructions will be with the rental car agreement." He looked from one to the other. "You have your passports?"

Rosie held up her satchel. "Packed days ago."

"Good." Bourne was relieved. He did not want to call Deron, his contact in DC, for forged passports because of the delay it would cause. Besides the Domna, he had to assume both FARC and the *federales* would at some point be after them. The fire in the tunnel and now the conflagration at Vegas's house were signs that even the somnolent Colombian military could not ignore. On the other hand, they could not know whether Vegas and Rosie were alive or dead—the same for him, for that matter.

He checked the time. They had almost two hours before their flight left and then, in Bogotá, ninety minutes more until the departure of their overseas flight at 8:10 PM. He was certain they would make their plane here, but Bogotá might be a different story. He needed a plan.

He excused himself. Perales was a small, regional airport. He knew he would have better luck finding what he needed in Bogotá, but if the airport in the capital was being surveilled that would be too late. It was here or nowhere.

There were four shops in the departures terminal: a drugstore, a clothing store, a newsstand that also sold sundries aimed at travelers' needs, and a souvenir shop, the bright yellow, blue, and red horizontal strips of Colombia's flag in evidence on everything from T-shirts to bandannas to pennants. They weren't ideal, but then nothing ever was.

He spent the next fifteen minutes limping from shop to shop buying what he thought he would need. He paid cash for all of his purchases.

When he returned to where the couple were sitting, he divvied up the purchases. Then they all went off to the restrooms.

"Is this really necessary?" Vegas said as he set out the shaving paraphernalia on the stainless-steel ledge above the line of sinks.

"Get on with it," Bourne said.

Shrugging, Vegas splashed his face with hot water, applied shaving cream, and began to take off his beard and mustache.

"I haven't seen this part of my face in maybe thirty years," he said as he rinsed off the disposable razor. "I won't recognize myself."

"No one else will, either," Bourne said.

He took the buzzer he had bought and began to give himself a "high-and-tight," the military haircut preferred by marines. Then he opened up the various pots of cosmetics he had purchased and started applying color to darken the lower half of Vegas's newly shorn face to match the rest of it. He made his own lips ruddy, his cheeks hollow and sunken. By the time he was finished, Vegas had emerged from a stall in the new outfit Bourne had picked out for him: shorts, flip-flops, a straw porkpie hat with a yellow, blue, and red band, and a T-shirt with MEMBER: COLOMBIAN CARTEL emblazoned across the chest.

"*Hombre*, what have you done to me?" he complained. "I look like a fool."

Bourne had to stifle a laugh. "All anyone will notice is the T-shirt," he said.

Taking up a pair of scissors, he slit the left leg of his new jeans. He threw a new roll of gauze at Vegas and said, "Bind up my leg from just below the knee to the bottom of my calf."

Vegas did as he asked.

Bourne put on the pair of magnifying glasses he had bought and said, "Let's go see how Rosie looks."

"I can't wait," Vegas said with an exaggerated grimace.

At the last moment, he pulled Bourne away from the door and said in a low voice, "*Hombre, escuchamé*. If anything should happen to me—"

"Nothing's going to happen to you. We're all going to talk to Don Fernando together."

His grip on Bourne's elbow tightened. "You'll take care of Rosie."

"Estevan—"

"What happens to me is of no concern. You'll protect her no matter what. Promise me, *amigo*."

The intensity in Vegas's voice struck Bourne hard. He nodded. "You have my word."

Vegas withdrew his grip. "*Bueno. Estoy satisfecho.*"

Bourne opened the door and they stepped out into the terminal, Bourne limping noticeably.

Rosie was waiting for them. The clothes Bourne had bought for her fit her perfectly—maybe too perfectly, as Vegas's eyes seemed about to pop out of his head when he saw her standing there, hands on shapely hips.

The clothes clung to her curves like a second skin, the low-cut shirt showing off the tops of her breasts to electrifying effect. The skirt was short enough that more than half her powerful thighs were revealed.

"*¡Madre de Dios!*" Vegas exclaimed. "With that display even dead men will get an erection."

Rosie gave him what looked like a Marilyn Monroe moue before breaking out into giggles. "Now I'm ready, sugar," she said to Vegas. "I feel as strong as Xena, the Warrior Princess."

"That's the spirit." Bourne looked around. "Now all we need is the wheelchair."

Hendricks, on his way to the conference room a floor below his office, was possessed with the desire to call his son, Jackie. Instead, he was stuck in his meeting with Roy FitzWilliams, the head of Indigo Ridge, who it seemed already had some problems with the details of Samaritan.

Last night, after dropping Maggie off, he had spent an hour tracking Jackie down. Good thing he was secretary of defense, otherwise he would have gotten nowhere with the Pentagon concerning his son's deployment. Jackie, as it turned out, was in Afghanistan. Even worse, he was heading up black-ops patrols scouring the cave-riddled mountains between Afghanistan and western Pakistan, which were inhabited by both Taliban tribal chieftains and the elite al-Qaeda cadres guarding bin Laden. Hendricks had lain awake the rest of the night thinking alternately about Jackie and Maggie.

Entering the conference room with his satellite aides, he settled himself at the head of the table. One of his aides laid down the sheaf of folders dedicated to Samaritan and opened them for him. Hendricks stared down at the computer printouts, trying to anticipate FitzWilliams's objections, but his mind was elsewhere.

Jackie. Jackie in the mountains of Afghanistan. Maggie had done this to him, opened up his heart. He had kept his desires locked up tight, but now he wanted his son back. His dinner with Maggie, such a simple thing, had been a night of normalcy after years of being out of the flow of life, of immersing himself so deeply in the sinkhole of his work. He had ignored—or was it resisted?—the current urging him onward.

FitzWilliams was late. Hendricks channeled his anger away from himself, toward the head of Indigo Ridge, so that when FitzWilliams came bustling in, all energy and bonhomie, Hendricks barked at him.

"Sit yourself down, Roy. You're late."

"Sorry about that," FitzWilliams said, sinking into a chair like a punctured balloon. "It couldn't be helped."

"Of course it could have been helped; it can always be helped," Hendricks said. "I'm sick of hearing people use excuses instead of taking responsibility for their actions." He flipped the pages of the Samaritan file. "No one's fault but your own, Roy."

"Yessir." FitzWilliams's cheeks were flaming. His voice seemed caught in his throat. "Definitely my bad. Won't happen again, I assure you."

Hendricks cleared his throat. "Now," he said, "what's your problem?"

Five, Rue Vernet, which housed the Monition Club, was a large, vaguely medieval-looking building constructed of pale gold stone. To one side there was a sunken formal garden with curving gravel paths looping back on themselves, lined with sheared boxwood hedges. In the center was a boxwood fleur-de-lis, ancient symbol of the French royal family. There were no flowers, giving it an austere beauty all its own.

Soraya allowed Aaron to take the lead, standing just behind and to one side of him as he rang the front doorbell. Amun stood directly behind her, so close she could feel his heat. It was odd how the three of them had become a triangle simply because Amun had willed it into being.

As the door opened and they were led inside, she wondered whether her love for Amun was real or imagined. How could something that had seemed so real last week dissolve into a mirage? She was appalled at the thought of how easy it was to fool yourself into believing an emotion was authentic.

They were led through the interior of the building by a young woman unremarkable in every way: medium height, medium build, dark hair pulled back in a severe bun, a detached expression that squeezed all personality from her face.

Soft indirect light illuminated their way down corridors lined in expensive wood and small framed illuminated manuscripts, which were hung at precise intervals. Their footfalls made no sound on the plush charcoal-colored carpet into which they sank as if in a marsh.

At length, the young woman stopped before a polished wooden door and rapped softly. She responded to an answering voice and opened the door. Stepping aside, she waved them into the suite beyond.

The first room of the suite appeared to be a study as well as an office. It was dominated by a hardwood refectory table and floor-to-ceiling library shelves filled with oversize tomes, some of which looked very old. A number of chairs upholstered in fragrant leather were scattered around the room. To one side was a large globe showing the world as it was known in the seventeenth century. Beyond this space was another distinct room that appeared to be a living room in a residence, modern and lighter in tone and decoration than the study.

When they entered, a man atop a low rolling stepladder twisted his torso, peering at them over a pair of old-fashioned half spectacles.

"Ah, Inspector Lipkin-Renais, I see you have brought reinforcements." Chuckling lightly, he came down off his perch and approached their group. "Director Donatien Marchand, at your service."

Amun shouldered past, interrupting before Aaron could complete introductions. "Amun Chalthoum, head of al Mokhabarat, Cairo." His stiff, formal bow had about it a vaguely threatening aspect that caused Marchand a brief hesitation, a startle in the depths of his black eyes, before his mouth returned to its business-like smile.

"I understand you've come about M. Laurent's unfortunate demise."

Aaron cocked his head. "Is that how you would characterize it?"

"Is there another way?" Marchand meticulously dusted off his fingertips. "How may I help you?"

He was a shortish man whom Soraya judged to be in his mid- to late fifties, but quite fit. His long hair was graying at the sides, but his widow's peak was still pure black. It possessed the peculiar metallic gloss of a raven's wing, spinning invisible light into an oil slick of colors.

Aaron consulted his notes. "Laurent was run down on Place de l'Iris, at La Défense, at eleven thirty-seven in the morning." He looked up abruptly into the director's eyes. "What was he doing there?"

Marchand spread his hands. "I confess I have no idea."

"You didn't send him to La Défense?"

"I was in Marseilles, Inspector."

Aaron's smile was sharp as an arrow. "M. Laurent had a cell phone, Director. I assume you do, too."

"Of course I do," Marchand said, "but I didn't call him. In fact, I had no contact with Laurent for a number of days prior to my leaving for the south."

Soraya noticed that Amun seemed to have lost interest in the conversation. He had broken away and was studying the books that lined the director's study.

Aaron cleared his throat. "So what you're claiming is that you have no knowledge of what business M. Laurent had in the Île de France Bank building two days ago."

Very clever, Soraya thought. *Aaron waited until now to mention the Île de France Bank.*

Marchand blinked as if blinded by a very strong light. "I beg your pardon?"

"Until M. Laurent's murder—"

"Murder?" Marchand blinked again.

Now Aaron had him, Soraya thought.

"Until his murder, M. Laurent was your assistant, is that not correct?"

"It is."

"Well, then, M. Marchand. The Île de France Bank." There was a slight edge to Aaron's voice, and he had picked up the pace of his questioning. "What was M. Laurent doing there?"

Marchand's voice turned abrupt, waspish. "I have already told you, Inspector." He seemed to be losing his temper, which was the point.

"Yes, yes, you claim you don't know."

"I *don't* know."

Aaron consulted his notes, flipped a page, and Soraya felt a little spark of glee rise up in her. Aaron opened his mouth. *Here it comes*, Soraya thought.

"Your answer interests me, Director. My research has revealed that much of the funding for this branch of the Monition Club comes from accounts in the Brive Bank."

Marchand shrugged. "What of it? A number of our senior members have their accounts at Brive. These men are large annual donors."

"I applaud their altruism," Aaron said lightly. "However, after no little digging it has come to my attention that the Brive Bank is a subsidiary of the Netherlands Freehold Bank of the Antilles, which, in turn, is owned by, well, the list goes on and on and I don't want to bore you. But at the end of the list is the Nymphenburg Landesbank of Munich." Here Aaron took a breath, as if to emphasize the exhaustion brought about by the amount of digging he'd had to do.

"Is Nymphenburg Landesbank wholly owned? Indeed it is. And for a time this stopped me in my tracks. But then I decided to turn my supposition upside down. And what do you know? Early this morning I discovered that for the past five years the Nymphenburg Landesbank of Munich has been quietly buying up pieces of..." Now he shrugged. "Need I say it, Director?"

Marchand was standing stock-still, his hands in midair. Soraya, looking at them, had to give the man credit: His hands were rock-solid, not a tremor to be seen.

Aaron grinned. "Nymphenburg Landesbank now owns a controlling interest in the Île de France Bank. The takeover was devilishly difficult to detect mainly because both the Landesbank and Île de France are private institutions. As such, they are not required to divulge changes in policy, key personnel, or control."

He stepped toward Marchand a pace and lifted a forefinger. "However, it occurred to me that there might be another reason for my difficulty in unearthing the connection."

The silence grew so thick that finally Marchand said through gritted teeth, "And what would that be, Inspector?"

Aaron closed his notebook and put it away. "À *bientôt*, M. Marchand." Until next time.

With that, he turned on his heel and left. Soraya followed in his wake, but not before grabbing a handful of Amun's jacket and dragging him away from his study of the book spines.

Outside, the sun was shining and the birds were chirping, flitting from tree to tree.

"How about some lunch?" Aaron said. "My treat."

"I'm not hungry. I'd rather get back to our hotel room," Amun replied.

"Well, I'm hungry enough for two," Soraya said, avoiding Amun's dark glare.

Aaron clapped his hands. "Splendid! I know just the place. Follow me."

Soraya sensed that Amun didn't want to follow Aaron anywhere, but unless he could find a taxi station, he had no choice.

"Why didn't you tell me what you had discovered?" Soraya said as she came up alongside Aaron.

"There wasn't time."

Soraya suspected this was only partially true. But she held her tongue because she sensed that Aaron hadn't wanted her to say anything to Amun.

They returned to the Citroën and when they were all settled in, Soraya next to Aaron up front and Amun in back with his carry-on bag, Aaron fired the ignition. But before he could put the Citroën in gear, Amun leaned forward and put a hand on his arm.

"Just a moment," he said.

Soraya, acutely attuned to both these men, felt immediate alarm. If Amun was going to start a fight she had to find a way to head it off.

"Amun, let's just go," she said in as even a voice as she could muster. She had been witness to Amun's temper; she did not ever wish to be on the receiving end of it.

"I said wait," he said in that tone of voice that turned lesser human beings to stone.

Aaron took his hand off the gearshift and half turned in his seat. To his credit, he was content to be patient.

"That was a good piece of work in there." Amun stared straight into Aaron's eyes. "I admired the technique."

Aaron nodded. "Thank you."

It was clear he had no idea where this was going. Neither did Soraya.

"You hit a nerve with Marchand and you left him wondering and frightened," Amun continued. "It's too bad you didn't plant a bug in his office. Then we could have found out who he's calling right now."

Aaron appeared slightly put out by Amun's denseness. "This isn't Egypt. I'm not allowed to bug people's offices or homes without proper authorization."

"No, you aren't." Amun unzipped his bag and pulled out a dull black box about the size of a first-generation iPod. It had a grille on the top. "But I can."

He flipped a hidden switch and at once they heard Donatien Marchand's voice caught in midsentence. They were able to listen to the rest of the phone conversation.

"*—God alone knows.*"

. . .

"*Not really, no, it's not the first time I've had an inquiry from the Quai d'Orsay.*"

. . .

"*Certainly, but I tell you this one feels different.*"

. . .

"*No, I don't know why.*"

An unusually long silence.

"*It's the Egyptian. Having the head of al Mokhabarat—*"

. . .

"*Bullshit, you wouldn't like it, either. The guy gave me the creeps.*"

. . .

"*Now I don't know what—*"

. . .

"*You try that, then. You didn't look these people in the eye.*"

. . .

"*Really? I haven't even mentioned the woman—Soraya Moore.*"

. . .

"Well, you may know her, but I don't. She worries me most of all."

. . .

"Because she says nothing and sees everything. Her eyes are like X-ray machines. I've had the misfortune of meeting several people like her. Inevitably, it's gotten messy—very messy. And with this Laurent business, messy is the last thing we need."

. . .

"Oh, you do, do you? And who would that be?"

There ensued what seemed to be a shocked silence before Donatien Marchand's voice started up again.

"You can't be serious. Not him. I mean to say, there's got to be another alternative."

. . .

"I see."

Marchand sighed in what sounded like resignation.

"When?"

. . .

"And it has to be me?"

. . .

"All right then." Marchand managed to inject a girder of steel into his voice. *"I'll give him his orders immediately. The usual price?"*

A moment later the connection was broken. The three eavesdroppers sat in silence, their bodies very still. The atmosphere was suddenly stifling, the musk of men and woman mingling into a thick stew. Soraya felt the slow, heavy beat of her heart. It was one thing listening in on a conversation, quite another when a key part of that conversation concerned you.

"Interpretation?" Aaron said a bit breathlessly.

"It sounds as if Marchand has been ordered to contact a hit man."

Aaron nodded. "That was my take, as well." He turned his head. "Amun?"

The Egyptian was staring out the Citroën's window and didn't bother to answer. "Here he comes," he said, pointing to Marchand, whom they could see emerging from the Monition Club. He got into a black BMW and took off.

As Aaron put the Citroën in gear and pulled out after him, Amun said, "I assume you've both lost your appetite."

The *federales* were looking for Bourne, all right. At least the identity Bourne had used to enter Colombia. Of course, that identity no longer existed. Neither did the man in the blurry wire photo the cops were passing around the international departures terminal in Bogotá.

"Don't worry," Bourne said from his seat in the wheelchair, "it's me the *federales* have an interest in, not you or Rosie."

"But the Domna has connections—"

"In this case," Bourne cut in, "I very much doubt they'd want the *federales* involved. Too many questions would be asked."

Nevertheless, as Vegas pushed Bourne across the concourse, he exuded nervous energy the way the sun generates heat. This was a problem— of what magnitude Bourne could not yet determine—for cops could smell fear from a thousand yards away.

Directing them to the business-class lounge, Bourne presented their tickets to one of the attendants, a slim, deeply tanned young woman, who personally showed them the best place to park the wheelchair, then went to get a server for them. There were definitely perks to being perceived as disabled, Bourne thought, but right now the most important one was throwing the *federales* off his trail.

When the server appeared, Bourne ordered a stiff drink for Vegas to calm him down. Rosie ordered her own; Bourne wanted nothing.

"I'll be fine once I see Don Fernando again," Vegas said.

"Stop looking around," Bourne said. "Concentrate on me." He turned to Rosie. "Hold his hand and don't let go, no matter what."

Rosie hadn't said a word since they disembarked their regional flight from Perales, but Bourne sensed little fear in her. Her innate trust that Vegas would protect her come what may appeared to insulate her from their precarious situation.

The moment she gripped Vegas's hand, he relaxed visibly, which was lucky since, at that moment, a pair of *federales* stepped into the lounge and started querying the receptionists. Both of them shook their heads when they looked at the photo of Bourne. Nevertheless, the two cops decided to make a circuit of the lounge.

Vegas had not yet seen them, but Rosie had. Her eyes locked on Bourne. He grinned at her, he laughed as if she had made a joke. Understanding, she laughed back.

"What's going on?" Vegas said. "What the hell is so damn funny?"

"In a minute or two, a pair of *federales* will pass by here." Bourne saw the fear bloom anew in the older man's face. He was a country fellow, unused to the confines of the big city, and here in the lounge there was nowhere to run.

He had already consumed more than half his drink. His face was pale. Bourne could see the bones of his skull clearly beneath the suddenly waxy skin; dead men looked better. Seeking to distract him, Bourne asked him about the oil fields—his early days, when he was learning the trade, when the danger was the most acute. He became animated, as Bourne had hoped. Clearly, he loved his work and was adept at its every nuance. All the while, Rosie listened as attentively as if she were a geological engineer.

The *federales* were fast approaching their area, strutting with their chests out, their hands on the butts of their sidearms. Tension ratcheted up. Even Rosie was not immune, Bourne saw.

"I saw the tamarind tree out back," Bourne said, "and the cross that marked the grave."

"We do not speak of this," Vegas said, shaking.

"*Mi amor, cálmate.*" Rosie kissed him on the cheek. "He couldn't know."

"I had no intention—"

Rosie lifted a hand to stop him. "You couldn't know," she said grimly. She offered Vegas a wan smile that guttered like a candle in the wind. She turned back to Bourne. "Our son, nine days old and already he held the entire world in his eyes." A tear slid down her cheek, which she immediately wiped away with the back of her hand. "This is how it is with children, before they are corrupted by the adult world."

"His death was a complete mystery." Vegas's words seemed squeezed out of him, as if each one gave him pain. "But what do I know? Only where I've been. I don't know where I'm going."

"They have to be protected, the children," Rosie said. Something in what Vegas had just said disturbed her deeply.

The *federales* were only steps away.

Bourne said, "You can have the chance to protect another one."

They both stared at him.

It was Rosie who spoke. "But the doctor said—"

"That was a doctor in the middle of Colombian nowhere. There are specialists in Seville, in Madrid. If I were you, I wouldn't give up hope."

The pair of *federales* swaggered past. Their eyes glancing over the tourists: the man in the wheelchair, whom they took to be an American war vet; the old man with the T-shirt emblazoned with its stupid logo that set them laughing. But mostly they let their gazes linger over the high breasts and long legs of the woman whose sensuality took their breaths away.

And then, like a storm cloud passing, they were gone, and the entire lounge seemed to breathe a sigh of relief.

Maggie—Skara thought of herself as Maggie now; it was effortless—was due for her daily report to Benjamin El-Arian. She luxuriated in bed, only a top sheet covering her naked body, and regarded the encrypted cell phone she used only for communicating with El-Arian. Then she turned away and stared at the pale blue-gold light of morning pearling the loose-weave curtains of her bedroom. At this hour, it was so quiet she could almost hear the faint crackle and spark of the light, as if it were the only thing stirring, shifting easily as the sun slowly dissolved the darkness.

Her mind was filled with many thoughts, some of them conflicting. But mainly she knew she did not want to speak with Benjamin. He was like a tether, dragging her back to another life, one she had chosen, true enough, though far from willingly.

It was funny, she thought now, how the exigencies of life forced you to make decisions. That there could be any form of control was an illusion. Life was chaos; attempts to control or even contain it could only end in tears.

She had shed enough tears for several lifetimes. The last time, when she saw her mother on the coroner's slab in the chill house of the dead, when she broke down sobbing with her two sisters, she had promised herself she would never shed another tear again. And she had kept that promise until last night. What was it about Christopher Hendricks that had shattered her resolve? For hours, while his presence still throbbed through her like a fever, she had lain awake thinking about this question. She had traced and retraced their evening together, combing through each nuance of voice and gesture like a starving tramp pawing through bags of garbage.

Around four o'clock she had finally given up, turning on her side, curling up, and closing her eyes, willing herself to drift off, as she often did, by thinking of her two sisters. Mikaela was dead now, killed in the pursuit of their revenge, but Kaja was very much alive, though, by mutual agreement, they'd had no contact with each other for years. Maggie imagined the two of them together, touching foreheads as the triplets had done when they were very young, that particular feeling of a shared warmth flowing through them, a closed circuit that made them special and kept the outside world—the hateful world of their childhood, of Iceland, the betrayal of their father—at bay. He'd left them and their mother to kill, to, finally, be killed, all in the name of what? The shadow organization to which their father belonged. She thought of their father now, walking out the door into the snow glare of a Stockholm winter. She had watched him go, never to return. And then nothing, until she had uncovered the news that he had been killed by his intended target, Alexander Conklin. A chill had flashed down her spine, a feeling she had not been able to share with her sisters. She closed her eyes on the bleakness of Stockholm, on the image of her father walking away from her—from all of them. She wanted to dream of him, which was why she held the memory of him close to her as she drifted.

With sleep drawing her into its arms, a dream rose like a ghost from the grave, but her father wasn't in it. She and Christopher were at a sports complex. It was completely empty, save for them. Moonlight shone on a vast pool. She looked down and saw Christopher smiling at her. He waved up to her, and she realized that she was standing on a high-dive board.

Go on, he said. *You needn't wait for me.*

She had no idea what he meant, but she knew she was going to dive. She stepped to the end of the board and curled her toes around the edge. She flexed her knees, felt the spring in the board, the coiled power of it, and it gave her great courage.

She sprang up and out in a beautiful arc. Her arms were in front of her, her palms together as if in prayer. She saw the water coming to meet her as she dropped through the night. Moonlight silvered the pool, turning it into glass, into a mirror. She saw herself diving down to meet the water, but it wasn't her she saw just before she cleaved the water. It was Christopher.

That's when her eyes flew open. Across the room, she saw the curtains patterned with dawn light, which to her half-dreaming mind looked thick and aqueous. For a moment, she thought she was underwater, deep in the belly of the pool, on her way up. Then recognition flooded her, and she knew with a certainty she felt in her bones. She and Christopher were so alike she felt chills ripple through her.

She sat up in bed, her pulse beating in her ears.

"Dear God," she said aloud, "what is to become of me?"

Peter awoke in an ambulance, siren wailing, rocketing along the city streets. He was lying strapped to a gurney, feeling as weak as a preemie.

"Where am I? What happened?"

His voice was thin and reedy, unfamiliar against the insistent ringing in his ears.

A face bent over him, a young man with blond hair and an open smile.

"Not to worry," the blond said, "you're in good hands."

Peter tried to sit up, but the restraints prevented him from moving. Then, all at once, like an oncoming locomotive hurtling out of the mist, he remembered walking across the underground garage, pressing the button on his key fob to start his car's engine, and then a crack like the end of the world. His mouth felt dry and sticky. There was a metallic smell in his nostrils that made him queasy.

Peter thought about Hendricks. He needed to brief his boss on what had happened. He also needed to find out why he had been targeted and by whom. He moved his right hand, forgetting that he was restrained.

"Hey," he said thickly, "take off the straps. I need to get to my cell."

"Sorry, buddy, no can do." The blond smiled down at him. "Can't free you while the vehicle is in motion. Rules and regs. If you get hurt you can sue my ass off."

"Then have the driver pull over."

"Can't do that, either," Blondie said. "Time is of the essence."

Peter was regaining his wits with every second, but he still felt physically exhausted, as if he'd just finished running a marathon. "I assure you I'm feeling much better."

Blondie produced a rueful expression. "I'm afraid that you're not in the best position to judge. You're still in shock and not thinking clearly."

Peter raised his head. "I said, have the driver pull over. I'm a federal agent reporting directly to the secretary of defense."

The smile faded from Blondie's face. "We know that, Mr. Marks."

Peter's heart began to race as he struggled with the restraining straps. "Let me the fuck up!"

That's when Blondie showed him the Glock. He laid the barrel gently against Peter's cheek. "This says lie back and enjoy the ride. We've got some time to go."

Which meant he wasn't being taken to a hospital. Peter stared up into Blondie's face, which was now as blank as a bank vault door. Were these the people responsible for wiring his car with explosives?

"Sorry to disappoint you."

Blondie looked down at him, took the Glock away from his cheek.

"I know you expected me to die in the explosion."

Blondie stroked the barrel of the Glock lovingly.

"What impresses me is how you got past security to wire my car."

Blondie delivered a wry smile to someone out of Peter's field of vision. "Who says it was wired in the garage?"

So these were the people who had targeted his car, and they knew where he lived. He still didn't know who they were working for or—more to the immediate point—how many of them were in the ambulance with him. He assumed three—Blondie, the driver, and whoever Blondie had grinned at just now—but maybe there was a fourth riding shotgun up front. One thing was clear: These people were well trained and well funded.

The ambulance swerved around a corner. Peter felt the gurney wanting to slide to one side, but it was locked down. Fortunately, the turn loosened the straps so that he could get his left hand free. Moving it down off the top of the gurney, he searched for the lever that would unlock it. A bit of surreptitious fumbling brought his fingers to the right spot, and he held on tight.

Blocks passed, and Peter was despairing of ever getting his chance, but then he felt the centrifugal force begin to kick in as the ambulance went into another turn. He pushed down on the lever at the apex of the turn. The gurney slammed into Blondie's knees, then caromed back the other way. Peter freed his right hand, and when Blondie fell over him, Peter grabbed his Glock. As Blondie tried to right himself, Peter slammed the pistol into the side of his head.

The second man came into Peter's view, lunging at him. Peter fired and the man spun backward. His heavyset frame careened into the rear doors. Peter unsnapped the straps holding him down and slid off the gurney.

At the same time, the ambulance was slowing; the driver was probably alarmed by the gunshot. Peter wasted no time. Leaping over the two bodies, he wrenched open the doors and jumped out. He hit the ground and rolled on his hip, but having used the last reserves of his strength, he was having difficulty even getting to his knees.

Several yards farther on, the ambulance had pulled over. The driver jumped out, running back toward where Peter lay. Peter knew his only chance was the Glock, but he had lost it during his fall. He desperately looked around and saw it lying in the gutter. But the driver was on him before he had a chance to crawl the few feet toward it.

He was plowed under by the driver's fists. He had no strength left with which to adequately defend himself, let alone retaliate. Bright spots of light exploded behind his eyes and waves of blackness rolled over him. He struggled against unconsciousness, but it was a losing battle.

A drowning man going under for the last time could not have felt more despairing than Peter did. He never imagined a moment like this, a defeat this unexpected and complete. And then, after a maelstrom of violence, a concentration of pain, the last wave reaching up to pull him down, there was a soft breeze on his face. Sunlight. The sweet smell of a motorcycle's exhaust.

And a face, blurry and indistinct as a dark cloud, loomed large in his limited field of vision.

"Not to worry, Chief, you're not dead yet."

15

IN THE DEWY light of morning, Jalal Essai went for a walk along the curving seaside streets of Cadiz. The day was already bright, with only a handful of white fluffy clouds way off to the south. The air was fresh, tangy with salt and phosphorus. Out on the water, several sailboats tacked, taking advantage of the wind. Many of the tourist shops were still closed, their metal gates rolled down like castle walls, and Essai caught a glimpse of the melancholy that invades coastal cities in the winter.

He carefully chose the seaside café, passing up a cluster of others nearer to Don Fernando's house for the one with the blue-and-white-striped awning emblazoned with a red anchor. Seating himself at a small round table in the second row from the sidewalk, he ordered breakfast.

Bicyclists whirred by like giant insects and occasionally a car or a delivery truck rumbled past, otherwise the early hour had scoured the sidewalks clean. His coffee and pastry arrived. He sipped the coffee tentatively, deemed it good, and added just a touch of milk. Then he bit into his chewy, sweet pastry and sat back, breathing the humid air deep into his lungs.

He began his ritual of plan review. Every day variables cropped up that interfered with the plan or caused it to be altered in vital ways. It was like working out a delicately balanced puzzle that subtly changed each time you looked at it. Human beings were usually at fault—those involved both voluntarily and unwittingly. They were far too often unpredictable in their responses, and therefore had to be monitored carefully. It was exhausting work, worth the trouble only if the payoff was sufficiently valuable or desirable. In this case, Essai thought, the payoff was both.

Unfortunately, monitoring each human element was not always possible. Estevan Vegas, for instance, was an old friend of Don Fernando, but he meant nothing to Essai. But Bourne—well, Bourne was the constant in Essai's plan. Bourne's innate honor made him utterly predictable in life-or-death situations. This current situation was a case in point. Benjamin El-Arian had finally made a major mistake by assigning Boris Karpov to kill Bourne, had failed to understand that the results of a collision between Bourne and Karpov were unpredictable and would likely be wholly unexpected. El-Arian did not know Bourne the way Essai did—in fact, he knew next to nothing about him. Essai was counting on that, just as he was counting on Bourne to bring back Vegas and the woman from Colombia.

He was congratulating himself when he saw movement out of the corner of his eye. He did not turn, he did not move. He simply stared straight ahead and watched Marlon Etana emerge out of the trembling morning sunshine and make his way beneath the blue-and-white-striped awning with the red anchor.

This way," Lana Lang said. "Quickly!"

Karpov followed her through the cluttered streets of Munich until they reached a small, dark green Opel. Fitful showers fell from a swollen sky the color of sheet metal.

"Get in," she said as she slid behind the wheel. Then she looked up at him, still standing on the sidewalk. "Come on, what are you waiting for?"

Boris was waiting for inspiration. Walking down the street with someone he didn't know was one thing, but getting into a small, enclosed, mobile space with her was something else altogether. Every instinct was screaming its paranoia in his mind.

"Hey," she said, clearly irritated. "We don't have time for this."

There's never time for anything, Karpov thought, getting in. *Leastways, anything important.* His life was filled with a constant flow of needs, obligations, accommodations, and reciprocal gestures—large, small, and everything in between. A political dance, in other words, that he could never ignore, or even take the least little break from, for fear that when the music stopped his chair would be taken over by someone else. And then, despite all his years of devotion, hard work, and the accretion of small atrocities for the state that hung invisibly on his uniform like medals of the secret wars, he would be looking at life from the outside in, which, in Russia, meant no life at all.

Lana Lang drove very hard and very fast through the maze of city streets. She drove, Boris observed, like a man, with great competence, nerve, and not a lick of fear, even though the rain fell harder, the streets slick. Here was her area of competence, he thought, whereas in the *biergarten* she had seemed like a silly, fashion-obsessed female whom he had no business accompanying, let alone trusting with his life.

Every few seconds her eyes alternated between the rearview and side mirrors. She went through lights at the last possible instant, and often doubled back on what Boris assumed was their route.

"Where are we going?" he asked.

She smiled a secret smile, and that, too, was different about her.

"Somewhere no one can find me, I assume."

"Not exactly." That secret smile expanded. "I'm taking you to the one place no one would think to look for you."

She put on a burst of speed, and Boris felt his torso pressed back into the seat. "And that would be where?"

She shot him a mischievous look, then returned her gaze to the traffic ahead. "Where else?" she said. "The Mosque."

Paris was laid out like a shell in the water of the Seine. Each district—or arrondisement—spiraled out from the center, the higher the number, the farther from the heart of the city. The outermost arrondisements were inhabited by immigrants—Vietnamese, Chinese, and Cambodians. Just beyond were the *banlieues*, or outskirts, which were given grudgingly over to the North African Arabs. Isolated on the cramped, unsightly fringes of the city, these disenfranchised were denied jobs or any meaningful contact with everyday Parisian life, culture, schooling, or art.

Aaron followed Marchand's BMW into one of the northernmost *banlieues*—the filthiest, most congested and degraded outskirt any of them had ever seen.

"Allah, this stinking place looks like Cairo," Amun muttered under his breath.

Indeed, the streets were narrow, the sidewalks cracked, the ugly whitish buildings looking like the worst of the British council flats, tumbled one on top of the other without any space between them.

Soraya, still on high alert, felt a renewal of tension between the two men and wondered at its origins. She sensed that Aaron was becoming more and more uncomfortable. As they rolled down the unlovely street, faces dark and tight with a toxic mingling of hatred and fear turned in their direction. Old women, their arms dragged down by bulging mesh shopping sacks, hurried away from them. Groups of young men came off the walls where they had been lounging or crouched, smoking, pulled toward the unfamiliar car like street dogs to a scrap of meat. She could feel the hostility directed at them from waves of black eyes, coffee-colored lips. Once, a bottle, thrown in a high arc, smashed against the Citroën's flank.

Ahead of them, the BMW had turned left into an alley. Aaron pulled over to the curb and parked. He was the first out of the car, but Amun said, "Considering the atmosphere, it might be better if you stayed with the car."

Aaron bristled. "Paris is my city."

"This isn't Paris," Amin said. "This is North Africa. Soraya and I are both Muslims. Let us take care of this part of the operation."

Soraya saw Aaron's face go dark. "Aaron, he's right," she said softly. "Take a step back. Think about the situation for a minute."

"This is my investigation." Aaron's voice was shaking with barely suppressed emotion. "Both of you are my guests."

Soraya engaged his eyes with her own. "Think of him as a gift."

"A gift!" Aaron seemed to crush the words between his teeth.

"Don't you see? He's used to these Arab slums; he can connect with the residents. Considering the way in which the investigation has turned, it's a great stroke of luck having him help us."

Aaron tried to push past her. "I don't—"

She blocked him with her body. "We wouldn't even have this lead without him."

"He's already gone," Aaron said.

Soraya turned and saw that he was right. Amun wasn't wasting any more time, and she understood—coming this far, they didn't want to lose Marchand now.

"Aaron, stay here." She began to follow Amun down the alley. "Please."

The alley was narrow, crooked as a crone's finger, and twilight-dark. She could just make out Amun's back as he slipped through a battered metal door. Racing ahead, she caught the door before it closed. As she was about to enter, she saw a rail-thin young man at the far end of the alley. She squinted. She could make out his red polo shirt, but the light was so dim she couldn't tell whether he was looking at her or at something else.

Inside, a grimy iron staircase led downward. The area was lit by a single bare bulb, hanging from a length of flex. Ducking below it, she moved cautiously down the stairs. As she descended, she strained to hear the sounds of Amun's footsteps—anyone's footsteps—but all that came to her were the creakings and protestations of an old, ill-maintained building.

She came to a tiny landing, and she continued down again. She could smell the dampness, mold, the sharp odors of decay and decomposition. She felt as if she had entered a dying body.

Approaching the end of the stairs, she found herself on slabs of rough concrete. Cobwebs brushed her face, and, now and again, she could hear the click and chitter of rats. Soon enough, other small noises came to her—hushed voices opened up the darkness. Doggedly, she groped her way forward, guided by the voices. Within fifty feet, she began to make out a wavering light that illuminated what appeared to be a war-ren of cave-like rooms. She paused for a moment, struck by the similar-ity between these spaces and those used by Hezbollah when they were preparing to cross the border for a raid into Israel. There was the same stench of sour sweat, anticipation, forgotten hygiene, spices, and the bit-ter, metallic smell of ordnance being prepped for detonation.

She was close enough to make out the voices—there were three of them. This brought her up short. Had Amun engaged them already? But no, now that she had crept close enough, her ears told her that only one of the voices was familiar—the miserable liar Donatien Marchand.

Approaching a corner, she peeked around. Three men stood in the dim fizzy light of an old-fashioned oil lamp. One was very young, thin as a reed, dark-eyed and hollow-cheeked. The other was only a bit older with a full beard and hands like ax heads. Facing them was Marchand. From the tone of their voices and their body language, it appeared they were in the middle of a difficult negotiation. She risked a glance around. Where was Amun? Somewhere close, she had to assume. What was his plan? And how could she get close enough to hear what the men were arguing about? Looking all around, she saw nothing that would help her. Then, directing her gaze upward into the shadows, she saw the massive beams that crisscrossed the space, keeping the entire building from col-lapsing into the Arabs' basement lair.

Using a series of boxes she found strewn over the floor, she climbed up until she could loop her arms around one of the beams. Hauling her torso upward, she wrapped her ankles across the top of the beam and, using that leverage, swung fully up. She had to be careful not to disturb the accumulated filth—grime, sticky cobwebs, iridescent insect shells, and rat droppings—which, raining down, would announce her presence. On her belly, Soraya inched along the beam until she was more or less above the three men.

"No, man, I say triple for that."

"Triple is too much," Marchand said.

"Shit, for that bitch triple's too little. You got ten seconds, then the price goes up."

"Okay, okay," Marchand said after a short pause.

Soraya could hear the slither of bills being counted out.

"I'll have a photo downloaded to your cell phone," Marchand said.

"Don't need no pho-to. That Moore bitch's face is etched in my brain."

Soraya shuddered. There was something grimly surreal about eavesdropping on the plans for her own imminent demise. She could feel her heart hammering in her throat as the meeting broke up.

She hated these Arabs, but she remained motionless. The mission was to discover whom Marchand had called after they had scared him half out of his wits. These Arab thugs couldn't tell her; only Marchand could do that. He would never have talked on his own territory, but now that she had caught him in a compromising position with these hit men, he might be more inclined—

She started as Amun came racing out of the shadows. The older of the Arabs turned, a switchblade already in one hand. He stabbed outward, forcing Amun to change direction. The younger Arab smashed his fist into the side of Amun's head, knocking him down.

Soraya dropped feet-first from the beam, her knee catching the younger Arab in the small of the back. He went down, his head striking the concrete, which shattered his front teeth. Blood spattered from his split lip. He groaned and lay still. Amun scrambled away from the older Arab's knife, and they both vanished into the darkness.

That left Soraya and Donatien Marchand. He stared at her with the fixed intensity of a trapped wolf. His eyes seemed yellow with hatred.

"How did you know where I was coming?" When she didn't answer, he glanced around. "Where's the Jew? Too timid to make it down here?"

"You're dealing with me now," Soraya said.

Before she could say another word, Marchand bolted away. She tore after him, back toward the stairs. Part of her mind was with Amun and his fight with the Arab. Were there more down here? But she couldn't think of that now; she couldn't let Marchand get away.

He reached the bottom of the stairs and leapt upward, faster and more agile than she had expected. She pounded after, through the wan, gritty light, up through patches of darkness, past the tiny landing, ascending the second part of the staircase, up toward where the bare bulb emitted its waxen light.

Marchand was running so hard he hit the bulb with his shoulder. It swung back and forth on the end of its flex, casting wild and disorienting shadows across the stairs. Soraya redoubled her pace, closing the distance to her enemy.

All at once Marchand stopped and, whirling, drew a small .22 with silver grips. He fired once, wildly, and then again as she closed, the second bullet tearing through the shoulder of her jacket but leaving her unharmed.

Barreling into him, she drove the edge of her hand into his wrist, knocking the .22 out of his grip. With a series of bright, hard clangs, it bounded down the stairs and lay half in the shadows.

Soraya grabbed the front of Marchand's coat, drawing him to her, but he had reached up and, before she knew what had happened, looped the electrical flex around her neck. He pulled tight and she gagged. Her hands reached up to loosen the flex, but Marchand, standing behind her, only pulled it tighter.

Her fingers scrabbled futilely at the flex cutting into her neck and throat. She tried to draw a breath, but it was no use. A moment later she began to lose consciousness.

16

BOURNE ARRIVED IN Seville with his two passengers without further incident. Interpol hadn't been waiting for the plane in Madrid, and in Seville the trio passed through the arrivals terminal unnoticed.

As promised, a rental car was waiting for them along with an Internet address. Bourne entered it into his cell phone's browser and up came a map of the area from Seville to Cadiz. A purple line indicated the route Essai expected them to take. At the end was an address in Cadiz, the place, he assumed, where Don Fernando Hererra was waiting for their arrival.

They climbed into the car, and Bourne started it up then drove them out of the airport. He had spent the air time trying to figure out Jalal Essai's game. There was no doubt that Essai had fed him a brew of truth and lies, so whether he was ally or enemy was still to be determined. Bourne had also spent much of the time brooding over his friend Boris Karpov. If it was true he had been ordered to kill Bourne, he hadn't shown up yet. But would he? Essai wanted something from Bourne, something he knew Bourne wouldn't do if Essai asked him straight-out. Did it have to do with Boris? Bourne felt a vast net beginning to tighten around him, but as yet he had no idea of its size or origin.

Someone wanted him—but why and for what?

"You don't talk a lot, do you?" Rosie said from the seat next to him.

Bourne smiled, staring straight ahead as he navigated the road. He was concerned about tails, but so far the traffic behind them appeared normal.

"You're not like anyone I've ever met."

"*Dios mio*, Rosie," Vegas said from the backseat, "stop peppering him with questions."

"I'm only making conversation, *mi amor*." She turned to Bourne, but her eyes did not meet his, sliding away into shadow. "I know what it's like to be alone—really alone, crouched in the shadows watching the sunlight."

"Rosie!"

"Hush, *mi amor*." She addressed Bourne again. "Here is what I can't understand: Why would someone do this voluntarily?"

"You know," Bourne said, "you don't speak like someone from the backwater of Colombia."

"I sound educated, yes?"

"I admire your vocabulary."

Her laughter was deep and rich. "Yes, someone like you would."

"You don't know anything about me."

"No? You are alone, always alone. I think this is the essential thing about you—it defines how you think and everything you do." She cocked her head. "You have no answer for this?"

"I don't know a single thing about you."

She touched the scars on her neck and chest. "But I think you do."

"The margay."

"She was so beautiful," Rosie said, "but I got in her way."

"No," Bourne said. "You frightened her."

Rosie looked away, out her window at the passing scenery, which was nothing much, a series of hypnotically undulating hills, some covered in groves of gnarled, dusty-looking olive trees.

Bourne glanced again in the rearview mirror. There was a red Fiat he was keeping an eye on, though he doubted any professional tail would be driving a red car.

"Stumbling over a margay's den," he said, "that doesn't sound like the kind of behavior I'd expect from someone who was born and raised in the Cordilleras."

"I was running. Crossing a stream, I slipped on a mossy rock and hurt my knee. I wasn't looking where I was going; I was frightened."

"You were running away."

"Yes."

"From whom?"

Rosie tossed her head. "You're always running. You should know."

"I was told you were running away from your family."

She nodded. "That is true."

"I've never done that."

"And yet you're alone, always alone," she said. "It must be exhausting."

Vegas leaned forward. "Rosie, for the love of God!" He turned to Bourne. "I apologize for her."

Bourne shrugged. "The world is full of opinions."

"I know why you run," Rosie said. "It is so nothing will touch you."

Bourne's eyes flicked again to the rearview mirror, the red Fiat, then to Rosie's face, but once again her eyes were averted.

"I suppose there's not much call for a psychologist in Ibagué," he said. "Is that where you were born?"

"I am Achagua," Rosie said. "From the serpent line."

Bourne, an expert in comparative languages, knew that the Achagua had named their different family lineages after animals: serpent, jaguar, fox, bat, tapir.

"Do you speak the language—Irantxe?"

A slow smile lifted the corners of her lips. "Nice try. I'm impressed. Really. But no, Irantxe is its own language. The Achagua spoke any number of Maipurean dialects depending on whether they lived in the mountains or the Amazon basin." Her smile broadened. "Please tell me you don't speak any of those languages."

"I don't," Bourne said.

"Neither do I. They were spoken a very long time ago. Even my father had no knowledge of them."

Bourne's eyes returned to the rearview mirror. He could no longer see the red Fiat and, instead, began to concentrate on the black van up ahead. Over the past fifteen minutes, it had had several opportunities to change lanes and speed, but it hadn't done so. Instead it had maintained its position four vehicles ahead of him.

Checking his side mirror, he waited for a break in the traffic, then, without signaling, shot forward into the left-hand lane. Within seconds he had passed the black van. He watched it firmly planted in his rearview, receding slowly from view. Then it changed lanes and accelerated.

Now he began to look for the box, a tailing maneuver extremely difficult to shake since it involved vehicles in front and behind.

"What's happening?" Vegas said.

Bourne could feel the anxiety radiating from him like waves of heat.

"There are people on this road who shouldn't be here," Bourne said. "Sit back."

Rosie gripped the handle above her door but said nothing. Her face was set in neutral. She knew when to keep quiet, Bourne thought.

The black van had established a position a car's length behind him. Apparently, the driver understood he had been made.

Bourne checked ahead, but saw no other black van. He saw two-seater sports cars, a bus full of Japanese tourists, cameras held in front of their faces, and sedans with families. There were also a wide variety of trucks, including a semi, but none of these vehicles seemed likely to be part of the box.

He tried varying his speed, noting how each vehicle in front of him reacted, but he got no definitive read. He thought it interesting—and worrisome—that though the black van had announced itself, the second vehicle was still incognito. He wondered what that meant because it wasn't part of the box playbook, which dictated all-in or all-out. Once one of the vehicles in the box was made, usually the two vehicles either peeled off or closed in.

Suddenly the black van made its move, coming up on Bourne's left. He switched into the center lane and, moments later, it followed. He kept going, into the right-hand lane even though the semi was now in front of him. If the black van followed, he could always swing around the semi's left.

With a burst of speed, the black van cut off a chugging sedan as it swerved into the right-hand lane behind Bourne. Bourne looked for a break in the traffic to switch to the center lane, but even as he plotted vectors the black van came up dangerously close behind him. He accelerated, and, at that precise moment, the rear of the semi slammed down, its edge casting off a shower of sparks as it dragged along the roadbed.

The moment Bourne saw it, he understood. The rear panel had been retrofitted as a ramp. The black van then gently rear-ended him, urging his rental car farther toward the ramp and the yawning empty interior of the semi, the box's second vehicle. These people never meant to tail him, never meant to kill him: They meant to capture him, seal him in, and take him out of the field permanently.

Soraya, struggling to stay conscious, dug her heels into the grit of the staircase. At the same time, she swiveled her hips to the left, moving them out of the way of her right elbow, which she drove into the soft spot in Marchand's throat.

Marchand reared back, so shocked that he took his hands off the flex to belatedly protect his vulnerable throat. With her right hand, she tore the flex away from her throat. She slammed her knee into Marchand's crotch. He gasped, bent over double, and she wrapped the flex around his neck, pulling on both ends so hard he collapsed to his knees.

He made little gasping sounds like a fish on the deck of a boat. He looked up at her, his watering eyes bloodshot and bulging. He tried to swipe at her with his right hand, then his left, but her grip on him was terminal.

She bent over, shoving her grim face in his. "Now, M. Marchand, you're going to tell me what I want to know. You're going to tell me now or by Allah I will take your life and your soul and I will grind them both to dust."

He stared at her. His face was becoming bloated, dark with pooled blood. Tears of pain spilled out of his eyes. She could see the whites all the way around.

"Ak, ak, ak" was all he could manage.

The moment she loosened the flex the smallest amount he lashed out at her, but she slammed her forehead into the bridge of his nose, resulting in a spray of blood that covered his upper lip, cheeks, and chin.

"Now talk," she said. "Who did you call after we left your office?"

His eyes opened even wider. "How...how did you know?"

"Tell me."

"Why bother? You will kill me anyway." His voice sounded sodden, as if he were speaking to her from underwater.

"And why not? You were planning my death," she said. "But unlike you, I might have a measure of mercy inside me. That's the chance you'll have to take."

All of a sudden his shoulders slumped and he shrugged. "So I tell you. What does it matter? You won't get out of here alive."

Soraya had had enough of him. Her desire to break him into little pieces became overwhelming. Taking his broken nose in her hand, she turned it like a water faucet until new tears sprang from his eyes and he was panting like a pack animal about to collapse. Then and only then did she loosen the flex sufficiently.

She stared hard into his eyes. "Five seconds, four, three—"

He jabbed upward, his fist connecting with her left breast. Soraya saw stars and, staggering back, almost pitched off the stairs. Seizing his moment, Marchand sprang at her, his face purple, his cheeks blotchy, and his breath sawed raggedly from his throat. His hands throttled her, bending her backward as he attempted to pitch her off the staircase down into the blackness at the bottom.

Also struggling for breath, Soraya cursed herself for letting down her guard, while working to spread his forearms and mitigate his attack. But Marchand was out for blood.

Soraya punched and punched, but she lacked leverage, so her blows were having a minimal effect. Lights were bursting behind her eyes and she was having trouble thinking. She struggled mightily, but that only seemed to worm her deeper into his grip. Slowly, inexorably, he pushed her backward against the railing, until her back was arched painfully.

Light and shadow danced spastically, eerily, as the bulb swung to her ever more desperate movements. She found herself staring at the light bulb, a miniature sun emanating from the coils. Then she blinked. She was at the tipping point and felt him marshaling his energy to heave her over the side. Her arm shot up. Grasping the base of the bulb, she slammed it into Marchand's left eye.

He screamed as the glass shattered, piercing his eyeball. Soraya, feeling the pressure come off, shoved the broken base deeper in.

The corona of the electric shock spun her backward like a giant hand slap. She sucked in deep, shuddering breaths, desperate to return oxygen to her system. She felt harrowed, hollowed out.

Then she smelled burning flesh and almost gagged. She stood up straight, groaning, every muscle in her torso sore and aching. Marchand was on his knees. His hands were glued to the base of the bulb, which was buried in his eye socket. Muscles jumped and spasmed even as he fell over, his heart short-circuiting.

17

THE ONCOMING BLACK van was behind Bourne, the semi ready to scoop them up in front. To the right was a two-foot shoulder ending in a galvanized-steel guardrail, beyond which was a steep drop-off into an olive grove clinging to the side of a hill. On his left was a convertible Mercedes, the oblivious driver bobbing his head to the music pouring out of his speakers. There was no time for thought, only instinct forged by years of training and hard experience.

Bourne accelerated, closing the car's-length distance between him and the ramp. Then he was on the ramp itself, the nose of the rental car pointed up.

"What the hell are you doing?" Vegas shouted.

Halfway up the ramp Bourne turned the wheel hard to his left and, at the same time, stamped the accelerator to the floor. The car shot up and off the ramp. Airborne, it passed over the Mercedes, the undercarriage clearing the driver's head by inches even before he instinctively ducked. Horns blared, brakes screeched. Bourne clipped the rear end of the car in the far left lane, regained control, and kept going. Behind him, cars piled into one another in a chain reaction, but the rental car was free now, accelerating away from the semi and the black van, both of which were caught in the expanding chaos of a massive crash.

"*¡Madre de Dios!*" Vegas cried. "Is my poor heart still beating?"

Rosie released her grip on the handle above the door. "What Estevan means is thank you."

"What I mean is I need a drink," Vegas muttered from behind them.

The day was spent, the sun, yellow bordering on orange, pressed down against the hills in the west like a fried egg. Twilight swept across the olive groves, lending their tortured branches a spooky aspect. They were racing west, toward the darkness of night and a sprinkling of first-magnitude stars.

The atmosphere in the car had altered. Bourne could feel it as surely as you feel the onset of winter, a drop in the pressure, a tiny shiver of a premonition. Following their escape from the box, a subtle shift in the balance of his two charges had occurred. It was as if Vegas, the competent oil man, felt like a fish out of water away from his mountains and his oil fields. Whereas their journey away from Ibagué had caused Rosie to blossom like a flower in sunlight.

He thought about the elaborate box, which had the hand of the Domna all over it. The Domna had tracked him down. Had Jalal Essai told them? Bourne wouldn't put it past him. Essai remained a complete mystery to Bourne.

Painful as it might be, everything Rosie had said was true: He was running away from everything and everyone. And of course, it was clear why. Once, he had cared deeply for a handful of people. Now all of them save Moira and Soraya were dead. Perhaps some of them, because of him. *No more*, an insistent voice inside of him cried. *No more*. His new philosophy, developed without his even being aware of it, was simple: Keep running. He knew he couldn't get hurt running. But the downside, the collateral damage that Rosie had so cleverly pointed out to him, was that he felt nothing. Was that living? Was he even alive? And if he wasn't, what was the state of being in which he found himself?

To distract himself, he turned to Rosie. "Why were you running away?"

"The usual reasons."

She had a knack of answering questions as he would have, without revealing any pertinent information. "There are no usual reasons," he shot back.

This made her laugh, a sound he found intriguing. It was deep and rich, launched from her stomach. There was nothing shallow or phony about that laugh. "Well, you're right about that."

She was silent for some time. Bourne caught a look at Vegas, asleep in the backseat. He looked drawn, exhausted, as if he'd traveled from the Cordilleras to just outside Cadiz on foot.

"I was not a good girl," Rosie said, after a time. She was staring out her side window. "I was, what do you call it, the black sheep. Whatever I did made the people around me angry."

"Your family."

"Not just my family. There were friends affected, too. That was one of the things my family couldn't forgive me for."

They rode on in silence, the wind cracking and moaning through the car. Rosie pushed her hair back behind her ear, revealing a small tattoo on the inside of one of the whorls.

"I see you keep a serpent with you at all times," Bourne said. The snake was striped orange and black.

She touched the pink shell of her ear. "It's a skytale."

"It looks mythical. Does it breathe fire?"

"Huh! I've yet to hear about a creature that breathes fire."

"You haven't met some of the Russians I have."

That laugh again, filling the car as if with perfume.

Bourne hesitated only a moment. "But you have met some bad people."

The wind floated her hair over her ear, obscuring the tiny dragon. "Pretty bad, yes." Before he could follow up, she said, "Why are you running?"

"I pissed off some very powerful people. They had plans and I got in the way."

Rosie gave Vegas a quick glance over her shoulder. "If it's the Domna, then good for you."

This brought a wry smile to Bourne's face. "What do you know about Estevan's involvement with them?"

Rosie hesitated, possibly considering whether or not to violate a confidence. Then she said, "His involvement wasn't voluntary, I can tell you that."

"How did they trap him?"

"His daughter."

"I thought she ran off with a handsome Brazilian?"

"Who told you that? Suarez?" When Bourne said nothing, Rosie shrugged and went on grimly. "That is the story Estevan decided on. It made sense, it was plausible. But the truth is the Domna kidnapped her. Where she is, I have no idea. Every week, Estevan received a photo of her holding a dated newspaper so he knew she was alive."

"But Estevan rebelled," Bourne said.

She ran her hands through her hair. "Essai told him that the Domna didn't have his daughter. They had taken her, but long ago she escaped. No one knows how or where she is. The only thing that Essai could tell Estevan was that the two men who had kidnapped her were found dead, their throats slit. The rest is a complete mystery."

"And the photo they sent him every week?"

"Photoshopped. They apparently used a girl built like her, then put Estevan's daughter's head onto her shoulders." She shuddered. "Ghoulish."

"I assume Estevan has never heard from her."

"Not a word."

Bourne turned off the highway at the exit for Cadiz. "Not long now."

"Thank God," Rosie said under her breath.

"She must have had help," Bourne said thoughtfully.

"Estevan and I talked about that a lot." She shrugged. "For all the good it did."

Bourne could see the city up ahead, like a shining ball of Byzantine brass. He rolled down the window all the way and drew the rich scent of the sea into his lungs.

"How much does Estevan know about the Domna?" Bourne asked. He remembered Essai telling him that if Estevan couldn't tell him what the Domna's new plan was he would surely know someone who could.

Rosie shifted in her seat. "The fact that he had to be coerced into working for them should tell you all you need to know."

"He was a cog in a wheel."

"Everyone except the directors is a cog. It's safer that way; compartmentalization provides complete security. In Estevan's case, he provided an invaluable service."

"Which was?"

"Oil rigs are under constant stress, parts wear out, clog, snap. New parts are always on order, the older ones being shipped back to the various manufacturers, you get the idea."

Bourne did. "What was Estevan smuggling in and out of Colombia for them?"

Rosie shrugged. "Drugs, weapons—for all I know, human beings. Honestly, it could have been anything."

"Estevan never told you?"

"He never knew. The sealed crates came and went. They were marked in a certain way. He was prohibited from opening them. He was simply the conduit."

"Curiosity is part of the human condition," Bourne said. "He never peeked?"

"They were sealed in a specific fashion. Anyway, if he found a way in, he never spoke about it."

"Would he keep something like that from you?"

"As you have seen for yourself, Estevan is extremely protective of me. He would die rather than expose me to danger."

When is a response not an answer? Bourne thought. *When Rosie provides it.*

They had entered the streets of old Cadiz, ablaze with light and sharp shadows. The filigreed architecture of North Africa was all around them. It was as if they had immigrated into another world, one suspended on the ocean, balanced between East and West, part of both, belonging to neither.

The light of day looked fatigued; the sharp odor of a storm was in the air. Night was already beginning to gather.

They drove on, down crooked streets, hearing the calls of street vendors in Spanish and Arabic, inhaling the incense of history.

Where did you learn to pilot a boat?" Marlon Etana said as he sat on the sailboat's bench.

"I'm full of surprises," Essai said. "Even to a man like you."

"A man like me sent to kill a man like you."

Essai laughed. "The best-laid plans."

After meeting up at the café early in the morning, the two men had shared a coffee. They talked about home, about nothing at all. Then they went for a long walk, but even then nothing of consequence passed between them. This was how they wanted it, how it had to be. Theirs was a relationship so buried in conspiracy, deceit, and deepest cover they often had difficulty communicating simply as human beings.

Essai had reserved a sailboat at the rental dock, and they had set sail just after lunchtime, when the world of Cadiz was still drowsing in siesta. All the other boats had pushed off just after dawn, so they wouldn't return until late afternoon. No one saw them; no one but the rental agent was around, and his sole interest was in the euros that crossed his greedy palm.

The day was clear, just some high clouds passing, the sun beating down, flattening the water to beaten brass. Still, the wind was up, and Essai maneuvered the small sailboat expertly, effortlessly, as if he had been born on the water. The edge of Cadiz slipped away, a Saracen's massive scimitar, its hilt encrusted with jewels winking in the sunlight.

It wasn't until the sun lowered, the western sky turning into a palette full of gaudy colors, that they got around to talking.

"El-Arian still thinks you hate me, yes?" Essai said.

"More than ever, I think." Etana's skull was gilded, but his thick beard extinguished the light. "I wanted to go after Bourne, but Benjamin assigned me to you."

"The wily bastard recruited Viktor Cherkesov. Cherkesov has Boris Karpov in his back pocket; he's the only one who does."

From his seat in the cockpit, Etana stared down into the water, cobalt with streaks of orange interspersed with an inky black. "I don't think that's the only reason he recruited Cherkesov."

Essai turned from checking the wind, one hand on the wheel. "Oh?"

Etana pulled into himself, elbows on stringy, muscular thighs. "Cherkesov's first assignment wasn't meeting with Karpov. El-Arian sent him to the Mosque."

Essai felt a chill run through him. The light was wavering before his eyes, turning from gold to blue-black. "The Mosque in Munich?"

"The very same."

"But why?"

Etana sighed. "I'd have to be a sorcerer to know that."

"He sent a Russian ex–FSB director to the Mosque?" Essai shook his head. "El-Arian must be mad."

Etana raised his eyes to Essai's. "We need to come up with a better explanation, and quickly."

"What about the plan?" Essai didn't want to think about the Mosque. The Mosque and the people who now ran it were the reason for the hatred burning inside him.

"El-Arian briefed the directors before I left Paris, but of course I wasn't part of the meeting. No one has said a word."

"I wouldn't expect them to."

The wind changed and the sails were beginning to luff, rippling like a flag. Essai rose briefly, made an adjustment, then returned to the cockpit and tacked starboard.

"Careful," he said.

With a crack of the sail, the boom swung past them.

Essai kept the boat close-hauled, the quartering wind pushing out the sails like a fat man's cheek. They skimmed through the water, roughly paralleling the shore.

Etana steepled his brown fingers, long as a pianist's. "I admit you were right, Jalal. There's no doubt the Mosque's influence over the Domna is increasing every day."

"This is Abdul-Qahhar's doing," Essai said bitterly. "Servant of the Subduer, indeed!"

"But how did El-Arian come under their control?"

Essai kept the boat steady on its course. "One has to go back decades, to a man named Norén, a deep-cover operative who infiltrated the Domna. Now and again, the Domna required a bit of wet work, and they used Norén. He was a ghost—a reliable ghost—which is the most important thing. But all the while he was on assignments for the Domna he was compiling lists of names, dates, facts, and figures."

"To use against the Domna."

"They were used. We lost twenty-one operatives in the span of three weeks."

"But who was he working for?"

"No one knows, though many people within the Domna and under its control tried to find out." Essai squinted off to the west, where thunderheads were building. The wind grew gusty, the water choppy, and he turned the wheel, heading for shore. "Norén was killed."

"What happened?"

"He was overmatched on one of his assignments."

Etana grunted. "Who was the target?"

Essai maneuvered the boat so that it was running before the wind, the hull cleaving the water, spray slapping them in the face with each wave crest.

"A man named Alexander Conklin shot him dead." Essai gave his companion a glance. "Heard of him?"

Etana shook his head.

Essai kept one eye on the roiling thunderheads. "Conklin was the head of Treadstone. In fact, he created it. One of the primary missions of Treadstone was to take down the Domna hierarchy. That's why Conklin became a target."

"And after Norén?"

"The whole idea of terminating Conklin was deemed too risky," Essai said. They were nearing the shore now, the gusty wind pushing them fast, so that he had to begin a long tack in order to slow them.

"Here, take the wheel and hold it steady."

With Etana's hands on the wheel, Essai stepped out of the cockpit, went forward, and reefed the jib in order to cut their speed even more. He could feel the storm's damp slap on his face, though it hadn't yet broken.

When he returned to the cockpit, he retook the wheel.

"Conklin and Treadstone scared the Domna," he said. "That was when El-Arian reached out to Abdul-Qahhar."

"Without getting the other directors' prior consent?"

"Just like El-Arian. I have a strong suspicion that he and Abdul-Qahhar had a prior relationship when they were young men—though I haven't been able to substantiate it yet."

"That would make sense."

"But what is clear is that Treadstone's assault was the excuse El-Arian needed to forge an alliance between the Domna and the Mosque." Essai shook his head. "That kind of Arab influence goes against the Domna's charter of East-West cooperation. It was a watershed moment for the Domna; it was when everything changed."

Etana was sitting very still, his hands had a death grip on the bench, and he seemed green around the gills. Essai said nothing, out of respect, and, soon enough, he reefed the mainsail and they glided into the dock. He threw the bowline to the rental agent.

"I was getting worried," the man said as he drew the boat slowly in. "This storm front looks very bad."

"No need to worry about us," Essai said. "No need at all."

Don't you pass out on me," Tyrone Elkins shouted.

Peter Marks, his arms tight around Elkins's waist, rode the motorcycle, dizzy and weak. There was a fire raging through his body, and he kept going in and out of consciousness, like an exhausted swimmer in the surf. That drowning reference again. Dimly, he wondered where that came from.

"Is that you laughing back there?" Tyrone shouted across the wind.

"Maybe," Peter said. "I don't know." He let his cheek rest against the thick leather of Elkins's jacket. Since when did CI allow one of its operatives to wear a leather jacket, he wondered. Then the thought was lost in the swirl of the inner surf that buffeted him.

"No hospital," he said.

"Gotcha the first time, Chief."

Peter gave a start of deep-seated anxiety. Who knew who was after him, what places they'd be watching? And waiting. "Please."

"Fear not, Chief," Tyrone said. "I know jus' where to go."

"Someplace safe," Peter mumbled.

"Please," Tyrone said. "Gimme a fuckin' break."

They arrived at Deron's house in Northeast DC seven minutes later, Tyrone having broken every traffic ordinance known to the district. Tyrone, brought up in this African American ghetto, had never held any truck with traffic laws, and now that he worked for CI he never gave them a second thought. Any cop stupid enough to pull him over got a face full of his federal ID and backed off faster than a rat looking at a cat.

Back in the day, Tyrone had worked for Deron, a tall, handsome black man with a British education and cultured accent that stood him in good stead with his international clientele of shady art dealers trafficking in Deron's magnificent forgeries. Deron also created all of Jason Bourne's forged documents, and some of his weapons as well. It was because of Bourne's friend Soraya Moore that Tyrone had decided to heed Deron's advice, leave the hood behind, apply himself, and train for work at CI. He'd never worked harder in his life, but the rewards had been many and worth it.

"What the bloody hell happened?" Deron said, as he helped Tyrone carry Peter into the house.

"Fucking meat grinder is what happened."

Peter seemed delirious, rambling incoherently about making calls, dire warnings, pieces of a puzzle.

"Any idea what he's on about?" Deron asked.

Tyrone shook his head. "Shit, no. All he was goin' on about on the way over was I shouldn't take him to a hospital."

"Hmm, Jason wouldn't want that, either."

Tyrone helped his former mentor lay Peter on the sofa.

"Details," Deron said.

Tyrone recounted the scene with the ambulance, the men shot, the driver beating up on Peter. "I brought him right over here," he concluded, handing over the Glock he'd snatched up from the gutter before helping Peter onto his motorcycle.

"I hope you didn't handle it too much."

"Little as I could," Tyrone said.

Deron nodded, clearly pleased. After carefully putting the gun into a plastic bag, he surveyed the battleground of Peter's body. "You know him?"

"Yeah. He Soraya's pal, Peter Marks. Used to work with her at Typhon before she was canned."

Deron went to fetch his extensive first-aid kit. Peter was still softly raving. "Call him, tell him . . ."

Tyrone bent over him. "Who, Peter? Who do you want to call?"

Peter just thrashed, mumbled words tumbling from his bloodstained lips.

"Hold him down so he doesn't hurt himself," Deron said.

"This here Peter left CI," Tyrone went on. "Don't know what he been up to since then, but seeing him like this, it sure as fuck can't be healthy."

Deron returned, knelt down beside Marks, and opened the case. "Son, you have got to work on your King's English."

"Say what?"

Deron gave a short laugh. "Never mind. We'll work on your pronunciation later." He administered a shot into Peter's arm.

"No, no!" Peter cried, his eyes not quite focused. "Must call, must tell him . . ." But then the anesthetic took him and, calmed, he slipped into unconsciousness.

Deron pulled apart Peter's shirt, sticky with blood. Peter's chest was studded with glass and metal shards, a miniature graveyard. "Right now, Tyrone, let's you and me make this man right."

Soraya heard the pounding of feet, and she turned, in a half crouch, ready to defend herself. But it was Amun, sprinting into the feeble light of the staircase.

"Are you all right?" he said from the foot of the stairs.

She nodded, unable for the moment to speak coherently. She was still reeling from Marchand's second attack on her, and her chest hurt like hell. Marchand had seemed like the quintessential academic; she had never thought him capable of such viciousness, and thereby she had learned an important lesson.

Amun, taking the stairs two steps at a time, said, "That the whore-son, Marchand?"

She nodded again. "Dead." It was the only word she was capable of uttering.

"It's over now. They're all dead down there. What a rotten nest of vipers. We should—"

His head exploded and he pitched forward into her arms. She screamed, staggering backward. He was deadweight. She saw a moving shadow, caught a glimpse of a red polo shirt. The man at the far end of the alley! Then a flash of metal. Another shot clanged off the stair railing, and, with her burden, she somersaulted backward, pitching down into the blackness.

Two shots followed. Then another, loud as a cannon shot.

Then nothing, not even an echo.

Oblivion.

18

WAIT!" BORIS SAID. "Stop!"

"What?"

Despite the steady rain, Lana Lang was driving very fast down a street that paralleled the Mosque's west side. The moment they had slewed into the dark, gloomy street, the hairs on the back of Karpov's hands began to rise and he felt an unpleasant stirring of anxiety in the pit of his stomach.

"Stop!" he shouted. "Back up!"

"What for? We're almost there."

Leaning over, he grabbed the gearshift and began to jerk wildly on it.

"What the hell are you doing?" she cried.

"Reversing out of here!"

"Cut it out." She fought him. "You're stripping the goddamn gears."

"Then you do it." He wouldn't give up. "Step on the fucking—"

A hail of bullets smashed the windshield, struck Lana Lang in the face, making her dance like a puppet. Boris, ducking down in the foot well, depressed the clutch with one hand and shoved Lana's foot down on the accelerator with the other.

The car screeched and moaned like a banshee. The drumbeat of rain sounded on the roof as it reversed, scraping along a brick wall. A shrieking commenced as sparking metal was stripped off the car's passenger's side. The door started to cave in, slamming into Boris's right side. He fell across Lana's lap. Her torso was being held upright by the seat belt across her chest, but there was no life left in her. Blood was everywhere, a fountain of it, a pool, a river running through the careening car.

More bullets, shattering the headlights, shredding the front fenders. Then Karpov had pulled the wheel over and the car straightened out. It shot out of the street like a streak of lightning.

The screech of brakes, the war-like blare of horns, shouts of fear and outrage. The fusillade had stopped and Boris risked looking up above the scarred dashboard. The car sat crosswise, blocking the street. Lana's corpse was preventing him from getting behind the wheel.

Just then an air horn sounded, deep and braying. He looked in the other direction and saw an enormous refrigeration truck bearing down on him. It was going too fast—in the foul weather he knew the shocked driver wouldn't be able to stop it in time.

He turned and tried to open the door, but it was so crumpled it was jammed shut. No amount of tugging and hammering was going to open it. And anyway, it was too late. With the roar and squeal of a rabid animal, the truck was on top of him.

We owe you a great debt," Don Fernando Hererra said. "You did us a great service."

"And now I'd like my payment," Bourne said. "I'm not an altruist."

"Oh, but you're wrong, Jason." Don Fernando crossed one elegant leg over the other, opened a beautifully filigreed humidor, offered a robusto to Bourne, who declined. Don Fernando plucked one out and went about the elaborate ritual of cutting and lighting it. "You're one of the world's last true altruists." He puffed, getting the cigar going. "In my opinion, that is what defines you."

The two men were sitting in Don Fernando's comfortable living room. Vegas was lying down in one of the bedrooms, Don Fernando having administered a light sedative. As for Rosie, she'd disappeared into one of the guest bathrooms, saying she was in desperate need of a long, hot shower.

That left Bourne and his host, a man whom he had gotten to know first in Seville, where they had matched wits and sparred verbally, and later, more intimately, in London following the violent death of the old man's son.

"I want half an hour alone with Jalal Essai," Bourne said.

A smile haloed Don Fernando's lips. He leaned forward. "More sherry?" He refilled Bourne's glass, which stood beside a plate of Serrano ham, pink and smoky, and rough-cut chunks of Manchego cheese.

Bourne sat back. "Where is Essai, anyway?"

Don Fernando shrugged. "Your guess is as good as mine."

"Then I can start with you. Why are you friends with him?"

"Not friends. Business partners. He's a means to an end, nothing more."

"And those ends?"

"He makes me money. Not drugs."

"Human beings?"

Don Fernando crossed himself. "God forbid."

"He's a liar," Bourne said.

"True enough." Don Fernando nodded soberly. "He knows no other way of operating. It's pathological."

Bourne sat forward. "What I really want to know, Don Fernando, is the nature of your connection with Severus Domna."

"Also a means to an end. At times, these people can be useful."

"They will compromise you, if they haven't already."

Don Fernando's smile was like a slow signal waxing. "Now you underestimate me, my young friend. I should be offended, but with you…" He waved a hand, dismissing the thought. "The fact is, ever since they formed an alliance with Abdul-Qahhar's Mosque in Munich, I felt it incumbent on me to keep an eye on them."

Seeing Bourne's expression, he chuckled. "I see I have surprised you. Good. You must learn, my friend, that all knowledge doesn't reside with you."

Rosie stepped into the shower and was immediately wrapped in a column of steam. The water cascaded down her shoulders, her back, her breasts, and her flat stomach as she slowly turned. Closing her eyes against the spray, she felt her muscles melt into the heat. Lifting her arms, she ran her fingers through her hair, moving it back and off her face. She turned her face up to the spray, and the hot water streamed against her eyelids, nose, and cheeks. Slowly, she turned her head to one side and the other, the jets massaging her muscles. The water hit her ears, creating a roaring sound that reminded her of surf, the vastness of the sea, and for a time she lost herself in this image of unplumbed depths.

The hot water struck the small tattoo on her ear, rat-tat-tatting against it, and gradually, the color began to fade and run, the serpent seeming to uncoil as it dissolved into a tiny pool of water tinged by the dye, running down her neck like tears, swirling down the drain.

Don Fernando contemplated the glowing end of his cigar.

"It all started with Benjamin El-Arian," Bourne said, "didn't it?"

Rain had come at last, hard and tropical in its fury. It beat against the windowpanes, whipped the palm fronds in the atrium beyond the glass. A gust of wind rattled a loose tile on the roof.

The old man stood, unfolding like an origami, and stepped to the French doors out to the atrium. He stared out, one hand at his temple.

"I wish it were that simple," he said at length. "A simple villain, a simple goal, yes, Jason? It's what we all crave because then we are free of complications. But we both know that life rarely affords us time to wrap things up so neatly. When it comes to Severus Domna—nothing is simple."

Bourne rose and followed Don Fernando, standing next to him. The rain sheeted down the glass, bounced off the paving stones. Runnels of water sluiced out of the copper downspouts, overrunning the grass and plant beds. The earth was black as pitch.

Don Fernando heaved a sigh. His cigar sandwiched between two fingers, all but forgotten.

"No, I'm afraid there is a terrible kind of circular logic at work here. Listen, Jason, it all started with a man named Christien Norén."

Don Fernando turned, peering into Bourne's face to see if the name triggered a spark of recognition.

"You don't remember, do you?"

"I don't remember ever hearing the name *Christien Norén*. Tell me about him."

"That's not for me to do." Don Fernando placed a hand on Bourne's shoulder. "You must ask Estevan's woman."

"Her name isn't Rosie," Bourne said, "is it?"

Don Fernando stuck the cigar in his mouth, but the ash was cold and gray. "Go find her, Jason."

Clean and ruddy, Rosie stepped out of the shower, swaddled herself in a thick bath sheet, then wrapped a smaller towel around her hair, making a turban and tucking the end under. Wiping the fog from the mirror with her fingers, she leaned in over the sink, pushed up the makeshift turban, and stared at herself.

Her hair was now its natural tawny blond, the last dregs of the dye ringing the shower drain. Holding her head still, she plucked the contact lens out of her right eye. There she was, one eye dark as coffee, the other the cerulean blue she was born with. One half of her in one world, the other in a second. Swinging open the mirror, she found inside the medicine cabinet everything she had asked for: nail clippers, file, an array of face scrubs and moisturizers. She removed what she needed.

And that was how Bourne found her, as he opened the door to the bathroom. Rosie stared at his reflection in the mirror.

"Don't you knock?"

"I think I've earned the right to come in on you unannounced," he said.

She turned slowly around to face him. "When did you figure it out?"

"In the car," Bourne said. "You'd never look at me directly. Then, when you turned to check on Estevan, I saw the edge of the contact lens."

"And you didn't say anything?"

"I wanted to see how it played out."

Cupping a hand, she bowed her head, popped the lens out of her left eye, and threw it in the trash can under the sink.

"Is that your real hair color or another dye job?" Bourne asked.

"This is me."

He stepped closer. She seemed utterly unafraid. "Not quite. Though the snake tattoo is gone, you still have a nose typical of native Colombians." He peered more closely. "The operation was masterful."

"It took three separate reconstructions to get it just right."

"That's a lot of trouble to go through to pass for an indigenous Colombian."

"Hiding in plain sight, my father used to say, is hiding completely."

"He's right about that, your father. Christien Norén, is that right?"

Rosie's eyes opened wide. "Don Fernando told you then."

"I suppose he thought it was time."

She nodded. "I suppose it is."

"So, then. It's you, not Estevan, who is so important to Don Fernando and Essai."

"It was me those people on the highway were after."

"Who are they?"

"I told you I was running."

"From family, you said."

"In a way, it's the truth. They're the people my father worked for."

Bourne stood very close to her. She smelled of lavender soap and citrus shampoo. "What shall I call you?"

She gave him an enigmatic smile. She came toward him, so close there was scarcely a handbreadth between them.

"I was born Kaja Norén. My father was named Christien, my mother, Viveka. They're both dead."

"I'm sorry."

"You're very kind."

Kaja laid one hand on his cheek, stroking it gently. With the other, she drove the nail file she had palmed through skin and layers of muscle.

Book Three

19

CLUTCHING THE HIGH-HEELED shoe he had ripped off Lana Lang's foot, Boris attacked the bullet-shattered windshield just as the truck plowed into Lana's car. The front and side air bags deployed, saving him from a dislocated shoulder. Still, he almost lost consciousness. Pulling himself together, he hacked at the windshield, using the heel like a hammer.

The truck driver slammed on the brakes, but the momentum of the two-ton vehicle was too much. The truck dragged the car along with it. The brake pads started to smoke, something fell out of the bottom of the car, sparks flying as it scraped the wet roadbed.

Arms crossed over his face, Boris sprang through the ruined windshield, the crack and tinkle of safety glass in his ears. The car shuddered beneath him like a shot deer. He rolled across the hood, then dropped awkwardly down onto the road. Pain stabbed briefly through his foot and up into his leg. Rain beat down on him, soaking him instantly. The car and truck, now one grotesque unit, continued on, slewing heavily, overheated, tortured metal screaming. The truck's brakes seized up and the mass skidded, like a planet thrown out of orbit. Then truck and car both jumped the curb and plowed through a plate-glass storefront. With a horrendous sound like an animal screaming in pain, they smashed the interior to smithereens and impacted the rear wall.

By that time Boris had staggered to his feet amid a chaotic mass of shouting pedestrians, blaring sirens, and stalled traffic. People in herky-jerky motion were everywhere, their umbrellas clashing into one another. Faces peered at him, hands grabbed for him, beseeching him for answers: Was he all right, what had happened? The crowd swelled into a mob that spilled out into the adjoining streets. People seemed to be running from every direction, splashing in the running gutters.

Boris was busy wrenching himself free of the mounting chaos. That was when he spied the human machine knifing through the crowd. The human machine grinned at him and said something Boris couldn't make out. It was Zachek, the mouthpiece for Konstantin Beria, the head of SVR. Zachek, who had detained him at Ramenskoye airport. What was he doing here? Boris asked himself.

"Believe me when I tell you that we can make your life a living hell," Zachek had warned him.

In that moment he saw everything as if a curtain had been lifted, revealing the poisoned feast laid out on a table. As he reeled drunkenly away, clawing through the dense clusters of chattering gawkers, Boris knew that it was SVR. SVR was responsible for Lana Lang's death, fucking with him here in Munich.

Do you ever think about them?" Kaja said.

Bourne, lying on the floor of the bathroom, stared up into her piercing blue eyes. She was sitting astride his stomach, one fist grasping the end of the nail file she had used as a makeshift knife. He felt very little pain. He suspected that the file hadn't gone very deep, that, in fact, one of his ribs had deflected it from its path. He could have dislodged her, but what was the point? She hadn't wanted to kill him, or even to hurt him badly. She had something to tell him, something he wanted—possibly even needed—to hear. So he lay still, breathing deeply, his thoughts going deep, gathering his resolve.

"The people you've killed?" she continued.

And then, staring into her eyes, the past rose up and melded with the present. Her blue eyes became the eyes of the woman in the bathroom of the Nordic disco club. Lights strobed, music blared, and he was back there in time and place. She was sitting on the toilet, the small silver-plated .22—almost a plaything when it came to stopping a human being—aimed at him.

He did what Alex Conklin had sent him to do. He knew nothing about the woman, except that she had been marked by Treadstone for termination. Those were the days when he had done what he was told, as his training dictated. Before the incident when he had lost his memory, after which he had begun to question everything, starting with Treadstone's motives.

Just before he had completed his mission, she had said to him, *"There is no—"*

There is no . . . what?

Kaja's eyes, the dead woman's eyes, the same eyes.

And then Kaja said, "I saw her. The police came and took me to Frequencies in Stureplan to identify her. She was sitting there, they hadn't moved her, God knows why . . ." Her head trembled. "There was no reason for you to do what you did."

"There is no reason." That was what she had said just before he had killed her. *"There is no reason."*

Soraya fell into darkness. She landed on Amun's corpse, which, in death, protected her as Amun had done in life.

The man with the red polo was on her immediately, dragging her off Amun and throwing her to the side like a sack of garbage. For a moment, he stared down at Amun's face. Then he kicked it. The jaw cracked and teeth flew everywhere. He kicked again and Amun's nose collapsed.

Then he went to work on Amun's ribs, staving them in with kicks that became ever more vicious. He was panting like a dog in heat. His face was flushed with blood and his lips were drawn back from his yellow teeth.

Soraya, coming to, heard the man's imprecations. Because they were Arabic, she became momentarily disoriented, believing she was back in Cairo. Then her gaze fell upon Amun's ruined face and she shrieked like a banshee. The Arab was turning toward her as she landed on him, toppling him backward.

They hit hard on the bare concrete, and she grunted with a sudden pain flaring through her left side. The Arab tried to roll off her, but she dug in with clawed fingers. Despite an overwhelming dizziness, she held fast to him. He chopped down on one of her wrists, providing the opening she needed. Slamming the heel of her hand into his nose, she pushed herself off her left side and tried to knee him. He jerked away and she connected with his thigh instead.

That was all the opportunity he was going to afford her. He jabbed her throat with the tips of his fingers and she reared back, gagging, gasping for breath. Calmly and methodically, he drew out a switchblade, *snikked* it open, and prepared to slit her throat.

A pounding on the bathroom door caused Kaja to lock it.

Don Fernando's voice could be heard through the door. "Is everything all right?"

"Perfectly fine," Kaja said. "Jason and I are having a heart-to-heart."

"Don't do anything precipitous," Don Fernando said. "He knows nine hundred ways to kill you."

"You worry too much, Don Fernando," she said.

He rattled the doorknob. "Come out at once, Kaja. This was a mistake."

"No," she said, "it's not."

"He doesn't remember, Kaja."

"So you told me." Leaning down, her face close to Bourne's, she said softly, "You won't lay a hand on me, will you? Not until you learn what happened, and by then it will be too late."

He wondered what she meant by that.

"Do you even remember her, Jason? Do you remember Frequencies, the dance club in Stockholm?"

Bourne was still engaged in a duel with her eyes. "It was winter, snowing."

Kaja seemed mildly surprised. "Yes, the day she died it was snowing hard. The day you killed her."

Full understanding bloomed. "She was your mother."

For a moment, something dark and ugly swam in her eyes. "Viveka. My mother's name was Viveka." She leaned ever closer, their lips virtually touching. And all at once her face twisted with a demonic spasm. Her voice was clotted with emotion when she said: "Why did you kill her?"

The knife blade swung in a shallow arc. Soraya tried to lift one arm to fend it off, to protect herself, but still gasping for air, she lacked the strength. The Arab knocked her arm away as if it belonged to a doll.

Gripping her hair with one hand, he jerked her head back, exposing the long, vulnerable curve of her throat. He grinned. "Bitch," he said. Then other words that made her shudder. His body curved into one long blade, a weapon bent solely to take her life, as if he had been born to that one dreadful task.

He arched up and Soraya said a prayer, for life and for death. And then the Arab's head was surrounded by a pair of arms. A hand cupped his chin and, even while recognition came into his eyes, jerked his head to the right in the most violent motion imaginable. His neck cracked, snapped, and, as the hands let go, he slumped sideways, down into the darkness he had meant for her.

Soraya looked up as Aaron moved into the pale, fluttering light at the base of the stairwell. He reached down and, without a word, picked her up in his arms and took her out of the basement via the alternate route by which he had found his way in.

There is no reason.

He could tell her the truth or lie. It didn't matter; she wasn't listening. All she wanted was her pound of flesh, and now he knew what it was.

"She was a civilian. That was what my father told us just before he left us. 'Whatever happens to me, don't be concerned,' he said. 'You're safe. You're civilians.' I didn't know what he meant, until the day of the snowstorm, the day my mother…" A spasm of deflected energy went through her. Her face looked white-hot. "Why did you kill her? Tell me! I need to know!"

He felt briefly buffeted by her pain, as if a great gust of wind had slipped by him. What could he tell her that would mollify her? He considered the state she was in, the amount of time she'd had to work herself up.

This was a complicated woman, of that Bourne had no doubt; she had hidden in plain sight for a number of years, insinuated herself into Estevan Vegas's life. More than that, however, she had made his life her own. She had lived and breathed, she had become what she seemed to be. She was no longer Swedish. She had been mauled by a margay; she was Achagua, from the serpent line.

"You should make that tattoo permanent," he said. "That skytale was beautiful."

His words seemed alchemical, working a change in her. Her hand came off his shoulder and she sat back, abruptly exhausted. The dark, ugly thing in her eyes vanished. She seemed to have gone to another place, and was now back with him in Don Fernando's house in Cadiz.

"One afternoon I saw a skytale in the forest not far from Estevan's house," she said. "It is a beautiful creature; as beautiful, in its way, as the margay. I drew it myself, using the natural plant dyes of the Achagua."

"It's been a long journey," he said. "You are no longer who you were."

She looked at him, as if for the first time. "That's true for both of us, isn't it?"

She rose off him then and stepped back, watching him warily as he got up, took the nail file out of his side. Blood spread across his shirt, and he took it off. He turned on the hot water and soaped the wound. It wasn't serious at all.

"It's bleeding a lot," she said, from her safe distance.

Does she think I'll strike her now? Bourne wondered. *Retaliate in some way?*

"Unlock the door," he said as he tended to the wound. "Don Fernando is worried about both of us."

"Not until you tell me the truth." She took one hesitant step toward him. "Was my mother a spy, as well?"

"Not to my knowledge," Bourne said. He remembered now. The force of Kaja's emotion had dislodged the shard of memory from the lost depths of his past. "Your father was sent to kill the man who was then my boss. He failed. I was sent in retaliation."

Kaja made a noise. She seemed to be having trouble breathing. "Why wasn't my father—?"

"My target?" he finished for her. "Your father was already dead."

"And that wasn't enough?"

There was no possible answer he could give that would satisfy her—or, he thought, himself.

There is no reason.

Viveka Norén had been right. There had been no reason for her death, save Conklin's need for revenge. But who had Conklin been hurting? Norén's daughters were innocents, they didn't deserve to have their mother taken from them. Conklin's vindictiveness sent a chill through him. He had been Conklin's instrument, trained and sent out again and again to terminate lives.

He rubbed his hands over his eyes. Was there no end to the sins he had compiled in the past he couldn't remember? For the first time, he wondered whether his amnesia was a blessing.

"This isn't the answer I wanted," Kaja said.

"Welcome to the real world," he said wearily.

He thought she might cry then, but her eyes remained dry. Instead, she turned and unlocked the door.

Don Fernando, standing on the threshold, wrenched it open. He stepped in with an appalled expression as he took in Bourne's wound.

"My house has now become a *corrida*? Kaja, what have you done?"

She was silent, but Bourne said, "Everything is fine, Don Fernando."

"I should think not." He frowned at Kaja, who refused to look at him. "You have abused my hospitality. You promised me—"

"She did what she had to do." Bourne found a sterile gauze pad in the medicine cabinet and taped it over the wound. "It's all right, Don Fernando."

"On the contrary." Don Fernando was furious. "I helped you out of the friendship I had with your mother. But it's clear you've spent too long in the Colombian jungle. You've picked up some very nasty habits."

Kaja collapsed onto the edge of the tub, her palms pressed together, as if in prayer. "It was not my intention to disappoint you, Don Fernando."

"My dear, I'm not angry for myself—I'm angry for you." The older man put his back against the door frame. "Imagine what your mother would think of your behavior. She raised you better than that."

"My sister—"

"Don't talk to me about your sister! If I suspected you were anything like her I wouldn't have let you anywhere near Jason."

"Apologies, Don Fernando." Kaja stared down at her hands.

Bourne had never heard Don Fernando raise his voice before. Clearly, Kaja had hit a nerve.

Don Fernando sighed. "If only you meant it. We are all liars here, we are all pretending to be what we're not." He looked from Kaja to Bourne. "Don't you find it interesting that we all have a problem with identity?"

At last, Kaja lifted her head. "We're all ruled by secrets."

"Well, yes." Don Fernando nodded. "But it's the secrets that cause the problem with identity. To keep secrets is to lie, to lie is to cause a change of identity. And then time goes by, the lies become the norm, then the truth—at least our truth, and then...who are we?" His eyes cut away from Bourne's. "Do you know, Kaja?"

"Of course I do." But she had answered too quickly, and now she paused, thinking. A frown invaded her face.

"Are you Swedish," Bourne said gently, "or Achagua?"

"My blood is—"

"But blood has so little to do with it, Kaja!" Don Fernando cried. "Identity has no basis in reality. It's pure perception. Not only how others see you and react to you, but also how you think of yourself, how you react." He grunted in what seemed mock disgust. "I think Jason is right. You should make that snake tattoo permanent."

Kaja jumped up. "You were listening through the door!"

Don Fernando held up a key. "How else would I know whether I needed to open it."

"Jason hardly needed your help," she said.

"I wasn't thinking about him," Don Fernando said.

She looked up. "Thank you."

It was astonishing, Bourne thought, how far she had come from being Rosie, Estevan Vegas's Colombian mistress.

Don Fernando gestured. "I think we all could use a drink."

Kaja nodded and rose. As the three of them returned to the living room, she asked about Estevan.

"Sleeping off his fear, gathering his strength, which he will need." Don Fernando shrugged. "It is unfortunate. He only knows one life, and it's a far simpler one than the one in which he now finds himself."

"Why are you looking at me like that?" Kaja bristled. "Do you think I'm going to leave him?"

"If you do," Don Fernando said as he poured them some of his extraordinary sherry, "you are sure to break his heart."

She accepted the glass he handed her. "Estevan's heart was broken long before he met me."

"That doesn't mean it won't be again."

Bourne accepted the sherry and sipped it slowly. He sat on the sofa. The adrenaline was wearing off and his side burned as if Kaja had stuck him with a hot poker.

"Kaja—" Bourne broke off at the shake of her head.

She came over and sat beside him. "I know Estevan and I would never have made it here without you. For this I thank you. And..." She stared down into the golden depths of her sherry. She took a deep breath and let it out slowly. "So. The past is the past. I have buried it." Her head turned, her eyes engaged with his. "And so should you."

Bourne nodded and finished his sherry. He waved Don Fernando off when he offered a refill.

"It would help me," he said, "if you could tell me about your father."

Kaja gave a bitter laugh, then took a long sip of her sherry. Her eyes closed for a moment. "How I wish there was someone who could tell me about him. One day, he went away. He left us as if we were a bunch of playthings he'd outgrown. I was nine. Two years later, my mother..." She could have finished that thought; she took a small sip of sherry instead. Light winked off the rim of the glass as she tipped it to her mouth. She swallowed hard. "Thirteen years ago. It feels like a lifetime." Her shoulders slumped. "Sometimes several lifetimes."

"He was a spy, an assassin," Bourne said. "Who was he working for?"

"I don't know," Kaja said. "And believe me I tried to find out." Her eyes cut away for a moment. "I feel certain that Mikaela, my other sister, discovered who it was."

"She didn't tell you?"

"She was killed before she could say a word to either me or Skara."

"Triplets," Don Fernando cut in.

Now the pieces of the puzzle began to fall into place. "So you and Skara ghosted away, changing identities," Bourne said, "hiding, as you said, in plain sight."

"*I* did at least." Kaja put her head down, resting the sugary rim of the glass against her forehead. "I went as far away from Stockholm as I could."

"But your father's organization found you anyway."

She nodded. "Two men came. I killed one and wounded the other. I was running away from him when I surprised the margay."

Bourne thought for a moment. "Is there anything you can tell me about the two men?"

Kaja shuddered and took another deep breath. For the first time, she looked terribly young and vulnerable, the runaway girl from Stockholm.

And in that moment, Bourne caught a glimpse of the energy it took for her to maintain her Rosie identity.

"The men spoke to each other in English," she said at last. "But at the end, the one I killed said something just before he died. It wasn't in English. It was in Russian."

20

HENDRICKS WAS JUST wrapping up the eighth Samaritan strategy session in the last thirty-six hours—this one on staff deployment along the perimeter that had been established around the Indigo Ridge mine—when Davies, one of his half a dozen aides, entered the room.

"It's the POTUS on the secure line, sir," Davies whispered in his ear before departing.

"Okay, out," Hendricks said to the participants. "But stand by for final orders. We deploy personnel in four hours."

After everyone had filed out and the door was closed, Hendricks swiveled his chair and, for a moment, stared out the window at the pristine, newly mowed lawn, bordered by the picket line of massive concrete anti-terrorist blockades that had been erected in 2001. Someone, perhaps in a fit of irony, had placed a row of flowerpots atop them. *Like planting flowers on a battleship*, he thought. The blockades stood immutable; their purpose could not be mitigated. Tourists milled on the other side of them, but the lawn was spotless, not a single weed allowed to show its face. Something about that deserted expanse depressed Hendricks.

Sighing inwardly, he picked up the receiver connected to the secure line to the White House.

"Chris, you there?"

There was a hollow sound, peculiar to the encryption program that scrambled their words every ten seconds.

"I'm right here, Mr. President."

"How's the boy!"

Hendricks's stomach contracted. The president's voice evinced that false heartiness it typically took on when he had some bad news to impart to the recipient.

"Tip-top, sir."

"That's the spirit. How are the plans for Samaritan progressing?"

"Almost complete, sir."

"Uhm-hum," the president said, by which he meant he wasn't listening.

Hendricks reached into a drawer for the box of Prilosec he always kept on hand for emergencies.

"It's Samaritan I want to talk to you about. It so happens that this morning I had breakfast with Ken Marshall and Billy Stokes."

The president paused to allow the two names to sink in. Marshall, who had been in the initial Samaritan meeting in the Oval Office, and Stokes, who had not, were, respectively, the Pentagon's and the DoD's most powerful generals.

"Anyway," the POTUS continued, "with one thing and another, the conversation eventually came around to Samaritan. Now listen here, Chris, it's Ken and Billy's considered opinion that as far as Samaritan is concerned, CI's gotten the short end of the stick."

"You mean Danziger."

Hendricks could sense the president taking a breath while he counted to ten.

"What I mean is that I agree with them. I want you to give Danziger a larger role in the operation."

Hendricks closed his eyes. He swallowed a Prilosec even as he felt a headache beating a tattoo against his forehead. "Sir, with all due respect, Samaritan is already set."

"Almost. You said it yourself, Chris."

Was it possible to scream at yourself? Hendricks wondered.

"This is my operation," he said doggedly. "You gave it to me."

"The Lord giveth, Chris, and the Lord taketh away."

Hendricks gritted his teeth. It was no use telling the president what a perfect little shit M. Errol Danziger was. The president had appointed him. Even supposing the POTUS shared Hendricks's opinion, he would never admit that he'd made a mistake, not in the current perilous political climate. One false move would set alight the worldwide blogosphere, which would in turn ignite a firestorm of talking heads on CNN and Fox News, which would spawn endless op-ed column inches. The poll numbers the president and his advisers scrutinized every month would plummet. No, these days even the president of the United States needed to be ultra-cautious with both his choices and his statements.

"I'll do what I can to soothe the ruffled feathers," Hendricks said.

"Music to my ears, Chris. Keep me informed on your progress."

With that fiat, the president disconnected. Hendricks didn't know what gave him more pain, his stomach or his head. He knew Danziger was aiming for complete control of Samaritan, which would surely end in disaster. Danziger was a career opportunist. Amassing power was his sole objective. He had come over to CI from NSA and for the past year he had been remaking CI into a carbon copy of NSA. NSA being an extension of the Pentagon, this was not good news for the American intelligence community. The military relied far too heavily on remote surveillance: eyes in the sky, spy drones, and the like. CI's stock in trade had always been human eyes and ears in the field. The intercom buzzed, interrupting his misery.

"Sir, everyone's out here waiting." Davies's voice crackled over the intercom. "Do you want to resume the briefing?"

Hendricks rubbed his forehead. A fierce streak of rebelliousness bubbled up in him. "They have their orders. Tell them to put the deployment into effect immediately."

Russian," Bourne said. "What form of Russian?"

Kaja stared at him. "I beg your pardon?"

"Dialect. Was it southern or—"

"Moscow. He was from Moscow."

Bourne put his glass down onto a table inlaid with Moroccan tiles. "You're certain?"

Kaja spoke to him in the Russian dialect used by Muscovites.

"Your father was working for the Russians," Bourne said.

"That's the first thing I considered when I heard him," Kaja said, "but it doesn't seem credible."

"Why not?"

"Both my parents hated the Russians."

"Perhaps your mother did," Bourne said carefully. "But as for your father, if he was working for the Russians his hatred for them would be part of his cover."

"Hiding in plain sight."

Bourne nodded.

She got up then. Don Fernando caught Bourne's eye. Bourne could see that the Spaniard didn't want him to continue this topic. Kaja stood in front of the window, staring at her reflection much as Bourne himself had done at Vegas's house the night before the helicopter attack.

A terrible silence invaded the room, but it was Kaja's silence. Neither Bourne nor Don Fernando felt it wise to break it.

"Do you think it's true?" Kaja's voice seemed to come from another place.

At length, she turned back in to the room and looked from one to the other, repeating her question.

"From what you've told us," Bourne said, "it seems the likeliest possibility."

"Fuck," Kaja said. "Fuck-fuck-fuck."

Don Fernando stirred, clearly uncomfortable. "There's always the possibility that Jason is wrong."

Kaja laughed, but there was a bitter edge to it. "Sure. Thank you, Don Fernando, but I'm long past the age where I can believe in fairy tales." She turned to Bourne, hands on her hips. "So. Any ideas?"

Bourne knew she meant who, specifically, her father might have worked for. He shook his head. "Since he was a foreign national working outside Russia, the SVR—Russia's equivalent of America's Central Intelligence—is a possibility. But frankly, he could just as easily have been recruited by one of the *grupperovka* families."

"The Russian mob," Kaja said.

"Yes."

She frowned. "That would, at least, be a more logical choice for him to make."

"Kaja," Don Fernando said, "I caution you against trying to apply logic here."

"Don Fernando is right," Bourne said. "We have no idea of your father's situation. For all we know, he may have been coerced into working for the Russians."

But already Kaja was shaking her head. "No, I know this much about my father: He could not be coerced."

"Even if your life and the lives of your sisters hung in the balance?"

"He left us flat." Her expression was set firm. "He didn't care about us; he had other things on his mind."

"He killed for a living," Bourne said. "It takes a special kind of human being to do it, an even more special kind to be successful at it."

She engaged his eyes with hers. "My point exactly. No pity, no remorse, no love. Full disconnection from humanity." She drew her shoulders back, defiant. "I mean, that's what makes it possible to kill not once, but over and over again. Disconnection. It's not so hard to put a bullet in the back of the head of a thing."

Bourne knew that she was talking about him as much as her late father. "There are times when killing is necessary."

"A necessary evil."

He nodded. "Whatever you choose to call it doesn't make it any less of a necessity."

Kaja swung back to confront the night, shimmering dimly just beyond the panes of glass.

"Leave Christien Norén to the unknown," Don Fernando said. "Trust me when I tell you that his life, his fate, are over and done with. Kaja, it's time for you and your sister to move on."

Kaja gave a dark laugh that was more like a bark. "You try telling Skara that, Don Fernando. She has never listened to me, and I can assure you she won't start now."

"Do you know where she is?" the Spaniard asked.

Kaja shook her head. "When we parted, we swore an oath not to look for each other. We have had no contact in more than ten years. We were children then, and now..." She turned back to him. "Everything has changed. Nothing has changed."

"It would be tragic if that were true. At least, for you." Don Fernando unfolded on creaky knees and crossed the room to stand beside her. He placed a hand on her shoulder. "There is hope for you, Kaja. There always was, I sincerely believe that. As for Skara..." His last words hung ominously in the room.

"She's doomed, isn't she?"

Don Fernando looked at her, a terrible sorrow informing his features.

Bourne stepped toward her. "Why do you say that?"

Kaja looked away.

"Because," Don Fernando said, "Skara suffers from dissociative identity disorder."

Kaja's eyes locked on Bourne's. "My sister has six distinct alter egos, all of them as real as any of us in this room."

Any meeting with M. Errol Danziger was fraught with both tension and peril—the man had a hair-trigger temper and all too often took offense at even the smallest perceived slight. For some reason he could not quantify, Hendricks felt unprepared, and so he put off the meeting until late in the afternoon, when he knew he should have taken Danziger to lunch.

He took Maggie to lunch instead. This meant—because she requested it—picking her up outside The Breadline on Pennsylvania Avenue, where she had bought enough food for their picnic on the National Mall.

The hazy sun moved in and out of the cloud cover as they walked through the grass. Hendricks's security detail, none too happy with their boss's choice of venues, nevertheless dutifully followed orders, staking out a suitable patch of grass around which they formed a strict perimeter.

Hendricks and Maggie sat facing each other, cross-legged like kids. She spread out the food she had bought. He was almost giddy with the child-like delight that comes from playing hooky. Here he was with Maggie, eating sandwiches, drinking iced tea, and basking in her smile and her scent.

"You surprised me with your call." She took a small, precise bite of a ham and Brie with jalapeño mustard. Her golden hair was drawn back in a thick ponytail. She was wearing a scoop-neck black-and-white polka-dot dress cinched with a wide black patent-leather belt. She had taken off her low heels, her bare toes wriggling in the grass.

"I'm just glad you weren't tending to my roses," he said.

"Who said I wasn't?" she said with a wry smile. She took another bite, small and precise. "I would have come anyway."

This statement so pleased him that his sandwich caught in his throat. He took a couple of sips of tea to wash the food down. Looking at her now in this idyllic setting he realized that he was falling in love. His first instinct was to be skeptical, to admonish himself for being foolish, adolescent, and, worse, possibly vulnerable. And then the thought was washed away. Looking at her now he experienced the sensation of falling, of a delicious weightlessness that he associated with his dreams, though he could not dredge up any one in particular. He was happy, and in his life happiness was the rarest of commodities.

Maggie cocked her head. "Christopher? What are you thinking?"

He set his sandwich down. "Sorry."

"Don't be."

"I was thinking about a meeting I scheduled for the end of the day." Hendricks hesitated. It occurred to him that a fresh perspective might help him get a grip on dealing with Danziger and the president. "The individual I'm meeting with is extremely difficult."

"That can mean so many things."

Hendricks could see by Maggie's expression that he had her undivided attention, and he was pleased. "He's an egomaniac," he said. "He's come up in the world riding other people's coattails—mainly my predecessor's." This was as specific as he planned to get with her. He might seek her opinion, but he was also unfailingly security-conscious. "Now a situation has arisen where he's insinuating himself into a position of power on an initiative of mine."

Maggie looked thoughtful. "I don't see a problem. A man who makes his living riding other people's coattails can't be very competent."

"But that *is* the problem. If he gets what he wants he's sure to screw the pooch."

"Then let him."

"What? You must be joking."

Maggie carefully rewrapped the uneaten half of her sandwich. "Consider, Christopher. This man screws the pooch, as you so colorfully put it—"

"But it's *my* pooch he'll be screwing."

"—and you ride in to the rescue." Maggie took out a chocolate chip cookie and broke off a small piece, which she held between her fingertips. "The people who are backing this individual will be so humiliated they're sure to withdraw their support of him." She popped the bit of cookie into her mouth, chewed slowly and luxuriantly. "In chess it's known as retreating one square to take the board."

Hendricks sat back, watching as she broke off another piece of cookie and handed it to him. He chewed thoughtfully, the chocolate melting in his mouth. What she was proposing ran against every protocol he had set for himself. Give in? Give Danziger his head? What a hellish thought.

He swallowed, and Maggie handed him more. *But then again why not?* he asked himself. After all, it was what the president wanted. Not only was the POTUS's head on the block, but so were those of Marshall and Stokes. Hendricks thought it would feel mighty fine to take them all down a couple of pegs, especially the two generals who were a constant pain in his ass. And think of the humiliation Danziger himself would suffer.

Thinking of Danziger and Indigo Ridge reminded him: Why the hell hadn't he heard from Peter Marks?

Far beyond the periphery of the straining mob, Karpov paused long enough in his flight to take inventory. His leg hurt like hell, but otherwise he was unhurt. If he were a God-fearing man he would have said a prayer for Lana Lang, who'd had the foresight to buy a car with side air bags.

The rain had abated. Water still sluiced along the gutters, but the clouds were lifting and only a slight drizzle remained of the storm. He looked around and realized that he had no idea where he was. He must still be in the Mosque's district, but that bit of information did him scant good.

He was in Munich, under attack from the SVR, and he still had no idea why Severus Domna had sent Cherkesov to the Mosque. Perhaps, he thought in a moment of weakness, it was time to cut his losses and escape this godforsaken city. He had only days to complete Cherkesov's mission. He should call Bourne, set up a meet, and get the hell out of here. But then, leaning against a brick wall, his mind jumped to a different track. Running would do him no good and might actually hurt him. The SVR would still make his life miserable and he'd be no closer to finding out what Cherkesov was up to. He needed leverage to get himself out from under Cherkesov's thumb. He was hoping to find that leverage here in Munich.

Then he thought about that bastard Zachek. *Of course he's still tracking me*, he thought. And then he realized that Zachek, who got him into this shitstorm, could be the one to get him out of it.

He went on through the narrow streets, which had, if not exactly an Arab flavor, then a distinctly Muslim one. Halal butchers proliferated. He could smell the spices of the Middle East. Women were modestly dressed, their heads covered.

His winding route led him to circle blocks until he found what he wanted. He then loitered on a corner as if waiting for a friend—which wasn't so far from the truth. He was waiting for Zachek, who did not disappoint him. When Boris saw him, he took off, his limp a good deal more pronounced than it needed to be.

It was odd, he thought, as he picked up his pace, how much better his leg felt the more he used it. He ducked into a clothing store, went through, and stepped out the back, a simplistic maneuver he fully expected Zachek to anticipate. He limped down the back alley lined with those same galvanized-steel garbage cans with the spiked lids. Zachek emerged from the rear of the clothing store. Boris was already nearing the end of the alley. He heard a shout behind him and, an instant later, one of Zachek's hatchet men stepped into the end of the alley toward which Boris was limping. He pulled out a Tokarev pistol and aimed it at Boris's chest.

Without missing a beat, Karpov snatched up one of the garbage can lids and jammed the spikes into the hatchet man's face. The gun went off; the bullet pierced the lid, but missed Boris. As the hatchet man staggered back, Karpov grabbed the Tokarev, but before he had a chance to curl his forefinger around the trigger he felt the cold deadweight of a gun muzzle against his right temple.

A second hatchet man, who had appeared out of nowhere, said in guttural Russian, "Go ahead. Give me the chance to blow your brains out."

The slam of the front door sent Don Fernando hurrying out of the living room.

Kaja stood very close to Bourne, staring at their reflections in the French doors. Then she turned the lever and stepped outside. Bourne followed her. It was chilly and she shivered a little.

"Let's go back inside," he said, but she made no move.

The wind lifted her hair. It was odd to see her as a blonde, as she really was. Then Bourne realized that for a very long time no one had seen him as he really was, not even Moira. He was heavily defended, even from himself. Was that what he wanted? he wondered. Or were his defenses necessary in order for him to keep going? Though he couldn't remember it, he was absolutely certain there had been a time he hadn't felt the need to be like this.

"I noticed Skara's peculiarities early on," Kaja said. Her arms were wrapped around herself. "There was no help for her. None at all. She freaked our mother out."

"I thought you said you were the black sheep of the family."

"I lied." She gave him a wan smile. "Skara taught me. She said she had no choice, that in order to live a more or less normal school life, all her personalities had learned to lie convincingly."

"It must have been difficult for you," Bourne said.

"At first. I used to have nightmares about her turning into some kind of monster—a vampire or a succubus." She turned to him. "But what stumped me was where the personalities went when they were dormant. And how did they cycle? By what mechanism was it decided which personality should pop up next?"

"Did you ever get answers?"

"Skara had no idea. She said it was like being on a roller-coaster ride that never ended."

"Did you ever worry that the same thing would happen to you?"

"All the time." Kaja shuddered. "Did you ever see *High Noon*? It's like that. I'm waiting for the train with the killer to come."

The president of the United States picked up the phone and called his securities broker. "Bob, gimme a quote on NeoDyme."

"Sixty-seven and a quarter," his broker said.

"What?" The president sat up straight. "It came at twenty-three, if I remember right, and that was, what? Three days ago?"

"There's been a shitload of buying, sir," Bob said. "The stock has gone vertical."

The president closed his eyes and rubbed his temples. "Jesus, I don't know."

"If you don't buy now, sir, you'll kick yourself when it breaches a hundred."

"Okay, buy five hundred now through the usual shell corp, and another five when it pulls back to...what would be reasonable?"

"With any other stock, I'd say it'd retrace a third, sir. But with NeoDyme, well, it's acting like an IPO from the go-go Internet days. Simply astounding. Hold on."

The president could hear Bob working his keyboard. "I mean, every day since it came it's been up on heavy volume. It might pull back ten per, but honestly I wouldn't bet on a deeper dip."

"Then put the order in for the second five at sixty."

"Done," Bob said. "Anything else, sir?"

"Nothing else matters," the president said sourly and hung up.

His phone buzzed almost immediately. Checking his watch, he saw that he had seven minutes to manage this call and get to the john to pee before his next briefing. Sighing, he picked up the receiver.

"Roy FitzWilliams for you, sir."

"Put him on," the president said. The line clicked several times, then he said, "Fitz, d'you have an answer for me?"

"I think I do, sir," FitzWilliams said from his office in Indigo Ridge.

"Tell me you found a method to get the rare earths out of the ground more quickly."

"I wish that were so, sir, but I think I've found the next best thing. As you know, all computer motherboards use rare earths. I think if we start a government-wide recycling program immediately, we might be able to scrape together enough of the elements to get the DoD its first weapons order in, say, eighteen months."

"Eighteen months!" The president literally sprang out of his chair. "The Joint Chiefs tell me DoD needed the first shipment yesterday, but it will settle for eight months."

"Eighteen is the best I can do," FitzWilliams said, "unless the government makes wholesale upgrades on all its computers immediately."

Good Lord, the president thought, trying to calculate the cost. *The*

Congressional Oversight Committees will have my ass in a sling. He knew he was between a rock and a hard place.

"I'll see what I can do, Fitz," he said, "but you have to get Indigo Ridge up and running ASAP."

"I'll go to the NeoDyme board and see about a massive hiring initiative."

The president grunted. "With the stock on a rocket ride to the moon money won't be a problem."

FitzWilliams laughed. "Yes, sir. My fortune is already made."

Don Fernando reappeared. "Essai has returned, Jason, and is asking for you. He's in the library. It's on the east side of the house. Meanwhile, Kaja and I will go prepare dinner."

Bourne crossed the living room, went down a side hallway to the library. It was a square room, light and airy, unlike most libraries. A number of bookcases lined the walls on either side of the double windows. The room was furnished with a scattering of comfortable-looking chairs and throw pillows in Moroccan-patterned fabrics.

Jalal Essai was standing in the center of the room, his fingers steepled in front of him. He turned just as Bourne stepped into the room.

As usual, his mood was unreadable. "I imagine you have a number of questions to ask me." He gestured to a pair of high-backed wing chairs. "Why not be comfortable while we talk?"

The two men sat, facing each other.

Bourne said, "Essai, there's no point in talking if you continue to lie to me."

Essai folded his hands in his lap. He appeared completely at ease. "Agreed."

"Are you still working for Severus Domna?"

"I am not; I haven't for some time. I did not lie about that."

"And that sad tale about your daughter?"

"Unfortunately, also true." Essai lifted a forefinger. "But I did not tell you the whole story. She was killed, yes, but it wasn't by agents of the Domna. They would never have condoned such a thing." He took a breath and slowly exhaled. "My daughter was murdered by agents of Semid Abdul-Qahhar." He cocked his head. "You have heard of this man?"

Bourne nodded. "He's the leader of the Mosque in Munich."

"Indeed." He leaned forward slightly, a certain tension informing his torso. "It was Abdul-Qahhar who took advantage of circumstances to forge a deal with Benjamin El-Arian."

"What circumstances?"

"Ah, now we arrive at the crux of the matter." Essai jerked his head. "That woman in there. She told you her story?"

Bourne nodded.

"Her father is the key to the mystery of why the Domna allowed Abdul-Qahhar to invade their precincts."

"It wasn't a deal?"

"Oh, yes, but the question is what kind of deal," Essai said. "The vulnerability the Domna felt when your old organization, Treadstone, targeted them led El-Arian to make his deal with the Mosque."

Bourne said nothing. This was the second time he'd heard about the Domna's sense of vulnerability. The problem was he simply didn't believe it. Either Essai was lying to him yet again, or Essai truly didn't know the real reason Semid Abdul-Qahhar had been welcomed into the organization. What bothered Bourne the most was that from all he had been able to find out, the Domna had been set up to bridge the cultural and religious gap between East and West—a noble attempt to teach the two cultures to live in peace with each other. Why, then, would Semid Abdul-Qahhar, an Arab extremist masquerading as a benign Muslim, be allowed to upset Severus Domna's carefully calibrated balance? Nothing added up. Bourne stared hard at Essai. Once again he was at a loss to classify the man as friend or enemy.

"You want to know who Christien Norén worked for, is that it?"

"Everyone in this house wants to know," Essai said, leaning back. "We thought Kaja would know, or at least be able to give us some clue, which is why Don Fernando wanted me to fetch her along with Vegas."

"Why didn't you tell me all this back in Colombia?"

"Her father went after your old boss. Word is the two of you were close. I couldn't be sure you'd do what needed to be done if you knew who she really was."

This explanation sounded logical, and possibly it was true, but with Essai you never knew. Don Fernando had warned him about Essai's pathological lying, not that Bourne hadn't already suspected as much. On the other hand, it was helpful to get confirmation of his suspicion.

"And if I hadn't come along?"

Essai shrugged. "I was negotiating with Roberto Corellos to help me when you fell into my life like a gift from Allah." He smiled. "You make a habit of it." His hand briefly lifted and fell. "But believe me, that's all water under the bridge."

Holding a conversation with Essai was an exhausting experience, listening to him and trying to ferret out what he was really saying—or, more often, not saying. "Unfortunately, none of this brings us any closer to discovering what the Domna is up to."

"There's something else." He sat forward again and, as he did so, lowered his voice. "Benjamin El-Arian has been taking secret trips to Damascus. I discovered their existence purely by accident, through, of all people, Estevan Vegas. Going through Estevan's bills of lading, I discovered a discrepancy in moneys that I traced to a round-trip first-class ticket from Paris to Damascus. Digging further, I turned up El-Arian's name, along with the fact that this wasn't his first trip to Damascus. El-Arian was paying for the trips by skimming off profits from the exports filtered through the oil fields in Colombia that Vegas manages for Don Fernando."

"Any idea what El-Arian was doing in Damascus?"

Essai shook his head. "In that regard, I've hit a dead end. But I think it has something to do with the group Christien Norén worked for."

"That makes no sense," Bourne said. "The men who came after Kaja and her sisters are Russian."

Essai rose. "Nevertheless, from what little my contacts in Damascus could glean, I think there's a connection."

Bourne wondered why Essai was so keen on finding out the truth about Christien Norén's affiliation. Then, like a flash of lightning, the answer came to him. Essai didn't believe the story about how El-Arian had come to make a deal with the Mosque, either. He was as skeptical as Bourne himself. He was convinced that the true reason would become apparent only when the mystery of Christien Norén was solved.

"Have you told Don Fernando any of this?"

Essai gave him an enigmatic smile. "Only you and I know."

Boris stood very still. The alley stank of fish and stale frying oil. The noise of the traffic was like a hive of angry wasps. Zachek sauntered up as if he didn't have a care in the world. His eyes were on Karpov all the time. He looked dapper in a long black cashmere coat, black kid-skin gloves, and mirror-finish brogues with soles so thick Boris was certain they must contain a tongue of steel. This was an old trick dating back to the KGB: the steel useful for vicious stomping sessions. Some things, Boris thought, never went out of style, even among the Internet generation.

When Zachek came up to where the two men stood at the mouth of the alley, he said, "Fuck, Karpov, maybe you wouldn't make such a good mentor, after all."

Boris gestured with his chin. "Why not ask your comrade with a face full of metal for his opinion?"

Zachek opened his mouth, threw his head back, and laughed. "You old guys," he said.

That was when Boris jammed his right elbow into the gunman's Adam's apple. At the same time, he shoved the gun away with his left hand. It went off, deafening all three of them. Boris shot the gunman point-blank with the Tokarev and the man arched back and slammed against the brick wall, where he left a mealy-looking Rorschach blood-blot.

Zachek was just starting to come out of shock when Boris grabbed him by the back of his soft, pelt-like collar and smashed his face into the blood-blot.

"What do you see there, Zachek, eh? Tell me, you little prick." Boris dragged Zachek back. He switched to an upper-class-British–accented English. "I say Zachek, old bean, you've gotten blood all over your five-thousand-dollar cashmere overcoat. Not to mention those shiny shoes. What are they? John Lobb?"

Zachek, clearly out of ideas, tried to kick Boris with one of his steel-soled shoes, but Karpov danced out of the way. "Uh-uh," he said, delivering a mighty slap to the back of Zachek's head. "Clearly, you need some lessons in how to behave."

Zachek had given up trying to extricate himself from Karpov's grip and was wiping the blood off his face. He had a split upper lip and the flesh over his right eye was puffed up, rapidly turning a deep purple-blue.

Boris shook him until his teeth rattled. "Any more of your SVR pals around?"

Zachek shook his head.

"Answer me when I speak to you!" he ordered.

"There . . . was just the three of us."

"You figured that was more than enough to handle an old man like me, right, little prick? Don't shake your head, I know exactly what's in that pea brain of yours."

"You . . . you've got it all wrong. Oh shit." Zachek snorted a clot of blood out of his nose. It stuck on the wall in the middle of the widening blot.

"Okay, little prick, tell me how I'm wrong." He shoved the Tokarev's muzzle into the soft flesh where Zachek's lower jaw met his neck. "But if I don't like your answer—*boom!*"

"I . . . I need to sit down." Zachek was hyperventilating. Beneath the smears of blood, his face looked pale.

Boris dragged him back down the alley, all the way to the other end, where a number of wooden crates that smelled of fresh oranges were stacked. Zachek collapsed gratefully onto one and sat slumped over, his hands crossed over his head, as if he was expecting Boris to beat him senseless.

There was less vehicular traffic beyond this end of the alley, but the foot traffic was heavy. Luckily, it was rush hour. Everyone was hurrying home, lost in their own thoughts; no one so much as glanced into the alley. Nevertheless, Boris didn't want to stay there any longer than he had to.

"Pull yourself together, Zachek, and tell me what you have to say."

Zachek gave a little shudder, pulled his stained cashmere coat more tightly around himself, and said, "You think we set that ambush for you and the woman."

"Don't pretend you don't know who she was."

"The fact is I don't." Zachek's ashen face looked like a battlefield. The man was spent. "I didn't come here following you. I didn't set that ambush, that's what I was trying to tell you in the crowd back there."

Boris remembered Zachek shouting something at him, but in the roar of the mob and the screams of police sirens, he hadn't been able to hear a word.

"You're making no sense," Boris said. "You have precisely ten seconds to rectify that."

Zachek flinched. "Beria sent me here to keep an eye on Cherkesov."

All the blood drained out of Boris's face. "Viktor is here?"

Zachek nodded. "I had no knowledge of you being in Munich until I saw you in the street. Believe me, I was as shocked to see you as you were to see me."

"I don't believe you," Boris said.

Zachek shrugged. "So, what can I expect?"

"Give me a reason."

Zachek's nose had begun to bleed and he tipped his head back. "I can get you an interview inside the Mosque."

"Tell me."

Zachek closed his eyes. "As easy as that? No, I don't think so. I want your word that I get out of this alive."

Boris watched Zachek's body language, which he had found a virtually foolproof method of discovering whether or not a person was lying.

"The only way you get out of this alley alive is if you become my eyes and ears in SVR."

"You want me to spy on Beria? If he finds out he'll kill me."

Boris shrugged. "Make sure he doesn't find out. For a smart little prick like you that shouldn't be difficult."

"You don't know Beria," Zachek said sourly.

Boris grinned. "That's why I have you."

Zachek looked up at him as he licked his bruised and swollen lips. His right eye was almost completely closed. Boris crossed his arms over his barrel chest. "It seems, little prick, that we need each other."

Zachek rested his head against the building wall. "I'd appreciate it if you didn't call me that."

"I'd appreciate some answers. Are you in or out?"

Zachek took a shuddering breath. "It looks as if you'll be mentoring me, after all."

Boris grunted. "If you didn't set the ambush, who did?"

"Who knew you were coming to Munich?"

"No one."

"Then 'no one' set the ambush." Zachek's lips twitched in a parody of a smile. "But of course, that's not possible."

Of course it isn't, Boris thought. All at once he had trouble breathing.

Zachek must have seen the change on his face because he said, "Life's more complicated than you thought, eh, General?"

This time, could the little prick be right? Boris wondered. *But it's impossible. Absolutely unthinkable.* Because there was only one other person who knew he was going to Munich: his old and trusted friend Ivan Volkin.

21

CHRISTOPHER HENDRICKS FOUND any face-to-face with M. Errol Danziger thoroughly unpleasant, but he had every confidence that this time would be different.

Lieutenant R. Simmons Reade, Danziger's sycophantic pilot fish, appeared first. He was a thin, weasel-eyed individual with a contemptuous demeanor and the manners of a demonic marine drill sergeant. The two spent so much time together that, behind their backs, they were known as Edgar and Clyde, a cutting reference to J. Edgar Hoover and Clyde Tolson, the Beltway's most infamous closeted gays.

Danziger looked the part. He was short and, unlike his days in the field, was running to fat around his middle, a sure sign that he liked his steaks, fries, and bourbon too much. He had a head like a football and a personality to match: tough, a will to get over the goal line, and always the possibility of fumbling short of the first down. The problem lay in his constant promotions. He had been deadly in wet work, near brilliant as the NSA's deputy director of Signals Intelligence for Analysis and Production, but a total bust as the director of Central Intelligence. He had no sense of history, didn't know how CI worked, and, worst of all, didn't care. The result was akin to trying to jam a dowel into a square hole. It wasn't working. The reality, however, had done nothing to stop Danziger's headlong reaving of the hallowed halls of CI.

"Welcome to the director's suite at CI," Lieutenant Reade said with all the officiousness of a palace chancellor. "Take a pew."

Hendricks looked around Danziger's vast suite and wondered what he did with all the room. Bowl? Hold archery contests? Shoot his Red Ryder BB gun?

Hendricks smiled without an ounce of warmth. "Where's your shark, Reade?"

Reade blinked. "Beg pardon, sir?"

Hendricks swept the words away with the back of his hand. "Never mind."

He chose the chair that Danziger had sat in the last time they'd had a meeting here.

Reade took a military step toward him. "Uhm, that's the director's chair."

Hendricks sat down, working his buttocks into the cushion. "Not today."

Reade, face darkened, was about to say something more when his master stepped into the room. Danziger wore a fashionable pin-striped suit, a blue shirt with unfashionable white collar and cuffs, and a striped regimental tie. A tiny enamel American flag was pinned to his lapel. To his credit, his pause at seeing where Hendricks had seated himself was minuscule. Still, Hendricks didn't miss it.

Forced into the facing chair, he made a project of lifting the fabric of his trousers over his knees, then shooting his cuffs, before he uttered one word.

"It's good to see you here, Mr. Secretary," he said with a closed face. "To what do I owe this honor?"

But of course he knew, Hendricks thought. He had gone crying to his general buddies at the Pentagon, who had petitioned the president. *Who's your mommy, Danziger?* he thought.

"Does your visit have an amusing component?" the DCI said.

"Ah, no. Just a passing thought."

Danziger spread his hands. "Care to share?"

"A *private* moment, Max."

M. Errol Danziger hated being called by his first name, which was why he had shortened it to an initial.

Reade was still in the room, thinking of filing his nails, for all Hendricks knew.

"Does the boy need to be here?" It was interesting, Hendricks thought, to see how both Danziger and Reade bristled at precisely the same moment.

"Lieutenant Reade knows everything I know," Danziger said after a frozen moment.

Hendricks kept silent, and, after several moments, Danziger got the point. He raised a hand in the lazy fashion of Old World royalty, and, following a murderous glare at Hendricks, Reade departed.

"You really shouldn't have embarrassed him like that," Danziger muttered.

"What is that, Max? A threat?"

"What? No." Danziger shifted uncomfortably in his chair. "Nothing could be farther from the truth."

"Uh-huh." Hendricks scooted forward. "Listen, Max, let's get something straight. I don't care for Reade, and I certainly don't give a shit about his feelings. That being the case, I don't want to see or talk to him the next time we meet. Is that clear?"

"Perfectly," Danziger said in a strangled voice.

Without warning, Hendricks rose and stepped toward the door.

"Wait a minute," Danziger said. "We haven't even—"

"The job is yours, Max."

Danziger jumped. "What?" He trailed after Hendricks.

At the door, Hendricks turned toward him. "You want Samaritan, it's yours."

"But what about you?"

"I'm out, Max. I've pulled my people."

"But what about the preliminary work they've done?"

"Shredded this morning. I know you have your own methodology."

Hendricks pulled open the door, half expecting Reade to have his ear to it. "As of now, you're in charge of security at Indigo Ridge."

Maggie heard the encrypted cell phone even in her sleep. The ring was "The Ride of the Valkyries." She was no fan of that Nazi Richard Wagner, nevertheless she dearly loved the Ring cycle. She turned over, her eyelids heavy, gluey with sleep. Returning to her apartment after her lunch with Christopher, she had crawled into bed and immediately fallen fast asleep. She'd been in the midst of a dream in which she and Kaja were engaged in the same argument that had defined pretty much their entire childhood. In fact, her throat ached as if she had been screaming in her bedroom as well as screaming in her dream. Screaming at Kaja had never worked. Why had she continued to do it? Their relationship, the secrets they knew about each other, made conflict inevitable. Had they been brothers, they surely would have beaten the crap out of each other. They had worked with what they had, which was precious little, and in the end they could no longer stand the sight of each other. If circumstance hadn't pulled them apart, they would have parted anyway. And yet, in dreams Maggie missed her sister. Mikaela never appeared in her dreams, but Kaja did. And seeing her, Maggie cried dream-tears, her dream-heart breaking. But when their dream-conversations began, they were invariably acrimonious from the very first words: the bile of two sisters who loved each other but could find no common ground. In latter days their arguments had revolved around their father. Their memories of him were so different, as if he were two people. The arguments, grown ever more bitter and vitriolic, saddened as well as angered her.

With the Valkyries riding herd on her consciousness, she rolled over and stared balefully at the cell phone atop the nightstand. She knew who was calling her: Benjamin El-Arian was the only one with the number.

She dug her thumbs into her closed lids to haul herself into full wakefulness, but ignored the call. Instead she stared at the evening's dusty shadows extending across the ceiling. Mid-note the Valkyries ceased to ride. In the eerie silence she thought about Benjamin. It was a mystery how she ever could have been attracted to him. He seemed part of another life, another person.

America had changed her. She had traveled to many places in the world, but never, before this, to the United States. Benjamin had planted the idea of America as corrupt and evil, a country that had become weak after a string of diplomatic and military defeats. But she'd had no hands-on experience on which to base that idea. Now that she was here, now that she had spent time at Christopher's side in the core of capitalism's prime engine, so to speak, she found America to be dynamic, vital, filled with the thrilling cross-currents of dissent. In short, quite agreeable.

And with that road-to-Damascus moment had come understanding of the speciousness of Benjamin's bitterly anti-American screed. She had pretended to buy into it, to get close to him, but it was only now, having come into contact with Benjamin's avowed enemy, that she realized the depth of his self-delusion.

Even now, after having spent so much time with him, she didn't know whether he had kept his extremist views hidden from the other Domna directors until he was in a position of power, or whether they had been grafted onto him later by Semid Abdul-Qahhar.

She despised the leader of the Mosque, a man animated by a hatred so pure and unrelenting there was no room in his world for compromise. If there were Evil in the world, Evil with a capital *E*, as the Catholic Church preached, she was certain it must be cultivated and maintained by such hatred.

At first she had been confounded by the alliance between the two men, but gradually, from incidents she witnessed, it became clear that Benjamin was using Abdul-Qahhar as his enforcer to maintain and consolidate his power, to keep the other directors in line. She had seen the result of Abdul-Qahhar's handiwork on a director who had been foolish enough to publicly defy El-Arian. His corpse had been a sight so diabolically foul that, as a matter of self-preservation, she had immediately consigned it to the realm of nightmare. Only Jalal Essai, of all the directors, had managed to survive as a dissident, and now sought to challenge Benjamin's leadership. Abdul-Qahhar's slaughterers had failed to silence his voice, which was why El-Arian had dispatched Marlon Etana to take care of Essai.

She was acutely aware of what a dangerous game she was playing with Benjamin, but she remained resolute in her desire to continue on the path she had chosen. She knew El-Arian found it amusing to have her—the daughter of Christien Norén—under his thumb. She had been meticulous in her planning, careful to give him what he wanted: someone subservient to his will. Her father—secretly working for another entity—had betrayed the Domna. This was a sin Benjamin would not forgive. She understood that the sin of Christien Norén would one day be visited on her. The tricky part lay in clearing out before that day arrived.

And now here she was in America, a place in which, ironically, she felt safe. It wasn't the luxuries of American culture she responded to; she'd had her pick of luxuries while in Paris. It was the freedom to say what she thought, to be who she wanted to be without fear of ridicule or reprisal. A new life so different from her childhood, which might just as well be light-years away. There was a reason it had been known as the New World, and in certain circles still was. Was it any wonder she didn't want to return to her life inside the Domna, at Benjamin El-Arian's side? And it was becoming clear to her that the time was near when she would be free of El-Arian and Severus Domna. Either that, or she would be dead.

The Valkyries rode again, making her teeth clench. This time she knew she had to take the call.

Picking up the phone, she hesitated for a moment, then activated it. "This is an inconvenient time," she said.

"Every time seems an inconvenient time for you." There was no misconstruing Benjamin's displeasure. "You are two days late with your report."

Maggie closed her eyes and imagined thrusting a knife into his heart. "The field is the field," she said. "I've been busy."

"Doing what, precisely?"

"What our plan set out to do: discredit Christopher Hendricks in order to protect FitzWilliams from scrutiny during our acquisition phase."

"And? I have not seen any negative reports concerning Hendricks."

"Of course you haven't," she said shortly. "Do you think something like that can be established in seventy-two hours? He's the United States secretary of defense."

El-Arian was silent for a moment. "What progress *have* you made?"

Maggie sat up, pushing the pillows behind her back. "I don't care for your tone, Benjamin." Then she sat, silent and waiting, determined not to say another word until he relented.

"The field is the field, as you pointed out," El-Arian said after allowing the silence to stretch on past a normal length.

Figuring that was as much of an apology as she was going to get, she relented. "Do you think anyone but me could have gotten to Hendricks in such a short time?"

"I don't, no."

Another concession. *How lucky can a girl get?* she thought.

"The legend you prepared was pitch-perfect," she said.

Actually, it was people lower on the Domna food chain who had prepared her Margaret Penrod identity, but it never hurt to use a little sugar. *Especially*, she thought, *now that I'm walking such a perilous tightrope.*

"And what of Hendricks himself?" El-Arian asked.

"Hooked," she said, "completely." It was curious—and not a little frightening—how much disquiet saying this out loud to Benjamin caused her.

"Well then, now is the time to reel him in."

"Slowly," she said. "We can't afford to have him become suspicious at this point."

El-Arian cleared his throat. "Skara, in twenty-four hours the acquisition period will come to its end phase. We need you to meet that ETA."

Twenty-four hours, she thought. *That's all the time I have left?*

"I understand perfectly," she said. "You can count on me."

"I always have," he said. "À *bientôt.*"

Skara threw the phone across the room.

Hendricks stood in the garage at what had been the Treadstone building, but which he had ordered abandoned immediately following the car bomb explosion. This was his second visit to the crime scene, the first being less than an hour after the explosion had detonated. At that time, having ordered a phalanx of federal agents to do a secure search of the immediate area and Peter's house, and not knowing whether Peter Marks had been blown to kingdom come, he had assembled a task force to investigate the matter.

The forensics team had determined that Peter had not been in the car. So far, so good. Then where was he? The task force had had no luck finding him. Hendricks called Marks's cell but, as before, got his voice mail. Next, he called Ann at the temporary offices he had secured for the Treadstone personnel, but she hadn't seen or heard from Marks. He gave up and departed the crime scene.

Hendricks arrived home early and unannounced. While his security team scoured the interior for electronic listening devices, as they did twice a week, he went into the kitchen and poured himself a beer. He stood watching the suits go about their business, controlled and precise as ants. Picking up the phone, he tried again to call Jackie, but his son was still in a forward position in the Afghanistan mountains, maintaining communications blackout.

He'd finished half his beer when the team members nodded on their way to take up positions outside. He put down his glass and went into his study, closing the door behind him. The windows were fitted with wide-slatted jalousies, which he kept closed all the time. Sitting down at his desk, he removed a small key from his wallet and inserted it in a lock in the lower left-hand drawer. He took out a tiny disc approximately half the size of his thumbnail. He knew what it was but he had never seen the design before. What he couldn't understand was why his security team had failed to find this electronic bug in their continual sweeps of his house.

He had discovered it ten days ago purely by accident. He had been in a hurry, his hand sweeping across the desk to snatch up a file that had been delivered by courier. In the process, he had upended a glass Eiffel Tower, swirls of color embedded in it, that Amanda had bought him the first time they had been in Paris. As such, it was a beloved token, a way to keep her close after her death. The tower's four feet were covered in felt, but when he'd upended it he'd seen that one of the felt discs had been replaced by this curious and frightening electronic bug.

Two possibilities had immediately occurred to him. The first was that someone on his security team had planted it and was deliberately ignoring it during the sweeps. The second was that this bug was so sophisticated, it was invisible to the electronic sweeps. Neither hypothesis was comforting, but the second one disturbed him more because it meant an unknown entity was in possession of surveillance equipment that far outstripped the US government's own. He had made several discreet inquiries, pulling in favors from people deep inside the intelligence community whom he thought might be able to tell him if a cabal inside the government was working against him. So far, no hint of such a group had surfaced.

He stared at the bug now, a dull silver-green, scarcely distinguishable from the felt pads on the bottom of Amanda's gift. He had quite deliberately kept it live, putting it on his desk, making innocuous calls and such because he did not want its owner to know that he had discovered its existence. It was this bug that had prompted him to form the complex communications system with Peter Marks. He replaced it, shut the drawer, and locked it.

Opening his laptop, he logged onto the government server on which his files resided, navigated to the encrypted file, and opened it To Peter's credit, he had figured out the system and accessed the encrypted file on Hendricks's computer. A message detailed what Marks had discovered. At a regional meeting in Qatar in the spring of 1968, Fitz was listed as a consultant for El-Gabal Mining, a now defunct government-run company. What interested Marks—and now Hendricks himself—was that Fitz had neglected to list El-Gabal on his CV.

In light of Marks's own investigation, it might not be so surprising that he hadn't reported in, Hendricks thought now. If Marks had found something further on Fitz, then, following the attempt on his life, he might have gone undercover to check it out himself. Maybe he had contacted Soraya. Hendricks rang her cell but, again, got no answer. He pulled out his cell and went out of the study, down the hall, and into a bathroom, where he turned on the taps.

It was after nine in Paris, so he called Jacques Robbinet at home. His wife told him that her husband was still at the office. Apparently there was an international incident he'd had to handle. Worried now, Hendricks called Robbinet's office. While the connection was being made, he stared out at his deserted house and not for the first time wished with all his heart that he could hear Amanda puttering about, cleaning out the closets as she loved to do. It depressed him to think that the closets hadn't been touched since her death. He wondered what the house would be like with Maggie in it permanently.

Robbinet finally answered. "Chris, I was just going to call. I'm afraid there's been a bit of an incident."

"What kind of incident?" Hendricks listened with sweaty hands as Robbinet related the meeting with M. Marchand, how Soraya, Aaron Lipkin-Renais, and the Egyptian Chalthoum had followed Marchand, and all that had happened.

"So Chalthoum is dead." *Christ, what a fuckup*, Hendricks thought. The head of al Mokhabarat murdered on French soil. No wonder Robbinet was still at the office; he'd probably be there all night. "Is Soraya okay?"

"As far as Aaron knows, she is."

"What the hell does that mean?"

"She's still unconscious."

Hendricks's stomach began to throb like a second heart. He pulled open the door to the medicine cabinet, shook out another Prilosec, and swallowed it dry. He knew he was taking too many, but what the hell.

"Will she live?"

"The doctors are still evaluating—"

"Dammit, Jacques, you've got to keep her safe."

"Aaron says the doctors—"

"Forget Lipkin-Renais," Hendricks said. "Jacques, I want you with her."

Silence for several heartbeats. "Chris, I'm knee-deep in *merde* over the Chalthoum murder."

"He was killed by North African Arab extremists."

"Yes, but on French soil. The Egyptian embassy has gone ballistic."

Hendricks thought a moment. "Tell you what, I'll take care of the Egyptians if you take care of Soraya."

"Are you serious?"

"Absolutely. Jacques, I consider this a personal favor."

"Well, it'll be a personal favor on both sides if you can get the Egyptians off my back. We already have enough problems with the Arabs here without the stink this will cause when it hits the news."

"It won't," Hendricks said grimly. "Jacques, do what you have to do, but get my girl back on her feet."

"I'll be in touch as soon as I have some news, Chris." He gave Hendricks his new, encrypted cell number. "Try not to worry."

But Hendricks couldn't help it. *Dammit*, he thought as he cut the connection and scanned his phone book for the number of the Egyptian president, *what the hell is happening to my people?*

Don Fernando was waiting in the hallway when Bourne and Essai emerged from their meeting.

"Jason, a word, if you don't mind."

Essai gave a curt nod and disappeared down the hall.

"How did it go?" Don Fernando asked

"We'll see," Bourne said.

Don Fernando removed a cigar from his pocket, bit off the end, and lit up. "I suppose you're wondering why I've chosen to keep Estevan in the dark," he said around clouds of aromatic blue smoke.

"How you deal with your friends is your business," Bourne said.

Don Fernando eyed Bourne for a moment. "I like you, Jason. I like you very much. Which is why I don't take offense at your implied rebuke." He paused for a moment, took the cigar out of his mouth, and stared at the glowing end. "Friendship can take many forms. Being a man of the world, I assume you know this." His eyes raised to meet Bourne's. "But I know you're not this sort of man. You are a dying breed, my friend, a true throwback to the days of conscience, honor, duty, and friendships that are sacred."

Still, Bourne said nothing. He resented being told what kind of man he was, even if it was the truth.

"So now we come to the difficult part." Don Fernando stuck the cigar back into a corner of his mouth. "Kaja has her eyes on you."

"That's a quaint way of putting it."

Don Fernando nodded. "All right. She's fallen in love with you."

"That's insane. Despite what she said, she hates me for killing her mother."

"Part of her does, unquestionably. But that part is someone who had never met you, who was driven by the sight of her mother dead on a marble slab. She built a fantasy around that. And then you appeared, a flesh-and-blood man. Along with that came the details surrounding her mother's murder. None of which, I believe, she was prepared for."

Don Fernando took more smoke into his mouth. "Consider this from her point of view. You appear and save her and Estevan not once, not twice, but three times—from both the Domna and the people whom her father worked for. She knows nothing about you, least of all that you killed her mother. She's two people now, one fighting against the other."

"That isn't my concern," Bourne said.

Don Fernando sucked on his cigar, enveloping them both in a cloud of smoke. "I don't believe you mean that."

"Is she in love with Vegas?"

"You'll have to ask her that."

"I mean to," Bourne said. "Circumstances are already complicated enough without Vegas blowing up in a jealous rage."

"She's out in the loggia."

"You can't see the loggia from here," Bourne said.

"I know where all my guests are."

Bourne wondered about that; he hadn't noticed video surveillance cameras.

Don Fernando smiled. "Go find her, Jason. Straighten this out before it turns into a blood feud."

This is how it will go," Zachek said. "The contact is waiting at the side entrance to the Mosque. You will say to him, 'There is no God but one God,' and he will reply, 'God is good. God is great.'"

Boris and Zachek, engulfed in blackest shadow, huddled one block from where the Mosque rose, dark and ominous against the seething Munich sky.

"You know this man," Boris said.

Zachek nodded. "Ostensibly he works at the Mosque, but—"

"I understand," Boris said.

Zachek checked his watch. "It's time," he said. "Good luck."

"The same to you." Boris gave him one last look. "By the way, you look like shit."

Zachek gave him a sorrowful smile. "Nothing lasts forever."

Boris left him then, stepping out onto the street, merging himself with the ebb and flow of pedestrian traffic. He paced himself carefully; he was expert at blending in. Better than Zachek would ever be. Fleetingly, he wondered whether he could trust the SVR agent. There were no sure things in his business, all you could do was home in on a person's psyche and try to push the right buttons. Their time together had been short, but it had been as intense as two soldiers inhabiting the same foxhole in wartime. Life had been compressed; he felt he'd gotten a good psychological read on Zachek.

He was approaching the Mosque's side entrance and there was no help for it now. He had to trust Zachek.

Two men lounged in the doorway, speaking in low tones, but as Boris approached, one broke away and left. Boris stepped toward the remaining man, who was small and square-shouldered. His full, curling beard reached to his chest. He smelled of tobacco and stale sweat.

"There is no God but one God," Boris said.

"God is good, God is great," the man replied, and, turning, led Boris into the Mosque.

He removed his shoes and washed his hands in the font of a stone fountain. Boris followed suit. The man took Boris down a narrow, poorly lit corridor, past cubicles without doors in which shadows moved and whispered voices conversed like the soft drone of insects. Farther away, Boris heard the massed chanting of prayer, the high-low ululations of the muezzin as he spoke to the faithful. The atmosphere was close, oppressive, and Boris strained to see ahead.

They turned left, then right, then right again. The place was a labyrinth, Boris thought. Not an easy place to get out of quickly. At length, the contact stopped outside a doorway. Turning to Boris, he said, "Inside."

"You first," Boris said.

As soon as the man had turned his back, Boris put his right hand on the grips of his Makarov. The man turned around and, shaking his head, held out his hand. Boris froze.

"It's the only way," the man said.

Boris produced the Makarov, unloaded it, and put the bullets into his pocket. Then he handed over the pistol.

The man took it, stepped across the threshold, and Boris followed. Boris found himself in a small square room with one window above chest height, the glass translucent; it was illuminated like a rose window by either daylight or streetlight.

A heavyset man with a greasy-looking beard sat cross-legged on a prayer rug. He was talking to two men who immediately rose and stepped away. Boris noted that they took up positions on either side of the room with their backs to the walls.

The heavyset man ran thick fingers through the tangle of his beard, which was as black as his eyes.

"You are SVR?" he said in a phlegmy voice. "From Zachek?"

Boris nodded.

"You want to know about Viktor Cherkesov," the man said. "Why he came here, whom he saw, and what was conveyed."

"That's right."

"This is difficult information to obtain. Furthermore, it puts me in a precarious position." The heavyset man cleared his throat. "You are prepared to pay."

Since it wasn't a question, Boris remained silent.

The man smiled now, revealing a pair of gold incisors. The rest of his teeth looked mossy, and there was an unpleasant odor wafting off him, as if food were rotting in his mouth or stomach. "Let us proceed, then."

"How much—?"

The man raised a meaty hand. "Ah, no. I have no need of more money. You want information from me; I want the same from you."

Boris was keeping a clandestine eye on the two men at the walls. They seemed to be interested only in the light filtering through the window. "What sort of information?"

"Do you know a man named Ivan Volkin?"

The question almost took Boris's breath away. "I've heard of him, yes."

The heavyset man pursed his lips, which were red and full. They looked obscene surrounded by the beard. "This is not what I asked."

"I've met him," Boris said cautiously.

Something changed in the man's dark eyes. "Perhaps, then, the information we exchange concerns the same subject."

Boris spread his hands. "I don't see how. I want to know why Cherkesov was sent here. I have no interest in Volkin."

The heavyset man hawked and spat into a small brass bowl at his side. "But you see, it was Volkin whom Cherkesov came here to see."

Bourne found Kaja, arms wrapped tightly around herself, standing in the loggia. She was watching a nightingale flit through a tree as if trying to find its way back home. He wondered whether Kaja was trying to do the same thing.

She stirred when she heard him but didn't say a word until the nightingale had settled on a branch and begun its lovely song. By that time, Bourne was standing beside her.

"You don't seem surprised to see me," he said.

"I was hoping you'd come. Then it would be just like it is in the movies."

"You haven't struck me as the romantic type."

"No?" She moved beside him, shifting from one hip to the other. "How have I struck you?"

"I think you're someone who will do anything to get what she wants."

She sighed. "You think I'll break Estevan's heart."

"He's a simple man, with simple needs," Bourne said. "You're anything but."

She looked down at her feet. "Suppose you're right."

"Then Estevan was a means to an end."

"For five years I gave him pleasure."

"Because he believed what you told him." Bourne turned to her. "Do you think he would have fallen in love with you if he'd known who you really are and what you needed him for?"

"He might have, yes."

She turned to face him. Moonlight struck her cheeks, but her eyes remained in shadow. Here in Don Fernando's garlanded loggia, all the ripe lushness of her figure was on display. Bourne had no doubt that she had deliberately positioned herself for maximum sensual effect. She knew very well the powers at her command, and she was unafraid to wield them.

"I don't want to talk about Estevan anymore."

"Perhaps, but I need to know—"

She put her hands on either side of his face, her lips close to his. "I want to talk about us."

And then Bourne understood. He could see the desire burning in her eyes; a desire not for him in the traditional sense. He, like Vegas before him, was a means to an end. All she wanted was to find out the truth about her father. Men could do this, not women, which was why she had turned herself into a serial lover. She attached herself to whichever man she sensed could get her closer to her goal.

"Don Fernando is under the misapprehension that you're in love with me."

She frowned. "Misapprehension?"

Then she stepped toward him and kissed him hard on the lips. As she did so, she plastered herself to him. Bourne could feel every hill and valley of her womanly body.

"Don't," he said, pushing her away.

She shook her head, her lips slightly parted. "I don't understand."

He wondered whether she had tricked herself into believing that she loved him. Was that how she had so successfully deceived Vegas, by deceiving herself?

"You understand perfectly well," Bourne said.

"You're wrong." She shook her head. "Dead wrong."

Amun!" Soraya cried when she returned to consciousness.

"He's gone, Soraya."

Aaron bent over her, his face filled with concern.

"Remember?"

And then she did: the descent into darkness, being nearly strangled to death by Donatien Marchand, Amun running up the stairs, the shots, the blood, and then the fall. Her eyes burned as they welled up and tears spilled out the corners, running down her cheeks, dampening the pillow.

"Where—?"

"You're in a hospital."

She turned her head, suddenly aware of the tubes running into her arm.

"I need to see him," she said.

But when she attempted to rise, Aaron pushed her gently back down.

"And you will, Soraya, I promise you. But not now, not today."

"I have to." She became aware that her struggle was for naught; she had no strength. She could not stop crying. Amun dead. She looked up into Aaron's face.

"Please, Aaron, wake me up."

"You *are* awake, Soraya. Thank God."

"This can't be happening." Why was she crying? Her heart seemed to have cracked open. The question of whether her love for Amun was real or not seemed irrelevant now. They had been colleagues, friends, lovers—and now he was gone. She had dealt with loss and death before, but this was on a completely different scale. Dimly, she was aware of her sobbing, and of Aaron holding her, the smell of him mixing with the sickly sweet odors of the hospital. She clung to him. But it was so odd that with Aaron holding her she should have the sense of being alone. Yet she did, and in a sense she felt more alone than she ever had before. Her work was her entire life. Like Jason, she had made little room in it for anyone else—save Amun. And now . . .

Jason entered her head then. She thought of the losses he had suffered, both professional and personal. She thought mostly of Martin Lindros, the architect of Typhon, her boss, and Jason's closest friend at the old CI. She had been rocked by Lindros's death, but how much worse it must have been for Jason. He'd moved heaven and earth to save his friend, only to fail at the very end. Thinking of Jason made her feel less alone, made her feel the oppressiveness of her surroundings, gave her the understanding that she needed to get away, to think, to sort matters out.

"Aaron, you've got to get me out of here," she said with a depth of desperation that startled even herself.

"You have no broken bones, just some bruised ribs. But the doctors are concerned about a concussion—"

"I don't care," she cried. "I can't bear to be in here a moment longer."

"Soraya, please try to calm down. You're understandably distraught and—"

She pushed him away, as roughly as she was able. "Stop treating me like a child and listen to what I'm saying, Aaron. Get me the fuck out of here. Now."

He studied her face for a moment, then nodded. "All right. Give me a moment and I'll clear it with admissions."

The moment he left the room, Soraya struggled to a sitting position. This made her head hurt, but she ignored it. She peeled back the tape and slipped the needle out of her arm. Carefully, she swung her legs over the side of the bed. The floor felt cold. Her ankles tingled when she tried to put weight on her legs. She waited for a moment, breathing deeply and evenly to bring more oxygen into her body. Holding on to the bed, she took several tentative steps—one, two, three—like a toddler learning the basics. Painfully slowly, she made her way across the room to the closet and took out her clothes. She was acting now purely on instinct. Walking stiff-legged like a zombie, she made it to the door and hung on there, renewing her energy while she breathed.

Then she hauled open the door and peered out, looking both ways. Apart from an old man shuffling away from her, holding on to the rolling rack that held his fluid drip, no one was about. Across the corridor was a utility room. She steeled herself and stepped out. The moment she did, she heard voices approaching. One was Aaron's. He wasn't alone. Willing her legs to move, she lunged for the handle of the utility room door, swung it open, and stepped inside. Just as the door sighed shut she caught a glimpse of Aaron flanked by two doctors heading for her room.

Bourne and Essai found Kaja and Vegas in the entryway. The front door was open and, beyond, Don Fernando could be seen directing two cars up his driveway.

"It's ten o'clock," Kaja said. As if she sensed that Bourne and Essai, having appeared together, wanted to talk with her, she added, "Dinner time is sacred for Don Fernando."

Bourne approached them. "Estevan, how are you feeling? You've been asleep for hours."

Vegas steepled his fingers against his forehead. "A little groggy, but better."

Don Fernando stepped into the doorway. "Our transportation has arrived."

Their destination was a seafood restaurant on the other side of Cadiz. Its expansive terra-cotta-tiled terrace abutted a stone seawall that overlooked the southern part of the harbor. Boats lay at anchor, bobbing gently in the swells. A launch pearled the water as it passed by, leaving a fast-dissolving froth in its wake. Moonlight lay on the water like a silver mantilla; overhead were handfuls of stars.

The maître d', making a fuss over Don Fernando, showed them

outside to a round table near the seawall. The restaurant was filled with glamorous types. Gold and platinum baubles on the wrists of slender women in Louboutin shoes gleamed in the candlelight. Jewels graced their throats and long necks.

"I feel like an ugly duckling," Kaja said as they seated themselves.

"Nonsense, *mi amor.*" Vegas squeezed her hand. "No one here outshines you."

Kaja laughed and kissed him with what seemed great affection. "What a gentleman!"

Bourne was sitting on the other side of her, and he felt the heat of her thigh pressing against his. She was turned toward Estevan, their hands still clasped. Her thigh slid back and forth against him, the friction creating a clandestine link between them.

"What's good to eat here?" he asked Don Fernando, who was seated on his right hand. Don Fernando's answer was drowned out by the roar of Vespas swinging along the sea road outside the restaurant.

The waiter uncorked the first bottle of wine from the stash Don Fernando had brought with him. They all drank a toast to their host, who told them that he had already ordered.

Bourne took his leg away from Kaja's, and, when she turned to look at him inquiringly, he gave her a brief but emphatic shake of his head.

Her eyes narrowed for the space of a breath, then, announcing her need to leave the table, she pushed her chair back hard and stalked across the terrace. Don Fernando shot Bourne a warning look.

Vegas put down his napkin and was about to rise when Don Fernando said, "Estevan, *calmaté, amigo.* This is a security matter; I'd rather have Jason keep an eye on her."

Bourne got up and, crossing the terrace, stepped into the closed-in part of the restaurant, where he was assailed by the aromatic scents of seafood being cooked with Moroccan and Phoenician herbs and spices. He spotted Kaja exiting the front door, and he snaked his way around the tables crowded with boisterous patrons.

He caught up with her on the narrow sidewalk. "What do you think you're doing?"

She pulled away from him. "What does it look like?"

"Kaja, Estevan will suspect something."

She glared at him. "So? I'm tired of all you men."

"You're acting like a spoiled child."

She turned and slapped him across the face. He could have stopped her, but he felt the outcome would be worse.

"Feel better now?"

"Don't think I don't know what's happening here," she said. "Don Fernando is terrified I'll tell Estevan who I really am."

"Now would not be a good time."

"Say what you mean. Never would be a good time."

"Just not now."

"Why not now?" Kaja said. "He treats Rosie like a child. I'm not a child anymore. I'm not Rosie."

Bourne kept an eye on the road, the clouds of young men on Vespas laughing drunkenly, vying with one another as they rode at a daredevil's pace. "It was a risk bringing both of you to Cadiz, but the alternative would have meant both your deaths."

"Don Fernando should never have gotten Estevan involved in smuggling for the Domna," she said. "It's clear he's not cut out for that kind of life."

"Don Fernando wanted a way in," Bourne said.

"Don Fernando used Estevan," she said, disgusted.

"So did you." Bourne shrugged. "In any case, he could have refused."

She snorted. "Do you think Estevan would refuse that man? He owes Don Fernando everything."

"*Querida!*"

They both turned to see Vegas emerge from the restaurant, his expression filled with concern.

"Is everything all right?" He came toward her. "Did I do something to make you angry?"

Kaja automatically turned on her megawatt Rosie smile. "Of course not, *mi amor.*" She had to raise her voice over the revving Vespas. "How could you do anything to make me angry?"

Taking her in his arms, he swung her around, her back to the street.

Three shots buzzed past Kaja's shoulder and head, and blew Estevan backward, out of her embrace, and Bourne leapt onto her, covering her as the white Vespa with the gunman accelerated away from the curb. Bourne dragged her to her feet.

"Estevan!" she cried. "Estevan, oh, my God!"

Vegas had landed in a bloody heap against the restaurant's front. The white stucco was spattered with his blood. Bourne kept her away, pushing her into the arms of Don Fernando, who had run out of the doorway.

"They tried again!" Bourne shouted. "Keep her inside!"

Then he stepped off the curb, corralled a young rider who had just stopped to gawk at the bloody body, and yanked him off his Vespa.

The boy stumbled over the curb, landing on his backside. "Hey! What?" he cried as Bourne roared away down the traffic-choked road.

22

PETER MARKS FLOATED in and out of consciousness like a swimmer caught in a rip current. One moment, his feet seemed to be on solid footing, the next they were sliding away as a wave crashed over him, taking him off his feet, spinning him down into a reddish darkness distinguished by vertigo and pain.

He heard his own groans and the voices of unfamiliar people, but these seemed to be either at a great remove or filtered through layers of gauze. Light hurt his eyes. The only thing he could get down was baby food, and this only occasionally. He felt as if he were dying, as if he lay suspended between life and death, an unwilling citizen of a gray limbo. At last he understood the phrase *bed of pain*.

And yet, there came a time when his pain lessened, he ate more, and, blessedly, limbo faded into the realm of dreams, only half remembered, receding as if he were on a train speeding away from a dreadful place in which it had been stalled.

He opened his eyes to light and color. He took a deep breath, then another. He felt his lungs fill and empty without the crushing pain that had gripped him for what seemed like forever.

"He's conscious." A voice from above, as if an angel were hovering, beating its delicate wings.

"Who..." Peter licked his lips. "Who are you?"

"Yo, it's Tyrone, Chief."

Peter's eyes felt gluey, there were coronas around everything he looked at, as if he were hallucinating. "I... Who?"

"Tyrone Elkins. From CI."

"CI?"

"I picked you up offa tha street. You were fucked up."

"I don't remember..."

The black head turned. "Yo, Deron, yo, yo, yo." Then Tyrone turned back and spoke to Peter again. "The ambulance. Remember the ambulance, Chief?"

Something was forming out of the haze. "I..."

"The bogus EMS guys. You got yourself outta the ambulance, shit, still don't know how."

The memory started to form like a cloud building on the horizon. Peter remembered the garage at the Treadstone building, the explosion, being hustled into the ambulance, the realization that he wasn't being taken to the hospital, that these attendants were the enemy.

"I remember," he murmured.

"That's good, that's very good."

Another face along with Tyrone's. Tyrone had called him Deron. A handsome black man with an upper-class British accent.

"Who are you?"

"You remember Tyrone? He's from CI. A friend of Soraya's." The handsome man smiled down at Peter. "My name's Deron. I'm a friend of Jason's."

Peter's brain took a moment to click into gear. "Bourne?"

"That's right."

He closed his eyes, blessing the good luck that had landed him in the safest place in DC.

"Peter, do you know who those people were in the ambulance?"

Peter's eyes popped open. "Never saw them before." He felt his heart beating and sensed that it had been working hard for some time, working to keep him alive. "I don't know..."

"Okay, okay," Deron said. "Save your breath." He turned to Tyrone. "Can you get on this? There must be a police report on the shootings. Use your creds and see if you can get IDs on the dead men."

Tyrone nodded and took off.

Deron picked up a plastic glass of water with a bendy straw in it. "Now," he said, "let's see if we can get some more liquid in you."

Placing one hand behind Peter's head, he lifted it gently and offered him the straw. Peter sipped slowly, even though he was parched. His tongue felt swollen to twice its size.

"Tyrone told me the whole story," Deron said, "at least as much as he knew." He took the straw out of Peter's mouth. "It sounds like you were being kidnapped."

Peter nodded.

"Why?"

"I don't..." Then Peter remembered. He'd done intensive research on Roy FitzWilliams and the Damascus-based El-Gabal, to which Fitz had had ties. Hendricks had been absolutely paranoid about security on the issue of Roy FitzWilliams. Peter groaned.

"What is it? Are you in pain?"

"No, that would be too simple," Peter said with a gritty smile. "I fucked up, Deron. My boss warned me to be careful and I did some back-door research on a company computer, which runs through the government server."

"So whoever was tapping in got scared and sent the extraction team."

"Well, they tried to kill me first." Peter described the explosion in the garage. "The extraction team was there as a backup."

"Which speaks both of meticulous planning and an organization with influence and deep pockets." Deron rubbed his jaw. "I would say you've got big problems, except for the fact that Ty tells me you're director of Treadstone. You've got plenty of firepower yourself."

"Sadly, no," Peter said. "Soraya and I are still getting Treadstone back on its feet. Most of our current personnel are overseas. Our domestic infrastructure is still hollowed out."

Deron sat back, forearms on his knees. Losing his English accent, he said, "Damn, homey, you done washed up at da right place."

Bourne took the Vespa around a corner, speeding after the gunman. He could see him up ahead on the white Vespa, weaving in and out of traffic as he followed the road along the waterfront, heading south. It was difficult to make up ground, but slowly, by running the bike full-out, Bourne was gaining. The gunman had not looked behind him; he didn't know that someone was on his tail.

He went through a light as it was turning red. Bourne, hunched over the handlebars, judged the vectors of the cross-traffic and, with a twist to the left, then the right, shot through the intersection.

Down the block the gunman had pulled over to the curb behind a black van. He popped open the rear doors and, with the help of the van's driver, hoisted the Vespa into the interior. Then he slammed the doors, and both men climbed into the front. Bourne was still going full-out, and as the van pulled out into the flow of traffic he was no more than two car lengths behind.

The van soon turned off the sea road, heading into Cadiz itself. It followed a tortuous path down the city's narrow, crooked streets. At length, the van pulled over and stopped along a street of warehouses. The driver got out and unlocked a door that rolled up electronically, then returned to the van. Bourne ditched the Vespa and sprinted as the van drove through into the interior. The door rattled down and Bourne dived through with just enough room to spare.

He lay on a bare concrete floor that stank of creosote and motor oil. The only illumination came from the van's headlights. Doors slammed as the two men jumped down onto the concrete. They didn't bother to unload the Vespa. Bourne rose to one knee, hiding behind an enormous metal barrel. The gunman must have gone to a switch box, because a moment later light flooded the interior from a pair of overheads, capped with green shades. There seemed to be nothing in the warehouse except more of the barrels and two stacks of wooden crates. The driver switched off the headlights, then the two men crossed to the crates.

"Is she dead?" the driver said in Moscow-accented Russian.

"I don't know, everything happened too fast." The gunman laid his pistol down on top of one of the crates.

"It is unfortunate that you didn't stick to the plan," the driver said with a tone of lamentation only Russians could exhibit.

"She came outside," the gunman protested. "The temptation was too great. Hit her and run. You would have done the same."

The driver shrugged. "I'm just happy I'm not in your shoes."

"Fuck you," the gunman said. "You're the other half of this team. If I missed her it's going to fall on both our shoulders."

"If our superior finds out," the driver said, "our shoulders won't be supporting anything worth talking about."

The gunman picked up his weapon and reloaded it. "So?"

"So we find out if she's dead." The driver squared on his companion. "And if not, we rectify your error together."

The two men stepped behind the stack and opened a narrow door. Before he went through into what Bourne surmised might be the office, the gunman extinguished the lights. Bourne crept to the van, carefully opened the driver's door, and rummaged around until he found a flashlight. In the rear, he went through a box of tools and picked out a crowbar. Then he stepped to the stack and squatted down so that the crates were between him and the rear door. Switching on the flashlight, he played the beam over the crates. The wood was an odd greenish color, smooth and virtually seamless. The beam slid across the surface, and he felt his heart rate accelerate. The crates were marked with their origin, Don Fernando's oil company in Colombia.

Boris felt his blood run cold. "Cherkesov came *here* to meet with Ivan?" He shook his head. "This I cannot believe."

The heavyset man signaled to one of the men along the wall, who stepped forward. Boris tensed as the acolyte reached into his robes, but all he brought out was a set of grainy black-and-white photos, which he held out to Boris.

"Go on, take a look," the heavyset man said. "Because of the lighting, you'll be able to tell that they were not doctored in any way."

Boris took the photos and stared down at them, his mind working a mile a minute. There were Cherkesov and Ivan speaking together. A bit of the Mosque's interior could be seen behind them. He took note of the date the camera had printed in the lower left-hand corner of the photos.

He looked at the heavyset man kneeling on the prayer rug. He hadn't budged since Boris had been shown into the room. "What were they talking about?"

A smile formed on the lips of the heavyset man. "I know who you are, General Karpov."

Boris stood very still, his gaze not on the kneeling man, but on his acolytes. They seemed to have as little interest in him as they had before. "Then you are one up on me."

"I beg your pardon?"

"I don't know who you are."

The smile broadened. "Ah, curiosity! But it is far better for you that you don't know." He unlaced his fingers. "We must concentrate on the matter at hand: Cherkesov and Volkin." He locked his red lips. "I am, shall we say, acutely aware that FSB-2, of which you are now the head, and SVR are locked in a deadly power struggle."

Boris waited out the silence. He was getting to know this nameless man, his predilection for dramatic pauses and declarations, the way he meted out information in precise bits and pieces.

"But that power struggle," the man continued, "is far more complicated than you know. There are powers lining up on either side that far surpass those of FSB-2 and SVR."

"I assume you're referring to Severus Domna."

The heavyset man raised his eyebrows. "Among others."

Boris's heart skipped a beat. "There are others?"

"There are always others, General." He gestured with a hand. "Excuse my poor manners. Come. Sit."

Boris stepped onto the prayer rug, careful to sit in the same position as his host, though it pained his hips and flexor muscles.

"You asked me what Cherkesov and your friend Volkin were talking about," the heavyset man said. "It was the Domna."

"Do you know that Cherkesov left FSB-2 to join the Domna?"

"I heard as much," the heavyset man acknowledged.

Boris didn't believe him. He sensed his host was withholding information. "Cherkesov has ambitions that, for the moment at least, outstrip his power."

"You think he had a plan in mind when he allowed himself to be lured away from FSB-2."

"Yes," Boris said.

"Do you know what it is?"

"It's possible one of us does."

The heavyset man's belly began to tremble, and Boris realized that he was laughing silently.

"Yes, General Karpov, that is quite possible." Boris's host considered for a moment. "Tell me, have you ever been to Damascus?"

"Once or twice, yes," Boris said, alert that the conversation had suddenly veered in a new direction.

"How did you find it?"

"The Paris of the Middle East?"

"Ha! Yes, I suppose it once was."

"Damascus has beautiful bones," Boris said.

The heavyset man considered this for a moment. "Yes, Damascus possesses great beauty, but it is also a place of great danger."

"How is that?"

"Damascus is what Cherkesov was sent here to discuss with your friend Volkin."

"Cherkesov is no longer welcome in Russia," Boris said, "but Ivan?"

"Your friend Volkin has a number of, shall we say, business interests in Damascus."

Boris was surprised; Ivan had let it be known that, apart from consulting, he was retired. "What kind of business interests?"

"Nothing that would keep him in good standing with the *grupperovka* bosses with whom he has done business for decades."

"I don't understand." The moment the words were out of his mouth, Boris knew that he had made a fatal error. A key aspect of his host's face changed radically; all its intimacy and friendliness disappeared like a puff of smoke.

"That is a pity," the heavyset man said. "I was hoping that you could shed some light on why Damascus has become the focus of both Volkin and Cherkesov." He snapped his fingers and the two men on either side produced Taurus PT145 Millenniums, small pistols with a big .45 punch.

Boris jumped up, but two more men, armed with Belgian FN P90 small-profile submachine guns, appeared in the doorway.

Behind them came Zachek with a death's-head grin. "I'm afraid, General Karpov," Zachek said, "that your usefulness is at an end."

Bourne had just inserted the crowbar into the gap between the top and side of one of the crates when the rear door opened. He snapped off the flashlight an instant before the two Russians emerged. Before one of them could reach for the light switch, he tossed the flashlight across the warehouse. When it struck the floor, the Russians started, reached for their weapons, and ran toward the sound.

He was closer to the gunman, the driver having taken the lead. Swinging the crowbar, he slammed the end into the gunman's hand, and his pistol dropped to the floor. The gunman howled, the driver pulled up short and turned on his heel just as Bourne flung the crowbar. It hit the driver square in the face, knocking him backward so hard his head slammed into the concrete, cracking his skull, killing him instantly.

The gunman, his fractured right hand hanging at his side, pulled out a stun baton with his left hand. It was a sixteen-incher that could deliver a nasty three-hundred-thousand-volt kick. The gunman swung it back and forth, keeping Bourne at bay while he advanced on him, pushing him back along the side of the van. His plan seemed to be to get Bourne into a corner where he would have no room to maneuver away from the baton. One touch of it and Bourne knew he would be writhing helplessly on the floor.

He retreated along the length of the van. The gunman had his eye on where he wanted Bourne to end up, so he was a beat slow in reacting as Bourne swung open one of the van's rear doors, using it as a shield between him and the baton while he scrabbled in the toolbox.

The gunman was swinging around the end of the door when Bourne uncapped the aerosol can of enamel paint and sprayed it into the gunman's eyes. The gunman reared back, hands to his face, gasping, and Bourne slammed the bottom of the can against the fractured bones. The gunman groaned, the pain bringing him to his knees. Bourne took the baton from him, but the gunman lunged forward, wrapping his arms around Bourne's legs in an attempt to bring him down. His mouth opened to sink his teeth into Bourne's thigh when Bourne connected with the side of his head. All the breath seemed to go out of him and he lay on his back, the fingers of his good hand trying to dig the paint out of his eyes.

Bourne grabbed his hand and pulled it away. "Who do you work for?"

"Go fuck your mother," the man said in his guttural tone.

Bourne dialed down the charge on the baton and gave the gunman a shot in the side. His body arched up, the heels of his shoes drumming against the concrete.

"Who do you work for?"

Silence. Bourne raised the charge slightly and applied it again.

"Fuck, fuck, fuck!" The gunman coughed heavily and began to choke. His mouth was full of blood; in his frenzy he had bitten his tongue almost clear through.

"I won't ask you again."

"You won't have to."

The gunman's jaws ground together and, a moment later, his chest convulsed. A bluish foam mingled with the blood in his mouth, bubbling over to coat his lips. Leaning over, Bourne tried to pry open the jaws, but it was too late. A distinct odor of bitter almonds wafted up to him and he reared back. The gunman had bitten open a cyanide capsule.

23

PARIS AT NIGHT was not such a bad place for a single woman to be. She sat in a café, drinking bad coffee and thinking about taking up smoking. Soraya was surrounded by young bohemians, with which Paris was always teeming, no matter the era. The thing about Paris's inhabitants she loved so much was that they were constantly reimagining themselves. While the city itself—its grand boulevards, its martial lines of horse chestnuts, its magnificent parks, its beautiful fountains around which were arrayed timeless cafés where one could sit for hours and watch the world go by—remained constant, its young people were busy remaking themselves.

The water of the Canal St. Martin was as black and shiny as vinyl. She was surrounded by lovers, bicyclists, laughing college kids, tattooed writers, and sloe-eyed poets, scowling into the night as they scribbled their random thoughts.

Each café was a nexus of its neighborhood, and though each had its own patrons, there was always room for the occasional guest. Waiters, long-haired and slim-hipped, came and went, dispensing plates of *steak-frites* and carafes of pastis. It wasn't only French she heard spoken at the adjacent tables, but German and English as well. The endless existential arguments remained the staple of the city's café society.

Her head hurt so much that she rested it in her hands. Her eyes closed, but this only caused her to become dizzy. She opened her eyes with a start and a muttered curse. She had to keep herself awake until the danger from a concussion had passed. Flagging down a passing waiter, she ordered a double espresso, gulped it down while the waiter was still standing beside her, then asked for another. When this came, she dissolved three teaspoonfuls of sugar in it and sipped slowly. The dual jolts of caffeine and sugar elbowed away the exhaustion. For the moment, the pain in her head eased and her thoughts became clearer.

She wondered whether it had been a mistake to run away from Aaron. She had needed to get out of the hospital immediately—the place reminded her of too many colleagues' deaths. He had been unwilling to help her and she had neither the strength nor the inclination to explain. Besides, she needed to be alone. She needed to think about Amun.

She was torn up inside. It was as if the dark thoughts she'd had about him had conspired to kill him. On the surface, she knew this was crazy, but right now she was feeling just a bit crazy, just a bit out of control. She had thought she'd loved Amun, then had come his anti-Semitic remarks, and her confidence in her own feelings had been shaken. Her love for him could not have been real if it had been destroyed by one nasty incident. But she couldn't know that for certain, and now she would never know. She looked out at the canal, seeing Amun's face, wanting him to speak to her. But the dead could not speak; they could not defend themselves or apologize. They could not proclaim their love.

Her eyes welled up and tears rolled down her cheeks. The world seemed empty and endless. Amun was dead and it was her fault. She had asked him to join her in Paris to help her investigation, and, out of love, he had come. There was a finality about what had happened, as well as an inevitability. She never should have allowed herself to become involved with him. She should have taken a page out of Jason's book and kept herself at a healthy remove. But this wasn't why she was crying.

I *should have been punished*, she thought. *Not Amun.*

Unable to bear her sanctuary a moment longer, she rose and, throwing several euros down on the table, walked off across the glistening cobbles into the secret heart of Paris. Three blocks later, holding on to a lamppost for dear life, she doubled over, vomiting up the contents of her stomach.

Before Bourne rose, he searched both the Russians, hoping to find a clue to the identity of the organization to which they belonged. Apart from keys to the van and the Vespa, twenty thousand euros, three packs of cigarettes, and a cheap lighter, there was nothing, no rings or jewelry of any kind. Opening up the driver's mouth, he dug out his cyanide capsule and pocketed it. Then he stripped them, figuring he might be able to identify their affiliation from their tattoos, but they had none. He sat back on his haunches. Now he knew these men were not part of a *grupperovka* family, and yet they didn't look like SVR agents, either. The mystery deepened.

Rising, he grabbed the crowbar and went through the rear door. Beyond was a short, evil-smelling corridor that led to a bathroom whose stench made his eyes water, and, at the end, a tiny office, furnished with a scarred metal desk, a swivel chair, and a steel filing cabinet. A single window looked out on a grimy air shaft.

The drawers in the cabinet and the desk were empty, not so much as a paper clip left behind. There was, however, a manila folder taped to the underside of the desk's kneehole. Bourne opened it to find twelve shipping labels, matching the number of crates in the warehouse proper. They were all going to the same recipient: El-Gabal, Avenue Choukry Kouatly, Damascus, Syria.

Now he really wanted to know what was inside those crates. He was closing the folder when he heard the rumble of the front gate opening up and the burble of a car engine. Quickly he stowed the folder back in its hiding place. He heard voices raised, then shouts of alarm. Stepping to the window, he threw it open and climbed through.

There was no direct egress; he had to go up the shaft. Turning, he closed the window, which would give him a couple of minutes at least.

The building was white stucco, affording no hand- or footholds. Grasping a drainpipe, he began his ascent.

Five, Rue Vernet was lit up like it was New Year's Eve. At least half a dozen Quai d'Orsay vehicles were parked in front and the area was cordoned off, patrolled by policemen gripping submachine guns.

Jacques Robbinet found Aaron inside the Monition Club, directing a cadre of operatives as they combed through the labyrinth of offices. The club's skeleton crew of nighttime personnel looked on, frozen in shock.

"What are you looking for?" Robbinet said.

"Anything. Everything," Aaron said.

"And Soraya Moore?"

"She's missing."

"I beg your pardon?"

"I left her room for a moment and when I got back..." He shrugged.

"So now you're here instead of searching for her?"

"I combed the hospital. Then I sent two units out in a grid search."

Robbinet stared at him. "But you didn't see fit to go yourself."

"Listen, sir, M. Marchand was in league with a group of Arab terrorists. This has become a matter of national security."

"You're telling me what's a matter of national security?" Robbinet took Aaron by the elbow and led him away from the others. In a voice so low only Lipkin-Renais could hear, he said, "I asked you to take care of this woman, Aaron, and I expected you to do so. She's an extremely important person."

"I understand," Aaron said. "But the incident in the basement precludes any—"

"Any orders I gave you?" Robbinet finished for him. "The Moore woman is co-director of an American intelligence agency. The American secretary of defense, a friend as well as an opposite number, asked me to do him a favor. Now she is injured and missing, and what are you doing? Standing around here watching your men stuff papers into boxes. Delegate, Aaron. There are any number of colleagues you could have tapped for this."

"I wanted to oversee the confiscation of all the computers myself. It's there we are most likely to find—"

"That was not your choice to make, Inspector. But since you've made it, keep at it." Robbinet's icy tone conveyed his fury. "This, at least, I know you're competent at." He began to walk away, then turned back for a moment. "Agents with limitations have limited careers."

Using the drainpipe, Bourne hauled himself up the warehouse facade. Halfway up, the stucco gave way to horizontal timbers. They were so rough-hewn he was able to gain toeholds to help him ascend. He was nearing the roof when he heard a noise and froze. The scrape of a match left him certain someone was on the roof, and he continued upward slowly and silently. When he was just beneath the lip of the roof he could smell the cigarette smoke and make out the two voices conversing in low tones.

He rose a bit more, until he could take a quick look over the parapet. Two men, submachine guns slung over their shoulders, were talking languidly in Russian about girls and sex as they smoked. Neither was turned in his direction.

The drainpipe rang dully when Bourne kicked it. A moment later one of the Russians peered over the parapet. Bourne reached up and grabbed him, dragging him across the cement. The Russian tried to chop down on Bourne's wrist, but was forced to shoot an arm out to keep himself from toppling over. He jerked a knife free and stabbed down toward the spot between Bourne's shoulder and neck. Bourne gave one final jerk, which launched the Russian headlong over the parapet and down the air shaft.

Bourne shinnied the last foot up the drainpipe and, as the second Russian appeared, levered his legs and torso upward. His ankles scissored around the submachine gun, and yanked it away from the Russian.

For a moment, Bourne lay atop the parapet, balancing himself. The Russian struck at him furiously, knocking him back so that his head and shoulders hung off the roof. The Russian's hands found Bourne's throat, his fingers closing around Bourne's windpipe.

Bourne brought his forearms up, inside the Russian's arms, and slammed them outward, breaking his hold. Then he kicked the Russian in the face. As he stumbled back, Bourne swiveled off the parapet onto the tarred roof and came after him. He grabbed him by his shirt and slammed the back of his head against the roof. Then, taking advantage of the man's dazed state, he reached into his mouth and dug out the cyanide capsule disguised as a tooth.

"Who are you?" he said. "Who do you work for?"

The Russian's eyes cleared, and his jaw began to work.

Bourne held out the poisonous tooth. "Searching for this?"

The Russian went into a frenzy then, but Bourne was prepared for this and, once again, he slammed his head into the rooftop.

"There's no escape," Bourne said, "no easy death."

The Russian looked up at him with eyes the color of dirt. "I know you. You fucked the Domna. We should be working together, not trying to kill each other."

"Who do you work for?"

"I'll take you to my boss. He'll tell you."

Bourne relieved the Russian of all his weapons, then allowed him to rise.

"You're a hero to us," the Russian said.

Bourne gestured with his head. "Let's go."

That was when the Russian broke away. Bourne sprinted after him across the roof. He caught him at the edge of the parapet, but instead of fighting to free himself the Russian grabbed Bourne and dragged both of them onto the lip of the parapet. As they teetered on the brink, Bourne realized the Russian's purpose. He struck the man under the nose; his grip loosened, and Bourne tore himself away just before the Russian followed his colleague down into darkness.

The moment he received the news of M. Marchand's death in an Arab-town basement, Benjamin El-Arian hastened to the bank building at La Défense. There he had made certain to lock out the Monition Club computers from the servers he had set up in Gibraltar. He had created this fail-safe mechanism for just such a time, not believing, however, that it would ever come. Now that it had, he was doubly grateful for his prudence.

Staring out into the blank night, he reviewed all the decisions he had made during the past six months. Had he made mistakes, and if so, how serious would they turn out to be?

With a disgusted sound, he turned away from the window and, sitting at the head of the conference table, fired up his iPad. What had caused Marchand to go see his terrorist contacts?

Using his twenty-digit password, he logged into the Domna servers and downloaded the phone records for the past three days from the Paris office. Using a software filter, he found all the calls Marchand made, then cross-referenced them against his database of phone numbers. All of them were to parties known to El-Arian, save one. Approximately an hour before the incident in Arab-town and—here he double-checked the timing—just minutes after the visit from the Quai d'Orsay inspector and his guests, Marchand had placed a call to a number that wasn't in the Domna database.

For a moment, El-Arian sat back, staring at the number. Why had Marchand called it and not him, as he should have done? He snatched up a phone and called a contact in the Paris Préfecture de Police. El-Arian woke him up, but that was all right, he was being paid a generous amount to be on call. El-Arian gave him the number, and the contact said he'd call back as soon as he had an answer.

El-Arian rose and made himself some Caravan black tea at the sideboard. At this hour of the night he needed a good shot of caffeine to keep his mind clear. Marchand had made a fatal error; that wasn't like him. Something must have occurred during the visit by the Quai d'Orsay to have severely rattled him. But to bring the Arabs into the picture was about the worst move he could have made. El-Arian sipped his tea. It was almost as if Marchand had decided to self-destruct and take the entire Paris Monition Club with him.

El-Arian sighed. The Domna's Paris operation had moved in all but name. The Monition Club had outlived its usefulness, especially now that the cache of Solomon's gold was lost. He consoled himself with the fact that the American operation was proceeding on schedule. He glanced at his watch. Skara had twenty hours to complete her part and then every loose end would be tied up. The economic destruction of the United States would be ensured.

The phone rang and El-Arian grabbed it. "Did you get the information?"

"Yes," his contact said, "but it wasn't easy. I had to get through three firewalls to find the owner of that number."

When he told El-Arian the name, Benjamin dropped his teacup and saucer. He didn't even notice the Caravan tea stains on the bottom of his trousers.

No, no, no, he thought. *It can't be.*

24

NIGHT. STILLNESS REIGNED throughout Don Fernando's house. Through the open windows, the sound of the sea could be heard. The scents of its endless expanse flowed like waves through the rooms. Dinner seemed like weeks ago. By the time Bourne had returned to the restaurant, Don Fernando had dealt with the police and phoned the mortuary.

Kaja went straight to her room as soon as they entered the house and Essai bade them good night. For some time, Bourne and Don Fernando sat in his study dissecting the violence that had occurred earlier. Bourne was wary. Don Fernando was involved in this mystery up to his eye-teeth. He had initiated the Domna's contact with Estevan Vegas, ostensibly so that the organization could use the oil field in Colombia to hide their shipments to, it now seemed, Damascus. Don Fernando claimed he was playing a double's game, using the shipments to gather intel on the Domna—specifically Benjamin El-Arian, who had been taking trips to Damascus without the Domna's knowledge. So far, so good. But tonight's revelation that the warehouse and shipment belonged to the Russian outfit bent on killing Kaja blew that story to smithereens. Was

Don Fernando colluding with this Russian group? If so, he was keeping the identity of the group Kaja's father worked for a secret from all of them. Once again, Bourne was faced with the question of whether Don Fernando was friend or foe. Therefore, he made no mention of the dozen crates, or that he had discovered their destination. Neither did he tell Don Fernando about his encounter with the Russians on the warehouse roof. In his altered version, the incident ended with the deaths of the gunman and his driver outside the warehouse.

Don Fernando drank several brandies much too quickly. "I have lost a good friend tonight," he said. He turned to stare out the door to the study. "I don't think I can bear to have her under my roof for much longer."

"It's not her fault."

"Of course it's her fault." Don Fernando sloshed more brandy into his snifter. "I made a mistake, I gave her too much leeway. Finding out about her father's secret life has turned into a reckless obsession. The bitch brought this on us all."

It was three o'clock by the time Don Fernando showed Bourne to his bedroom, which, along with the other guest bedrooms, was grouped in a wing on the opposite side of the house from the master suite. Don Fernando lit a cigar and puffed on it contemplatively. He seemed to have calmed down from his brief tirade, but who could really tell?

"You did well tonight," Don Fernando said, but now his thoughts seemed far away.

"I'm going to look in on Kaja," Bourne told him.

Don Fernando nodded, but as Bourne turned to go, he caught Bourne's arm. His eyes had snapped back into focus. "Listen, Jason, if anyone can take the Domna down, it's you. But be warned, the Domna is a modern-day hydra. As of this moment, Benjamin El-Arian is its head, but there are others waiting in the wings."

"I've been thinking about that," Bourne said. "Maybe it's not El-Arian I need to concern myself with. Maybe it's Semid Abdul-Qahhar."

Bourne knocked softly on the door to the bedroom Kaja was meant to share with Vegas. He heard a muffled sound, opened the door, and stepped into the room. The lights were off. Moonlight fell across the bed, bathing Kaja in blue light as she lay staring up at the ceiling. With her face mostly in shadow, it was impossible to read her expression.

"Did you get him?"

"The gunman is dead," Bourne said. "Along with several others."

She sighed. "Thank you."

A soft wind blew through the partly open windows, and the curtains shivered.

"I killed Estevan." Her voice, raw with emotion, betrayed her; she had been crying.

"Don't do that," Bourne said.

"Why not? It's true."

"You should have thought of that before you used him as cover."

She threw an arm across her eyes. "I did think about it," she said. "But I was concentrated on my own survival."

"You're only human." Bourne came and stood by her bed. "You should get some rest."

A laugh that was half a cry was torn from her throat, and she took her arm away to look at him. "You must be joking."

He sat on the bed beside her. Her scars shone livid in the pale light. She turned her head to one side and, in a strangled voice, said, "I bring death wherever I go."

"Now you're being melodramatic."

"Am I? Estevan is dead because of me. Don Fernando doesn't want any part of me; I'm sure he told you as much."

When Bourne put a hand on her wrist he could feel her pulse, steady and strong. "Staying here is a dead end."

The wind fluttered the curtains like owl's wings. The moonlight made the bedspread glitter.

Her head turned toward him. "The men you killed, were they the Russians?"

"Yes. Not *grupperovka*, though."

"SVR."

"Not like any government operatives I've ever encountered or heard about."

She rose up on her elbows. "Who, then? Please tell me."

The brief conversation with the Russian up on the roof swirled through Bourne's head. *"You're a hero to us."* "Whoever they are," he said, "they're working against the Domna."

Her eyes glittered. "I don't understand."

"Your father worked for them even while he was employed by the Domna to kill Alex Conklin."

A sharp intake of breath. "He was a mole?"

"I believe so, yes."

Bourne took a deep breath and let it out. "I also think Don Fernando is working for them."

Don Fernando, wreathed in smoke as if he were on fire, watched Bourne disappear down the hallway. Then he turned and rapped softly on one of the bedroom doors. A moment later Essai poked his head out.

Don Fernando nodded to him, and he slipped out of his room, closing the door behind him. Stepping across the hall, he opened the door to Bourne's bedroom.

"Good luck," Don Fernando whispered.

Essai nodded.

"He's exceedingly dangerous."

"Please," Essai said, entering Bourne's room.

He shut the door silently, and Don Fernando melted away down the hallway.

Essai sat in a chair in the corner of Bourne's darkened bedroom. The curtains were drawn back from the window that looked out the south side of the house onto a grove of palms. Piercing the glass, moonlight threw blue smears across one wall. Otherwise, shadows hung in the room like bats. Essai was completely invisible.

Waiting, he thought about his life, about the path he had chosen and others he might have taken instead. He was not content. As far as he was concerned, there was time to be content when he was dead. Life was a constant state of flux, which meant anxiety, tension, and conflict. But what lay most heavily on his mind was how easily friends became enemies by betraying you. He had believed in Severus Domna, had for a time even believed in Benjamin El-Arian. Possibly in the case of El-Arian he had engaged in self-delusion masquerading as wishful thinking. Looking back on it now, he could link small incidents like a string of rotten pearls that should have alerted him to El-Arian's true purpose. Not the least were his trips to Munich and then, more recently, Damascus. In hindsight, it was clear that in Munich he had been meeting secretly with Semid Abdul-Qahhar, plotting the alliance that would ultimately corrupt the Domna beyond its founders' recognition.

A faint sound, no more than the scratching of a field mouse, brought him to full alert. On either side of the window the curtains shifted, and, with them, the pattern of moonlight on the opposite wall. Like a cloud passing in front of the moon, a shadow appeared. For long moments it remained stationary. Then, ever so slowly, it moved against the windowpanes, so gently that if Essai hadn't known better he might have mistaken it for the fluttering of a moth.

He watched, gimlet-eyed, as the window slowly slid up until there was enough space for the shadow to climb silently through.

Only when the shadow turned toward the bed did Essai say, "He's not here."

"Where is he?" Marlon Etana said.

"I warned you," Essai said.

Etana turned slowly around. "I never cared for your warnings."

"I need Bourne. I told you quite clearly this afternoon on the boat."

"I didn't see much point in paying attention."

Essai cleared his throat. "You're going to have to explain that."

"Why?"

Essai brought the Makarov pistol he was holding into the moonlight. It had a suppressor screwed onto the muzzle.

Etana eyed it with what appeared to be a mixture of amusement and resignation. "You see, Essai, this is the difference between us. I shouldn't have to tell you; you should know why Bourne has to die."

Essai waved the Makarov. "Humor me."

Etana sighed. "Bourne killed our people in Tineghir last year. In particular, he murdered Idir."

"Idir Syphax, yes." Essai nodded. "So it's true, then."

"What are you talking about? You know Idir and I had been friends since childhood."

Essai tilted his head to one side. "Rather more than friends, it now appears."

"I don't know what you mean."

"Save it." The flat of Essai's hand cut through the air. "I am not so much a hypocrite as other Arabs. I only care about your sexual orientation as it affects me. Bourne killed your lover—"

"Idir had a wife and children."

"The fact that Bourne killed your lover doesn't make it right to seek revenge."

Etana let out a cruel laugh. "You're a good one to talk. Your entire life is bent toward revenge against your daughter's death."

"Bourne is a dead man walking. As you very well know, he is being stalked by a general of the FSB-2, who, frankly, has a far better chance of—"

"Russians," Etana said contemptuously. "But who cares? You're protecting Bourne now."

"For the moment, yes. Without him I can't bring down the Domna. You have to forget about him. His death is foretold, but not by your hand."

Etana stiffened. "It must be by my hand."

Essai sighed. "Give it up, Marlon."

"I can't," Etana said. "I won't."

"You have no choice." Essai rose.

Etana was on him before he had fully reached his feet. The two of them tumbled over the back of the chair, but, despite the Makarov, Essai was in the vulnerable position. When the back of his knees struck the chair seat he lost his balance and couldn't get a clear shot off. Instead he swung the elongated barrel, opening a red crescent just below Etana's eye. Etana struck him a vicious blow on his sternum, and stars exploded behind his eyes. His breath felt hot in his throat and his lungs had trouble sucking in air.

The two men fought silently and efficiently. They were evenly matched, if not in strength, then in their intimate knowledge of each other, accumulated during their years of friendship. None of that mattered now, the shared history, the scheming together, watching each other's backs. Now only a desperate struggle for survival mattered. One of them would not leave the bedroom alive, and they both knew it.

Essai heard the metallic click, sensed Etana's switchblade, and drove his elbow hard into Etana's stomach. He could see the blade then, thin and wicked looking. It reflected the moonlight as it arced in toward him. But Etana's pass at him was off the mark. The tip of the blade grazed his shirt, the fabric rent open. His skin prickled as if being overrun by ants.

He drove Etana back, fighting to break away so that he could use the Makarov and end the battle. But Etana grabbed hold of him with one hand and would not allow him to gain advantage. Close in, the switchblade was the weapon of choice. If wielded correctly, it could do more damage in one swift cut than a five-minute pounding by a pair of fists.

Essai struck Etana in the mouth. The lips split and blood filled Etana's mouth, staining his teeth vermilion. He spat blood into Essai's eyes and, as Essai reeled back, slashed him with the knife. Essai felt the hot slash and gasped inwardly. He tried for Etana's mouth again, missed, his fist smashing into Etana's cheek instead.

Etana reeled away, taking Essai with him. Essai's hip struck a night table, the lamp tilting against him. He snatched it up and slammed the base against the back of Etana's hand. The switchblade skittered across the floor, fetching up on the rug at the edge of the bed. Etana swung

Essai around and smashed his arm against the wall. He tried to claw the
pistol out of Essai's hand, and Essai drove his elbow into Etana's rib cage.

The two men stumbled backward and hit the floor, rolling over. The
pistol went off as it hit the floorboards, the bullet burying itself in the
ceiling. Etana's head struck the bed frame, and Essai began a flurry of
punches that had Etana's head swinging back and forth like a pendulum.
Etana slumped over, and Essai glimpsed the switchblade out of the corner of his eye. Shoving Etana off him, he stretched out to grab it. As he
did so, Etana chopped the edge of his hand down on the back of Essai's
neck. Snatching up the switchblade, Etana pulled Essai's head back and
slashed his throat from ear to ear.

Patterns of shadow and light crawled across the hotel room's standard-
issue carpet, mimicking the vehicular traffic on the street outside. Maggie stood in the room to which she was supposed to bring Christopher.
One hand was at her temple, the other at her side. Silently, she counted
the lenses of the miniaturized video cameras: in the bar, the TV cabinet,
one corner where the ceiling met the wall. Even the bathroom had one
hidden in a strategic position. The microphones were all on standby, waiting for a word to be spoken. Through one of its many subsidiaries, the
Domna had rented this room for a month. The day after it was booked,
three of its techs spent several hours painstakingly installing the electronic equipment then, using plaster and paint, covering up their work.

It was lonely in here, and she felt the pain of that loneliness as if it
were a loss of a limb. The room had been prepared so lovingly, and yet
now she hated it with every fiber of her being. She was not the same
woman who had arrived in Washington, DC, to do Christopher in. The
change had occurred magically, overnight, and it staggered her. She sat
on the bed now, head in her hands as the lozenges of shadow and light
danced slowly around her.

She had less than twenty hours to lure Christopher up here, to
seduce him into a constellation of compromising positions, and get him
to say the words that would lead to his disgrace. Weeks ago the plan

seemed stellar; it also seemed like fun. Unlike other countries, which the Domna had successfully infiltrated through political and financial means, the United States had proved far more difficult, due to its diverse population, vast expanses, and resounding resilience. It, among all the developed nations, had a highly elaborate network of checks and balances that had foiled the machinations of even the Domna hierarchy.

She had been against attacking America's currency through manipulations of the worldwide gold market, which had been the Domna's plan until Jason Bourne had stopped it cold last year. But she had to admit that changing the target to the Indigo Ridge mine and its vast rare earth riches was brilliant. Members of the Domna's Chinese arm had been successful in choking off the export of rare earths, and now the US military's orders for cutting-edge weaponry were at a complete standstill. Phase One complete. Phase Two, far more difficult to achieve, was the Indigo Ridge mine itself. Through its American operatives, the Domna had received advance word of the US government's intention of reopening the mine by floating an IPO on the stock market. Security was bound to be the primary issue on the American president's mind. Benjamin El-Arian had made a list of the people the president was likely to appoint to direct security at Indigo Ridge. Maggie had seen the shockingly short list, which contained only three names: Brad Findlay, the head of Homeland Security; M. Errol Danziger, the director of Central Intelligence; and Christopher. Danziger was out because, as Benjamin told her, CI's bailiwick was outside the precincts of the United States. The obvious choice was Findlay, but Benjamin knew that the president trusted Hendricks over the others. In El-Arian's opinion, the extreme high priority of the security mission made Hendricks's appointment a fait accompli. Therefore Christopher had been targeted. The idea was to cause a scandal that would derail the security plans while, at the same time, diverting key people's attention from Indigo Ridge during the time the Domna needed to accomplish Phase Two.

But now...Now Maggie didn't know. From one breath to the next everything seemed to have shifted around her, or maybe she was seeing the world with different eyes. Which was why she had taken the

astonishing opportunity Christopher had laid in her lap during their picnic lunch. She had advised him to give up duty at Indigo Ridge—she
knew precisely what he had been alluding to—and dump it into Danziger's incompetent lap. That was the only way she could think of to
save Christopher—and, by extension, herself. Once off Indigo Ridge,
he would be of no use to the Domna. She could fold her operation and
flush it.

She wondered why Benjamin hadn't called her yet. Surely he would
have gotten word of the security shift by now. The suspense was like
a knife in her gut. With a soft groan, she reached over for the phone,
dialed room service, and ordered a porterhouse, steak fries, and creamed
spinach. She might as well eat well in her misery.

She lay back on the bedspread, her arms outstretched on either side.
She inhaled the recycled air of the room while she stared at the ceiling.
Traffic sounds filtering in from outside now seemed cold, alien, lethal.
She shivered, even though her body seemed feverish. Shadows sliding
along the pale blue ceiling created images like clouds in the sky. Star-
tlingly, she saw her father. When she dreamed of him, he was always
leaving, the shadow of his great woolly overcoat filling the doorway to
their house in Stockholm. Beyond, there was only the snow, sparkling
in the wan northern sunlight like piles of sugar. And always he would
fade into that sea of whiteness, as if he had never existed. She would
wake from these dream-memories thinking that she knew what his life
had been like. Other times, she wasn't so certain. And sometimes she
was afraid that her memories of him were part of a fantasy she had con-
cocted as a child, afraid that it would all fall apart in the light of day. But
no, she had to have faith, she had to believe the path she had chosen
was the right one, the only one she could have taken. Yet so much blood
had been spilled, so much grief and heartache. Her mother gone, and
Mikaela dead. She had to believe that these deaths had a purpose, otherwise she would lose her mind.

Just as she was turning over, the Valkyries began to ride on her enci-
phered cell phone, and she thought, *Even here, in the New World, I'm
tethered to my old life*. Lunging for the cell, she answered.

"Where are you?" Benjamin's thin, echoey voice slapped her from across the Atlantic.

"In the hotel room, making sure everything is ready for Hendricks."

"There's been a change of plan."

She shot up, her heart pounding in a leap of hope. "What do you mean?"

"Hendricks has been relieved of security at Indigo Ridge."

"What?" She poured disbelief into her voice. "How could that happen?"

"In the madhouse of American politics, who can say?"

She rose, swung her long legs off the bed, and padded over to the window to stare out at the passing traffic. Her heart lifted and the vise around her lungs released. For the first time in days, she took a deep breath.

"So, where do we go from here?" she said, though she knew perfectly well. "After I close the mission down."

"The mission is still active."

Her breath froze in her throat. "I...I don't understand." Her heart seemed to be flogging her chest to death.

"Hendricks is on to Fitz; he assigned one of his people, Peter Marks, to look into it."

Maggie stared out at the street, where young couples window-shopped arm in arm. A mother jogged by while pushing her baby in one of those special strollers. Horns blared, testament to their drivers' impatience. Maggie wanted desperately to be in one of those cars, to be moving away, to be anywhere but in this room, talking to anyone but Benjamin El-Arian.

She cleared her throat. "Give me two hours. I can get Hendricks to shut the investigation down."

El-Arian didn't bother to ask her how she would do it. "Too late," he said. "Marks found something. We've taken care of him, but that still leaves one loose end."

Maggie pressed her forehead against the window, trying to transfer the coolness of the glass to her burning body. "You don't expect me to kill him?"

"I expect you to follow orders." Benjamin's voice was like a wasp in her ear.

"He's the secretary of defense, Benjamin."

"Get creative, but just get it done," El-Arian said.

There was a long silence during which Maggie could hear the blood rushing in her ears.

"Are you there?"

"Yes," she said, almost inaudibly.

"You know the only way it can be done."

"Yes." Her breath leaving her, as if forever.

"Skara, you knew before you left what this mission could turn into."

She closed her eyes, trying to will herself to remain calm. Nevertheless, her voice held the slightest tremor when she said, "I did."

"Well, then, now you know for certain." El-Arian's voice, like a wasp, delivered its sting. "You are on a suicide mission."

Bourne heard the muffled sound and immediately identified it as a shot with a suppressor-enhanced pistol. Peering out of Kaja's window, he was just in time to see Marlon Etana emerging from his own bedroom window. Etana eeled through a stand of palms, then leapt a low wall. Bourne opened the window and leapt through. He took a line that got him to the wall and over it faster, and he was on Etana within the space of a hundred yards.

They hit the ground together, rolling. Bourne struck first, but Etana managed to tumble away and was up on his feet and running again. Bourne sprinted after him, out of the stand of palms to the verge of the sea road, then across it, dodging speeding Vespas as he headed toward the dockside area.

Ducking into a shipwright's workshop, Etana snatched up an awl, threw it behind him. Bourne ducked and kept on, vaulting over the hull of a boat whose outside was being re-tarred. He grabbed a four-foot length of wood and threw it like a javelin. It struck Etana on the left shoulder, spinning him around even as he staggered, his arms flailing to keep his balance. He struck a wall, which saved him from losing his feet, and he reeled onward, out the other side of the shack, into the spangled night.

The water, rippled with moonlight, was on their right, the seawall on their left. Etana lurched to the left in an attempt to mount the wall, but Bourne cut him off and he was obliged to head the other way, out to the boat slips.

Etana ran out onto one of the long slips, boats on either side. Bourne was gaining on him. He saw this and leapt onto one of the vessels, vanishing behind the cockpit. Instead of heading directly for him, Bourne sprinted toward the adjacent boat, leaping onto it as Etana appeared holding a Taurus PT145 Millennium. Etana looked around, baffled as to where Bourne had gone.

Headlights swept the docks, illuminating for Bourne the path he needed to take; crouching low, he scuttled to the starboard side of the boat and made the jump onto Etana's boat. At once Etana appeared, no doubt having felt the slight rocking Bourne's weight had caused.

The two men stalked each other, using the contours of the boat to shield themselves as they moved about. Etana fired at Bourne as he showed himself briefly. Now that he knew where Etana was, Bourne doubled back, vaulted onto the cockpit, rolled over it, and dropped down on Etana. The Taurus went off again, and then, with Bourne's second blow, it went skittering across the deck.

Etana drove a fist into Bourne's cheek and blood spurted out of Bourne's mouth. He followed that up with a vicious kidney punch that dropped Bourne to the deck, writhing in agony. Etana turned and, snatching up the Taurus, turned back in time to receive a kick that flattened his nose. He staggered backward, blood gushing over his face, but still managed to bring the Taurus into firing position. But before he had a chance to squeeze off a shot, Bourne drove the end of his fingers into the spot just below Etana's sternum.

All the air went out of Etana, he doubled over, and Bourne grabbed the Taurus out of his hand. He jammed the muzzle of the pistol into the side of Etana's head.

"Stop!" a voice called from dockside. "That's enough!"

Bourne turned and saw Don Fernando standing in a spread-legged shooter's stance, arms straight out in front of him.

"Put the Taurus down, Jason, and step away." When Bourne hesitated, Don Fernando cocked the hammer of the Magnum .357 Colt Python. "Now or never. It will only take one shot."

Book Four

25

I'D KILL YOU right here, General Karpov, but killing isn't allowed in the sacred grounds of the Mosque." Zachek prodded Boris in the small of his back. "Not that I wouldn't mind."

The two men with him grinned, waving their weapons as if they were flags.

Outside, the night had formed a gritty layer, a tense gray band that seemed at any moment ready to snap back into its original shape. They waded through this as if it were the shallows of the ocean.

Zachek bundled Boris into a waiting car. He was squeezed in between Zachek and one of the gunmen.

"How does it feel?" Zachek said. "To be on your own, no direction home?"

The second gunman slid in beside the driver, and they took off, crossing the river, driving deep into Sendling, one of Munich's two industrial districts. At this time of night, there were few vehicles on the streets and no foot traffic whatsoever. The driver pulled to the curb along Kyreinstrasse and they got out. The driver unlocked a door and they entered what appeared to be an abandoned building. The stench of the past was strong in Boris's nostrils. The walls were peeling, a chair with a broken leg lay on its side, cartons were falling apart. Everywhere he looked was decay, as if they were inside a huge animal slowly dying.

While the two gunmen looked to their weapons, Zachek led Boris to the rear wall and turned him so his back was facing it. "This is where it will happen," he said.

"As long as it's quick," Boris said.

"We're all professionals here." He pulled Boris's arms behind his back, but instead of tying his wrists, he placed Boris's Tokarev into his waiting hands. Then he moved back smartly and stood to one side, so that both the gunman and the driver, leaning casually against a crumbling pillar, were in his line of vision. He, too, held his hands behind his back, slipping a Taurus from beneath his jacket where it had lain inside his belt.

He raised his voice. "Any last requests, General? Never mind, there's no one to pay them any mind."

The gunmen chuckled as they raised their weapons. Boris brought his right arm around in front of him and squeezed off two shots. As both gunmen fell, bullets through their brains, Zachek shot the driver through the heart.

In the smoking space, amid the deafening silence that comes after gunfire, the two men stood looking at each other. Zachek's eye was still closed, the flesh around it multihued and puffy. He was the first to lower his weapon. Boris followed suit, walking toward the other man.

"What is it about little pricks," he said, "that makes them so reliable?"

Zachek grinned.

When Robbinet arrived at the hospital where Aaron had taken Soraya, he discovered that the doctors who had treated her were all off shift and had left for the night. He looked at his watch: It was the hour before dawn. He asked for the best neurologist on staff, was told he was busy, and then produced his credentials. Within five minutes a dapper young man, with longish hair that marked him as something of a maverick, appeared and introduced himself as Dr. Longeur. To his credit, he was already leafing through Soraya's chart.

"I don't think she should have checked herself out," he said with a frown. "There are a number of tests—"

"Come with me, Doctor," Robbinet said crisply, leading him out of the hospital. He told Longeur that Soraya was missing. "My job is to find this woman, Doctor. Your job is to make sure she is physically sound."

"It would be best if she returned to the hospital."

"Under the circumstances, that may not be possible." Robbinet scanned the dark streets. "I have to assume she will be unwilling to return."

"Is she phobic?"

"You can ask her that when we find her."

Together they questioned the area habitués, people who, Robbinet was sure, had been there when Soraya had fled. Robbinet showed them a photo of Soraya.

"These people need help. Some desperately," Robbinet said.

Dr. Longeur shrugged. "The hospital is already overloaded with patients in worse shape, what would you have us do?"

They went on with their interviews. Finally, they found a disheveled woman who claimed to have seen Soraya and the direction in which she went. She held out a trembling hand and Robbinet gave her some euros. He turned away, disgusted; it was impossible to know whether she was telling the truth.

They sat in his car while the driver waited for instructions. Robbinet called Soraya's cell phone again and got no answer, but then he wasn't expecting any. The patrols Aaron had sent out had yet to find her. He didn't think they would. She was a highly skilled field agent. If she didn't want to be caught, she wouldn't be. He sensed that she was following her own lead, that after her friend's murder she didn't want to be encumbered by anyone, even the Quai d'Orsay. He didn't agree with her decision, but he understood it. Still, he feared for her life. She had been near death and had lost someone close to her. It seemed likely that when it came to her own condition she was not thinking clearly.

He gave his driver the address of the Monition Club, but when he arrived the place was lit up like a Christmas tree and there were so many Quai d'Orsay and police personnel around, he knew she hadn't come back here. Where then?

He glanced at his watch again. The sky to the east was lightening. He reviewed the situation. He knew everything Aaron knew, but it was possible Soraya knew more. She had been certain that the murder trail led back to the Île de France Bank, outside of which her contact had been run down. He tried to put himself in her head. If she had a goal, why go to ground? Maybe because at night she could not gain access to wherever she needed to go. He leaned forward; his gut told him where she was headed. He was taking a gamble, but he did not know what else to do.

"Place de l'Iris," he told his driver. "La Défense."

It was where he would go if he were her.

Jason, please step away," Don Fernando said. "I won't ask you again."

"This is a mistake," Bourne said.

Don Fernando shook his head, but the muzzle of the Magnum never wavered. Bourne took a step back and Don Fernando fired. The bullet struck Etana between the eyes. He was thrown back so hard he flipped over the railing, tumbling into the sea. The water darkened with the spread of his blood.

Bourne glanced over the side of the boat. "Like I said, a mistake." He looked back at Don Fernando, who was advancing toward him across the dock. "He could have told us a lot."

Don Fernando stepped onto the boat, the Magnum held at his side. "He would have told us nothing, Jason. You know these people as well as I do. They have no conception of pain. They have suffered all their lives; martyrdom is all they think about. They are only shadows in this life; they are dead men walking."

"Essai?"

"Etana slit his throat before he leapt out the window." Don Fernando sat down on the wooden cowling. "Etana came to kill you, Jason, for what you did in Tineghir last year. Essai tried to talk him out of it, but Etana was a stubborn man. So Essai and I hit upon a plan. I'd keep you out of your room while he slipped in and waited."

"He was waiting for Etana."

"That's right."

"It's a pity Essai is dead."

Don Fernando passed a hand across his eyes. "There are too many deaths on my plate these days."

Bourne thought about the shipment lying in the warehouse across the city waiting to be delivered to El-Gabal in Damascus. What was in those twelve crates, who was the real sender—the Domna or the organization Christien Norén had worked for—and was Don Fernando a member of that same group? It seemed the answers lay at Avenue Choukry Kouatly.

He tensed as a police cruiser appeared, heading down the dock as slowly and purposefully as a shark approaches a dead fish.

Don Fernando took out a cigar, bit off the end, and lit it. "Easy," he said as the cruiser slowed to a halt. "I called them."

Two uniforms and a detective in a suit piled out. Don Fernando directed them to Etana. While the uniforms went to inspect the corpse floating by the side of the boat, the detective headed straight to Don Fernando, who offered him a cigar.

The detective nodded, bit off the end, and lit up. He made no attempt to inspect the murder scene or glance Bourne's way.

"The dead man's a foreign national, you say." The detective's voice was deep and phlegmy, as if he was fighting a chest cold.

"In Spain illegally," Don Fernando said. "A drug dealer."

"We have very harsh penalties for drug dealers," the detective said around a cloud of smoke. "As you know."

Don Fernando inspected the end of his cigar. "I saved the state a lot of money, and you, Diaz, a great deal of time."

Diaz nodded sagely. "True, Don Fernando, and for this service you have the gratitude of the state." He let out another cloud of smoke and stared up into the spangled sky. "Let me share my thoughts as I was driven here. Our precinct is a poor one, Don Fernando, and with the debt crisis, budgets are cut and then cut again."

"A sad state of affairs. Please allow me." Don Fernando reached into his breast pocket and drew out a folded wad of euros, which he pressed into the detective's hand. "Leave the body to me."

Diaz nodded. "As always, Don Fernando." Then he turned on his heel and shouted to his men, "¡Vámanos, muchachos!" He strode off, the two uniforms in his wake.

When the cruiser had backed up and taken off down the sea road, Don Fernando gestured. "The way of the world never changes, eh, Jason?" He gestured. "Come, now we attend to Marlon Etana."

"Not you," Bourne said as he went back to the side of the boat. "I'll do it."

Reaching down, he removed a boat hook from the side of the cockpit, snagged the collar of Etana's jacket, and hauled him up until his head, arms, and torso balanced on the gunwale. Don Fernando grabbed Etana's belt and dragged him the rest of the way into the boat. For a moment he stared down at the corpse, which was spewing seawater out of its open mouth. Then he crouched down beside Etana, his knees creaking.

Bourne watched as Don Fernando's hands pulled aside Etana's jacket and went through all his pockets as skillfully as a sneak thief. Don Fernando handed Bourne Etana's phone, wallet, and keys. Then he rose and hauled the anchor out of its compartment in the bow of the boat. Unhooking the chain from its attaching ring, he wrapped it around Etana's corpse.

"Let's get him over the side," Don Fernando said.

"In a minute." Crouching down, Bourne pried open Etana's mouth and tested his teeth. A moment later he held up the false tooth that contained the cyanide capsule. When he rose, he produced the false tooth he had taken off the Russian in the warehouse. Holding one in each hand, he showed them to Don Fernando.

"Where did you get that?" the older man said.

"I went inside the warehouse, where I killed the gunman and his driver," Bourne said. "The gunman bit into his while I was questioning him. This one is from the driver." When Don Fernando said nothing, Bourne added, "This hollow tooth is an old NKVD trick to keep its members from talking if they were captured."

Don Fernando pointed to Etana. "I can't get him over the side myself."

"Only if I get answers."

Don Fernando nodded.

Bourne pocketed the suicide capsules and they hoisted Etana up over the gunwale and into the water. He sank out of sight immediately.

Don Fernando sat on the gunwale, facing Bourne. He seemed very tired, and suddenly old, shrunken in on himself. "Marlon Etana was put in place to inform on the Domna."

"In other words, he was Christien Norén's replacement."

"Precisely." Don Fernando rubbed his hands down his trousers. "The problem was, Etana went rogue."

"El-Arian turned him?"

Don Fernando shook his head. "He made a secret deal with Essai when Essai became a dissident."

"Etana belonged to the same organization that Christien did, that you do." Bourne dealt the older man a hard look. "It's past time you told me about it."

"You're right, of course." Don Fernando ran a hand across his eyes. "Maybe if I had, Essai would still be alive." He waited for a moment, as if deciding how best to explain the next part. At length, he pushed himself off the gunwale. "It's time for a drink and some serious talk."

Don Fernando chose a seaside café that looked closed, but wasn't. Many of the chairs were overturned on the tabletops and a young boy with hair down to his shoulders was sweeping the floor in a desultory manner, as if he were already asleep.

The proprietor waddled out from behind the bar to shake Don Fernando's hand and escort them to a table. Don Fernando ordered brandy but Bourne waved away the notion of alcohol. He wanted his head clear.

"When my father died, everything changed," Don Fernando said. "You must understand: My father was everything to me. I cherished my mother, yes, but she was ill, bedridden much of my life."

When the snifter was set upon the table, Don Fernando stared into the amber liquid. He wet his lips with it before he began. "My father was a big man in every way imaginable. He was tall, and powerful, both physically and in spirit. He dominated every room he walked into. People were frightened of him, I could see it very clearly in their eyes; when they shook hands with him, they trembled."

The proprietor appeared with a glass of sherry and set it down in front of Bourne, even though he hadn't ordered it. He shrugged, as if to say: *A man should not engage in serious conversation without proper fortification.*

"Starting when I was seven, he took me hunting," Don Fernando continued when the proprietor had returned to his place behind the bar. "This was in Colombia. I shot my first gray fox when I was eight. I had tried for a year but could not pull the trigger. I wept the first time I saw my father shoot one. My father took me over to it, dipped his fingertips into its blood, and smeared my lips with it. I recoiled, gagging. And then, under his stern gaze, I felt ashamed. So I screwed up my courage, returned to the fox, bloodied my own fingers, and stuck them in my mouth. My father smiled, then, and I never before or since felt such a sense of complete satisfaction."

Bourne sensed that these memories unnerved Don Fernando, that he was privileged to be hearing them.

"As I said, when my father died everything changed. I took over his business, for which he had been training me for years. It was difficult to see him on his deathbed, so frail, laboring to take a breath, this man who had felled trees and enemies with equal ease and zeal. We all come to this point in our lives, I know, but with my father it was different because of what he had trained me for, what was waiting for me the moment he passed."

Don Fernando had drained his glass. Now he signaled for more. The proprietor came with the bottle, filled the snifter, then left the bottle.

Don Fernando nodded his thanks before he went on. "In the last years of his life, my father introduced me to a number of men. All of them were Russian, all of them frightened me on some"—he waved a hand—"I don't know, some primitive level. In their eyes I saw a world filled with shadow, piled with death." He shrugged. "I don't know how else to explain their effect on me.

"Gradually, though, I grew used to them. The darkness that had fallen over me didn't recede, rather it became understandable. I was introduced to death, and then I had cause to recall my first blooding, and I was never so grateful for how my father helped me. Because these men dealt in death—as, it turned out, did my father."

Don Fernando held out his hand and when Bourne extended his, he gripped it tightly, clapping his other hand over them both.

"As I said, Jason, all of the men my father introduced me to were Russian—all, that is, save one. Christien Norén."

26

I NEED A CELL," Peter Marks said. He was sitting up in bed, though he was able to walk now without panting like an overtaxed engine.

Deron dug out a burner cell in a blister pack. "You may be surprised to know that whoever was after you is even more powerful than we thought."

Peter cocked his head. "Nothing would surprise me now. How's that?"

Deron slit open the blister pack, freeing the phone. "I sent Ty to the Metro police to find out about your kidnappers. They claim they have nothing. Someone did make a nine-one-one call, but by the time a patrol car arrived on the scene, there was nothing to see, no bodies, no ambulance, and obviously, no you."

Peter sighed. "Back to square one."

"Not exactly." Deron handed over what appeared to be a human tooth. "Ty found this at the scene and grabbed it before he helped you onto his motorcycle. You must have knocked it out of one of your kidnappers."

Peter turned the tooth over in his hands. "How does it help me?"

As he probed at it, Deron said, "Watch it!" and snatched it out of his hand. "This only looks like a tooth. It's actually hollow, filled with liquid hydrogen cyanide."

"A suicide pill?" Peter said. "I thought that went out with the NKVD."

Deron rolled the tooth between his fingertips like a marble. "Apparently not."

"But it *is* Russian in origin."

Deron nodded. "So now we know the country of origin of your kidnappers. Does that help?"

Peter frowned. "I'm not sure yet."

Deron activated the phone, added a package of minutes, and handed it to Peter. "You have twenty minutes of time, overseas included," he said. "After that it's trash."

Peter nodded gratefully. Deron knew his security backward and forward. After Deron left the room, he punched in the cell number of Soraya's contact in Damascus whom he'd called days ago when he first read about El-Gabal, the defunct mining company Roy FitzWilliams had consulted for before he was hired by Indigo Ridge.

"Ashur," he said when the voice answered, "this is Peter—"

"Peter Marks? We thought you had been neutralized."

A trickle like ice water rode down Peter's spine. "Who is this? Where's Ashur?"

"Ashur is dead. Or nearly so."

Peter felt a prickle at the nape of his neck. Using the suicide tooth as a cue, he said, "*Kahk dyelayoot vlee znayetye menya?*" How do you know me?

"Ashur told us," the voice replied in kind. An evil chuckle. "He didn't want to, but in the end he really had no choice."

What the hell are Russians doing in Damascus? Peter asked himself. "Why did you try to kill me?"

"Why are you interested in El-Gabal? It's been out of business for years."

Peter's anger kicked in, but he was careful to keep it in check. "If you kill Ashur—"

"His death is already assured," the voice said with a maddening serenity.

With an enormous effort, Peter put Ashur aside and gathered his thoughts. As a stab in the dark, he said, "El-Gabal isn't defunct. It's of too much importance to you."

Silence.

I'm right, El-Gabal still exists. "I have the suicide tooth from one of your men. Once I pried it out of his mouth, he talked. I know El-Gabal is the center of everything."

More silence, hollow and somehow eerie.

"Hello? Hello?"

Dead air pulsed in his ear. Peter hit REDIAL, but got nothing, not even Ashur's voice mail. The tenuous line of communication had been cut.

Your friendship was with the girls' father, not their mother," Bourne said.

Don Fernando nodded.

"And you never told them."

He took another sip. It might have been a trick of the light, but his eyes now seemed to be the precise color of the brandy. "I only know Kaja. The truth is far too complex for her to—"

"She's been looking for answers to who her father was all her adult life," Bourne said with some force. "You should have told her."

"I couldn't," Don Fernando said. "The truth is far too dangerous for the girls to know."

Bourne disengaged his hand from the older man's. "What gives you the right to make that decision?"

"Mikaela's death gives me the right. She found out; the truth killed her."

Bourne sat back, regarding Don Fernando. He was like a chimera. Every time you thought you had him figured out, he changed shape the way Bourne himself changed identities.

Don Fernando, gazing deep into Bourne's eyes, shook his head. "At least give me a fair hearing before you find me guilty."

Your eye looks terrible," Boris said. "I'll get you a steak to put on it."

"No time," Zachek said, closing the connection on his cell phone, "Cherkesov was spotted going through security at the Munich airport."

Boris stepped to the curb and flagged down a taxi. "Where is he headed?"

"Damascus," Zachek said as they climbed in.

Boris told the driver their destination, and he headed toward the nearest entrance to the A 92 Munich–Deggendorf Autobahn.

"Syria." Boris sat back against the seat. "What the hell is he doing in Damascus?"

"We don't know," Zachek said, "but we intercepted a call on his cell phone. He's been given instructions to go to El-Gabal, a mining company on Avenue Choukry Kouatly."

"Curious."

"It gets curiouser," Zachek said. "So far as we've been able to ascertain, El-Gabal has been defunct since the 1970s."

"Clearly, your intel is wrong," Boris said drily.

"I'll try not to revert, if you don't," Zachek said.

"We made a deal that's satisfactory to both of us," Boris said. "That doesn't mean I have to like you."

"But you have to trust me."

"It's not you I worry about," Boris said. "It's SVR."

"You mean Beria."

Boris stared out the window, relieved that he was getting out of Germany. "I take care of Cherkesov and you take care of Beria. It's a straightforward bargain." But he knew nothing was straightforward in their line of work, where lying was not only endemic, but necessary for survival.

"It's a matter of trust," Zachek said, punching in a coded number on his phone. "It always is." He spoke into it for several moments, then disconnected. "We have a ticket waiting for you at the airport. Cherkesov took the four PM flight. We got you on the six forty. You'll arrive in Damascus just after two tomorrow morning. The good news is your flight is shorter. You'll have an hour in Damascus before he arrives." He was texting a message. "We'll have a man waiting to take you to—"

"I don't want one of your men looking over my shoulder."

Zachek glanced up. "I assure you—"

"I know Damascus as well as I know Moscow," Boris said with such finality that Zachek shrugged.

"As you wish, General." He put away his phone and cleared his throat. "We are putting our lives in each other's hands."

"That's not wise," Boris said. "We scarcely know each other."

"What's to be done about Ivan Volkin?"

Boris understood Zachek's point. Boris and Ivan went back decades. Their friendship had not protected him from Volkin's betrayal.

"You won't be safe until he's planted," Zachek said in such an offhand manner that Boris laughed.

"First things first, Zachek."

The other man smiled. "You called me by name."

Bourne willed himself to relax. "Go on."

"Almaz was born during the dark days of Stalin and his chief enforcer, Lavrentiy Beria." Don Fernando cupped the snifter, inhaling the brandy fumes before drinking again. He did it slowly, as if it was a ritual that calmed him, brought him back to himself. "As you doubtless know, Beria was named head of NKVD in 1938. From that moment on, the secret police became the state-sanctioned executioners Stalin lusted for. At Yalta, Stalin introduced him to President Roosevelt as 'our Himmler.'

"Beria's bloodthirsty ways are well documented, but, believe me, the truth is far more dreadful. Kidnappings, torture, rape, maiming, and death became the order of the day for his enemies and their families— women and children, it was all the same to him. And as the months turned into years there were those within the NKVD who became disgusted with the unrelenting cruelty and violence. It was impossible to voice their dissent, so they went underground, forming a group they called Almaz—diamond—because diamonds are hidden, created under tremendous pressure deep within the earth."

Don Fernando's eyes were blue again, glinting like the morning sea. He had finished his brandy and he poured himself another.

"These men were clever. They knew their survival depended not only on the absolute secrecy of Almaz, but on expanding it beyond the borders of the Soviet Union. Allies were their only long-term hope, both in terms of power and influence, and also as an escape conduit should the need arise to flee the motherland."

"That's where your father came in," Bourne said.

Don Fernando nodded. "My father started in Colombia working the oil fields, but soon became bored. 'Fernando,' he used to say to me, 'I am plagued with a restless mind. You are forbidden to follow in my footsteps.' He was joking, of course, but only slightly. He shipped me off to London, where I took a First in economics at Oxford. But the truth was, I enjoyed physical labor, so when I returned to Colombia, much to my father's horror, I went to work in the oil fields, working my way up. I found great satisfaction in eventually buying my former bosses out.

"My father, meanwhile, turned his restless mind to international banking, founding Aguardiente Bancorp." He knocked down his third brandy and attacked the bottle again. "My three brothers were, unfortunately, of no use whatsoever. One died of a drug overdose, another died in a cartel shoot-out. The third died, I think, of a broken heart."

He waved his hand again. "In any event, it was through Aguardiente's increasingly lucrative international deal-making that my father came in contact with the dissidents of Almaz. There is no more ardent capitalist than a converted socialist. So it was with my father. He sympathized completely with Almaz and pledged to help them in any way he could. Not without compensation, however. Almaz systematically raided Stalin's coffers. My father laundered their money, then invested it most wisely, including his generous cut. They all grew rich and increasingly powerful.

"By the time Beria was finally forced out by Khrushchev and his allies, Almaz was a force to be reckoned with, so much so that its members could have surfaced, but they had learned not to believe in any form of Soviet government. Besides, they were comfortable in the shadows, and that is where they chose to remain, influencing events behind the scenes."

"But their ambitions outgrew the Soviet Union," Bourne interjected.

"Yes. They foresaw the Soviet Union's demise. With my father's urging, they diversified."

"And by this time I imagine your father was a full-fledged member," Bourne said. "Joining Almaz was what he had trained you for."

Don Fernando nodded. "I joined Christien Norén as the first non-Russian members of Almaz."

"You were the brains and he was the brawn, the enforcer."

Don Fernando finished off his brandy, but didn't refill his glass. His eyes had taken on a slightly glassy, alcohol-fueled look. "It's true that Christien was very good at killing people. I think he might have actually enjoyed it."

He threw some bills on the table and both men rose, strolling out of the café and up the sea road toward Don Fernando's house. The night was exceptionally clear, the moon the palest yellow, riding high in the cloudless sky. Rigging clanged arrhythmically against masts in the gusts of salt wind off the sea. The far-off roars of Vespas lent the end of the night a melancholy note.

"If Christien was a mole inside the Domna," Bourne said, "then I assume the two groups were antagonists."

"I would say, rather, that their spheres of influence overlapped. Then Benjamin El-Arian made his deal with the devil."

"Semid Abdul-Qahhar."

Don Fernando nodded. "It was then we realized we had made a terrible mistake. We started the rumor that Treadstone had targeted the Domna. We knew that the Domna would dispatch Christien to terminate your old boss."

"You wanted Alex Conklin dead."

"On the contrary, we wanted Christien to recruit Conklin into Almaz."

Bourne knew that Conklin was of Russian extraction. He had hated the communists with every fiber of his being. Almaz would have had a good chance of recruiting him to its cause.

"It would have been the ultimate coup," Don Fernando continued, "accomplished right under the Domna's nose."

Up ahead, Don Fernando's street came into view, the lights in his house warm and beckoning.

"But the plan went wrong," Bourne said. "Conklin killed Christien and El-Arian made his deal with his own enforcer, Semid Abdul-Qahhar."

"Worse, the Domna became aware of Almaz as its implacable enemy, and now we are in a state of all-out war."

There were a number of ways into a bank and Soraya knew them all. Ten AM found her walking down Avenue Montaigne and into the Chanel boutique, where she bought a day outfit that fit her perfectly. It reeked of moneyed status. In a nearby boutique she used her Treadstone credit card, which had no spending limit, to purchase a pair of Louboutin shoes that complemented her ensemble. As she was signing the receipt, she was overcome again; directed to the bathroom by a concerned saleswoman, she rushed in, slammed the door behind her, and had just enough time to make it to the toilet before she retched so violently she imagined she was giving up the lining of her stomach. Now she began to worry; vomiting was a common symptom of a serious concussion. Her heart was like a trip-hammer in her chest and, feeling abruptly weak, she grabbed onto the stall door. Gritting her teeth, she took deep breaths and carried on.

It took her ten minutes to wash her face, rinse out her mouth, and recover sufficiently to be seen, but by that time her headache had bloomed into a violent pounding. She was so pale, the saleswoman offered to call a doctor. Soraya declined politely, but asked where she might purchase makeup.

Out on the street, the sunlight hurt her eyes and increased the pain in her head. Half an hour later, after she'd spent nearly three hundred euros, having designer makeup professionally applied, she looked more or less normal. Then, wearing a pair of outsize sunglasses she had selected at the shop, she strode down the street, entered the Élysée Bank branch a block from the Seine, and tapped into the Treadstone account.

She had a bank officer call her a taxi, asking for a late-model Mercedes. While she waited, she called her destination and, in her best, clipped Parisian French, made an appointment with the vice president under the name of Mademoiselle Gobelins. When the Mercedes arrived, she gave the driver the address of her destination.

Ignoring the intermittent pounding in her head, she pushed through the glass doors of the bank building at the stroke of eleven thirty. A receptionist's podium rose imposingly in the center of the space, flanked on either side by large potted traveler's palms. Directly behind the podium were the glass doors to the bank. She stood in front of them for a moment, feeling lost, ill, and slightly fearful, but then a feeling of elation gripped her, as if she had reached the end of her investigation. With an effort, she put aside the grief and despair of last night and drew on her anger to help her concentrate on her mission.

Inside, the bank was an open space with long pedestals for people to write on. To the right, a line of teller cages stretched away, to the left a gated wooden half wall led to a row of cubicles inside which bank officers dutifully listened to customer requests or brought their paperwork up to date. At the rear of the room was a high wood-paneled wall in the center of which were a series of digital clocks showing the time in Paris, New York, London, and Moscow. On either side were staircases leading up to the second-floor offices where the highest-ranking bank officers worked. That was where Soraya needed to go.

She gave her name to the information officer, who immediately picked up a phone and called upstairs. Moments later a guard came and accompanied her across the room. She was buzzed in through a gate, and the guard brought her to the center of the rear wall. At the touch of a button, a panel slid open and Soraya stepped into a sumptuously appointed elevator. The guard accompanied her up to the second floor, directing her to the right, down a softly lit corridor. Soraya could hear the discreet *tap-tap-tap* of fingernails on computer keyboards as she passed open doorways to right and left.

Her appointment was with M. Sigismond, a tall man, slim but

powerful looking, with light brown hair, parted on one side, who sprang around his desk to greet her. Extending his hand, he said, "So very nice to make your acquaintance, Mademoiselle Gobelins." His French contained a slight Germanic starchiness. Holding her hand by the tips of her fingers, he kissed the back, then indicated a plush sofa on her right. "Please have a seat."

When he had settled himself beside her, he said, "I understand that you would like to make the Nymphenburg Landesbank of Munich your financial institution of choice."

"That's right," Soraya said. She thought M. Sigismond's brown eyes were the product of colored contacts. "Now that I've come into my inheritance, your Wealth Management Division has been recommended to me as being the best in Western Europe."

M. Sigismond's smile could not have been warmer. "My dear, it is gratifying, is it not, to know that all one's hard work has had its desired result."

"It certainly is."

"And your complete wish is?"

"To open an account. I have a sizable sum to deposit with more to come. And I will require investment assistance."

"But of course. Splendid!" M. Sigismond slapped his hands decisively on his thighs. "Now, before we proceed further, I would like to introduce you to the gentleman behind the grand success of our Wealth Management." He rose and opened a door in the wall that Soraya had not previously noticed. In strode a man of distinctly Middle Eastern descent. He was dark in every way imaginable, and almost magnetically handsome.

"Ah, Mademoiselle Gobelins, what a pleasure to meet you," he said, gliding toward her. "My name is Benjamin El-Arian."

Bourne stopped them as they were nearing Don Fernando's house.

"What is it?" Don Fernando said.

"I don't know." Bourne moved them into the clattering shadows of the palms on the sea side of the road. "Something's wrong. Stay here."

"I don't think so." Don Fernando raised the Colt Python. "Don't worry, I won't slow you down."

Bourne knew there was no point in arguing. Together the two men moved from shadow to shadow until they were opposite the street where the house sat. They stayed there, still and silent, until Bourne caught a shadow darting across one of the lighted windows. It was too large to be Kaja. He pointed, and Don Fernando nodded. He had seen the shadow and understood its implications.

Bourne turned to the older man. "I'm going in through the bedroom window Etana used, but I need a diversion."

"Leave that to me," Don Fernando said.

"Give me three minutes to get into place," Bourne said before he set off across the almost deserted road.

He moved silently from shadow to shadow, approaching the house via an indirect route. Ahead of him, between the street and the stand of palms through which he had chased Etana, was a patch of open ground lit up by streetlights. Moving around to the other side of the house, he saw that the neighboring home was quite close. Bundled telephone and electrical wires stretched down lower and lower house-to-house from the high metal pole on the sea road. He had little time to second-guess himself. He unbuckled his belt, then scaled the side of the neighboring house. Tossing the buckle end of the belt over the wires, he grasped both ends and slid down the wire bundle until he reached the shadows of Don Fernando's house, and climbed down.

As he ran through the shadows at the rear, he heard gunshots. Racing to his bedroom window, he climbed through into darkness.

He stood absolutely still, listening with every part of his body. The smell of industrial-strength cleanser came to him, but no trace of Essai's blood. There was no sign of the corpse; Don Fernando's people were both fast and efficient. Bourne stood just inside the door, controlling his breathing. He could hear the soft hum of the heating system, the squeak of the window sashes as gusts of wind buffeted them. Then he heard the creaks of the floorboards. Kaja's weight was not great enough to create that sound, so at least one man was in the house. Then a second creak, in a different room, told him there were at least two men in the house. Where was Kaja? Tied up? Wounded? Dead?

Passing through the partially open door, he picked his way down the long corridor that led to the living room and the front of the house. His nostrils flared as he smelled the alien presence. Pushing the door to Kaja's bedroom open, he found it empty. The coverlet was unrumpled; he didn't smell her. Whatever she had done after Don Fernando had left, she hadn't been in the room. He passed the kitchen, which was empty.

The end of the hallway opened up into the living room. Through the French doors, the enclosed garden looked windblown and abandoned. She wasn't out there, either. Bourne saw the two armed men. One was at the front door, the other was coming back inside after checking the cause of the gunshots.

"Nothing," he said to his partner in Russian. "Must have been a truck backfiring."

Bourne launched himself at them, knocking the one on the right flat on his back. He landed a heavy blow on the point of the Russian's chin, then twisted his torso to give himself enough leverage to engage the one on the left. He had just locked his hand over the barrel of the Glock when Don Fernando burst through the front door. His cell phone was clapped to one ear, his Colt Python pointed at the floor.

"Stop! All of you!" he cried. "Jason, these men are Almaz!"

Bourne relaxed his body and the two Russians stirred. The one he had punched groaned and rolled over.

"What are they doing here?" Bourne said, gaining his feet. "Where's Kaja?"

Don Fernando took the phone from his ear. "She's gone, Jason."

"Kidnapped?"

The second Russian shook his head. "She was observed leaving here on her own. That's why we were dispatched."

Don Fernando glowered at him. "And?"

The Almaz agent sighed. "She's gone. We could find no sign of her in the area, no clue inside the house as to where she went." He looked up at Don Fernando. "She's ghosted away."

Skara stared at herself in the hotel's bathroom mirror and saw a face she scarcely recognized. One thing was for certain, she was no longer Margaret Penrod. *Who am I?* she wondered with a shiver like ice water down her back. The question terrified her; the reality of it brought her unbearable grief. Her fingers curled, the nails like knife blades as she scored welts on her palms. She felt the fire, but it was only skin-deep.

She'd had every intention of going back to her apartment, but had stayed in the rigged hotel room, either out of self-punishment or spite, possibly both.

She closed her eyes. Memories flooded back like blood from an open wound. Her father had told her to keep Mikaela safe before he left for the last time. Skara was the only one who had known he was never coming back. He had confided in her, though it was only much later that she understood why; he never said a word about his life to Viveka. Possibly he had seen something of himself in Skara; certainly he had passed things on to her, had taught her how to take care of herself and her sisters. But the Russians had come in the middle of the day when she had mistakenly thought it would be safe to get food. She had left Mikaela with a gun, she had been gone only fifteen minutes, but as it turned out they were the last fifteen minutes of her sister's life. That was when she and Kaja had decided to leave Stockholm, leave Sweden altogether, split up and have no contact with each other.

She stared at her reflection in the mirror. The welts she had scored on her palms seemed to pulse in the fluorescent light, as if alive. When she switched off the light it seemed to her that she had winked out of existence.

Padding across the room, she reached into the mini-bar for a bottle of vodka. It was so small, she poured it and a second into a thick, heavy-bottomed lowball glass she took off a metal shelf just above the half fridge. She drank off a quarter, then put the glass down on the night table.

She disrobed slowly and provocatively, performing for the video cameras as if they were switched on. Kneeling with her legs apart, she gripped her bare breasts, squeezing until tears ran down her cheeks.

Then she lay on her stomach, her hands beneath her at the fulcrum of her thighs, working her fingers in a way that sent a mixture of pleasure and pain through her as she wept into a pillow.

She dragged out the pleasure-pain as long as she could, riding the crests until she fell over onto the other side. When it was over, her body drained, her mind empty, there came a respite, but so brief she winced when the responsibilities of her current life flooded back.

She was trapped in a morally perverse world, trapped in a place and time she had worked toward, but now regarded as repellent. For the first time in many years, she wished Kaja were with her, or at least accessible so she could pour out her current agony before the only other soul on earth who might understand. But she had no idea of Kaja's whereabouts, or even her current identity. There was no hope on that score.

Then what about Christopher? The room's air conditioner started up, and a cold wind blew across her back, raising goose bumps. She had run out of options—there was Christopher and then there was Benjamin, the two opposing forces in her current life. Everything had changed during the last phone call with Benjamin; she had to ignore her heart, she had to stay as far away from Christopher as possible.

Making that decision heartened her, and she rose off the bed. She stared at the table on which rested the meal room service had delivered hours ago. She hadn't touched it and now never would. She picked up the tray and carried it to the door. Balancing it on one hand, she opened the door. The moment she did so, three men waiting in the hallway jumped her.

If he were to be honest with himself, Aaron was doing a whole bunch of nothing when he caught the call from his boss.

"She's not at the bank," Robbinet's crisp voice said in his ear. "You'd better hope she isn't lying somewhere in the gutter unconscious, or with a bullet through her head."

Aaron's mind raced. Like Robbinet, he had assumed that Soraya would head for the Île de France Bank in La Défense. He would have if he were her.

"Wait a minute," he said, suddenly remembering a certain detail of their interrogation of M. Marchand. "The finances of the Monition Club run through Île de France, but the managing entity is Nymphenburg Landesbank of Munich."

"Never heard of it," Robbinet snapped. "Is it represented in Paris?"

"Just a moment." Aaron did a Google search on his cell phone. "Yes, sir, there's one office. Seventy Boulevard de Courcelles. Just opposite Parc Monceau."

"Meet me there in fifteen minutes," Robbinet said. "And God help you if she's injured, or worse."

The plates, cutlery, and food went flying as Skara drove the edge of the tray into the leading man's throat, but the other two men shoved her back into the room with such force she tumbled into the table and went down on one knee.

The man she had struck slammed the door behind him, locking the four of them in the room together. He drew out a Glock and screwed on a suppressor, while the pair grabbed her arms and threw her onto the bed. He aimed the Glock at her while one of the pair pinned her ankles. The third Russian loosened his belt and climbed on top of her. He stank of garlic and cabbage. His legs pried her thighs apart and he put his face close to hers. She lunged her head upward, her bared teeth biting into his lower lip. He yelped and tried to rear back, but she held on, shaking her head like a dog, working her teeth deeper until she had ripped off a piece of flesh. Blood poured out and the Russian tried to roll off her.

"What's going on?" the Russian with the Glock said.

As the Russian on top of her struggled to rise up, she slammed his lower jaw upward and forced him to grind his teeth.

"I know who you are," she whispered into his ear as bloody foam began to leak out of his ruined mouth. She inhaled the scent of bitter almonds.

The Russian's eyes rolled up and he convulsed. She threw him against the Russian holding her down, who let go of her ankles in order to catch the corpse. She grabbed him and swung him around just before the gunman squeezed the Glock's trigger. The bullet struck the second Russian and he reared up, momentarily blocking the gunman's view of his intended target.

She tumbled off the bed and, as the gunman swiveled to find her, kicked him hard in the chest. Taken unawares, he reeled back onto the carpet. His Glock went flying across the room. She lunged for the glass on the bedside table, smashed it against the edge, and drove the jagged bottom into the gunman's eye.

He screamed and kept on screaming, his arms flailing, as she ground the glass deeper. The Russian's fists beat at her, driving the breath out of her, and he began to rise up, using his superior strength and weight against her. But she drove her knee into his throat and, using all her leverage, cracked through the cartilage. He choked, gasping for air he could no longer draw into his lungs.

She rose off him then, picking her way carefully around the glittering shards of glass to where the Glock lay. She picked it up and, turning, shot the Russian between the eyes.

She stood rooted to the spot for some time. Before the air conditioner clicked on she thought she could hear the sound of blood seeping. She went slowly over to the bed and sat down on the edge of it, elbows on knees, the Glock with its extended barrel hanging between her legs.

Her head bowed, tears came, and for a long time she did not want to stop crying.

Your time here is over, Jason," Don Fernando said. "You can no longer protect Kaja."

"You left her alone."

"There was an emergency. Besides, she was under surveillance."

"Little good it did."

Don Fernando sighed. "Jason, this woman has made herself an expert at running and hiding. I knew all along that if she wanted to leave, short of tying her up, there was nothing I or my people could do to stop her."

Bourne knew he was right, but it rankled him that Kaja was gone. She was a loose end. She had become an unknown in the complex equation.

Don Fernando produced a slim folder from his breast pocket and handed it to Bourne. "A first-class ticket to Damascus. There are several stopovers, but that can't be helped. You'll touch down by tomorrow morning. I'll have Almaz agents meet you."

"Don't bother," Bourne said, "I know where to go." When Don Fernando looked at him quizzically, he added, "I found the shipping labels for whatever is in the dozen crates in the warehouse."

"I see." Don Fernando nodded judiciously. As the two Almaz agents departed, he extracted a cigar from its aluminum tube, bit off the end, and, flicking open his lighter, sucked smoke into his lungs. When he had the Cuban going to his satisfaction, he said, "The crates are filled with FN SCAR-M, Mark 20 assault rifles."

"The Mark 20 doesn't exist."

"It does, Jason. These are prototypes. Their firepower is extremely destructive."

"And they're going to the Domna in Damascus. What for?"

"That's what you need to find out." Don Fernando blew out a cloud of aromatic smoke. "The Domna has been stockpiling these and other assault weapons for over a month, but in the last week the shipments have accelerated."

"We have the ability to stop this one."

"On the contrary, I'm doing everything I can to make certain they are delivered to the address you discovered. El-Gabal on Avenue Choukry Kouatly used to be the headquarters of a mining and mineral company. Now it's a vast complex of offices and warehouse-size spaces used as Domna's main staging area."

Bourne tensed. "Why would you let the weapons leave Cadiz?"

"Because," Don Fernando said, "those SCAR-Ms are filled with a powerful C-4 compound." He pressed a tiny plastic package and a small cell phone into Bourne's hand. "Each crate needs to be embedded with one of these identical SIM cards." He opened the package to show Bourne the stack of SIMs.

"This couldn't be done beforehand?"

Don Fernando shook his head. "Every delivery to El-Gabal is put through three different screeners. One is an X-ray machine. The chips would show up. No, they have to be planted by hand on site."

"And then?"

Don Fernando smiled like a fox. "You have only to press six-six-six on this phone's keypad, but you must be close and within line of sight of the SIMs for the Bluetooth signal to work. You will then have three minutes to get out of the building. The resulting explosion will destroy everything the Domna has stockpiled as well as everyone inside El-Gabal."

27

SAVE FOR THE heightened security, Boris found Damascus much as he had left it, a modern city painfully growing up around the oasis, sporting minarets, mosques, and sites dating back to the time the Book of Genesis was written, somewhere during the thirteenth century BC. At the head of his army, Abraham descended into Damascus from the land of the Chaldeans, north of Babylon. He ruled the city for some years, refreshing himself and his men, enchanted by this bejeweled city in the fragrant valley between the Tigris and Euphrates Rivers, before pushing on to Canaan. Subsequently, Damascus was conquered by Alexander the Great and, later, taken by the Roman general Pompey. Septimius Severus decreed it an official colony of Rome, but Christianity came to the city also. Saint Paul was struck down by holy light on the road to Damascus. Subsequently, he and Saint Thomas lived in Bab Touma, the city's oldest neighborhood. A crossroads of East and West of major importance, Damascus became the spiritual home of Severus Domna.

In modern times the city was made up of three distinct sections. The ancient Medina—as the Old City was known—and the French

Protectorate, whose lyrical architecture and ornate fountains dated from the 1920s, lay side by side like beautiful pearls, but what had accreted around them was the ugly sprawl of the modern city, with its brutal Soviet-style concrete buildings, shopping malls, and traffic-choked avenues.

Boris identified the SVR agents hanging around the arrivals terminal the moment he passed through immigration, trying without success to blend into the scene. He felt for them. At two in the morning there were no crowds to blend into. He entered the men's room, washed up, and stared at himself in the mirror. He scarcely recognized himself. Decades maneuvering through the minefields of the Russian clandestine services had changed him. Once, he had been young and idealistic, loving the motherland, willing to offer himself on the altar of making it a better place. And now, years later, he realized that Russia was no better off for his hard work. Possibly, it was worse off. He had squandered his life on an impossible dream, but wasn't that the mirage of youth: the dream of changing the world. Instead, he himself had changed, and the realization disgusted him.

Returning to the arrivals lounge, he found the one food stand open, bought a *meze* plate, and sat at a round table no larger than a Frisbee. He ate with his right hand while watching the arrivals board for the flight carrying Cherkesov. It was on time. He had forty minutes until it touched down.

He rose and went to the car rental desk. Fifteen minutes later he was sitting behind the wheel of a rattletrap, engine coughing and groaning. He used the time left to consider his pact with Zachek. An eye for an eye, a curious riff on *Strangers on a Train*, one of his favorite films, where two strangers talk about committing murders for each other to avoid becoming suspects. In the clandestine services, this kind of pact wouldn't work. Strangers wouldn't be able to get near Cherkesov or Beria. But those close to them could. Even after decamping to the Domna, Cherkesov remained a thorn in SVR's side—according to Zachek even more so now that his power had grown outside Russia's borders. Boris had offered to terminate Cherkesov for Zachek. In return, Zachek would plant Beria six feet under. He would assume control of SVR and Boris would have gained an ally instead of another enemy. Boris, of course, had his own reason for wanting Cherkesov dead. He owed his job to his former boss, but as long as he was alive Boris lived under his thumb.

Boris checked his watch. Cherkesov's flight had landed. By the time he pulled out of his space in the lot, passengers from the flight had begun drifting out of the terminal. Boris waited until he saw Cherkesov striding out. He smiled to himself because he was certain his former boss had picked up the SVR agents just as he had, and he knew that Cherkesov would believe they had been waiting for him.

As Cherkesov hurried to the short line of waiting taxis, Boris gunned the car around them. He pulled into the curb in front of the first taxi and, leaning over, threw open the passenger's-side door.

"Get in, Viktor."

Cherkesov's eyes opened wide. "You! What are you doing here?"

"The SVR is right on your heels," Boris said urgently.

Cherkesov climbed in. As soon as he closed the door, Boris threw the car in gear and pulled out with a squeal of rubber against tarmac.

At night, the wailing of the calls to prayer rang from minaret to minaret, enmeshing the city in a veil of language sung in alien ululations. At least, they seemed alien to Boris as he approached the city in the squeaking car. Green lights burned from the tops of the minarets, far more than he remembered. Cherkesov sat beside him, fuming while he smoked one of his vile Turkish cigarettes. Boris could feel the energy coming off him like electric sparks from a severed power line.

"Now," Cherkesov said, half turning to Boris, "explain yourself, Boris Illyich. Have you taken care of Jason Bourne?"

Boris took an exit ramp off the highway into the streets. "I've been too busy taking care of you."

Cherkesov stared at him openmouthed.

"After our talk about the SVR I went back to Zachek, Beria's man."

"I know who Zachek is," Cherkesov said impatiently.

"I made a deal with them."

"You did what?"

"I made a deal so I could find out why they're shadowing you."

"Since when have I been—"

"I spotted one of their agents out on the tarmac at Uralsk Airport. I wondered what he was doing there. Zachek told me." He turned the wheel and they headed down a darkened street lined with anonymous white concrete buildings. Somewhere a radio blared a muezzin's recorded voice. "Beria is very much interested in your new post inside Severus Domna."

"Beria could not know—"

"But he does, Viktor Delyagovich. This man is a devil."

Cherkesov chewed his lower lip in anxiety.

"So I have been following Beria's agents, from Moscow to Munich and now here, wondering what their orders are."

"Zachek didn't tell you?"

Boris shrugged. "It's not as if I didn't ask, but I couldn't press him. There was the danger of him becoming suspicious."

Cherkesov nodded. "I understand. You did well, Boris Illyich."

"My loyalty did not end when you bequeathed me FSB-2."

"Much appreciated." Cherkesov squinted through the fug of bitter smoke. "Where are we going?"

"To an all-night café I know of." Boris hunched forward, peering through the scarred windshield. "But I seem to have lost my way."

"I'd rather go straight to my hotel." Cherkesov gave an address. "Get back to a major intersection. From there, I'll know which way to go."

Boris grunted and turned right, moving along a slightly better illuminated street. "Why the hell is Beria so damn interested in where you go and who you see?"

"Why is Beria interested in anything?" Cherkesov said, an answer that gave away nothing.

Boris came to an intersection where the light was broken, not an uncommon occurrence in this neighborhood. The sound of the muezzin's canned voice seemed to be following them. Outside, the night was absolutely still. What trees they passed looked skeletal, stripped bare, like prisoners about to be slaughtered.

Boris came to a burned-out block, mostly rubble surrounded by a chain-link fence. He pulled over to the curb and stopped.

"What are you doing?" Cherkesov said.

Boris gently pressed the point of a ceramic knife between two of Cherkesov's ribs. "Why is Beria so interested in you?"

"He's always been—"

Cherkesov jumped as Boris dug the point through his clothes and drew blood. Reaching behind him, Boris opened his door. Then he grabbed Cherkesov by the shirtfront and, as he slid out of the vehicle, dragged his former boss with him.

"Some things never change," Boris said as he goaded Cherkesov toward the chain-link fence. He gestured. "This place makes a convenient killing field. The dogs rip the corpses to shreds before anyone bothers to contact the police."

Pushing Cherkesov's head through a gap in the fence, he bent over, following him through.

"This is a grave miscalculation," Cherkesov said.

Boris poked him again, so that he flinched back into Boris's grip. "I do believe you've made a joke, Viktor Delyagovich."

Boris pushed his victim on through the rubble until they reached the heart of the destruction. The same blank-faced high-rises rose all around them, dark and uncaring, but the lot itself was filled with the movement of the dogs Boris had spoken about. Sensing humans, they sidled and circled, their black snouts raised, sniffing for the first hint of spilled blood.

"Your death scents you, Viktor Delyagovich. It comes for you from all sides."

"What...what do you want?" Cherkesov's voice was a hoarse rasp; he seemed to have trouble breathing.

"A reminiscence," Boris said. "Do you recall a night about a year ago when you took me to a construction site on—where was it again?"

Cherkesov swallowed hard. "Ulitsa Varvarka."

Boris snapped his fingers. "That's right. I thought you were going to kill me, Viktor. But instead you forced me to kill Melor Bukin."

"Bukin needed killing. He was a traitor."

"Not my point at all." Boris jabbed Cherkesov again. "You made me pull the trigger. I knew what would happen to me if I didn't."

Cherkesov took a breath. "And look at you now. Head of FSB-2. You, instead of that fool Bukin."

"And I owe it all to you."

Shuddering at Karpov's ironic tone, Cherkesov said, "What is this? Revenge for a killing that got you where you wanted to be? You disliked Bukin as much as I did."

"Again, Bukin is not the issue. You are. Your use of me—or should I say abuse. You shamed me that night, Viktor."

"Boris, I never meant to—"

"Oh, but you did. You were reveling in your newfound power—the power the Domna had bestowed on you. And you reveled in it again when you forced me into the pact that would put me forever in your power."

A shadow of Cherkesov's oily smile returned. "We all make deals with the devil, Boris. We're all adults here, we knew this going in. Why are you—?"

"Because," Boris said, "you forced me into an untenable position. My career or another murder."

"I don't see the issue."

Boris slapped Cherkesov hard on the side of his head. "But you do see the issue, and this is why you chose me. Once again, you reveled in your power to compel me to kill my friend."

Cherkesov wagged his head back and forth. "An American agent responsible for countless deaths, many of them Russian."

Boris hit him again, and a streak of blood flew out of the corner of his mouth. The nearest dogs began to howl in counterpoint to the muezzin. Their gaunt bodies looked like scimitars.

"You wanted to break me, didn't you?" Boris said, dragging his head back. "You wanted me to kill my friend in order to keep everything I have ever dreamed of and worked for."

"It was an interesting experiment," Cherkesov said, "you have to admit."

Boris kicked the backs of Cherkesov's calves, and he went down. His trousers ripped. Blood seeped from his torn-up knees. Crouching down beside him, Boris said, "Now tell me what you're doing for the Domna."

That smile again, dark as pitch. "You won't kill me because then you will be marked as an enemy of the Domna. They won't stop until you're dead."

"You have it all wrong, Viktor. *I* won't stop until *they're* dead."

Still, the realization did not show in Cherkesov's eyes. "They have too many allies, some close to you."

"Like Ivan Volkin?"

Now a black terror transformed Cherkesov's face. "You know? How could you know?" His entire demeanor had changed. His face was sallow and he appeared to be panting.

"I'll take care of Ivan Ivanovich in good time," Boris said. "Right now, it's your turn."

Champagne or orange juice, sir?"

"Champagne, thank you," Bourne said to the young flight attendant as she bent over, a small tray balanced on the spread fingers of one hand.

She smiled sweetly as she handed him the flute. "Dinner will be served in forty minutes, sir. Have you made your choices?"

"I have," Bourne said, pointing to the menu.

"Very good, sir." The flight attendant's smile widened. "If there is anything you require during the flight, my name is Rebeka."

Alone in his seat, Bourne stared out the Perspex window as he sipped champagne. He was thinking about Boris, wondering why he hadn't shown himself. In this battle, Boris had the distinct edge. They were friends because Boris said they had been. Bourne had no memory of their first meeting, or what had happened. His first remembered encounter with Boris was in Reykjavik six years ago; before that was a complete blank. He had only Boris's word that they had been friends. What if Boris had been lying to him all along? This cloud of unknowing was the most frustrating—and dangerous—effect of his amnesia. When people popped up out of his past and claimed to be friends or colleagues he was required to make an instant determination about whether or not they were telling the truth. In the six years Bourne had known Boris, he had always acted like a friend. Two years ago Boris had been wounded in northeastern Iran. Bourne had found him and carried him to safety. They had worked side by side in a number of perilous situations. Bourne never had cause to doubt Boris's motivations. Until now.

Have you made your choices? An innocent sentence coming from a flight attendant, but it had many layers of meaning she wasn't aware of. Bourne had had his choices made for him when he plunged into the Mediterranean and surfaced without a memory of who or what he was. Since then, his life had been a struggle to understand the choices he had once made but could no longer remember, a struggle with the choices Alex Conklin had made for him. The latest case in point to surface from the murk of his past: killing Kaja's mother, Viveka Norén. It nauseated him that Conklin had sent him on a mission of personal vengeance, to— what? To teach a dead man a lesson for trying to assassinate him? The cruelty and heartlessness of Conklin's choice made Bourne sick to his stomach. And he had been the agent of death. He could not exonerate himself. *"There is no reason."*

No, he thought now, there was no reason.

So, Mademoiselle Gobelins," El-Arian said, "how may we best serve your needs?"

The moment he sat down beside her Soraya felt as if her skin had been seared. Invisible ants crawled over her flesh, and it was all she could do not to flinch away from him. Even his smile was dark, as if the emotion behind it came from a different place inside him. She felt his enormous psychic energy, and for the first time in her adult life she was afraid of another person. When she was five, her father had taken her to a seer in a seething backwater alley of Cairo. Why he did it, she had no idea. When her mother had found out about it afterward, she had flown into a rage, something Soraya had never before seen her mother do.

When the seer, a surprisingly young man with black eyes and hair and dark skin that looked like the hide of a crocodile, took her hand in his she felt as if the earth beneath her had crumbled, that she was falling into an abyss, that she would never stop falling.

"I have you," the seer said, as if to comfort her, but she felt like a fly caught in his web, and she had burst into tears.

On the way home, her father had not spoken to her, and she sensed that she had failed an important test, that he would never forgive her, that his love for her was slipping away like grains of sand through her slender fingers. Afterward, following her mother's terrifying outburst, she sensed that nothing was the same between her parents. Her father had broken some unspoken agreement between them and, just as he couldn't forgive Soraya, his wife couldn't forgive him. Six months later, her mother bundled her off to America. As a child or adolescent, she would never see Cairo again.

Soraya, sitting next to Benjamin El-Arian on the second floor of the Nymphenburg Landesbank, experienced again the same frightening sensation of falling into an unfathomable abyss.

El-Arian stirred beside her. "Are you well, Mademoiselle Gobelins?"

"Quite well, thank you," she said in a thickened voice.

"You look somewhat pale."

He rose and she took a quick breath, as if released from a vise.

Crossing to a sideboard, he said, "Perhaps a bit of brandy to revive your spirits."

"Thank you, no."

He poured the brandy anyway and brought it back in a cut-crystal glass. He sat down beside her and held out the glass. "I insist."

She saw his dark eyes scrutinizing her expression. *He knows*, she thought. *But what exactly?*

She brought a smile to her lips. "I don't drink alcohol."

"Neither do I." He set the brandy aside. "Are you a Muslim?"

She nodded. "I am."

"Arab."

She looked at him steadily. He tapped one long forefinger rhythmically against his lips. Slowly. One, two, three, like a hypnotist's metronome.

"That excludes Iranian, and you're not Syrian, surely." His eyebrows rose. "Egyptian?"

Soraya felt the need to gain some control over the conversation. "Where is your family from?"

"The desert."

"That could be almost anywhere," Soraya said, "even the Gobi."

El-Arian smiled like an indulgent uncle. "Hardly." A soft chime. "Excuse me." He rose and, digging out his cell phone, stepped out of the office.

Soraya rose and a wave of vertigo caused her to clutch the armrest of the sofa in order to steady herself. Ignoring the continued pounding in her head, she crossed quickly to M. Sigismond's desk, scanning the contents scattered across the top. Letters and files. Using the knuckle of her forefinger, she moved a sheet of paper slightly so she could read what was on the pages underneath. Her head came up as she heard El-Arian's voice briefly; when it faded away, accompanied by footfalls, she continued poking around. There were no photos, no mementos, nothing by way of a personal nature. The office was perfectly anonymous, as if it was used only sporadically. She started on the drawers. Wrapping a tissue from a box on the desktop around the handle of a letter opener, she used the blade to open each drawer and survey the contents. She was looking for some evidence that would link M. Marchand's traitorous dealings with the bank.

A moment later she heard El-Arian's voice approaching. She closed the drawer, dropped the letter opener, and was back at the sofa, using the tissue to blow her nose when he reappeared, M. Sigismond on his heels.

"My dear Mademoiselle Gobelins, my sincerest apologies for interrupting our meeting."

"It's quite all right," she said, stuffing the tissue away in her pocket.

"Ah, but first impressions are so important, don't you think?"

"I do."

He held out his hand and she took it, rising off the cushion.

"M. Sigismond has an appointment. In any event, I believe you will find my office more conducive to concluding our business."

He led the way down the hall and into a large office suite, this one furnished completely in a modern style. He stepped behind his desk, which held only an old-fashioned blotter, a set of fountain pens, a cut-crystal paperweight with the name of the bank engraved in gold, an ashtray filled with butts, and a multi-line phone. He gestured for her to stand beside him. "Please. I'm having papers drawn up for your intended deposit." He pulled out a printed card from a drawer. "But first, we must gather some basic information."

When she was at his side, he pressed a button and a video picture bloomed on the flat-screen panel across the room. Soraya saw herself in M. Sigismond's office as she rose from the sofa and almost staggered. Her eyes followed herself as she crossed to M. Sigismond's desk and began her clandestine work.

"I wonder," El-Arian said, "what you were looking for."

His hand clamped her wrist in an iron grip and did not let go.

Ivan Volkin was your friend for, what? Thirty years?"

"Longer," Boris said.

Cherkesov nodded. "And when the time was right, he sold you out." Some color had returned to his face, and though he was still kneeling, he was breathing more easily. "That's the way it is in our world. There's room for comradeship and alliances, but not loyalty. In our world loyalty is too costly. It's not worth the price." He tried to shift to get the pressure off his skinned knees. "You think it's any different with Jason Bourne? The man's a natural-born killer. What does he know about friendship."

"More than you."

"Which is nothing." Cherkesov shook his head. "I never had a friend in my life—not the way you figure it, anyway. How could I? It would leave me in a vulnerable position."

Boris turned the knife point slightly. "What the fuck do you call this?"

Cherkesov licked his lips. When he spoke, the words tumbled out, faster and faster. "Don't you understand what a favor I've done you? I've given you the opportunity to kill Bourne before he has a chance to betray you the way your friend of over thirty years, Ivan Volkin, has." Some words seemed to catch in his throat and he coughed, his eyes tearing with the effort. "Volkin has been advising the Domna ever since his so-called retirement from the *grupperovka* world. In fact, I'll tell you a secret: It was the Domna that put the idea of retirement into his head. Who knows how much the Domna paid him to come work for them?"

Boris sat back on his heels, considering the implications of what Cherkesov had just said.

Sensing an opening, Cherkesov pressed on. "Listen to me, Boris. I'm of more use to you alive than dead. You and me, we form an alliance. I tell you what the Domna is planning and you use the power of FSB-2 to take Beria and his people down. We can then merge FSB-2 with SVR with you at the head and me advising you. Boris, think of the possibilities of being in charge of clandestine services both inside and outside Russia. The entire world will open up for us!"

"Viktor, you surprise me," Boris said. "Beneath that thick crust of cynicism, you have a streak of positivity."

Cherkesov's fist connected with Karpov's jaw, knocking him to one side so that the knife pulled away from Cherkesov's flesh. Cherkesov grabbed for it, splitting a finger open on the edge. Using the spray of blood to blind Boris, he wrenched the knife away and jabbed it hilt-deep into Boris's belly.

28

BOURNE ROSE AND made his way through the darkened cabin to the first-class galley. He found Rebeka leafing through the latest issue of *Der Spiegel* as she stood against the stainless-steel counter. She turned when she became aware of him, a smile blooming on her face.

"Good evening, Mr. Childress, what can I get for you?"

"A macchiato, please."

"Can't sleep?"

"Bad dreams."

"Sadly, I know that scenario." She set aside the magazine. "I'll bring it to your seat as soon as I've brewed it."

"I'd rather stay here," he said. "I need to stretch my legs."

A slight flush ruddied her cheeks just before she turned away. "Of course." The scent of rose attar lifted off her. "Whatever you fancy." Her eyes were the color and shape of ripe olives, unexpectedly exotic against her Mediterranean skin and black hair. Like an Egyptian of ancient Alexandria, she had a Roman nose and delicate cheekbones, and stood very tall even in her flats. Perhaps as a child she had studied ballet.

Bourne watched her deftly making the macchiato. "Are you based out of Madrid?"

"Oh, no. Damascus." She produced a tiny cup, which she placed on the diminutive saucer. "I've been living there for the past six years."

"Do you like it?"

"It's difficult to make friends." She shrugged. "But it pays for me to be there. I get a yearly bonus."

"I haven't been back to Damascus in some time," he said truthfully. "I suppose there will be a lot of changes."

She pulled the espresso and slid it across the counter to him. It had just the right amount of foam. "Yes and no. The modern parts are terribly congested, the traffic is a nightmare, the polluted air stifling, but the Old City is still filled with the gorgeous covered arcades, the leafy squares, and, of course, space around the great mosques." She frowned. "But there are troubling aspects."

"The state sponsorship of Hezbollah, for one."

She nodded, her gaze falling gravely on him. "Also in the last year or so there's a growing conservative segment of the population that looks favorably on Iran."

Bourne seized the opening. "So there must be more in the way of security all over the city, starting with the airport."

Rebeka gave him a rueful smile. "I'm afraid so. The airport, especially. Al-Assad has clamped down at entry points, partly due to pressure from the West."

"There won't be any difficulties, will there?"

She laughed softly. "Not for you. Anyway, there's always a senior security official on hand when passengers deplane to guide you and answer questions."

Having gotten what he wanted, Bourne threw back his macchiato. Rebeka tore off part of a page from her magazine and wrote on it. As he turned to go, she slid it over to him.

"I'm off for the next three days." Her warm smile returned. "My number, in case you lose your way."

Instead of piercing Boris's flesh, the knife blade retracted into its handle. Laughing, Boris slammed the heel of his hand into Cherkesov's nose. Blood gouted, the cartilage cracked, and Cherkesov fell onto his backside.

Boris took back the knife. He pressed a hidden button on the handle and the blade popped out. He pressed the button again, locking the blade in place so it would not retract.

He knelt beside Cherkesov. "Now we get to it, Viktor." He shoved the tip of the blade into Cherkesov's right nostril. "There are many things, precious to you, I'm sure, you will give up before you tell me what I want to know."

Cherkesov stared up at him with reddened eyes. "I'll die first."

"You're a liar, kitty cat," Boris said.

"Huh?" Cherkesov looked up at him.

"You know what happens to liars? No? Wanna guess? No? Okay, they lose their noses."

With one flick of Boris's wrist, the blade slit open Cherkesov's already bloody nose. Cherkesov arched up; Boris shoved him back down with the flat of his hand.

"Let me the fuck up!"

"Forget it, Viktor, it's Chinatown."

"Fuck you, you cocksucker. I'm not telling you a thing."

"It's not a question of pain, Viktor, but you already knew that." Boris wiped the blade on Cherkesov's trouser leg. "It's a question of what you can tolerate living without." He smiled, almost benignly. "Not to worry, I won't let you die. There's no escape." The knife blade made a circuit of Cherkesov's face. "I mean what I say; I'm an expert, and I have all night long."

Hendricks was in his office, poring over the file of the three men found dead in Room 916 of the Lincoln Square Hotel. None of them was a guest, none had any identification on him. Their fingerprints had yielded nothing, and now their dental records were being sought, though this would probably be a dead end as well. According to the FBI, who had taken over the case from Metro Homicide, the dental work was definitely not American. Eastern European was the best they could do at the moment, but that covered a lot of territory.

Hendricks paused to drink some ice water.

The one strange thing about all of the victims was the suicide pill— the hollow tooth that contained liquid hydrogen cyanide, an old NKVD marker. Were these men Russians and, if so, what the hell were they doing in Room 916 of the Lincoln Square Hotel?

Hendricks turned the page. Room 916 was on a long-term lease through ServicesSolutions, a company with phantom headquarters in the Caymans. Hendricks had no doubt that ServicesSolutions was a shell corporation for God alone knew who. He rubbed his forehead. Whoever owned ServicesSolutions had some very nasty enemies. He called a colleague in Treasury, gave him what info he had on ServicesSolutions, and asked him to find out who actually owned it. Then he called the head of the task force he had assigned to find Peter Marks. Following the bombing of Peter's car in the Treadstone garage, the whole building was in lockdown. Everyone who worked or had recently worked in the building was being run down and questioned, but nothing so far. Hendricks had been extremely relieved to learn that no human remains had been found in the car. On the other hand, this concerned him, given Sal's testimony that he and Peter had been in the same elevator minutes before the explosion. The night watchman had exited at the lobby level, but he was certain Peter had continued down to the garage. So chances were good that Peter was in the garage when the car bomb was detonated, but had not been in the vehicle. What had happened; where was he? Had he gone to ground? That would be a reasonable assumption.

Hendricks rose and crossed the office to fetch more ice for his water pitcher. He stopped stock-still as something occurred to him. What if Peter had been injured? Back at his desk, he asked one of his assistants to call around to every hospital in the Greater DC area, starting with the ones closest to the Treadstone building. Then, as another thought occurred to him, he ordered the assistant to include all EMS and private ambulance services.

"Put every available person on it," he concluded.

He sat back, swiveled his chair around, and stared out the window. It was a dreary, windswept day. Beads of rain slid down the panes of glass, and, beyond, on the street, people in shiny raincoats were hunched over, umbrellas trembling like leaves, as they slogged their way to and from work.

At the sound of his intercom, he turned back.

"What?" His mind was buzzing with a thousand possibilities.

"Package just arrived for you, sir. It's been vetted by security."

"What's in it?"

"A DVD, sir."

Hendricks frowned. "Bring it in."

A moment later, one of his assistants placed the DVD on his desk. Hendricks looked up. "That's it? No note?"

"Nothing, sir. But it was addressed to you and was stamped PERSONAL AND CONFIDENTIAL."

Hendricks waved the assistant out, put the DVD aside, and returned to the case of the three dead men in Room 916. He studied the crime scene photos of their faces and bodies, noting that there were no tattoos, which ruled out the Russian mob. So who were these jamokes? They were armed, but that could mean anything. It certainly gave no clue as to their country of origin, let alone their affiliation. The FBI had concluded, however, that they constituted a hit team. Did that mean the team's target was more than one person? And where was he/she/they now? He turned another page. The FBI had questioned everyone who worked in the hotel, as well as all the guests on the ninth floor. No one had seen or heard anything. Possibly someone was lying, but the FBI report stated its operatives didn't think so. That left the other possibility: Whoever had been in that room knew how to get into and out of a public building without being spotted. All of this was interesting speculation, but Hendricks couldn't see how it would help them find out who these

people were and who their target was. It was imperative that he find
the answers to those questions ASAP. The threat of terrorism overhung
them all.

He needed something to make his day. He called a contact of his
at CI.

"How are the plans proceeding with security at Indigo Ridge?"

"The place is in a fucking uproar." The disgust in his voice was evi-
dent. "This isn't our thing and no one knows how best to go about it." He
took a breath. "We sure could use your help, Mr. Secretary."

"You want help, talk to Director Danziger," Hendricks said with a poisoned glee. "That's why he gets to sit in the big chair."

His contact chuckled. "You're killing us, Mr. Secretary."

"Not me."

"By the way, there's a minor buzz around here concerning your new
co-director of Treadstone, Peter Marks."

Hendricks caught his breath. "What about him?"

"Word is he's missing."

Hendricks said nothing.

"Peter still has a lot of friends here, Mr. Secretary. If there's anything
we can do."

"Thanks, I'll keep that in mind," Hendricks said before he disconnected.

He thought about how right Maggie had been in suggesting this
course of action with Danziger. Phoning his Indigo Ridge security group,
he told them they were back on standby. He could allow Danziger's fucking up to go only so far. Indigo Ridge needed to be secured.

But his pleasure at the prospect of riding to the rescue was short-
lived, what with an attempt on Peter's life, Peter missing, and the FBI
material on the triple homicide at the Lincoln Square Hotel staring him
in the face. Then his phone rang.

"No luck with any of the hospitals," his assistant said, "and we went
all the way out to Virginia and Maryland. Same with EMS."

Hendricks closed his eyes. A headache was starting way back behind
his left eye. "Have you any good news?"

"Well, that depends. One of the private ambulance companies reported a stolen vehicle not long ago."

"Has it been found?"

"No, sir."

"Well, dammit, find the fucking thing!"

He slammed down the phone so hard the DVD jumped off the desk. He looked at it, then picked it up, watching the rainbow rise and fall on its metallic surface. Opening the tray on his computer tower, he settled the DVD and slid the tray home. He heard the mechanism spinning up, then his video software program appeared full-screen and the DVD began to play. Out of the black screen, Maggie's face appeared like a vision from a nighttime mist.

Christopher, by the time you see this I will be long gone. Please don't try to contact me."

She paused, as if knowing Hendricks had reached for his cell phone, which he had. He felt his fingers tremble with the slender weight of it, as if he were touching the nape of her neck.

"My name isn't Margaret Penrod and my profession isn't landscape architecture. Almost nothing I told you is true, though the truth began to leak out despite myself."

Her eyes glittered, and even though Hendricks felt a fiery demon clawing at the lining of his gut, he was powerless to look away from her image, which shimmered like sunlight on water on the flat screen of his computer.

"You must hate me now, which I suppose is inevitable. But before you judge me, you must understand something."

Her expression changed, and Hendricks sensed that she was reaching out for something—a remote control, as it turned out. The frame drew back from her face to reveal her naked body. It was covered in blood.

Hendricks hunched forward on the edge of his chair. "Maggie, what the fuck?" Then he realized that the woman he was looking at, the woman to whom he'd made love, had possibly given his heart to, wasn't Maggie. "Who are you?" he whispered.

The lens moved back farther until Hendricks could see that she was standing in a hotel room. At that instant, he was overcome with what might have been a hot flash. He felt his gorge rising. And rising more, as the video camera moved lower and panned the floor behind his naked lover.

And there they were. Hendricks let out a low groan. The three members of the death squad, all dead. At his lover's hand? His mind seemed to implode. How was that possible? As if to answer his question, Maggie continued:

"These men were sent to kill me because I protected you. And now I have to leave Room Nine Sixteen, leave DC, leave America. I'm on my final journey." The camera returned to her, zeroing in on her face. "I was supposed to bring you here, Christopher. Room Nine Sixteen was to be our secret love nest where our every move, every word we exchanged would be recorded and then disseminated to the media. To ruin you. I couldn't let that happen. And now instead of a love nest, Room Nine Sixteen has become a charnel house. Perhaps that's a fitting end for the two of us, I don't know anymore." Her face was obscured for a few seconds as she brushed wisps of hair from her eyes. "The only thing I do know is that you're too precious to me to hurt. If I don't go now you will be in terrible danger."

Her smile was rueful, almost sad. "I won't say that I love you because it will only sound hollow and false to your ears. It sounds fatuous, stupid, even. How could I love you when we have known each other a matter of days? How could I love you when all I've done is lie to you? How is it that the earth is the third planet from the sun? No one knows; no one *can* know. Some things just are, sunk in their mystery."

Hendricks, scrutinizing her face through the squeezing of his heart, saw that she didn't blink, her eyes didn't cut away, two basic tells of the liar. She wasn't lying, or she was very, very good, better than any liar he had ever met. He looked into those eyes and was lost.

"Apart from my father, I have never loved anyone before you, and my love for him is very different than it is for you. Something happened when we met, a mysterious current went through me and changed me. There is no better way to explain it. That's all I know."

She leaned forward suddenly, her face blurring as she planted her lips on the lens. "My name is Skara. Good-bye, Christopher. If you can't forgive me, then remember me. Remember me when you are protecting Indigo Ridge."

A smear of colors, a vertiginous blur of motion as she pushed the lens aside. Then Hendricks was faced with blackness, the fizzing of the electronic void, and the painful galloping of his heart.

Dawn had broken and so had Cherkesov. Boris had done as much damage as he needed to do. Cherkesov, it turned out, was deathly afraid of going blind. A swipe of the knife blade just under his right eye had been enough for the resistance to bleed out of him. He handed over what he had been bringing from the Mosque in Munich to Damascus.

"It's a key," he told Boris, through thickened, bloodstained lips.

"What does it open?"

"Only Semid Abdul-Qahhar knows."

Boris frowned. "Didn't Semid Abdul-Qahhar give you the key to bring here?"

"Semid Abdul-Qahhar is here, not in Munich. I was to deliver the key to him in person."

"How?" Boris said. "Where?"

"He maintains a residence." Cherkesov's lips quivered in the parody of a smile. "You'll like this, Boris Illyich. His residence is in the Old City, in the former Jewish Quarter, in the last remaining synagogue still standing. It had been abandoned for years, ever since the Syrian Jews fled to America."

"So Semid Abdul-Qahhar took it over, figuring his enemies would never think to look for him there."

Cherkesov nodded, and groaned. "I need to lie down. I need to sleep."

"Not yet." Boris grabbed him by his sodden shirtfront as he was leaning back. "Tell me the time of the rendezvous and the protocol."

A thin line of pink spittle exited the corner of Cherkesov's mouth. "He's expecting me. You'll never have a chance."

"Leave that to me," Boris said.

Cherkesov began to laugh until he coughed up blood. Then he looked up at Boris. "Look at me. Look what you've done."

"It's a sad day for you, Viktor. I agree, but I can't sympathize." Boris shook his former boss until his teeth chattered. "Now, fucker, tell me the details, and you can cry yourself to sleep."

Soraya stood perfectly still. El-Arian's touch was toxic, as if he had somehow exposed her to polonium-210 and now she was rotting from the inside out, weak and defenseless.

"Who are you, mademoiselle?"

Soraya said nothing and stared straight ahead. The pounding in her head made it difficult to gather her defenses.

"It seems that we're a mystery to each other, M. El-Arian."

He wrenched at her wrists and she gasped. "Enemies by whatever names we call ourselves."

"Did Marchand order Laurent's death, or did you?"

"Marchand was a bureaucrat." El-Arian's voice was like the scrape of sandpaper. "His mind was fixed on petty things. He lacked the vision to conceive of the traitor's death."

She looked at him, then, a terrible mistake. She was riveted, paralyzed. Never before had she believed in the concepts of Good and Evil, but his mesmeric eyes struck her as windows into an unbearable evil.

She grabbed the paperweight and smashed it into El-Arian's temple. He relinquished his hold on her as he staggered back into the chair. It spun away from him on its casters and he pitched down onto the floor. Soraya turned and ran out of the office, down the hall. She heard a discreet alarm sound—El-Arian must have pressed a panic button. A security guard appeared, pulling a sidearm from a black leather holster. Rushing him, she smashed her elbow into his throat, and he went down. She bent to take his weapon, but he grabbed her and she had to kick him in the face to free herself. She passed up the elevator; it would be a death trap. Racing down the hallway, past open doors and startled faces, she reached the top of one of the staircases leading down to the ground floor. Behind her, she heard El-Arian cursing her.

She took the stairs two at a time, stumbling a bit because of the incessant pounding in her head, but managed to hold herself upright with one hand clutching the polished wooden banister. But she was less than halfway down when a pair of security guards converged from either side of the ground floor and rushed the stairs. Both men had their service revolvers out.

Soraya turned back, but El-Arian fairly flew down the stairs. He had a gun in his hand. He reached out and, as she tried to dive away from him, snatched her into his grasp.

29

BOURNE RETURNED REBEKA'S smile as he exited the plane. He could smell the light rose of her perfume all the way down the jetway. He saw the security officer standing by just as she described.

"Pardon me," Bourne said in Arabic. "This is my first visit to Damascus. Could you recommend a good hotel to stay at?"

The officer stared at Bourne as if he were an insect, then grunted. Bourne bumped against him as he was getting out of the way of a woman being escorted off the plane in a wheelchair. Bourne apologized, the security officer shrugged while he was writing down his recommendations. Thanking him, Bourne walked off with his clearance card.

He was already behind the rest of the debarking passengers and now he fell farther back. Then he saw what he was looking for: a door marked NO ADMITTANCE. OFFICIAL PERSONNEL ONLY. Beside the door was an electronic reader. He swiped the stolen card and pushed the door open. He had no idea who would be monitoring passengers going through Immigration, he only knew he didn't want to be identified entering Damascus by anyone, especially Severus Domna.

He took the back halls of the airport, unsure of where he was going until he found a fire-drill map of the area screwed to a wall. In fifteen seconds he had memorized the map and had worked out the route he wanted to take.

Soraya felt herself being dragged backward, the cold metal of the gun's muzzle hard against the side of her head. Seeing the security guards hesitate, she felt disoriented. Didn't these men work for El-Arian? Then they parted and she saw Aaron, Jacques Robbinet, and a young man she didn't recognize, who was scrutinizing her with a cold physician's eye. The entire ground floor had been evacuated.

"Put the weapon down," Aaron said. He was armed, as well, with a SIG. Aaron advanced between the two guards. "Put it down, let the woman go, and we'll all walk out of here peacefully."

"There is no chance of peace," El-Arian said, "here or anywhere."

"There's nowhere to run," Aaron said as he took a step forward. "This can end well, or end badly."

"It will surely end badly for her," El-Arian said, jamming the muzzle of the pistol into Soraya's head so hard that she made a low sound in her throat. "Unless you move aside and allow us safe passage."

"Let the woman go and we'll discuss it," Robbinet said.

El-Arian's lip curled upward. "I won't even dignify that suggestion with a response," he said. "I am not afraid to die." He rubbed his cheek against Soraya's hair. "The same cannot be said for your agent."

"She's not our agent," Aaron said.

"I'm done listening to your lies." El-Arian dragged Soraya down the stairs. "She and I are going to walk across the floor and out the door. We'll disappear and that will be the end of it."

As he took the last several steps down to the marble floor, Robbinet ordered the guards to move back. El-Arian smiled. Aaron looked into Soraya's eyes. *What is he trying to tell me?* she asked herself.

El-Arian apparently saw the look, too, because he said to Aaron, "If you kill me, you'll kill her as well. Her death will be your responsibility. Are you a gambling man? Are you willing to take on that weight?"

As he spoke, El-Arian moved across the floor. The space echoed with their footfalls, the vast empty space an arena where, Soraya supposed, the end of her life might play out. She knew that Aaron had given her a signal. If her head had been clear, if the pounding weren't making her wince with every agonizing throb, she would know what part he wanted her to play in the endgame, because she had no doubt Aaron had an endgame in mind. She would have, if she were in his position.

They were almost to the front door now, Aaron and Robbinet shadowing their every step. She felt helpless, like every damsel in distress in every action movie ever made, and this angered her to such a degree that she shoved the pain into a dark corner, holding it at bay while she tried to figure out...

Position! That was it! Aaron was moving into position to make a kill shot. He would do it just as El-Arian reached the door—that's when she would do it. She could see Aaron moving into position, approximately forty-five degrees to the rear of El-Arian's right shoulder. That was the vulnerable spot—the head shot.

But she had looked into her captor's eyes and she knew his heart, she knew that he would not go down easily, that his first instinct would be to shoot Aaron, not her. It would be the soldier's reflex action—to fire back at his attacker—one El-Arian couldn't control. He might shoot Aaron and then her before he went down, but for certain Aaron was in mortal danger. One man she cared about was already dead because of her. She would not allow another to die.

This decision was what drove the pain racking her skull down farther, the adrenaline pumping through her, the certain desire to do this one last thing that would give her a sense of rightness, of completion, of her life—and death—having meaning. Like El-Arian, she was not afraid to die. In fact, she had considered it an inevitability when she had chosen fieldwork. But she was not a martyr; she loved life, and there was a sadness in her even as she and El-Arian reached the door, as she saw Aaron's SIG come up, as she slammed the back of her head against El-Arian, as she drove an elbow into his kidney, as she became his assailant, not Aaron.

She heard Aaron shout, felt the air go out of El-Arian. Then she was in the eye of a monstrous thunderstorm that blew her sideways. She tasted her own blood, she was falling, the pain in her head vanished.

Then everything was obliterated by absolute stillness.

Damascus spread out before Bourne as he took a taxi in from the airport. The sun-washed morning bounced off the windshield and set fire to the hood as they rumbled through the streets. He had the taxi let him off several blocks from the section of Avenue Choukry Kouatly that was his destination, then walked the rest of the way, losing himself within the drifts of pedestrians. Taking a quick, covert circuit of El-Gabal's geometric Syrian modernist building, he scoped out the three entrances and the security at each. The front entrance, all glass and hammered steel, had no overt security presence, but taking his time paid off, as at intervals of precisely three minutes, he observed a pair of uniformed guards passing in front of the glass doors. On the west side of the building was a single-door emergency exit. The metal door looked solid, made to seem impregnable, but Bourne knew that no door was impregnable. In the rear was a wide loading dock, which was currently empty. Beyond the dock were four wide doors, at the moment all closed. A uniformed security guard sat smoking and talking on his cell phone. Occasionally, he turned his narrowed eyes on the street, peering back and forth, checking for anything suspicious or out of place. Unlike the guards in the lobby, who carried sidearms only, this man had an AK-47 strapped across his back. At each angle, Bourne looked upward, studying the roofline and the possible means of gaining its height. There were no trees or telephone poles, but the building itself looked scalable.

He was about to depart when he heard a truck coming down the alley. The guard heard it, too, because he broke off his conversation and pressed a buzzer just to the left of the left-most door. Almost at once, the four doors lifted up. A wizened man peered out, the guard said something to him, he nodded and disappeared into the dimness of the interior.

By the time the truck rumbled, turned, and backed up to the loading dock, two men appeared. They wore sidearms. The driver got out and, leaping up onto the dock, opened the rear door with a key. He rolled the door up and stood back as the two men entered the truck's rear. The guard had unstrapped his AK-47 and was now holding it at the ready. He was young and looked slightly nervous as he peered down the street.

Bourne shifted his position in time to see the two men unloading the first of the dozen long wooden crates containing the poisoned weapons he had seen in the warehouse in Cadiz. He recognized them by both their shape and the distinctive greenish color of the wood.

He needed to get inside to set the SIM cards, but that would have to wait until the darkness of night. He withdrew and went in search of the items he thought he'd need. He bought himself Syrian clothes that would allow him to better blend in, a glass cutter, a sturdy, wide-bladed knife, a length of electrical wire, two coils of rope of different lengths, and a pickax. Lastly, he purchased a duffel in which to carry everything, then took a taxi to the train station, where he stashed the duffel in a paid locker.

Then he went in search of a hotel, which proved problematic. The first three he entered had security personnel stationed around the lobbies. They might have belonged to the respective hotels, but he didn't think so. He went farther afield and, on the southern outskirts, found a run-down hotel. Apart from two dusty armchairs, a pair of even dustier palm trees, and a curve-backed receptionist, the lobby was deserted. Bourne booked a room on the top floor and paid with cash. The receptionist scanned his passport with little apparent interest, marking down name, nationality, and number, then handing it back, along with the room key.

Bourne took a protesting elevator up to the sixth floor, went down a bare, odorous concrete hallway, and entered his room, a Spartan cubicle with bed, dresser, badly streaked mirror, tiny closet inhabited by a couple of roaches, and threadbare carpet. One window faced west. Beyond the grid of the fire escape lay the teeming street, the city's unceasing daytime tumult boring its way through the glass. The bathroom, if you wanted to call it that, was down the hall.

Despite the meanness of the surroundings, Bourne had been in far worse places. He lay down and closed his eyes. It seemed like days since he had slept.

Where are you, Boris? he wondered. *When are you coming for me?*

He must have dozed off because the next thing he knew, the sun was thicker, deeper, slanting through the window, low in the sky. Late afternoon, shading into twilight. He lay still on the bed as if stunned. He felt groggy, which meant that he had been pulled prematurely out of deep REM sleep. He lay listening, but almost immediately identified a scratching at his door. It might be a rodent, but he didn't think so.

Silently, he rose and went to the wall just behind where the door hinged open. Reaching out, he watched as the lock was slowly opened from the hallway. The doorknob began to turn and he steeled himself for whoever was coming in.

That's when a shadow crossed his peripheral vision an instant before two men shattered the window as they leapt through.

Christopher Hendricks sat at his desk for fully an hour without moving or speaking to anyone. Once, his secretary came in, worried that he wasn't answering his intercom, but one look at his ashen face and she departed.

Alone at his desk, the image of Skara frozen on the screen in front of him, he felt an existential coldness creep over him. Maggie: Her face was now a matter of colored pixels, informed by a series of 0s and 1s. This was Maggie, a mirage, a dream, an electronic fantasy. Who, then, was Skara? How had she so successfully penetrated the government's vetting process, how had she pierced his own armor, how had she grabbed hold of his heart? Even now, with the shock of her revelations still running through him, his heart beat on to the rhythm she had set for it.

"I have never loved anyone before you."

He did not know whether to believe what she said in the video.

"Something happened when we met, a mysterious current went through me and changed me."

At last, at the end, had she told him the truth, or was that wishful thinking? Was her last message another lie, one to keep him from sending his people after her?

"I'm on my final journey." What the hell did she mean by that? The words tolled in his head like funeral bells, sending a shiver down his spine.

His head hurt, his thoughts frantically pinwheeling, getting nowhere. He no longer knew truth from fiction because he wanted what she said to be the truth, wanted it so badly it left a metallic taste like blood in his mouth.

She was an agent, that was clear enough, and a demonically clever one. But who was she working for, and how did she know about Indigo Ridge? His mind raced backward, reliving in reverse their short but intense time together. He thought of their picnic, of what he had revealed to her—a helluva lot less than she already knew, as it turned out. It had been her idea for him to dump security for Indigo Ridge into Danziger's lap, though he had, of course, not revealed names or places.

Why had she made that suggestion? He ran a hand across his eyes, but at once he snatched it away. He felt magnetized to her eyes, pulled toward the image on the screen. He wanted so badly to reach out and touch her—no, not merely touch her, he ached to hold her.

She had protected him, she said. What did that mean? *"Remember me when you are protecting Indigo Ridge."*

And then he understood. She had tried to protect him by taking him off Indigo Ridge. But how had she known he was on it? The depth and accuracy of her intel boggled his mind. No wonder she had been able to fool the vetting process. He made a mental note to overhaul the entire process.

A setup. He was meant to take a fall via a video taken in Room 916 that she would disseminate. Disgraced, he would be summarily removed from Indigo Ridge and, momentarily, at least, the security would be in turmoil.

That's when the people she was working for were going to strike!

He lunged for the phone and jabbed the red button.

"Remember me when you are protecting Indigo Ridge."

I will, he thought as he waited for the president to come on the line. *I swear I will.*

The two men were on Bourne even as he was turning to face them. The third man came through the door unimpeded. The three men converged on Bourne. They were big, grizzly men who stank of beer and fried corn.

They might be big, but they were undisciplined—street fighters, rough and tumble. They were partial to roundhouse punches with brass knuckles and swipes with switchblades. Ripping the mirror off the wall, Bourne slammed its edge into a brass knuckle. The mirror cracked into a dozen shards, and Bourne grabbed one of the larger ones, unmindful of how it sliced into his palm, and jabbed the pointed end into one of the men's arms. The man reeled backward into one of his compatriots.

The third man rushed at Bourne, knife held in front of him, expecting Bourne to retreat. Instead Bourne moved into the attack, grabbed the man's knife arm, pulling him into him, and embedded the mirror shard in the man's throat. Blood gouted as the man reeled backward. Bourne grabbed his shirtfront and shoved him into the two oncoming attackers. One man used his brass knuckles to sweep aside his dead compatriot while the other drew an ice pick and hacked down with it. Bourne, dodging, slipped past the attack. Three straight punches brought Ice Pick to his knees. Bourne kicked him in the face, and he toppled onto his side.

The third man, the largest of the three, leapt on Bourne, bouncing Bourne's head off the wall. Bourne went down and Knuckles dropped onto him. He swung, the brass knuckles connecting painfully with Bourne's left shoulder. Bourne kicked him, at the same time twisting his torso, slamming his elbow into Knuckles's midsection. Bourne threw Knuckles off him and, in a crouch, rushed him, slammed him into the wall, wrapped one arm around his head, and, joining his hands, jerked powerfully, breaking his neck.

As Knuckles collapsed, Bourne took a moment to check out a hunch. Going through the men's pockets revealed Colombian passports. This was a death squad sent by Roberto Corellos, who hadn't forgotten his vow of revenge against Bourne. How they had picked up his trail here in Damascus was anyone's guess. In any event, he had no time to try to find an answer—that would come later.

He was about to exit the room via the shattered window when he turned back, scooped the ice pick off the floor, and, stepping over bodies and through shattered glass, made his way out of the room, down the fire escape, and into the teeming twilight.

Damascus's Jewish Quarter, a warren of narrow ancient streets, scarred and twisted by time and cruelty, was filled with abandoned houses cordoned off by thick chains and brass padlocks. The place had an unmistakable air of sorrow and suffering, two things with which Boris was well acquainted.

The rendezvous with Semid Abdul-Qahhar wasn't until 10 PM, but Boris thought he'd better get the lay of the land before he tried what the late, unlamented Viktor Cherkesov had described as impossible. As he wandered the streets surrounding the old synagogue, he thought back to the vacant lot that had been his home last night. He could have left Cherkesov alive after his former boss had coughed up all his secrets, but that would have been foolish—worse, it would have been the height of sentimentality. When a man in his profession became sentimental, it was time to quit. And yet, not too many actually did quit or retire. Ivan was the latest example. Really, Boris thought now as he turned a corner, it was astonishing that he had fooled everyone into believing that he had retired, including Boris himself. But then Ivan's sincerity was always one of his most admired traits. It was, after all, what had led him to be trusted by all the *grupperovka* families. And he had never betrayed confidences to any of them. But now, it seemed brutally clear that he had betrayed every family's confidences to Severus Domna.

Boris shook his head. If he lived to the age of Methuselah he would never understand what could possibly motivate Ivan and then Cherkesov to turn against the motherland.

He had now made three complete circuits of the streets surrounding the old synagogue occupied by Semid Abdul-Qahhar and had set the map of the Jewish Quarter firmly in his head. Though his stomach was grumbling fiercely, he felt so encrusted with grime that he headed for Hammam Nureddin, at Souk el-Bzouriyeh, in another section of the Medina.

He paid his fee, hung his clothes in a wooden locker, and took a moment to study the key Cherkesov had picked up at the Mosque in Munich, which he was due in three hours to put into Semid Abdul-Qahhar's grubby little hand. It was gold, small, and oddly shaped. It looked ancient, but when he scratched at it with his thumbnail a thin line of patina came off. He examined his nail. It wasn't only the patina that had come off, but the gold color itself.

He looked at the key in a whole new way. Gold was soft, so it wasn't surprising that the key was made of a harder metal. Boris had speculated that the key was made of iron with an outer layer of gold. He turned the key over and over between his fingers. There was something vaguely familiar about its shape. It seemed unlikely that he had seen it before, nevertheless he could have sworn he had.

Standing in front of his locker, naked save for the towel wrapped around his waist, he set his mind to thinking about where he might have seen the key—perhaps in a book, a magazine article, or even an intel report at FSB-2. Nothing surfaced.

He secured the locker with an old-fashioned key on a red cotton wrist bracelet. The color indicated that he had paid for the full menu. He padded to the first of the many showers, steam rooms, and skylit massage facilities. What did the mysterious key open, and what made it so valuable that Cherkesov had to deliver it in person? And why Cherkesov? Surely the Domna and Semid Abdul-Qahhar had any number of trustworthy agents to handle the task.

These questions swirled through his mind like a school of fish as he showered, was scrubbed by an attendant, then padded into one of the great tiled steam rooms. He sat, a towel draped across his loins, bent forward, forearms on thighs, and tried to free his mind of questions, doubts, and the myriad responsibilities he faced. His head hung, his vision going out of focus as his muscles slowly relaxed. He could feel the exhaustion oozing out of him with his sweat. His overactive mind eventually calmed.

Suddenly his head snapped up. He opened his left hand and stared at the key lying in the center of his palm. A laugh bubbled up. He laughed so hard his eyes began to tear. Now he understood why Cherkesov had been chosen to go to the Mosque in Munich, even though he despised Muslims.

Twenty minutes later he was lying facedown on a massage table, having his muscles reduced to quivering jelly. He closed his eyes, listening to the slap of the masseur's hands on his back, humming to himself as his right hand played with the thick wooden peg under the tabletop that kept the parts together.

A shadow fell across his face and he opened his eyes and looked up to see Zachek, his face raw and red as just-butchered meat, swollen on one side. Below the neck, his body was pale as milk. His torso was completely devoid of scars. Boris remembered when his own body had looked like that.

"Fancy meeting you here, Boris." Zachek's smile was warm and ingratiating. "I saw what you did to Cherkesov." He clucked his tongue against the roof of his mouth. "A sorry end for a man of such power. But then, power is fleeting and life is short, eh?"

"You look like a fucking bureaucrat, Zachek. Go home."

Zachek's smile was lopsided, as if stitched there by a bad tailor. "What did Cherkesov tell you?"

"Nothing," Boris said. "He had bigger balls than I had imagined."

The smile froze. "I don't believe you, Boris."

"I'm not surprised. You're out of your league here in the field."

Zachek's eyes narrowed. "Aren't we partners now?"

Boris lay his cheek against his folded arms. He was getting a crick in his neck from keeping his head up. "You're supposed to be in Moscow, tending to your part of our bargain."

"To be honest, I didn't trust you would keep your end."

"But I have."

"Astonishing, really." Zachek flicked the key dangling from Boris's right wrist. "What was Cherkesov doing in Munich? Why did he come here?"

"I told you—"

Zachek leaned over Boris. "He was a mule, wasn't he? He was bringing something here. Was that it?"

"I have no idea."

Zachek lunged for the locker key. When Boris tried to slide off the table, the masseur held him in place.

"What the hell is this?" Boris said.

"You know what this is." Leaning over him, Zachek slid the wristband off. He held up the key. "Let's see what's in your locker."

As Zachek sauntered off, Boris tried again to rise, but the masseur, leaning in with all his muscled bulk, held him even more firmly in place.

He was not alone with the masseur for long. He saw another man enter the room. His face was triangular, vulpine, the black eyes never alighting on one thing for long. He was not a tall man, but he was nevertheless imposing. His body was squat and wide, chest and shoulders thick with matted hair like a bear's pelt. Despite his lack of uniform, Boris recognized him immediately.

He forced a smile onto his face as the man approached him. "Konstantin Lavrentiy Beria, at last we meet."

30

IN THE LONG Damascene twilight, Bourne walked down Straight
Street, the main artery of Bab Touma, the oldest section of the Medina.
Not knowing where it might be safe, he dug out the slip of paper Rebeka
had given him and called her. He heard the pleasure in her voice when
he identified himself.

"I live in an alley off Haret Al-Azzarieh," Rebeka said. "It's very near
the old Jewish synagogue, right around the corner, in fact. I'll come
down to meet you, otherwise, finding me the first time is pretty much
impossible."

Bourne liked that, and told her so. He saw her at the head of Haret
Al-Azzarieh, leaning against a crumbling brick wall that might have
been a thousand years old. She was dressed in woven leather sandals, a
long flowing cotton dress, and a brightly colored long-sleeved shirt in the
Syrian style. She seemed perfectly at ease.

"Are you hungry?" she asked, just as if they were old friends. "I know
a small place with excellent food not far from here."

Bourne nodded, and they wended their way down crumbling alleys
and narrow streets. Every city in the Middle East had a pervasive smell.

In Tunis it was jasmine, in Fez, cumin; here in Damascus it was coffee mingled with cardamom.

"What happened to your hotel reservation?"

"The room was unacceptable."

"There's no shortage of hotels in Damascus."

"But none as impossible to locate as your apartment."

She smiled as if she knew he wasn't telling the truth. Perhaps she believed that he was simply taken with her; if so, he had no intention of setting her straight. On the other hand he was curious about her. She did not strike him as a typical flight attendant: slightly bored, reserved, interested in her passengers for only as long as they were on her plane.

Walking along the streets of the Medina was like opening a pack of Advent cards. In each window, within each doorway, were a staggering array of artisans working in glass, silk, pottery, and upholstery. There were bakers and halal butchers, flower arrangers and tailors, basket weavers and dyers. On the street itself were vendors selling everything from steaming cups of thick Turkish coffee to cardamom ice cream dipped in almonds. Then there were the flamboyant water sellers, dressed in the ornate Ottoman style of the Umayyad Caliphate. The Umayyad caliphs had made Syria their home, even while their fierce armies were expanding their empire east to Baghdad and north across the Mediterranean into Spanish Andalusia.

When Bourne remarked on the number of Iraqi accents he was hearing, Rebeka said, "For some years the Medina was declining in population. Iraqis—Sunni and Christian alike—fleeing the long war changed all that. Now the Old City is packed."

The restaurant she took him to was tucked into an outdoor patio, jam-packed, and full of flavorsome odors. Vines climbed the walls and filigreed iron and brass lamps threw moonbeams of light across the tables and checkered tile floor. Niches in the black and ocher walls contained brightly colored mosaics of Ottoman sultans and Umayyad warriors.

The rotund chef bustled out from the kitchen. "*Marhaba,*" he said.

"*Marhabtayn,*" Rebeka replied.

He shook Bourne's hand and said something Bourne couldn't hear over the hubbub.

After they were seated, she said, "No menus. Baltasar will make us special dishes, probably *farooj*, because he knows it's my favorite. Do you know what this is?"

"Chicken with chilies and onions," Bourne said.

A plate of stuffed grape leaves was delivered to their table. Rebeka ordered *mate*, an Argentinian drink that had recently become beloved by many Syrians.

"So," Bourne said as they ate, "why do you live in Bab Touma?"

Rebeka licked olive oil off the fingertips of her right hand. "The history of the Jews is here. Of course there's history everywhere in the Medina, but the history of the Jews is the most evocative—stalwart, sorrowful, brave."

"You must be sorry they're mostly gone."

"I am, yes."

The *mate* appeared, a waiter pouring the beverage for them both. Bourne ignored it, waiting for it to cool, but Rebeka drank it hot through a silver straw.

"It's sad to see all the ruins," Bourne said, "the abandoned buildings, padlocked and dark. The synagogue most of all."

"Oh, the synagogue, at least, is no longer empty. It's been renovated recently."

"And worship has begun again?"

"There's an Arab living there now, not full-time, but still..." She shook her head. "Incredible, isn't it?"

"That's sometimes the end of things," Bourne said. "Sad and ironic."

She refilled her cup and shook her head again. "It shouldn't be that way. It mustn't."

The empty plate was whisked away, replaced by another piled with *falafel*.

"Tell me about the synagogue. Who lives there now?"

Rebeka frowned. "No one knows, really. At least, no one's saying. But then this city thrives on secrets."

"You live near enough. You must have seen the Arab coming and going."

She smiled, tilting her head so her eyes caught the light. "Why are you so interested in the synagogue?"

"I have business with the Arab who lives there."

She put down her cup. "You know his name?"

"I do."

"What is it?"

He popped a *falafel* ball into his mouth. "Why are you so interested in him?"

Her laugh was like velvet. "You and I have a mutual interest."

"So it would seem." Bourne swallowed some *mate*. "His name is Semid Abdul-Qahhar."

"Really? He's rather famous, isn't he?"

"In certain circles, yes, he is."

They looked at each other, and Bourne saw knowledge in her eyes that she had not spoken of. The *farooj* came, steaming and looking luscious. The babble of voices around them seemed to have built into a crescendo, forcing them to lean across the table to hear each other.

"Semid Abdul-Qahhar is a terrorist," Rebeka said, "though he pretends to be otherwise."

"How do you know that?"

"I'm Jewish," Rebeka said.

Now her interest in the Arab who had defiled the synagogue was clear.

Heₑ won't find anything of interest in my locker," Boris said.

"Zachek will decide that."

"I'm somewhat surprised to see you out of your Moscow Central bunker," Boris said.

"Some matters are worth pursuing yourself," Beria replied. "Otherwise, where is the satisfaction?"

"You're wise not to trust Zachek."

"You found that out the hard way." Beria folded his arms across his chest. "You know, General, your problem is you're too trusting. For the life of me I cannot fathom how you have persisted so long."

"Flourished," Boris said. "Use the correct term."

Beria frowned. "You certainly evince no fear. We'll soon fix that up." He smiled cheerfully. "Really, General, no one believes that you would allow Cherkesov to die without him spilling his guts."

Boris stared up at Beria. Then he crooked his forefinger, signaling for the SVR director to come closer. Beria glanced around as if he suspected a trap, then he leaned over, putting his head close to Boris's. He smelled of expensive cologne.

"Stalin wore cologne, too, Beria. Did you know that?" Boris clucked his tongue against the roof of his mouth. "Men who wear cologne . . ." He shrugged to the extent he was allowed by the masseur's weight on his back. "What can I say?"

Beria produced a pained smile. "Zachek will be back in a moment and then everything will change for you. If he finds nothing—"

"Trust me, he won't."

"If he finds nothing," Beria repeated with added emphasis on each word, "then we evacuate you to our safe house. I have men there, experts in their field."

"I probably know them either by name or by reputation," Boris said.

Beria looked at him quizzically. "I don't understand you, General."

"Few do." Boris unfurled his left hand and watched as Beria stared at the key.

Beria plucked the key up. "Is this it?"

"It is what Cherkesov was supposed to deliver to Semid Abdul-Qahhar."

Beria's head snapped up, his black, feral eyes boring into Boris's. "That terrorist is here?"

"According to Cherkesov," Boris said. "His residence is in the old synagogue in Bab Touma. Assuming I've been in this hammam for about an hour, the meet is set for two hours from now."

A flicker of suspicion momentarily crowded out Beria's expression of triumph. "Why are you telling me this, General?"

"I know when I've been outmaneuvered. And I have no wish to be evacuated to a safe house filled with sharp claws and teeth."

Beria sighed just as Zachek returned and threw the locker key on the floor, shaking his head. "My dear General, I do thank you for being so forthcoming," Beria said, "but I'm afraid I can't leave you here. You are a loose end, and I won't have that."

He raised his eyes to look at the masseur, and nodded. At once the masseur trapped Boris in a fierce grip. Beria turned, no longer concerned with Boris. He held up the key and Zachek nodded. As the two walked out, Zachek shot Boris one last look that could have meant anything. Boris paid him no mind; his attention was focused fully on what he had to do now.

The masseur was leaning over the table, his left forearm pressed down across the back of Boris's neck, his right knee on the small of Boris's back. Boris's right hand found the wooden peg under the table and pulled it with the same fierce determination he'd once used when pulling the firing pin on a hand grenade.

Without the peg's support, the front of the table collapsed. The masseur lost his balance, and, with it, the pressure he exerted on Boris's torso. Boris slid down the table, curled his legs, and twisted out from under the masseur's sprawled body. As the masseur struggled to rise, Boris punched him in the side of the face. When this had little effect, he drove his knee into the same spot. The masseur collapsed as if poleaxed.

Boris scooped up his locker key and found his way back to where his clothes still hung, careful not to run into Beria and his little prick of a lapdog. If he never saw another SVR agent in his life, he'd die a happy Russian. But he knew that was too much to hope for.

My head hurts." There was a ringing in Soraya's right ear that had nothing to do with the bandage covering half her head.

Aaron's face swam into view. "I know."

"I mean it *really* hurts."

"Be happy you're not dead. After that little stunt—"

"El-Arian?"

He responded to the anxiety in her voice. "Shot dead."

"You're sure?"

"Three shots to the chest and one to the head." He smiled thinly. "Yes, I'm sure."

Soraya relaxed visibly and licked her lips. "I'm thirsty."

Aaron took a plastic cup off a tray, poked a straw into the water he poured in it. He did something to the bed so that Soraya's head, shoulders, and torso lifted off horizontal without her having to take her head off the pillow.

She began to suck the water up.

"In the hospital again, I'm afraid." Aaron's smile turned tentative. "Not too much, we don't want it coming right back up." He placed the cup on the tray. When he turned back, his eyes engaged hers. "You almost got yourself killed."

"Almost doesn't count." When he failed to laugh, she said, "You're welcome."

"I owe you, Soraya."

She looked away. "You don't owe me anything."

He sighed, hooked his shoe through the rung of a chair, and brought it over so he could sit down beside her. "Why did you run away?"

"I hate hospitals."

He looked relieved. "I thought you hated me."

"Men," she said.

He looked down at his hands. "I'm sorry about Chalthoum."

Tears began to leak from Soraya's eyes and Aaron jumped up and used a tissue to blot the corners. Soraya jumped as if burned.

"Get away from me!"

He backed away, his face pale and drawn. Then he turned and stepped to the door. She waited until he pulled down the handle before saying, "Come back."

He hesitated, then turned. She could see in his eyes that he didn't know what to do. Something black burned inside her, reveling in her mastery over him. Then, as quickly as the spark flamed up, it died, leaving her empty and shaking.

"Which is it, Soraya?"

"Aaron. Please."

He approached her with a cautious step and sat gingerly on the edge of the chair, as if ready at any moment to flee. She looked at him. All the fight had left her. She felt as if she had gone through a terrible trial by fire, had seen loves, wants, and needs reduced to ash, leaving her naked, but no longer vulnerable. She sensed her strength returning, but it was a different form of strength, one that would require time to explore.

Her eyes fluttered closed for a moment.

"Soraya?"

She heard the anxiety in his voice and looked at him. "How am I?"

"Better than you have any right to be." He seemed relieved to be talking about a topic that was quantifiable. "When we brought you in here the doctors were very grave. Frankly, I don't think they gave you much of a chance. But the wound looked worse than it was. The bullet from El-Arian's weapon grazed your skull high enough so your vision wasn't impaired. And we've been assured that your hearing will return to normal in time."

"Nothing paralyzed."

"No, but the concussion you were walking around with will need time to heal, or surely something neurologically bad will happen. No running."

"Or falling off staircases."

He smiled. "Best to get out of that habit."

"I promise." Her fingers picked at the sheet as if she couldn't wait to get it off her. "I suppose, then, you'll have to take me to safer places."

His expression sobered. "Soraya, I promise to get you out of here as soon as I can. No more than a day or so while they finish tests, and then I'll use Robbinet's influence, assuming he's still talking to me."

"What happened between you two?"

"I lost you. He was ready to end my career if we didn't find you alive and well."

"I'll talk to him."

"Finally! I have a champion!"

He laughed and she joined in, even though it pained her a bit. She didn't mind. The pain reminded her that she was alive, and that felt so very fine.

"But you have to be good," Aaron said. "You still need plenty of bed rest."

"Don't worry, I now have a healthy respect for concussions." She grinned. "Lucky I have that hotel room, huh?"

He nodded. "But now you have to rest."

"In a minute. Please give me my cell phone."

He gave her a stern look but did as she asked, rummaging in the shallow closet. When he brought it to her, she turned it on and saw she had four messages from Hendricks, but none from Peter. She looked up at Aaron. "Okay, now scram."

His brow furrowed. "What does this mean?"

"Leave me alone."

He nodded. "I'll be right outside."

"Don't you have anywhere else to be?"

"I do." He crossed to the door and opened it. He grinned. "But I'm learning to delegate."

In all the noise of the restaurant Bourne almost didn't hear his cell phone. He was in the middle of finessing more information out of Rebeka on the building plan of the synagogue, and for a moment considered ignoring the call. Then he saw it was from Soraya and answered. But he couldn't hear a word she said, so, excusing himself, he went outside onto the street, walking several hundred feet away down a narrow alley, pressing himself against a crumbling building chained with a padlock.

"Where are you?" Her voice sounded tight and strained.

"Damascus." Bourne kept his eyes on the passing crowds. Between Boris and Corellos, he needed to be wary of death squads and lone assassins. "Are you all right?"

"Yes. Fine. I'm in Paris. I tried to call Peter but he isn't answering his cell, which is very odd. No one has seen or heard from him."

"Contact Tyrone. If he hasn't heard something, then he'll find a way."

"Good idea." She told him everything she had learned about the Monition Club, the Arab terrorist connection, and the fiduciary trail that led back to the Nymphenburg Landesbank of Munich. She did not mention Amun; she did not want to speak his name, let alone hear any expression of sympathy, however sincere. She concluded with Benjamin El-Arian's death, but omitted her injuries.

Bourne's mind was processing the information as fast as it was received. "What interests me is that the Domna's finances are handled through a Munich bank and Semid Abdul-Qahhar, the head of the Mosque in Munich, is also here in the same city where Severus Domna has its headquarters and staging area."

"Staging area for what?"

"Not sure, but I think it's an imminent attack on US soil."

"Target?"

"I don't—" Bourne broke off the conversation. He had seen someone, a flash of a face among the bobbing heads. Slamming his phone shut, he took off after the figure. As he drew closer, he was able to identify the familiar gait. Even without a clear look at the man's face, he knew it was Boris.

Bourne shouldered his way through the crowds as people squeezed together along the narrow streets. After several minutes he had a sense that Boris was headed toward the synagogue. What was he up to? Surely if he had followed Bourne here, he had lost the scent. But Boris did not give the impression of someone who was lost. On the contrary, his concentration was fierce; he was a man on a mission.

The entrance to the synagogue was down a narrow, unprepossessing alley, which gave out on a cobbled courtyard with an olive tree planted in its center. When he reached a spot where he could keep an eye on the alley, Boris melted back into shadow. He crossed his arms in front of him like an Egyptian mummy and stood absolutely still, waiting.

Bourne waited. Nothing happened. No one entered or left the alley leading to the synagogue. The sliver of sky visible was a carnival set, the night tinged a gaudy, electric blue from the lights atop the minarets.

Bourne took out his cell and dialed Boris's number. In the shadows, Boris started and grabbed for his phone. As he did so, Bourne stepped into the shadows beside him.

"Hello, Boris," he said. "I understand you've been sent to kill me."

31

JASON, WHAT IN hell are you doing here?"

"I could ask you the same question, Boris." Bourne studied his friend in the darkness. "The question is whether either of us will tell the truth."

"When have we ever lied to each other?"

"Who can say, Boris? You know far more about our relationship than I do. Right now, as far as I can see, nothing is what it seems."

"I couldn't agree more. I've been shafted by so many people these last couple of days my head is spinning."

"Friendship is a matter of trust."

"Once again, I couldn't agree more, but if you have to think about it, trust doesn't exist."

A bitterness in Boris's voice disturbed Bourne. "What's at the heart of this issue, Boris?"

"I just came from Munich. One of my oldest friends tried to have me killed there. As a matter of fact, you know him. Ivan Volkin never retired. He's been working for Severus Domna for years."

"My condolences."

"You don't seem surprised."

"The only surprise was that you two were friends."

"Well, we aren't." Boris turned his head away, peering down the street. "It seems we never were."

Bourne let a moment pass, in honor of Boris's sorrow. "Are you here to say your special form of hello to me," he said finally, "or to Semid Abdul-Qahhar?"

"No secrets from you, are there? Why am I not surprised." Boris laughed humorlessly. "Let me tell you something, my friend, several hours ago the man who forced me to make a decision between killing you and keeping my career was on the other end of my special form of hello."

"So you have removed the need to kill me."

"There was never any need, Jason. If I did what Viktor Cherkesov ordered me to do, there wouldn't be enough of me left to have a career." He grunted. "And by the way, how do you know that that prime dick Semid Abdul-Qahhar lives here?"

"How do you?"

The two men laughed together.

Boris slapped Bourne on the back. "Dammit, Jason, it's good to see you! We must have a toast to our reunion, but first I'm expecting Konstantin Beria, the head of SVR, and his little prick, Zachek, to show up here."

"How is that?"

Boris told him about the key that Cherkesov was tasked by the Domna to bring to Semid Abdul-Qahhar.

"You let Beria have it?" Bourne said.

Boris laughed. "For all the good it will do him. It's not a real key, it doesn't open anything. It's modeled after the keys in a Flash video game." Seeing the look on Bourne's face, he added, "Hard to believe, but someone inside the Domna has a sense of humor."

"What's hard to believe is that you know anything about video games."

"I need to keep up with the times, Jason, otherwise I'll get run over by the young technocrats coming to power. They use video games to keep their skills sharp and the smell of blood in their nostrils."

"You and I use the field."

"They're useless in the field, the young ones. They're always looking for shortcuts."

"For keys to unlock the next level."

"That's right. They don't think for themselves."

A cooling wind snaked down the street, bringing with it the scent of spices. The muezzins started up, the amplified calls to prayer drowning out all other noise. The street drained of people.

"The key was a test," Bourne said.

Boris nodded. "To see if Cherkesov was trustworthy and obedient."

"He failed."

"Miserably. But Semid Abdul-Qahhar doesn't know that yet. And Beria doesn't know I'm waiting for him." Boris put an arm across Bourne's chest. "Hold on. They're coming."

Bourne saw two men approaching. They wore long coats that reached down to the tops of their shoes, a clear indication that they were carrying long-barreled weapons. The older man was short and feral looking, the other younger and taller, with a face that looked like it had been put through a meat grinder. Bourne smiled as he thought of Boris's fists making vicious contact with the technocrat.

"I want these cocksuckers," Boris said. "They tried to kill me."

"It looks like they're carrying some heavy weapons," Bourne said.

"So I see."

Bourne was preparing himself when, from the corner of his eye, he saw a figure in a black robe and *hijab* come stealthily down the street from the other end. It was Rebeka.

The security for Indigo Ridge once more set, Hendricks did precisely what Skara had asked him not to do: He went looking for her. First, he tried her cell phone, but got a Chinese man who told him to go to hell in Mandarin. Next, he had a private conversation with Jonathan Brey, the head of the FBI. He and Brey went back a long time; they exchanged favors regularly.

"Anything you want, Chris," Brey said, "it's yours."

"I'm looking for someone who's dropped out of sight," Hendricks said, consumed with shame, humiliation, and the singular anguish of a jilted lover. "She may have already left the country." He paused. "She entered as Margaret Penrod, which was an alias, but I have no doubt she's now under another assumed name."

"Any idea what that might be?"

Again, those terrible emotions washed over Hendricks. "I do not."

"Photo?"

"I'll have one sent over." *The government vetting process must have one*, Hendricks thought, *otherwise I'll look even more like an idiot.* "Right now, though, I need two of your best investigators."

"Done," Brey said.

Hendricks met the agents at Skara's apartment. When the doorbell went unanswered, the agents broke in, sidearms drawn, even though Hendricks told them that wasn't necessary. Procedure, they said in almost robotic unison. Once they had secured the premises, they retired to the doorway, as Hendricks ordered, lurking like a pair of leashed guard dogs.

Hendricks took a tour around the small one-bedroom apartment. The living room was depressingly bare, exuding the stale air of abandonment. There was nothing to tell him that she had been there. Ditto, the tiny bathroom; only lint lay like sand on the narrow shelves of the medicine cabinet. The toilet tank held only water, the bathtub had been washed clean of sediment and hairs.

He stepped into the bedroom and immediately smelled her. He went through the drawers of the dresser, which were all empty. Pulling them out, he turned them over, looking for something taped to their under-sides. The closet was occupied by an assortment of hangers, nothing more. The bedside table had one drawer in which he found two paper clips, a card for her fake business, and the nub of a pencil.

With a heavy sigh, he sat down on the bed, feeling it give just the way her body gave under his weight. Wrists on knees, he bent over and stared at the floor. He missed her, there was no denying it. A hole gaped open inside him. He thought he had made sure he'd never feel that way again. His eyes swam out of focus, his thoughts swirled like water down a drain. At that moment his cell phone burred.

"Hendricks."

"Mr. Secretary, this is CI agent Tyrone Elkins."

The words slowly penetrated Hendricks's muzzy mind. "How did you get my number, son?"

"I have a message from Peter Marks."

Hendricks's brow furrowed and tension came into his shoulders and arms. "Where is Peter?"

"He's safe, sir. He's been under attack. He needs to talk with you."

"Well, put him on." There was a pause. "Peter?"

"Yes, sir."

"Are you all right?"

"I am, sir."

"What the hell has happened to you?"

Peter recounted the near miss with the car bomb and his escape from the ambulance with its impostor crew. "It was sheer luck that Tyrone was behind me," Peter concluded.

"Where the hell are you? I'll send people to—"

"All due respect, sir, after the breaches in security you warned me of and the breach at the Treadstone building, I'd rather no one know where I am for the moment. Soraya found me through Bourne."

"Bourne?"

"Both Soraya and Bourne know Tyrone, sir. That's all it's safe to say at the moment."

"And Soraya?"

"Still in Paris. She found out who ordered the murder of her contact. Benjamin El-Arian. He's dead." He continued on, telling his boss about the intel he had found that had triggered the attacks on him. "You've got to send a team to bring Roy FitzWilliams back to DC for questioning ASAP. FitzWilliams consulted for this Syrian mining company, El-Gabal, and failed to report it when he was vetted."

Another failure of the vetting process, Hendricks thought. It was a wonder this government was still standing.

Peter said: "We're looking at an imminent threat on US soil."

"Remember me when you are protecting Indigo Ridge," Skara had said.

"Indigo Ridge," Hendricks breathed.

"My thought exactly."

"Good work, Peter."

"Sir, I'm sorry I gave you a hard time. You were right about assigning me Indigo Ridge in this roundabout way."

"I'm just happy my decision didn't lead to your death."

"Your job is no bed of roses," Peter said. "But you do it well."

"Thanks." Hendricks thought a moment. "To maintain security until we have this situation nailed down, have Tyrone phone me every day at noon. I'll let you know as soon as FitzWilliams is in custody. You deserve to be in on the interrogation."

He closed the connection and called his Indigo Ridge field operations director, who was already getting flak from Danziger.

"Forget about him," Hendricks said. "I want you to take a detachment and take Roy FitzWilliams into custody."

"Sir?"

"You heard me. Assign your best man to fly him back to DC ASAP. I'll have an air force plane waiting for you. I want him delivered directly to me, is that clear?"

"As crystal, sir. Consider it done."

Hendricks called an air force general of his acquaintance and got him to authorize a jet to stand by. As he put his phone away, his gaze fell on Skara's card, lying in the drawer of the bedside table.

"Your job is no bed of roses," Peter had said.

Into his mind swam an image of Skara as he had seen her the day they met, kneeling in his tiny strip of a garden, tending his roses.

He snatched up the card. There was a rose planted squarely in its center. With his heart pounding, he jumped up and ran out of the apartment, leaving the bewildered FBI agents in his wake.

Rebeka no longer looked like a flight attendant; there was a certain intensity about her, sharply alert and purposeful. Her eyes were eager, her cheeks flushed, as if she were about to hurl herself at Fate head-on. She had transformed herself into an avenging angel. She had changed clothes since he'd left her in the restaurant, confirming what he had suspected: She had her own agenda concerning the occupants of the synagogue. All she'd been lacking was the trigger, which he himself had provided when he had given her the identity of the Arab who was desecrating the Jewish house of worship alongside which she had chosen to live. He now suspected that she was Mossad, but in the end it didn't matter. She was out to infiltrate the synagogue and assassinate Semid Abdul-Qahhar. The trouble was she was walking blind into a lethal crossfire between Semid Abdul-Qahhar's men and the SVR. He had to stop her.

He was preparing himself to block her way when she veered off. She wasn't headed for the alley that led to the synagogue after all. But because of their interrupted discussion over dinner concerning the synagogue's architectural plan, he knew where she was going.

Grabbing Boris, he headed down the street after her.

Boris pulled back. "Are you crazy? You're going to screw up everything."

Bourne turned back to him. "It's a matter of trust, Boris."

Hesitating only a moment, Boris nodded, then followed Bourne as he headed left, down an alley that ran more or less parallel to the one leading to the synagogue.

Up ahead, Bourne saw Rebeka vanish to the left. He picked up his pace, Boris right behind him. When he reached the spot where Rebeka had disappeared, he saw a passageway no wider than shoulder-width. He plunged in, summoning up the plan of the ancient synagogue as Rebeka had described it to him.

Abruptly he came to the end of the passageway. A blank wall faced him.

"What the hell is this, Jason?" Boris whispered.

"We're following a Mossad agent who knows another way into the synagogue."

"How? Did she melt through solid stone?"

They were engulfed in darkness. Bourne reviewed everything he had learned about the synagogue from Rebeka. He knew where it was in relation to the passageway, so he turned to the left and felt along the stone wall, searching for a lever or handle. Nothing. Then he stepped back a pace, almost bumping into Boris, and his right foot scraped against a metal grate.

Both men backed up enough for Bourne to kneel down and feel around with his fingers. The grate was square, large enough for a human being to fit through. Curling his fingers through the holes, he pulled upward. The grate gave easily and he stood it on end against one wall. Then he slipped his legs into the hole. His shoes struck something.

"There's a ladder," he said to Boris, who had squatted beside him.

The two men climbed down. The ladder was made of iron, flaking off beneath their grip, attesting to its extreme age. They arrived at the lower level, which was carved out of the living rock. To their left Bourne saw a soft glow, and he and Boris followed it until Bourne was certain they were beneath the synagogue. A set of stone steps led upward, and Bourne and Boris took them, moving with extreme stealth.

At the top of the stairs was a narrow door made of hand-planed hardwood, bound with wide bronze bands. Cautiously, Bourne depressed the iron lever and pushed the door inward. They stepped across the threshold and found themselves in a section of the synagogue that was still in the process of being renovated. Sheets of striated marble and black stone lay against one wall or across rough-hewn sawhorses, where they were being cut to size. Curtains of undyed muslin closed off the area to protect the rest of the interior against the stone dust.

They crept forward until they were at the muslin curtains. Bourne listened for any sounds of a struggle, but heard only the hushed sound of footsteps muffled by carpets, the occasional word or two of Arabic, spoken softly but urgently.

Parting the curtains, they slipped through into the central section, renovated in the Arabic style.

"This Mossad agent is going to get herself killed here," Boris whispered.

"The name she's going by is Rebeka, Bourne said."

"Maybe we'll get lucky and the SVR and Semid Abdul-Qahhar will kill each other," Boris muttered as he stared into the middle distance.

But Bourne could tell by his tone that he didn't believe it. Nothing in their world was ever so neatly wrapped up, there was too much rage and high emotion, too much blood already spilled, so much more to be poured out.

They moved forward. The great spaces the ancient architects of the synagogue had provided were now broken up into small rooms, all ornately painted and furnished, like a sultan's seraglio. There was none of the desert Arab's austere sensibility to be found. All the prayer rugs were opulent, woven of the finest silk in intricate, jewel-tone patterns.

"Where the hell are Beria and his lackey?" Boris whispered.

Bourne wondered where anyone was. He had no idea how many men Semid Abdul-Qahhar had with him or how heavily armed they were. He looked up and discovered a safe way to find out. The rooms were constructed with thick, hand-hewn beams of fragrant cedar that rose to a height of ten feet, well below the height of the original structure. There was no ceiling to the rooms, simply crossbeams to keep the vertical ones true, and swaths of fabric hung from beam to beam.

He signaled to Boris to go on ahead, then worked his way up one of the beams, finding footholds in the rough wood. The beams were massive six-by-sixes, allowing him to stretch out along them as he crawled from room to room. The fabric was sheer enough to make out figures, their positions in the rooms, and their movement inside them. He saw three of Semid Abdul-Qahhar's men, one alone in a room, preparing to pray, but no sign of either Rebeka or Semid himself. He knew that she must be as focused on Semid as he was; the men were just a temporary roadblock.

And then, in the fifth room, he saw her. She was with Semid, but there wasn't anything about the scene he liked.

Boris crept forward on little cat feet, as the poem went, one that he had memorized when he was a boy and repeated to himself each night before he went to bed, as if it were a prayer. Tonight, however, his heart was full of blood; all he could think of was Zachek and Beria. It occurred to him now that his line of work was defined by a chain of affronts and retributions. You just had to pray that you would survive them all . . . on little cat feet.

He entered a room where a man was kneeling on a prayer rug, his forehead pointing toward Mecca. A short-barreled assault rifle lay at his side. Boris could hear the muttered prayer, words falling like rain from the Arab's mouth as his torso rose and fell. Boris waited until his forehead touched the rug. Then he stepped silently up to him and, putting all his weight into it, slammed his shoe down on the back of the man's neck. He heard a series of sharp cracks, like someone puncturing bubble wrap, and the man collapsed.

Scooping up the assault rifle, Boris stepped over the corpse and continued on.

Two men were behind Rebeka. Bourne couldn't tell whether or not she was aware of them, so he leapt off his perch, crashing down through the fabric. He landed in a crouch. The men turned, and he swung a leg out, catching one of them behind the knees. He went down in a tangle, and Bourne was on him at once with both fists.

Rebeka struck the second man on the side of the head. He staggered back, but managed to raise his assault rifle and fire off a barrage of shots. She went down at his feet, and he lifted the butt of the weapon as if to slam it onto the top of her head, but first she drove her fist into his crotch. As he doubled over, she drew a slender knife from beneath her black cloak and slit open his belly from one side to the other.

Even as his eyes opened wide in shock, she was leapfrogging over him, stretching out to grab the hem of Semid Abdul-Qahhar's robe. He stumbled but used a wide-bladed dirk to cut away that section of cloth, freeing himself. He ran from the room.

Bourne rose from the floor and sprinted after Rebeka as she followed Semid out of the seraglio rooms and into the synagogue proper.

The moment Boris heard the rapid-fire blasts, he broke into a run. Beria and Zachek, both wielding AK-74 assault rifles, were spread-legged, standing side by side, as they mercilessly mowed down six of Semid Abdul-Qahhar's men.

Zachek spotted Boris as he ran into the entry space and turned his weapon, firing indiscriminately. Boris retreated behind the doorway through which he had entered. The firing was so blistering he had to wait, crouched, heart hammering, before he could make a reappearance. By that time, only the bodies of the six men remained, twisted and bleeding from multiple wounds. No sign of either Beria or Zachek.

Keeping his rage and frustration in check, he took each room one by one, listening as well as looking. Then he heard another burst of gunfire and headed off to his left. A bullet tore into his left calf as he crossed a threshold. He went down, his left leg collapsing under him, but landed on his right shoulder, tucking it in so that he rolled, coming up onto one knee and returning fire. He nearly took Zachek's head off, but the little prick pulled back just in time.

Boris moved, even though it pained him and his left ankle almost buckled. It was a good thing he did because Zachek's head and shoulders popped up as he fired at the spot Boris had just vacated. Swinging his assault rifle around, Boris clipped the corner of the wall behind which Zachek hid. Wood and plaster splinters fountained up, and Boris moved again, this time in the opposite direction, and when Zachek appeared again, firing at the spot where Boris would have been if he had continued in the same direction, Boris drilled Zachek's left shoulder.

As Zachek fell backward, Boris sprinted directly at him, holding his fire until Zachek came into view. Zachek squeezed the trigger of his AK-74 and more bits of wood and plaster blinded Boris momentarily. Still, he came on, knowing it was fatal to stay in one place.

Clearing his vision, he saw Zachek on the floor. His back was against a wall. Blood streamed from his shattered left shoulder. He was desperately trying to reload his weapon.

Sensing Boris, his head came up and he bared his teeth like a rabid dog. Then he grinned, threw the assault rifle away, and spread his hands.

"I surrender, General. Don't shoot, I'm unarmed."

Boris glimpsed the tiny derringer half hidden in Zachek's right hand. But even if the little prick had been unarmed, Boris knew it wouldn't have mattered. He pulled the trigger on his assault rifle and Zachek briefly danced like a marionette whose strings were being cut. In a mass of blood, he slipped sideways and his eyes went dark.

Something significant must have happened, Boris thought, because he saw that Beria had now begun his retreat from the synagogue. Boris was intrigued. He deduced that Bourne had somehow altered the situation irretrievably, and that Beria was pragmatic enough to get out while his skin was whole.

That wasn't going to happen.

Boris caught up with him in the entryway, already littered with six corpses. Beria, in full flight, chose the shortest distance between him and the front door. This route took him between two of the bodies. The instant he skidded in a puddle of blood, Boris, loping from behind at full speed, barreled into him. Something lurched in his left ankle and a javelin of fire scorched up his leg. The bullet from Zachek's assault rifle had gone completely through his calf, which was good, but the wound was bleeding profusely. The leg needed to be elevated and the wound seen to. Boris's leg gave way and he went down hard on one knee. A sea of pain swept through him. Beria, only partially recovered, swung the butt of his AK-74 across Boris's chin, knocking him flat.

Beria aimed the assault rifle, about to pull the trigger when he heard voices echoing suddenly and frighteningly. Unwilling to give away his position by firing, he whipped around and fled the synagogue as fast as his legs would carry him.

Bourne saw Semid Abdul-Qahhar take a swipe at Rebeka with his gleaming dirk. She countered with her thin-bladed knife, then closed with him, slipping inside his defenses, slicing his left cheek from just beneath the eye to the corner of his mouth, which opened wide, but made no sound. He struck her in the side with his fist, then delivered a vicious kick to her ribs, which slammed her against a wall.

He came in hard and fast, leading with the dirk while fumbling beneath his robe with the other hand. Rebeka was defending herself against the stab of the dirk. She evaded it with ease, but only because it was a feint.

Bourne saw before she did that Semid gripped a Mauser in his other hand. He leapt at Semid, knocking him back, wrestling the Mauser out of his hand. As Semid turned toward Bourne's attack, Rebeka contemptuously slapped aside the dirk and stabbed inward with her own knife. The blade penetrated Semid's chest just below the sternum, and, with a surgeon's deft hand, she twisted it upward and to the left, puncturing a lung, and then the heart.

Blood bubbled out of Semid's mouth as he sighed a fetid breath. She stared hard into his eyes while she held him up with her knife blade and her tensed arm.

"Rebeka," Bourne said.

She studied Semid as if he were a specimen pinned to a lab table.

"Rebeka," Bourne repeated, more gently this time.

She expelled a breath and, at the same time, withdrew the knife blade, and the body fell to the floor. Bourne expected an expression of triumph on her face, but when she turned to him, there was only disgust.

She stared at him for a long moment, and Bourne had the impression that he was facing a singular creature, precisely controlled and calibrated on the outside, but possessing an untamed spirit and a wild heart.

"You ran out on me," she said as she wiped her blade free of blood and gore, "and now I find you here."

"Lucky you." He smiled. "Don't tell me you're surprised."

Her eyes burned with a cold fury. "This is my territory."

"That's irrelevant now," he said evenly, trying to defuse her anger. "Semid Abdul-Qahhar is dead."

She kicked the corpse so it flopped over on its back. "Whoever the hell this is," she said, "he's not Semid Abdul-Qahhar."

32

THERE WERE TIMES—and this was one of them—when Hendricks resented the security detail that followed him around as closely as his own shadow. He resented the fact that they were surely speculating on what had caused him to drive hell-for-leather back to his house in the middle of a workday. Worse, they watched him from behind smoked-glass windows as he crossed to his rose garden, got down on his knees, and began rooting around.

One of them, Richards, he thought, exited his car and strode to where he knelt.

"Sir, are you feeling well?"

"Perfectly," Hendricks said with a distracted air.

"Is there anything I can do?"

"You can return to your car."

"Yes, sir," Richards said, after a short pause.

Hendricks, glancing over his shoulder, saw Richards shrug, signing to his compatriots that he had no idea what the boss was up to. Returning to his work, Hendricks tried to calm himself, but he found to his horror that his hands were trembling uncontrollably. The moment he'd picked up Skara's business card and seen the rose imprinted on it, he'd become certain that she had left the card for him to find. Only he would understand the rose's significance.

"I'm on my final journey."

He was terribly afraid that Skara was going to do something irrevocable. He could not imagine her killing herself, but then he knew so little about her. And yet, strangely, he felt that he had known her all his life. It was a complete mystery to him how someone could become a part of his life so quickly. She had crawled under his skin and, lodged there, refused to budge. Her sudden disappearance only made him more acutely aware of how she affected him.

"I'm on my final journey."

Was she going to do something terrible, some final act that one way or another would snuff out her life? This was the scenario that terrified him.

"I'm on my final journey."

He had convinced himself that she'd left him a clue to what she was about to do, that she wanted him to stop her, that he was the only one with the ability to do so. He desperately wanted to believe that she felt about him the way he felt about her. Hadn't she said as much on the DVD? But he harbored a suspicion that it had been a performance, that she had not really revealed what was in her hidden heart, and that now he would never know, because within days, or even hours, her life would be extinguished like a candle flame.

His shaking hands were covered with soil, his nails dark with grit. Starting at the left side of the rose garden, he was making his methodical way toward the right. At the base of each plant, his fingers dug into the soil, hoping to find something she had buried there for him to find after she had gone. But he came to the last rose and, digging in, found nothing.

He sat back on his haunches, resting his wrists on his knees while he stared at the flowers. He loved his roses, their colors and scents, but now all he saw were the thorns. Perhaps this time a rose was just a rose. He didn't want to believe it, but now he had to, because there was nothing else for him to believe.

Bitter tears rose into his eyes, and, ashamed and despairing, he covered his face with his filthy hands.

Boris was nowhere to be found. Bourne, making a quick inventory of the dead and dying, found no trace of either Boris, for which he was profoundly grateful, or the SVR chief, Konstantin Beria. Briefly, he wondered whether they had gone, but he had his own agenda to consider.

"I've been after Semid Abdul-Qahhar for three years," Rebeka said as they exited the synagogue the way they both had entered it. "He employs half a dozen doubles who look like him and talk like him. More often than not, they're the ones who appear in public. Semid Abdul-Qahhar himself can be seen in the periodic taped messages his people send to Al Jazeera. I've studied those tapes in detail. I know what the real Semid Abdul-Qahhar looks like. Virtually no one else outside his circle of lieutenants does."

That there might be body doubles changed Bourne's plan radically. Boris had told him Semid Abdul-Qahhar was in Damascus. Now he sensed that the synagogue was a ruse. If so, then he knew that the leader of the Mosque must be at El-Gabal. This had many implications, not the least of which was that the planning phase of the terrorist attack was at an end, the operations phase had begun, and Bourne had little time to infiltrate El-Gabal, plant the cloned SIM cards, and set off the charges inside the twelve crates of FN SCAR-M, Mark 20 assault rifles Don Fernando had spiked.

He wanted to go into El-Gabal alone, but he realized now that having Rebeka with him was vital. Only she could recognize Semid Abdul-Qahhar. If he really was in the building, Bourne was not going to let this opportunity to kill him pass. Semid was the real danger. With El-Arian dead, he was now the heart and soul of Severus Domna; without his support the organization would be so severely weakened that it could be dealt with by Soraya, Peter, and their team. But if Semid somehow survived, his grip on the Domna would become a stranglehold, and with its members in legitimate positions in business and politics, Semid's potential for launching terrorist attacks expanded exponentially. Bourne could not allow that to happen.

As they reached the street, he told Rebeka about El-Gabal and what he needed to do. "I think that's where Semid Abdul-Qahhar is. I know how to get in, just as you knew how to get into the synagogue without being observed," he concluded. "Either you're with me or we part ways here."

To her credit, she didn't hesitate an instant. They took a taxi to the train station, where he opened the locker and took out the duffel filled with the implements he had purchased earlier. Rebeka watched him with the ghost of a smile on her lips.

"What's so amusing?" Bourne said as they exited the terminal.

"Nothing really." She shrugged. "It's only that I was right and my superiors were wrong." Her smile widened. "It was no coincidence that I was working your flight from Madrid."

"Mossad was tracking me."

"You think I'm Mossad?"

He did not reply as he guided her along the wide streets that led to Avenue Choukry Kouatly. They both wore Syrian clothes, so no one gave them a second look. Rebeka's head was completely covered by her *hijab*.

"*I've* been tracking you," she said. "Once I had identified the connection between Semid Abdul-Qahhar and Severus Domna, I knew our paths were going to cross. Your false name didn't fool me; I'd seen your photo and matched it to ones we have in our files."

"So you didn't care that I ran out on you."

"Frankly, I expected it."

"I owe you for the check."

She grinned. "My treat."

"Now that I'm taking you in with me."

She laughed softly. "Everything my superiors think they know about you is wrong."

"Let's keep it that way," he said.

Within twenty minutes, they had reached the area around the El-Gabal complex. Lights were blazing inside, though it was after 2 AM.

Bourne, crouched in shadow, observed the uptick in both activity and guards. The loading dock and surrounding area were crawling with armed men. Trucks had not yet pulled up, but the first of them was rumbling down the street. He had less time than he had thought, an hour at the outside, probably less.

Rebeka, crouched in the shadows beside him, said, "You're sure you can get us inside? The building is crawling with armed guards."

Bourne unzipped the duffel. "Watch me," he said.

Boris sat at an all-night café with his left leg up on a chair. The doctor he had gotten out of bed to clean and dress his wound insisted on an outrageous sum of money, even though he knew Boris from previous visits. Boris was beyond caring.

When he had left the synagogue, he had spent a dizzying and unsuccessful half hour scouring the maze of surrounding streets in Bab Touma for Beria. His heart was a black pit in which he wanted to bury the SVR director. Then, like a switch being thrown, something changed. Most likely it was the pain, which had become so severe he could hardly stand on his left leg, and, with the adrenaline draining out of him, he felt overcome by exhaustion. Beria could wait; he needed to take care of himself.

Now, sitting with a cup of thick Turkish coffee laced with cardamom and a small plate of sticky sweets, he popped pills in his mouth—a painkiller and an antibiotic—and, with a grimace, swallowed them dry. He sipped his coffee, which warmed him heart and soul, and watched the intermittent comings and goings on the street.

After some consideration he thought that breaking off his pursuit had little to do with pain; he had endured much worse and kept going. He sensed that his change of heart stemmed, instead, from his reunion with Jason Bourne. That brief encounter had brought home that his life—his and Jason's—did not have to be predicated solely on a chain of affronts and retributions. There could, in fact, be a human element, and, after all, it was friends like Jason, even if Jason was the only one, who made this life bearable. Briefly, he thought about Jason, wondering where he was. It didn't matter; Boris was in no shape to be of help to him. Besides, Jason worked best when he was on his own.

Boris sighed and took a bite of a sweet, holding it in his mouth while the paper-thin layers of pastry dissolved and the honey melted on his tongue. He did not want to turn into a modern-day Ahab. He had made promises to himself, true enough, but their fulfillment could wait for another time, another place.

Wasn't revenge a dish best served cold?

Removing the length of electrical wire and the pickax from the duffel, Bourne attached the haft to one end of the longer coil of rope. He stood up, moving several paces away from Rebeka. They were both well in the penumbra of shadow cast by a stand of royal palm trees. The west side of the El-Gabal building was in front of them, the palms behind them and, beyond, a bank building, dark and brooding. Security lights blazed on either corner of El-Gabal, but there was a narrow stripe of shadow down the center of the building's side.

As Bourne began to swing the rope with the pickax at its end, Rebeka saw what he was about to do. "There may be guards on the roof," she said.

When Bourne said, "I'm counting on it," she shot him a quizzical look.

Bourne waited until the throaty roar of the trucks' exhaust rose through the night, then whirled the pickax over his head and let it go, watched it as it rose up into the night and landed on the roof. Whatever sound it made was masked by the burble of the trucks. Tugging on the rope, he pulled the pickax toward him until its curved head caught in the crack between the roof and the low parapet wall. He strapped the duffel across his back, and, without another word to Rebeka, began his ascent of the strip of shadowed wall.

When he was halfway up, she took hold of the rope and hauled herself up after him. The noise from the trucks had ceased, making them hypervigilant about any noise whatsoever. Bourne reached the parapet, grabbed hold of it with one hand, and rose up high enough to peek over the top. Two guards were visible. One was standing in the center of what looked like an enormous target painted onto the flat roof. Outlining its circumference were a series of small blue LED lights, which burned very brightly. The second guard was at the rear of the roof, his hands on the parapet as he leaned over, staring down at the increased activity on the loading dock.

Bourne launched himself over the parapet and crouched down onto the roof. A moment later, Rebeka joined him.

"They've got a helipad up here," she whispered in his ear. "The lights are on so they must be expecting a helicopter."

He nodded. "It looks like this is the way the real Semid Abdul-Qahhar is going to make his exit."

To one side of the helipad was a glass-covered hatch, large enough so that both men and matériel could be taken from inside the building to the helicopter, or vice versa. It was a neat solution to arriving and leaving quickly. Bourne signaled Rebeka to take the guard at the rear while he handled the one at the helipad.

The roof, made of a gravelly substance, was dotted with risers, water tanks, vents, and elevator and HVAC housings. He crabbed his way from one of these to the next. This was the easy part because he could keep to the shadows cast by the structures. The circle of light cast by the LEDs was another story entirely. As he came to rest behind the elevator housing, he picked up a loose piece of gravel and threw it so that it hit the side of a water tank twenty feet to his right.

The guard turned his head instantly and, unstrapping his AK-74, came cautiously toward the spot where the gravel had struck the tank. He walked around the tank. As he turned his back on Bourne's position, Bourne sprinted across the intervening space, leapt onto the guard's back, and, wrapping his arm around the guard's neck, snapped it. He lay the limp body down and took the automatic weapon from nerveless hands.

Scuttling back around the water tank, he made for the rear of the roof. He saw the second guard sprawled on the gravel. Above him was Rebeka, but she wasn't alone. A third guard, one hidden from both of them until now, was creeping up on her. Not wanting to fire his weapon, he ran toward her, but the instant the third guard was within arm's length, she whirled, struck away the muzzle of his AK-74, drove her fist into his gut, and grabbed him by the throat. The guard arched back, straining to fire his weapon so as to alert the guards on the loading dock. Rebeka was forced to relinquish her grip on his throat in order to pry open his hold on the assault rifle. As it clattered to the rooftop, something flashed in his hand and drove inward. Rebeka slipped her arm through his, twisted sharply, fracturing his elbow. The guard groaned, his knees giving way, and she slammed the heel of her hand into the base of his nose, jamming the cartilage back into his brain. He keeled over, dead before his body hit the gravel.

Bourne was at Rebeka's side. She grinned up into his face, then her eyes went out of focus and she slid into his arms, her head flung back, her face to the starry night. He saw the slick blackness, felt the warm flow of blood coming from the knife wound in her side. She was panting, her lips parted.

He lay her down and began to part her clothes in order to see the extent of her wound.

"Don't bother," she said. "You have a deadline to make. I won't be the reason you don't make it."

"Shut up." Bourne's fingers moved quickly and expertly over the wound. It was deep, but he couldn't find any evidence of organ damage. This was good, of course, but she was still losing blood at a rapid rate. If he didn't take immediate action, she would bleed to death. Ripping her cloak into strips, he wound them around her, binding the wound as tightly as he dared. The blood stopped flowing for a moment, but then it began to soak through the material.

"Listen to me," she said in an urgent voice, "the real Semid Abdul-Qahhar has a tic at the outer corner of his right eye. You'll see a tiny muscle pulsing. That's something that can't be replicated by his doubles."

Bourne nodded as he bound her with another layer. This was as much as he could do.

"Leave me now," she said.

Still, he hesitated.

"Go on." She gave up a tight smile. "I can take care of myself. I'm Mossad."

"I'll come back for you."

Her smile turned sardonic. "No you won't. But thanks, anyway."

He rose and peered over the rear parapet. The doors of the loading bay had been thrown open. He had to get to the stash of spiked weapons before they were loaded onto the trucks. He had no time to argue with her.

Without a backward glance, he ran to the hatch that led down into the building. Stripping off his clothes, he clad himself in the uniform of the guard he had killed. Then he surveyed the top of the hatch. Through it, he could see a storeroom, for the moment at least dark and deserted. A ladder led up from the floor to one side of the hatch. He wasn't surprised to see an alarm wire running around the edge of it. Instantly, he knew that without suction cups to hold the glass in place after he had cut it, the glass cutter was of no use. Setting down the duffel, he brought out the wide-bladed knife. He drove the tip of the blade into the base of the hatch, where it met the gravel. The tip broke off, leaving the end looking more like a screwdriver than a knife blade.

The hinges of the hatch were on the side opposite the ladder. Using the broken tip of the blade, Bourne loosened the screws enough to lift the hatch. He found the alarm trip wire, used the knife to cut through the insulation in two places, then wrapped the bare ends of the electrical wire to the bare spots to keep the circuit intact while extending the length of the trip wire. Then he raised the hatch far enough for him to slither through. He dropped to the floor of the storeroom, found the door, and stepped out into a long corridor that stretched to his left and right. Directly ahead of him was a half wall. Peering down, he could see the whole of the warehouse structure laid out below him. He looked for the twelve long crates and spotted them almost immediately. They were off to the right side. To the left were the open doors that led out to the loading bay. The first crates were being taken out to be loaded onto the trucks. He spent ten seconds memorizing the warehouse layout, then found the nearest staircase and began his rapid descent.

The upper floors were no problem—everyone was on the ground floor overseeing the loading of the war matériel. As yet, there was no sign of Semid Abdul-Qahhar, but Bourne was sure he wouldn't be far away. This shipment was much too valuable for him to leave its transit to subordinates.

He met the first guard one flight above floor level. The guard nodded to him, but as Bourne brushed past him, he reached for Bourne's left arm.

"Where is your weapon?" he said.

"Right here," Bourne replied as he slammed the guard's head back against the wall. The guard's eyes rolled up in his head as he slid down. Bourne took the AK-74 and continued on his way down. Judging by the pace of loading, he calculated he had ten minutes at the outside to set the SIMs in place and get out of the building before he sent the electronic signal that would blow the place sky-high.

The second guard stood just to one side of the bottom of the staircase. He nodded disinterestedly as Bourne came down off the last step. Bourne took one step past him, swiveled, and buried the butt of the AK-74 into the guard's belly. He doubled over and Bourne slammed the butt into the back of his neck. After dragging the body back into the shadows, he set off on a route that would take him quickly to the two stacks of spiked FN SCAR-M, Mark 20s.

He spent a precious minute blending into the swarm of men, directing a group away from Don Fernando's crates to a stack of wooden boxes on the other side of the poured concrete floor. He had twelve cloned SIM cards, one for each crate. Don Fernando had been quite specific as to where Bourne should place the SIMs on the side of each crate. The tiny cards had sticky backs. All Bourne had to do was peel off the covering film and slap them into place. He had affixed six of them when a commanding voice called out, "You there, guard! What are you doing?"

Bourne turned to see a man who looked like Semid Abdul-Qahhar.

He had stepped out from behind a wall of crates that were apparently not slated for departure tonight.

Semid's eyes narrowed as he beckoned Bourne over. "You are unfamiliar to me."

"I was assigned to the warehouse this morning."

Semid nodded to two men who had come up behind Bourne. They stuck the muzzles of their AK-74s into the small of his back and marched him behind the wall of crates.

"No one was reassigned to El-Gabal this morning," Semid said, "or any day this week." He stepped closer as one of his men stripped Bourne of his weapon. "Who are you? More importantly, how did you infiltrate the building?" When Bourne made no reply, he smiled. "Well, we'll deal with you the moment the loading is complete."

Bourne grabbed the arm of the guard on his right and swiveled from the waist, taking the man off his feet. Bourne chopped down on the other guard's wrist and, with his trigger hand clearly numb, ripped the AK-74 out of his grip and clubbed him over the head. The first guard, having reared back, charged Bourne with his head down. His face connected with Bourne's right knee, something cracked, and he collapsed.

Bourne turned right into the muzzle of a Makarov, which Semid pushed against his teeth. Bourne was close enough to see the tiny spasm at the corner of his right eye.

"Don't move," Semid said softly and fiercely, "or I'll blow the back of your head off." He patted Bourne down with great precision and expertise. "Hands at your sides." Finding nothing, he leaned in so that his nose was almost touching Bourne's. The overpowering scent of cloves filled Bourne's nose. "There is nothing more for you to do here. Five minutes from now this place will be deserted, except for the dead, which will include you."

Time was rapidly running out. It was now or never. Bourne laughed, one hand creeping into his pocket.

"What are you doing? Take your hand out of there." Semid Abdul-Qahhar waved the Makarov in Bourne's face. "Slowly."

Bourne did as he was asked.

"Open your hand."

Bourne did so. As Semid Abdul-Qahhar grabbed his hand, he leaned in to take a closer look, the Makarov wavered a little, and Bourne shoved one of the false teeth he had been carrying between Semid's teeth. At almost the same instant he slammed the flat of his hand into the bottom of the other man's chin, forcing his teeth together. The false tooth cracked and the hydrogen cyanide flooded Semid Abdul-Qahhar's mouth. Semid swallowed convulsively in order not to choke. Instantly his eyes opened wide and he brought the Makarov to bear. Bourne was ready for him, knocking the handgun away. Semid tried to grab a handful of Bourne's uniform to steady himself, but he slid to his knees. Bourne unknotted his fingers. A blue froth appeared at the corners of Semid's mouth. He made sounds without words, the stuff of nightmares. Then his eyes clouded over, and Bourne kicked him, dragging him back behind a niche in the wall.

Emerging from behind the wall of crates, he affixed the last six SIM cards in place. A contingent of four men was coming in his direction. Bourne pressed 666 on the cell's keypad. Three minutes until the building and everyone in it would be blown to atoms.

"These need to be taken onto the truck," Bourne said to the men.

The lead man frowned. "I thought they were to stay here."

"Change of plan," Bourne said in the clipped voice of authority all soldiers automatically obeyed. "Orders from Semid Abdul-Qahhar himself."

The man shrugged and beckoned to his men. They bypassed Don Fernando's crates and started on the ones behind. Bourne was now faced with a crucial decision. If he walked out onto the loading dock, past the guards, and into the back street, he would be leaving Rebeka behind, and he could not do that.

As soon as the men hefted the first crate, Bourne turned on his heel and retraced his steps, across the floor, up the stairs, and out onto the open hallway that led to the supply room with its ladder up to the roof and the longer but preferable route to safety.

He opened the door and stepped into the room, right into a small, silver-plated .22 Beretta aimed at him. It appeared identical to the gun Viveka Norén had aimed at him in Frequencies, the Stockholm disco, years ago. Holding it was a beautiful woman with blond hair and Viveka's light eyes. She looked exactly like Kaja, but from her formidable expression and the way she held herself he knew it couldn't be Kaja. It was her twin sister, the dangerous multiple-personality Skara.

33

FRACTURED LIGHT FELL like daggers through the skylight, piercing the shadows, illuminating sections of her face—cheek, nose, a triangle of forehead.

"Skara."

She frowned. "Who are you?"

"I've met your sister," Bourne said. "Kaja."

"Kaja." She traced her oval lips with the tip of her tongue, as if tasting the name. "Isn't she dead?"

Two minutes left. "Skara, we have to get out of here."

"*I* am getting out of here. Abdul-Qahhar and I together, leaving this hellhole of a country far behind."

She cocked her head to one side. "Hear that?" The roaring of rotors overhead. Lights played crazily across her face. Her eyes glittered. "It's the sound of the copter landing." She smiled viciously, baring her teeth. "It's also the sound of your death."

A heavy thump above their heads caused her attention to flicker, and Bourne leapt at her. She fired the Beretta, and he felt a small flame in his left shoulder. Then he had her. He tried to snatch the .22 away from her, but she was quicker and more tenacious than he expected, and she re-trained her grip on the handgun, trying to bring it to bear on his chest. He strode into her, pushing her back with his superior weight and strength so that the handgun was trapped between their bodies. The backs of her calves struck a box, and she stumbled backward. He made another grab for the .22, twisting it.

As they struggled for control of the Beretta her eyes were fierce in the dimness. There was something different about them, something familiar. "Kill me," she cried. "Kill me now and end this."

He tried to wrest the .22 away, but she resisted, the Beretta turned awkwardly, and her finger pulled the trigger twice in rapid succession. Blood fountained out of her, the bullets rupturing major arteries, including her aorta.

"Skara," Bourne called as he pulled her back toward him, but she was already beyond hearing him or anyone else.

The sleek black Sikorsky S-76C++ helicopter was waiting on the center of the target, its rotors spinning, whipping up a baleful wind. Bourne saw the pilot, but no one else inside. He ran, hunched over, to where Rebeka sat, her back against the rear parapet. Her eyes were closed and for a moment he thought she was dead, but when he lifted her in his arms her eyes fluttered open.

She was shivering. "You came back." Her words were ripped away like sheets of paper by the roaring of the helicopter. Her teeth chattered.

Bourne ran, bent over, his upper body protecting her. It seemed as if she hadn't lost much more blood. The pilot leaned over and opened the door, but as soon as he saw they weren't his expected passengers, he drew his sidearm. Before he could aim it, Bourne shot him between the eyes with Viveka Norén's silver-plated .22.

After placing Rebeka in the passenger's seat, he wrapped her in a cashmere blanket he found in the back and strapped her in. He ran around and, opening the pilot's-side door, hauled him out and climbed in, slamming the door behind him. At that moment a slew of guards erupted out of the rooftop hatch. Semid or one of the dead guards must have been discovered. The men began firing at the helicopter.

Working the controls, Bourne took off, banking toward the west. Enough adrenaline was still pumping that he didn't yet feel any pain in his left shoulder.

High in the sky, he turned and saw the fireball erupt, blotting out the buildings behind it, as the entire El-Gabal complex was obliterated. The shock wave manhandled the shuddering Sikorsky, which dipped and spun, but Bourne managed to regain control. He flew as low as he dared. He knew within minutes Syrian fighter jets would be screaming toward the explosion, along with fire, police, army, and emergency vehicles.

Rebeka stirred and said something he couldn't hear over the roar of the engines. Holding the steering oval steady between his knees, he leaned over, slipped a pair of headphones over her head identical to the pair he wore, then adjusted the attached microphone. Now they could speak to each other through the com center.

"Is Semid dead?" Even in pain and severely weakened by loss of blood, she had a one-track mind.

"Yes."

"You're sure it was him?"

"I saw the tic."

A sigh of contentment escaped her.

He saw the pilot's flight plan taped above his head and he stuck to it until the last minute, then headed due west.

She stirred beside him. "Where are we going?"

"Lebanon."

"Thirty-three, thirty-two, fifty-five, sixty-four north by thirty-six, oh-two, oh-four, fifty east."

She was giving him specific map coordinates. He punched them in and the helicopter banked left, then flew straight on.

"Radar," she said. Her voice was thin and reedy.

"I'm going in as low as possible," Bourne said. In the pearly light of dawn, he could make out the snaking line of barbed wire with the periodic signs warning of land mines. "Close now."

Overhead a silver flash drew his attention. The plane was too high to see whether it was a commercial flight or a Syrian army fighter. He flew on. Only several thousand yards now. The silver flash grew in his vision as the plane commenced a steep dive. It was a Syrian army jet.

Even before he heard the first volleys of machine-gun fire, he put the helicopter into a series of daredevil evasive maneuvers. The Syrian jet was coming fast, but now the barbed wire of the border was below him. The jet sent one last volley, hoping to set off one of the land mines, and then they were through. The jet veered off, climbing steeply until it vanished into the sunrise.

"We're in Lebanon." Bourne glanced over. Her head was lolling. "Rebeka?"

Her eyes opened and she drew a deep, shuddering breath. "I'm tired."

"Rebeka, we've crossed over."

A sphinx-like smile spread across her lips. "The Red Sea has parted." Momentarily revived, she peered out through the Perspex at the arid landscape, shimmering like copper. "Head southwest. Make for Dahr El Ahmar." She gave him the new coordinates.

Bourne saw pinpricks of blood seeping through the blanket. She must have been shaken up during his violent maneuvering. "Hold on," he said, making the course correction. "I'll have you down in no time."

She started to laugh, and when Bourne looked at her, she said, "You come to the end of your life and who are you with, a virtual stranger who has saved your mission." Her cough was thick and phlegmy, and she almost choked. "Don't you think that's funny?"

"You're not going to die, Rebeka."

"From your mouth to God's ear."

"I have enough experience to know. You need blood and a good surgeon."

"We'll find them both in Dahr. We have a field unit there. Your shoulder will be as good as new."

He was surprised that she had had the presence of mind to notice. "My shoulder is fine."

"Nevertheless..."

"Nevertheless what?"

"I have an obligation to see you restored to health."

"That works both ways."

Her sphinx-like smile reappeared, flickering like a guttering candle.

They flew on. Bourne could see the first outbuildings of Dahr El Ahmar, looking like sugar cubes in the morning's strong, slanted sunlight. They passed over clumps of sentinel palm trees, their fronds, like tongues, set wagging in the helicopter's backwash. Soon they would be down. His shoulder was on fire.

"El-Gabal." Rebeka shivered. "That felt like the end of the world."

Bourne put his hand over hers. "We survived."

Her eyes were half closed and she looked very pale. Her dark hair lay damp against her cheek. "In the long history of my people, that's the important thing."

"It's the only thing," he said.

Epilogue

IT WAS SNOWING in Stockholm, just as it had been the last time he had been there. Bourne, shoulders hunched against the wind-driven snow, crossed Stureplan, the crowded square that was the hub of Stockholm nightlife.

He had flown into Stockholm that morning in response to a brief but telling text that had shown up on his cell phone three days before:

Back home after 13 yrs. @ Frequencies evry nite from 9 till u come.

Kaja. The small package he had sent on ahead was waiting for him when he checked into the small family-run hotel in Gamla Stan, the island between Stockholm proper and Södermalm. He had the contents of the package tucked in the inside pocket of his fur-lined greatcoat as he crossed the busy street and stepped into the entrance of Frequencies. The electronic music hit him with the force of a jackhammer. Lights blazed across the ceiling, the dance floor was jammed with bodies bobbing to the trance-like beat that seemed to rise up from the floor, the shimmering air thick with sweat and perfume.

The long, underlit bar was three- and four-deep with guys trying to score and girls checking them out. It was a mystery how Bourne saw her amid all the throbbing mob and pinballing energy, but there she was, her mother's eyes shining. Her hair was its natural blond color and her tan was completely gone. She was standing near one end of the bar, a glass in one hand, slightly detached from the mingling crowd. As Bourne approached her, someone asked her to dance and she declined. She had seen Bourne by this time, handing her glass to the bewildered guy and moving toward Bourne. She was dressed in umber: snow boots, a three-quarter-length leather skirt, and a wool cable-knit turtleneck.

They met in a small, briefly calm space amid the swirl. There was no point in having a conversation amid the earsplitting noise. She took his hand and led him around the periphery of the club to the bathrooms. Inside the door marked DAMER, no one batted an eye when she led him across the tiled floor. The young women were too busy snorting coke and telling one another war stories about the guys out on the dance floor.

She opened one of the stall doors and they went in, the door closing behind them.

"Kaja," he said, "I have something for you." He took out the silver-plated .22 that had belonged to her mother and handed it over.

She studied it briefly, then looked up at him. There was something subtly different about her, but maybe it was her blond hair or how much she resembled Viveka Norén. Or maybe it had something to do with where they were, the Beretta between them.

"I don't understand," she said. "Why are you giving this to me?"

"It belonged to your mother, Kaja. She tried to shoot me with it."

"I'm not Kaja," she said. "I'm Skara."

For a moment time seemed to stand still, the throbbing noise from outside seemed to fade, and Bourne's mind ran in circles. "You must be Kaja," he said. "Skara was in Damascus with Semid Abdul-Qahhar."

"Kaja died in the destruction of El-Gabal," the woman said. "It was my sister, Kaja, you met there."

Kaja. Skara. One of them was lying, but which one? "Skara has dissociative identity disorder," he said, "which fits with the sister I confronted in Damascus."

"Well, that seals it, doesn't it? Kaja was the one with dissociative identity disorder."

Bourne felt as if the ground had fallen away under him.

As if divining his confusion, she said, "Let's go somewhere less charged."

She took him to a small café in Gamla Stan. It was filled with teenagers and twenty-somethings, which would include her, if Bourne's calculations were correct. The two remaining sisters had fled Stockholm when they were fifteen. They had been away for thirteen years. That made the woman sitting across from him twenty-eight.

"My sister loved to tell everyone that I was the one suffering from dissociative identity disorder. It was part of her problem."

The coffee and stollen they had ordered came, and she spent some time adding sugar and cream to her cup. "Kaja was a stellar liar," she said after she had taken her first sip. "She had to be, in order to keep her brain from flying into a thousand pieces. Every personality she displayed was at once authentic and a lie." She put down her cup and gave him a sad smile. "I see you don't believe me. It's okay, you're not alone. Kaja fooled everyone."

"Even Don Fernando Hererra?"

"She was a master at it. I'm quite certain she could have beaten a lie detector."

"Because she believed her own lies."

"Yes, absolutely."

Bourne took a moment to regroup. Now that he had been talking to this woman for a while he had begun to notice differences from the Kaja he had known—or, to be accurate, not known. He was becoming more and more convinced that the person sitting across from him was, indeed, Skara. Into his mind swam the final encounter in the storeroom at El Gabal. There had been something different in the woman's eyes, something achingly familiar. *"Kill me,"* she had cried. *"Kill me now and end this."*

Had that woman returned to being Kaja just before the end?

There was one way to be absolutely sure.

Bourne leaned toward her. "Show me your neck."

"What did you say?" She looked at him quizzically.

"Kaja was mauled by a margay. She has scars down the sides of her neck."

"All right." She pulled down her turtleneck, revealing a long, beautiful neck with skin a luminous pink, and perfectly clear. "Do I pass?"

Bourne relaxed, but there was a sadness inside him. *"Kill me now and end this."* Poor Kaja, tortured by the nightmare of personalities she couldn't control.

"What was Kaja doing with Semid Abdul-Qahhar?" he said at length.

Skara sighed as she rearranged her turtleneck. "One of her personalities hated our father. She wanted to strike back at him for walking out on us."

"So she told the truth about that."

Skara regarded him for a moment. "First of all, the best lies are always embedded in the truth. Second of all, the truth she told you is incomplete."

Bourne felt chilled. He took up his cup and drank off some of the coffee, black, bitter, but invigorating. "Tell me."

For a moment her gaze was lost in the dregs of her coffee. "I'd rather not."

"No?" Bourne felt a rising anger. The feeling of being manipulated was all too familiar.

"It's not for me to tell you." She smiled. "Please. Be patient just until tomorrow morning." She took a small leather notebook out of her handbag, wrote out an address, tore it off, and handed it to him. "Ten o'clock tomorrow morning." She raised her arm to summon the waitress and got their cups refilled.

Her eyes went to his left shoulder. "You were injured in Damascus."

"I'm fine," Bourne said. He was going to ask her how she knew about him and what had happened in Damascus, but decided against it. He sensed he would find out soon enough.

"Now tell me about the Beretta." She frowned. "I had no idea my mother owned a gun, let alone was armed when she was killed. Did you take it from her?"

"Your sister had it," he said. "I have no idea how."

Skara nodded, as if coming upon a fact that had been self-evident all along. "She must have given it to Viveka. That would be just like Kaja."

"At fifteen?"

"After my father left, we were all terrified. I can imagine Mother grabbing it without a second thought."

"There's more to this story, isn't there?"

Skara summoned up a bleak smile. "Unfortunately for all of us, there always is."

Sometime during the night, the snow had stopped falling. Sometime during the night, Bourne had called Rebeka, who sounded tired but happy to hear from him. In the darkness of the hotel room, their murmured conversation felt like a dream. Afterward, the deep, basso throb of the drowsing city lulled him to sleep. In his dream, a truck rumbled along a deserted highway, sounding lonely and forlorn.

When morning arrived and he stepped out of his hotel and into a waiting taxi, the sky was a sparkling blue, the sunlight intense, as if magnified by the clear, crisp air. He got out in front of a modern building on Birger Jarlsgatan. Across the street was Goldman Sachs International.

Skara was waiting for him outside the building and, linking arms with him, took him inside. The entire ground floor was taken up by the Nymphenburg Landesbank of Munich. The guards nodded to her as she took him across the checkered marble floor to an elevator that whisked them skyward. When they got out, she led him to a huge suite of offices, passing by a pair of secretaries and three assistant managers, through a door marked with an engraved plaque that read MARTIN SIGISMOND, PRESIDENT, and into an enormous office with a breathtaking view of downtown Stockholm. Sunlight glittered on the river.

Sigismond, a tall, handsome man, slim and very fit, with straight blond hair and blue eyes, was waiting for them. He wore a navy-blue suit. His tie was a tongue of flame. At his side was Don Fernando Hererra, wearing a pair of pleated wool trousers and, of all things, a smoking jacket.

"Ah, Mr. Bourne, it's a genuine pleasure to meet you," Sigismond said, extending his hand. "Don Fernando speaks very highly of you."

"Oh, please." Skara was on the verge of laughing. "Mr. Bourne, I'd like to present Christien Norén, my father."

After the shortest of pauses, Bourne took his hand. "Your grip is strong for a dead man."

Christien smiled. "I'm back from the dead, and none the worse for it."

The four of them sat together on facing sofas in one section of the president's office.

"To all intents and purposes I'm Martin Sigismond," Christien Norén said, "and have been for many years."

"As you can imagine," Don Fernando said, "Almaz produced all the identification papers Christien needed."

"Almaz is behind this entire scheme," Bourne said.

"I'm sorry I couldn't tell you everything," Don Fernando said. "We needed you focused on the connection between Severus Domna and Semid Abdul-Qahhar. More specifically, we needed you in Damascus to cut off their arms and legs."

"Semid Abdul-Qahhar had engineered an armed attack on Indigo Ridge, a rare earth mine in California," Christien said. "He had a man inside Indigo Ridge, Roy FitzWilliams, whom he had recruited to his cause years ago."

"That's where all the matériel was being shipped," Bourne said.

Don Fernando nodded. "Along with a cadre of handpicked terrorists. American-born Muslims, sad to say."

There was silence for a time, then Skara said, "Dad?"

Christien made a gesture acknowledging his daughter. "Mr. Bourne, Don Fernando and I owe you an enormous debt of thanks."

"What you owe me," Bourne said, "is a full explanation."

"And you shall have it." He looked abruptly rueful. "I have made many mistakes in my life, Mr. Bourne, but none more grievous than walking out on my family. My wife is dead and so are two of my three children. The fact is, I miscalculated grievously."

"No, Dad," Skara said with some vehemence, "you were lied to."

Christien seemed in no mood to abdicate responsibility. "I was already in a bind with the Domna. Benjamin El-Arian was growing suspicious of me, which is why he sent me to kill Alex Conklin. It was a test."

"We both made mistakes," Don Fernando said with a sigh. "I wanted to recruit Conklin into Almaz, and I thought Christien's mission was the perfect opportunity."

"Somehow," Christien said, "El-Arian found out. I faked my death so he would have no cause to go after my family. That was a terrible mistake."

Bourne shook his head. "Then why did Conklin send me to kill Viveka?"

"Another mistake, pure and simple. He thought she was a spy."

"No," Skara said, "it was Kaja's doing."

Bourne and Don Fernando looked at her in astonishment. Christien just looked sad.

"I didn't really understand until Mr. Bourne gave me this." She produced the silver-plated .22. "Mom had this on her when she was killed. She shot at Mr. Bourne, isn't that right?"

"It is," Bourne said.

"Kaja gave Mom the weapon," Skara said. "Just as in one of her personalities she hated you, Dad, in another she despised Mom."

Christien pressed his palms together as if in prayer. "Kaja became a scourge." His expression revealed the emotional body blow he had been delivered. "She had the advantage of looking three or four years older than she was. She was precocious and, in her own way, brilliant. I told no one about her—not even you, Don Fernando. For one thing, I was ashamed and horrified at the way in which she was trying to follow in my footsteps. For another, I thought I could control her. That was my biggest mistake." He stared down at his shoes. "No one could control Kaja."

"She used her body as well as her twisted mind," Skara said.

Christien shuddered. "Doubtless you're right." He shrugged. "In any case, Conklin discovered that I had been sent to kill him. That aborted the mission. But even after he heard I was dead, he sent you, Mr. Bourne."

Skara sat forward. "On the strength of Kaja's dreadful lie." She turned over the .22.

"At least the Beretta redeemed itself," Bourne said. "It saved my life in Damascus."

"Thank God for that," Don Fernando said fervently.

Another silence descended. It seemed they were all spent. When Christien rose, so did everyone else. Bourne shook his hand; there was nothing else to do.

"Skara," Christien said, "why don't you take the day off and show Mr. Bourne some of the sights he might have missed when he was here last."

Don Fernando embraced Bourne and kissed him on both cheeks. "Good-bye, Jason," he said, "but not farewell."

When Bourne and Skara had left, Christien turned to Don Fernando. "Do you think he suspects?"

"Not at the moment," Don Fernando said. "But I have no doubt he will put it all together once he returns to Washington and speaks to Peter Marks."

Christien frowned. "Are you certain that won't be a problem?"

"It's what we want." Don Fernando smiled. "You have bought enough shares of NeoDyme so that we have a controlling interest in Indigo Ridge. We will have wealth beyond even our imagining." He regarded his friend judicially. "I forgive you for keeping me in the dark about Kaja. Your plan to use the Domna's attack on Indigo Ridge as a diversion worked perfectly. The notables in the American government were too busy unraveling the Domna's scheme to investigate the companies we used to buy up all the NeoDyme shares."

Christien crossed to the window. He looked down as Bourne and his daughter exited the building and crossed the slushy street. "What will Bourne do when he finds out?"

Don Fernando joined him at the window. The sky had clouded up; more snow would soon be on the way. "With Bourne it's often difficult to predict. My hope is that he will come back here to have a talk with us."

"We need him, don't we?"

"Yes," Don Fernando said gravely. "He's the only one we can trust."

FICTION LUSTBADER
Lustbader, Eric
Robert Ludlum's The Bourne
   dominion : a new Jason
Bourne novel

R0118989447   EAST_A

EAST ATLANTA
Atlanta-Fulton Public Library